To Family

BANISHED *and* *Welcomed*

THE LAIRD'S RECKLESS WIFE

BY
BREE WOLF

Acknowledgments

A great, big thank-you to my dedicated beta readers and proofreaders, Michelle Chenoweth, Monique Takens and Kim Bougher, who read the rough draft and help me make it better.

Also a heartfelt thank-you to all my wonderful readers who pick up book after book and follow me on these exciting adventures of love and family. I love your company and savor every word of your amazing reviews! Thank you so much! There are no words!

BANISHED

and

Welcomed

THE LAIRD'S RECKLESS WIFE

Prologue

Greystone Castle, Scottish Highlands, Autumn 1806 (or a variation thereof)
Two Years Earlier

T he key turning in the lock sent a deafening sound through the small chamber, a chamber that had been hers for as long as she could remember. Never had it been a prison cell though. Never.

But that had changed the day Moira Brunwood, once a proud daughter of Clan Brunwood, had betrayed her own kin.

Swallowing, Moira rose from the chair she had occupied for the past hour, her gaze directed out at the land she loved, but would be forced to leave that very day. Her hands brushed over her gown, suddenly obsessed with smoothing out even the smallest wrinkle as she turned toward the door.

Slowly, it swung open, revealing the tall stature of Alastair Brunwood, Moira's brother. His features were hard as his blue eyes settled on her, anger burning in their depth as she had never seen before. His lips were pressed into a thin line, and the muscles in his neck were rigid as he jerked his head toward her. "Come," he all but growled, his voice harsh, revealing how deep her betrayal had cut him.

Still, Moira rejoiced at that single word for it was the first one she had heard him utter in many weeks. Or had it only been days? Moira could not say. Time had lost all meaning as she had been locked away, her heart and mind retreating from the world, from what she had done. How often had she sat in this chair, staring out at the land that was no longer hers?

She would never know.

And it did not matter, did it?

Her hands trembled as Moira stepped forward. She could feel tears stinging the backs of her eyes, and yet, she did not dare look away for this was her last day.

Her last day at Greystone Castle.

Her last day with her clan.

With her brother.

Bracing herself, Moira drew closer to where Alastair stood, her heart twisting painfully at the sight of his taut face. The way his eyes refused to meet hers almost brought her to her knees, and in that moment, all she wanted was to sink down and weep for the mistakes she had made, the illusions she had entertained. How had she not seen this coming? How could she have been so wrong?

Brushing a blond strand behind his right ear, Alastair stepped from the room, waiting for her to follow. He stood like a sentinel, eyes directed forward as though he did not even see her.

Or did not wish to.

For the first time in weeks, Moira stepped out into the corridor, the grey stones of the walls surrounding her as familiar to her as the back of her hand. Her whole life had taken place in this castle, and now it would have no place in her future. It was hard to believe, and a part of Moira felt as though this was no more than one of her dreams.

Dreams that showed her things that were not real but could be one day. They had been her downfall, and not a day passed that she did not curse the Fates for allowing her glimpses of a future that would now never be hers.

With her head bowed, Moira followed her brother down the back staircase. The day was still young, and only a dim glow of the autumn's light reached inside the thick stone walls. A chill crawled up her arms, and she drew her shawl more tightly around herself.

All was silent as they stepped out into the courtyard and turned toward the stables. Fog lingered all around her, shrouding everything in a thick blanket, and the air smelled faintly of salt, whispering of the sea nearby.

Her eyes swept over the familiar courtyard where they had danced not too long ago, celebrating their laird's happy marriage.

Connor's marriage to an English lady.

With her lips pressed into a thin line, Moira picked up her step and hurried after her brother. Not even now could she think of Henrietta Brunwood, Connor's wife, without feeling a stab to the heart. After all, it had been the slender, pale Englishwoman who had brought about Moira's downfall. She had bewitched Connor, stolen his heart as well as his hand, so that he had no longer been able to see Moira.

A lone tear escaped and rolled down her cheek as Moira quickly reached up and brushed it away. There was no point in falling to pieces now. She had cried all the tears she had possessed for the loss of her future.

The future she had seen in her dreams.

The future she had been promised.

And although it was lost to her now, her dreams still stayed with her as though to taunt her.

Every now and then when sleep took her, she would travel to the moment that had urged her to act, to conspire against Henrietta, the moment that had led her down a path of betrayal.

Again, she would see herself standing atop a lush green hill, Connor by her side, his arm wrapped around her shoulders as her head rested against his strong chest. Together, they gazed across the land, their eyes sweeping over the men and women and children of their clan, preparing for the Highland Games. Moira could see the Brunwood banner flapping in the strong breeze, and a smile would come to her lips.

Again, and again, she had seen this in her dreams. Dreams she knew to be a whisper of the future. It was a gift she had had since she had been a wee lass. A gift of the Old Ones. A gift she was to use to secure her clan's future.

And so, Moira had acted.

She had taken steps to rid her cousin Connor of his new English wife, believing - no, knowing! -that *she* -Moira- was meant to lead their clan by his side, not Henrietta. After all, her dreams had told her so, and never once had her dreams been wrong.

Until now.

Stepping into the stables, Moira breathed in the warmth of the animals mingling with the strong scent of hay and manure. She watched her brother lead two horses from their boxes, their saddles in place and a few belongings tied behind them.

Alastair kept his gaze firmly fixed on the task at hand, never once even glancing in her direction. He was a seasoned hunter, trained in combat, and had the instincts of a warrior. He knew without looking where she was and what she was doing. He always had, and Moira had always felt special because of it.

She was his little sister, and he was her big brother.

At least, they had been.

Once.

"Goodbye, Moira."

Spinning around, Moira stared at Connor standing only a few feet behind her, his bear-like stature blocking the door. He was tall and broad, but he moved with the same ease and precision as Alastair. His black hair and full beard gave him a somewhat darker countenance; however, Moira knew that Connor was a man full of laughter and mirth.

Only now, his eyes were hard, and his lips pressed into a thin line as he regarded her with the same sense of disbelief and disappointment she had seen in his gaze since he had learnt of her betrayal. Since he had realised that *she* had been the one to almost cost him his life. That *she* had been the one to threaten his wife.

A wife he loved with all his heart and soul.

Moira knew that now, but she had not known it then.

To her great dismay, fresh tears shot to her eyes, and she clenched her teeth, willing them to not show themselves. After all that had happened, all Moira had left was a small bit of pride, and she would fight to keep it. "I'm sorry," she said nonetheless; her voice, however, was even and free of the deep regret she felt. "I swear I never meant for ye to be hurt...or her." She swallowed. "I didna know what he had planned. I swear it."

Swallowing, Connor nodded. His gaze momentarily slid to Alastair standing somewhere behind her, tending to the horses, before he drew closer, his dark eyes fixed on her face as though he hoped to read her thoughts. "I believe ye, Lass, as Old Angus made no secret of how he used ye for his cause."

Moira drew in a shuddering breath at the memory of the hateful, old man who had seen Connor's English wife as a threat to the clan, a threat that needed to be eliminated. He had gathered men and led them in an attack against Connor, thinking him weak for allowing the British to infiltrate their home.

And to her shame, Moira had believed his lies and aided him in his quest.

In the end, it had been Henrietta's courage and Alastair's loyalty that had saved Connor's life. Moira still felt sick at the thought of how close he had come to dying that day.

And she would have been responsible.

"But ye betrayed me," Connor told her. "Ye betrayed all of us. I understand how Angus could have done what he did." He shook his head. "After the horrors of Culloden, he hasna been right in the head. But ye?"

Moira nodded. "I know. I canna believe it myself. All I can do now is apologise."

"And make amends," Connor told her, his eyes hard as they held hers. "Yer past is sealed. It canna be changed, but ye're still the master of yer future." Taking a step closer, he placed a hand on her shoulder. "I know ye've been misled and that ye're sorry, but that isna enough. Ye need to find a way to lead a good life." He sighed, "Ye know ye canna stay here."

Swallowing, Moira nodded.

Connor glanced over her shoulder, his eyes no doubt meeting Alastair's before he looked down at her once more. "For yer brother's sake,

I give ye this chance. Use it wisely for it shall be yer last." Then he took a step back, and his hand slid from her shoulder. "Goodbye, Moira. May yer dreams not lead ye astray again." Then he turned and walked away, severing the bond that had connected them since childhood. Their lives would now lead them down different paths, and Moira wondered if she would ever see him again.

As she followed Alastair out of the courtyard, feeling her mare's strong flanks beneath her legs, Moira drew in a deep breath. Her body shuddered with the weight of the moment that was finally upon her, a moment she had dreaded for the past weeks, and her eyes filled with tears.

And this time, she let them fall for her heart broke anew as they rode out of Greystone Castle, leaving behind a life, a family, a home.

Outcast.

Banished.

Exiled.

All these terms that had been coursing around in her mind these past few weeks spoke to one deep-seated fear: loneliness. Now, Moira was alone in the world with no one to care whether she lived or died. She would live among strangers, strangers who would no doubt look upon her with disgust and mistrust for her deeds had spread throughout the lands, even reaching the ears of those far away.

And Moira could not blame them. She had no defence, no justification, no excuse or explanation. Aye, she had been misled; still, the decision had been hers.

She had failed them as well as herself.

Glancing over her shoulder, Moira watched Greystone Castle vanish a little more with each step their horses surged forward, a heavy fog settling around its walls and upon its towers. It was as though the Old Ones, too, were punishing her, hiding those she loved from her view.

Always had Moira had the Sight, and now, she could not see.

Days passed in silence as they travelled onward across the land, and Moira's heart grew heavier. Her limbs felt weak, and it was a struggle to pull herself into the saddle each morning. Her mind was numb, clouded with guilt and fear as well as another moment of loss she knew would come.

When they spotted *Seann Dachaigh* Tower, home of Clan MacDrummond, around midday on their fifth day since leaving Greystone Castle, Moira felt an icy fist grab her heart and squeeze it mercilessly. She shivered against the cold that swept through her body, gritting her teeth as she fought for control.

Without so much as glancing in her direction, Alastair spurred on his horse as though he could not wait to rid himself of her. Her betrayal had indeed cut deep, and Moira tried to gain comfort from the fact that his hatred of her would not be so profound if he had not loved her as much as she loved him.

Seann Dachaigh Tower, home of their mother's clan, was situated on a small rise, surrounded by Scotland's rolling hills as well as a small village. Its grey stone walls stood strong, surrounding a fortified inner castle, with only a large front gate to grant entrance. To Moira, it looked like a prison from whence there would be no escape, and her breath caught in her throat when despair washed over her in a powerful, suffocating wave.

Birds called overhead, and the scent of pine and hazel trees drifted through the air. The breeze tugged on Moira's blond tresses and brushed over her chilled skin raising goose bumps. Still, the mild hint of salt she detected brought her a small comfort, a reminder of home. The sky shone in a light blue, but Moira spotted dark clouds on the horizon.

A bad omen?

Wishing she could simply turn her mare around and ride away in the opposite direction, Moira paused atop a small slope, her blue eyes gazing down across the valley at the imposing structure that would be her home henceforth. Her fingers tightened on the reins, and she could feel her mare's agitation as she no doubt picked up on the unease that coursed through Moira's veins.

Noting her delay, Alastair pulled up his reins and turned his gelding around, thundering toward her. His eyes narrowed into slits, and a snarl curled up the corners of his mouth. "Ye willna dishonour this family further," he growled. "I willna allow it, do ye hear?"

Swallowing the lump in her throat, Moira nodded, then urged her mare onward, her gaze distant as she did not dare look at her brother. Was this how they were to part? Was this how she was to remember him?

When they finally reached the old structure, entering through the wide-open gate into the bustling courtyard, Alastair pulled up short and addressed a man carrying a bag of grain on his shoulder. A few words were exchanged before the man pointed him toward a small group of women standing near a well, chatting animatedly.

Moira dismounted; her fingers tightly curled around her mare's reins as she glanced around the inner courtyard. Eyes watched her, narrowed and full of suspicion. She heard whispers and felt stares digging into the back of her skull.

They knew.

They knew of her. They knew her story.

They had known she would come.

And they did not like her.

In fact, they loathed her and wished her gone.

With all her heart, Moira wished she could do as they desired, but her hands were tied. In this, she had no choice.

Turning her head, Moira saw her brother striding back toward her, an older woman by his side. Her light brown hair had streaks of grey, and her face looked stern as her blue eyes swept over Moira in displeasure.

Stopping in front of her, Alastair turned to the woman by his side. "This is Aunt Fiona. She's agreed to give ye shelter." The tone in Alastair's voice rang with disapproval, and he looked at their late mother's older sister with a hint of apology as though he loathed burdening her with his dishonourable sister.

Fiona gave her a sharp nod. "I warn ye, Lass. Folks do not look kindly on those who betray their own kin. I suggest ye do as ye're told and keep yer head down." She sighed, her blue eyes gliding over Moira's appearance, the niece she had not seen since she had been a wee bairn. "But first, ye'll meet the laird." She turned to go. "Come."

Moira's heart thudded to a halt when she turned back to look at her brother, only to see him walking away. In a few strides, he had crossed to where he had left his gelding, taken up the reins and swung himself into the saddle.

Panic swept through Moira as she stared at him. Her lower lip trembled, and tears ran freely down her face. Would he not even say goodbye to her?

Alastair's face looked stoic as he stared straight ahead, eyes focused on the large opening in the wall. The muscles in his jaw tensed, and he kicked his horse's flanks with more vigour than necessary. The gelding surged forward, shaking its large head, no doubt confused about his master's unkind treatment.

Look at me! Moira pleaded silently as she watched her brother ride away. *Please, look at me!*

But he did not.

He rode on stoically.

Moira's breath came fast as her vision began to blur before her eyes. Her knees buckled, and she groped blindly for something to hold on to, something to keep her upright as the world began to spin, threatening to throw her off her feet.

"Ye canna blame him, Lass," Fiona grumbled beside her as she grasped Moira's hands, pulling her around to face her. "He's a proud man, and he loved ye dearly." Fiona shook her head, her blue eyes sharp as she watched her niece. "Nay, ye canna blame him. He needs time. A lot of time. Perhaps more than he has." Then she turned toward the castle's keep pulling Moira with her.

Together, they crossed the courtyard, climbed the steps to the large oak door and then entered the great hall.

Moira saw very little of her surroundings as her heart ached within her chest. With each step she took, she had to fight the urge to sink to her knees as tears continued to stream down her face.

"Pull yerself together, Lass," her aunt reprimanded her as she guided their feet down a long corridor that seemed to go on forever, leading them far away from the loud hustle bustle in the great hall. "Our laird is a kind man, but he willna take kindly to those who only weep for themselves." She scoffed. "I dunno why he granted ye sanctuary when yer laird sent word of what ye'd done. Many argued against it, but he has a way of knowing things others do not." Her aunt stopped, fixing Moira with her sharp blue eyes. "Dunna make him regret this small mercy, do ye hear me, Lass?"

Moira could only nod as she wiped the tears from her eyes, suddenly overwhelmed by the thought that strangers would see her in this state of despair. Of course, she could not expect compassion, sympathy or even pity.

And yet, her heart ached for it.

On they continued down the corridor until they came to a lone door at the very end of it. There, Fiona stopped and lifted a hand to knock.

"Come in."

The laird's voice rang strong and commanding, but not unkind, and Moira wondered what kind of man he was. Clearly, he was held in high esteem by the people of his clan, and she had only ever heard Connor speak with great respect of Cormag MacDrummond.

Their clans had been close long ago but had drifted apart since Culloden and the destruction of the Highland clans. The years had been tough, and trust had been hard to come by. What would it be like to live among another clan as one who had betrayed her own kin? Would they lock her in her chamber as well? Afraid she would betray them, too?

Moira swallowed, and a cold chill ran down her back as she followed her aunt into the laird's study.

Large with narrow windows, it was a simple room that held only the laird's desk as well as a couple of chairs and cabinets. It was not designed for comfort, but for practicality, for handling the clan's affairs.

Now, she too was a clan affair.

Straightening, Moira lifted her head, determined not to cower. As much as she felt like sinking to the ground, she would not give the MacDrummond laird the satisfaction. She would stand tall with her head held high. Aye, she would apologise and voice her regrets-as she had so many times before. She would accept the blame as it was rightfully hers. However, she would not allow him to frighten her, to force her to hide the pride that had always lived in her chest.

After all, she was of Clan Brunwood, a proud Highland clan, and even if her legs trembled with fear and her heart ached with loneliness, she would rather die than reveal her inner turmoil to a man who would no doubt look down on her with suspicion for the rest of her life.

As Moira followed her aunt and came to stand in front of the laird's large desk, her eyes swept over his tall stature as he stood with his back to her, staring at the wall for all she knew. He was a large man with broad shoulders and raven-black hair, and for a thoroughly terrifying moment, he reminded Moira of Connor. Would her past haunt her wherever she went?

Perhaps she deserved it.

"I present to ye my niece," her aunt spoke into the silence of the room, "Moira Brunwood. Her brother delivered her to me only moments ago."

Moira glanced at her aunt, wondering about the need to explain what she heard in the older woman's voice. Was Fiona afraid the laird would fault her somehow? Was she doing what she could to distance herself from her traitorous niece?

Moira sighed knowing she could not blame her aunt for what she did. Aye, it would have been nice to have someone on her side; however, she had to admit that she had not once thought about what her presence here at *Seann Dachaigh* Tower would mean for her aunt. How would it affect Fiona's life? How would people treat her? Look upon her?

The laird's broad shoulders rose and fell as he inhaled a long breath. Then he slowly turned around as though apprehensive to look upon her.

Moira gritted her teeth, feeling a surge of anger rise in her heart. Why on earth had he agreed to Connor's request if he did not want her here? Why would he-?

The breath caught in Moira's throat the moment Cormag MacDrummond's charcoal grey eyes met hers. Of all the things she had expected to feel in that moment-shame, regret, guilt, even fear-she was completely unprepared for the sudden jolt that seemed to stop her heart and make it come alive at the same time. Warmth streamed into her chest as though the sun had risen after a long absence, and she felt the corners of her lips curl upward, unable to contain the exhilaration that had claimed her so unexpectedly.

Overwhelmed, Moira clasped her hands together, needing something to hold onto.

Never had she felt like this before.

Not even Connor had ever inspired such...such...

In that moment, Moira finally realised that she had never been in love with Connor Brunwood.

Chapter One

A WITCH IN THEIR MIDST

Seann Dachaigh Tower, Scottish Highlands, Summer 1808

Two Years Later

"I hope ye slept well," Moira said as she poured a cup of tea for her aunt as well as for herself. Then she glanced out the window. "'Tis promising to be a beautiful day."

Fiona grumbled something unintelligible under her breath as she took the cup from Moira's hands.

Sighing, Moira sat down to sip her own tea. "I'll probably head out to gather some more herbs later today."

Again, Fiona grumbled something under her breath.

Although Moira had been allowed to live with her aunt-instead of being locked up in the castle's dungeon-the two women spent very little time together. As she had initially suspected, her aunt was far from happy to be duty-bound to shelter her traitorous niece; a sentiment, Moira had come to understand more and more when she had realised how adversely her presence affected her aunt.

Widowed with two grown daughters married outside of the clan,

Fiona MacDrummond was alone; still, the companionship of her close-knit clan had never allowed her to feel lonely. She loved to stop in the marketplace and chat with women she had known all her life, and her days were filled with people stopping by for advice or to issue an invitation to supper. Life had been good and comfortable for Fiona until the day her niece had come to live with her.

Moira knew that she was the reason her aunt's friends no longer included her in the same carefree way they had before. Always did they cast worrisome glances at Moira if she was nearby, whispering on the quiet about her odd behaviour and shameful past.

Even after two years with Clan MacDrummond, two years without incident, nothing had changed.

Moira was still an outcast, a black mark on an otherwise spotless gown. While Fiona tried to be kind to her, some days were harder than others. People always regarded Moira with suspicion, and few dared speak to her directly. Either they ignored her or told her off harshly so that Moira spent most of her time alone. She too missed the company of others; however, she knew that she was fortunate to be allowed to live so freely, to come and go as she pleased. Unfortunately, though, that proved worrisome to some members of the clan, who were constantly eyeing her with suspicion, wondering if she might eventually turn against them as well.

So, Moira kept her distance, and every now and then, she thought to see a spark of gratitude in her aunt's blue eyes.

It was all she could hope for these days.

With a basket slung around her arm, Moira walked across the meadows to the west of *Seann Dachaigh* Tower. Wildflowers were in bloom, and all around her bees buzzed with such vigour that it sounded like a waterfall was rushing nearby. Still, the small loch in the valley glistened peacefully in the sun; its calm surface only here and there disturbed as a fish rose to catch a bug.

Out of sheer boredom, Moira had begun to gather herbs trying to learn as much as she could about their healing abilities. Occasionally, she would steal into the large library located deep in the belly of the keep, trying to identify the many flowers she found. At first, it had been rather slow going; however, it had given her something meaningful to do, something to keep her mind occupied outside of her daily chores.

Her aunt sometimes suffered from severe headaches, and Moira was glad she was able to help her, to soothe the pain and see Fiona's face relax when relief found her. It was only something small, but it gave Moira a purpose. More than that, it made her feel proud.

Of herself.

Of something she alone had accomplished.

It was a rare feeling, but one to be treasured.

Most days, Moira was at peace with her situation at *Seann Dachaigh* Tower. Of course, a part of her still hoped for acceptance while another felt her loneliness acutely. However, most days passed in a pleasant manner...especially if one did not dwell on them too much.

Sitting down in the shade of a grove of trees, Moira watched a group of children racing through the meadows, their cheerful voices painting a smile on her face. Their laughter was beautiful and melodious, and it spoke to something deep inside her, reminding her of the childhood she herself had once had.

With Connor.

With Alastair's wife Deidre.

With her brother.

Moira swallowed, and as always, her throat closed as tears stung the backs of her eyes.

Two years had passed since she had last seen her brother, and in all that time, he had not once sent word. Every now and then, Moira wrote to him, apologising, vowing that she would never again do anything to cause him pain. She did it as much for herself as she did it for him, hoping that over time he would slowly come to believe her and no longer be burdened by her betrayal.

He deserved better.

He deserved to be happy.

To Moira's relief, Deidre, her brother's wife, was a woman with a wide-open heart and the ability to forgive. Long ago, she had set Moira's mind at ease, promising she would find a way to reunite her with her brother, and no matter how soft-spoken and yielding little Deidre often seemed, the woman had an iron will and loved Alastair beyond hope.

No, she would not allow him to suffer for the remainder of his days.

A hesitant smile sneaked onto Moira's face as she thought of her sister-in-law. One day, Deidre would find a way to break through Alastair's pride and stubbornness. Moira was certain of it, and it gave her hope like nothing else.

Something to look forward to.

Something to hold onto.

Something.

A little blond-haired girl of no more than five years broke away from the small group of children racing around the meadow, chasing one another, and headed straight toward Moira, a smile on her beautiful little face. "Are ye out gathering more herbs?" she panted, trying to catch her breath.

Moira smiled, looking down at the full basket sitting beside her in the grass. "Quite observant, little Blair." She glanced behind the girl, noting the way her brother Niall was eyeing them with suspicion. "Go ahead and play now. The others are waiting for ye."

Shrugging off Moira's words, the girl sank down into the grass, her blue eyes looking up into Moira's face with curiosity. "'Tis only my brother," she remarked, scrunching up her little nose as she glanced over her shoulder at the scowl on Niall's face. "I dunno why."

Moira sighed, knowing full well that it was indeed Niall's father, Ian MacDrummond, who'd instilled such hatred for Moira in his son. For a reason Moira could not name, the man detested her-beyond the familiar distrust and suspicion of the rest of Clan MacDrummond. He openly opposed her place in the clan and often tried to rally others against her. More than once, Moira had seen the man's distorted face as he had glared at her, his hands balling into fists as though he wished to attack her. Deep down, Moira knew that it would not take much for Ian's hatred to push him into acting against the decency and honour she knew he possessed.

"He's only looking out for ye," Moira counselled, enjoying the girl's company despite the glare in Niall's eyes as he continued to watch them. Blair was one of only a handful of clan's people who met Moira with unadulterated kindness and without even the smallest hint of suspicion. It was a balm to Moira's soul, and she would have loved to spend more time with the girl.

If it were not for Ian MacDrummond.

Blair tilted her head sideways, her blue eyes still as curious as before. "Are ye a witch?" she asked openly.

Moira chuckled, "What makes ye say so?"

Blair shrugged. "I've heard it whispered." Her eyes narrowed in contemplation. "Ye dunna look like a witch."

"What does a witch look like?" Moira asked, knowing she ought to send the child on her way.

Blair's gaze grew thoughtful. "I dunno. Are witches always bad?"

"I dunno." Moira shrugged. "I've never met one. Have ye?"

The girl shook her little head. "People say ye did something bad. Is that true?"

Hanging her head, Moira sighed, "Aye," she whispered before lifting her head and meeting the girl's eyes once more. "I did."

"Why?"

"At the time, I believed it to be the right thing."

Inhaling a deep breath as though to better absorb what she had been told, Blair nodded. "Ye made a mistake."

"A grave mistake," Moira pointed out, knowing that Ian as well as the rest of Clan MacDrummond had a very good reason to distrust her. After all, she was not an innocent in all of this.

"Are ye sorry?"

Sighing, Moira nodded. "Aye, verra sorry." To this day, she could not understand how she could have been so blind as to not see the wrong of her ways. The thought to be mistaken like that again, to act against others, believing she was doing the right thing, was constantly with her. After all, she had not seen it coming the last time either.

What if it were to happen again? What if this time someone did get hurt? The mere thought sent a shiver down her back.

A smile came to Blair's face. "Good." And with that, the issue seemed to be resolved for her. "Do ye like flowers?"

Moira nodded.

"I'll pick ye some," the girl exclaimed as she jumped to her feet.

"Ye dunna need to," Moira said, trying to stop her. She ought not encourage the girl's kindness. What would her father do if he found out? And judging from the look on Niall's face, he would.

"But I want to," Blair replied with a smile.

"Yer parents will worry about ye if ye spend yer time with me." Moira did not quite know what to say, how to dissuade the enthusiastic little girl, but she knew she at least needed to try.

Blair shook her head. "My mother always tells me to be wary of strangers, and ye're not a stranger," she reasoned, not a hint of doubt in her young eyes.

Moira smiled at the girl as her thoughts strayed to Maggie MacDrummond, who was the complete and utter opposite of her husband. Friendly to a fault, Maggie treated everyone with kindness and respect. She was a warm and loving woman, and Moira was always happy to exchange a word or two with her as Maggie had a way of making those around her feel at ease.

Still, Maggie's kindness toward her had initially surprised Moira for she had learnt that the dainty, young woman had not been born a Scot. In fact, she had grown up in England and had then married Ian MacDrummond upon visiting her mother's clan years ago. She had found a new home in the Scottish Highlands and loved its people with a fierceness that had long ago made her a true Scot in the eyes of her clan's people.

Still, she had been English once, and considering that Moira had been banished because she had conspired against her laird's *English* wife, she had expected Maggie to despise her more than anyone else.

But Maggie had not.

Moira wished she knew why.

"Come!" Blair's red-headed brother called, a stern tone to his voice as he took a careful step closer. "We needa head home." His green eyes were wary as he watched Moira as though he expected her to jump up and swallow him whole at any moment.

Blair merely shrugged, then all but rolled her eyes and whispered to Moira, "He's afraid of ye, but I dunno why."

Forcing a smile onto her face, Moira said, "Perhaps he too thinks I'm a witch."

Blair laughed as though the mere thought was ludicrous. Then she mumbled a quick goodbye and skipped up the small slope toward her brother.

Taking his sister's hand, Niall once more glanced over his shoulder before he leant down to Blair. "Ye know Father doesna approve. Why do ye always have to go and talk to her? She's a dangerous woman; perhaps even a witch." A shudder seemed to grip his small shoulders.

Blair snorted, "I'm too old to believe in fairy tales, and ye should be too." And with that she raced ahead, leaving her brother behind looking a little forlorn.

Despite the severity of the situation she found herself in, Moira could not help but smile at the girl's reply, wishing deep down that Blair's words could be true. If only her gift was something out of a fairy tale. Something that was not true, was not real, and could not hurt anyone. It certainly would have kept her from making the biggest mistake of her life and it would not constantly force her to make impossible decisions.

Always had her dreams come to pass, and Moira had come to trust in them without hesitation. And then her world had crumbled around her, teaching her a painful lesson. Blind faith would not be rewarded. Nevertheless, she knew she could not ignore her dreams.

After all, they came when they chose. What was she to do? How was she to know which to trust and which to be wary of? Which spoke of a danger to be prevented? Or of a promise that needed her aid to be fulfilled? And which were only a taunt, a tease, a test?

Each time, a new dream found her, Moira wished they would simply leave her alone. Long ago, she had felt honoured to have had such a gift bestowed upon her. But no more. Now, she had rather be like everyone else: unburdened and free.

Still, she had no say in the matter. The only choice she did have was whether to act...or not.

Again, she allowed her thoughts to stray to the dream that had come to her the night before wondering what she ought to do. Ought she pretend it had never happened and keep two people from finding one another? Or ought she to try and help and point them in the right direction?

Moira sighed. What she had always thought of as *helping*, others might call *interfering*.

Others like Ian MacDrummond.

And if he found out, he would not look kindly on her.

Chapter Two

A FAVOUR ASKED

Cormag's eyes lingered on the golden-haired, young woman sitting beneath the small grove of trees. He saw little Blair run up to her, a smile on her young face, and he noted the way her elder brother Niall watched the two of them with the same hateful distrust Cormag often saw in the lad's father.

Sighing, Cormag pressed his open palms to the rough stone of the parapet wall as he stood atop the walkway, which granted its visitors a spectacular as well as strategic view of the land surrounding *Seann Dachaigh* Tower.

Ian MacDrummond had always been a friend, a good friend, and Cormag cherished his friendship as much as he cherished Garrett's and Finn's. Despite their differences in temperament and character, the four of them had always walked through life side by side: training together, studying together, growing up together.

Now, they all were trying to find their place in this world. While Ian had married young, becoming a husband and father, Cormag had always known that he himself would take over as laird of Clan MacDrummond upon his father's passing.

That had been three years ago, and life had been different ever since.

No longer could Cormag allow the twists and turns of every day to guide his feet. While Finn and Garrett seemed to drift here and there, not bound to anything but their clan, Cormag knew that he needed to follow his head instead of his heart. He had a duty now. A duty that always came first.

It had to.

For the good of the clan.

As he watched Moira speak to little Blair, Cormag knew that when it came to the young woman from Clan Brunwood, he often failed to remain emotionally detached. Not that anyone would notice, for over the years Cormag had learnt to perfect a mask of interested indifference, one that had served him well in his position as laird.

No doubt, his mask was as perfect as it was because he worked every day to maintain a certain distance between himself and others, keeping it fixed in place to ensure that his head decided wisely without regard for his heart's momentary desires. Unfortunately, that distance seemed to slip away whenever Moira drew near.

The day she had walked into his study two years ago, Cormag had known that something was different. He had felt her standing on the other side of his desk, and without even laying eyes on her, he had sensed her spirit, her strength, her sorrow, but also her pride, her defiance, her recklessness. He had known that life would never be the same again if he allowed her to stay.

And yet, he had.

Cormag remembered well the moment he had drawn in a deep breath, bracing himself for the heart-stopping sensation of having her eyes looking back into his. He had turned with apprehension, and the moment he had seen the shimmering blue of her dark eyes, he had known that his life would never be the same again.

Indeed, it had been a constant battle ever since.

Closing his eyes, Cormag willed himself to turn away from the scene before him, and with determination, he strode down the wall-walk and headed back into the castle. His footsteps were heavy as he turned down the staircase and found his way back to his study. And all the while, his heart pounded with a fierceness that made him grit his teeth and curse the day Moira Brunwood had come to *Seann Dachaigh* Tower.

Closing the door behind him, Cormag strode purposefully toward his desk. After all, there were matters that needed his attention. Clan matters. People depended on him, and he would not let them down.

Focusing his thoughts in such a manner had often helped Cormag retrieve the balance he needed to be the laird his clan deserved. He knew what needed to be done. He knew his place, his purpose, and he would not allow anyone to interfere.

For the good of the clan.

An hour passed, and slowly Cormag felt his balance return. His heart beat steadily in his chest, and his mind was focused as it ought to be. However, just as he allowed a sense of relief to spread across his limbs, he sensed an emotional turmoil drawing near.

Someone was coming.

Someone agitated and distraught.

Cormag braced himself for the onslaught.

Ever since he had been a lad, Cormag had had the misfortune of reading others' emotions. He felt them as though they were his own, and as a young boy, he had often been overwhelmed by the sorrow and fear of those around him. His father, with his calm demeanour and strong voice, had guided his hand through those years of upheaval, urging him to train his body as well as his mind, to find a balance within himself, to feel but not to succumb.

Cormag had always been grateful for his father's understanding nature for he knew well that those who possessed gifts were often looked upon with suspicion.

As was Moira.

Perhaps that had been why Cormag had allowed her to stay. Why he had felt protective. Something deep inside him had urged him to keep her near. Still, ever since that day, he feared that this weakness would one day return to haunt him.

A knock sounded on the door, and Cormag sat up to focus his heart and mind as his father had taught him. "Come in."

The door swung open, and in walked Mrs. Brown, *Seann Dachaigh* Tower's cook. Her face was flushed as always, but she seemed outwardly calm. Still, Cormag noticed the way her fingers curled all but painfully into her apron, her eyes slightly widened as she fought to remain in control of the fear that now pulsed off her as though in waves. "I apologise for the intrusion," Mrs. Brown panted, a faint shimmer of sweat lingering on her forehead.

Cormag felt his own heart tighten as he too struggled for composure. "What can I do for you?" he asked calmly. "Is something wrong?"

Mrs. Brown nodded. "Aye, my sister sent word. There's been an accident, and she begs me to come." She swallowed hard, trying to catch her breath. "I assure ye that all is taken care of in the kitchen. Ye needna worry that-"

"There's no need," Cormag assured her. "Go and see to yer family and promise to send for me if there's anything ye need."

A grateful smile flitted across the woman's face, and Cormag felt his muscles relax when relief and gratitude lessened the strain her fear had on him. Rising from his chair, he escorted the older woman to the door, gently squeezing her hand as she looked up at him with relief. "I pray that all will be well."

Mrs. Brown nodded in agreement before she hurried through the door, her footsteps receding quickly.

With each step she took down the long corridor, Cormag began to feel more like himself, and he stepped up to the window, knowing the calming view over the rolling hills would bring him peace.

While everyday emotions now barely affected Cormag, those that went deeper, those that quickened one's heart and stole one's breath were still taxing for him, and he often wished he could simply rid himself of the *gift* the Old Ones had seen fit to bestow upon him. Granted, it gave him an advantage in all kinds of confrontations and negotiations. He simply knew whether others were lying or being truthful, and he could act accordingly, make the best possible decision. However, the price was still a steep one, and some days, Cormag was not certain it was worth it.

Did Moira feel the same? He could not help but wonder. While his own gift remained a secret-only his father had ever truly known-hers was whispered about near and far. No one knew. No one was certain, but stories flew through the land of her otherworldly gifts. Cormag did not know what was true and what not, but he suspected. He knew how to strip away embellishments and exaggerations and see to the core of things.

After all, that was *his* gift.

Unfortunately, most people did what they always did when faced with something unknown, something they could not understand.

They allowed fear to take over.

Cormag sensed that apprehension in almost all his clan members when faced with the blond-haired outcast from Clan Brunwood. Not all were hostile like Ian; however, most were fearful and tended to be cautious rather than too bold and risk harm.

Again, Cormag remembered the day she had first stepped across the threshold of *Seann Dachaigh* Tower. Even before she had set foot into his study, he had sensed her approach from up the corridor. Indeed, he had chosen this rather isolated room for his study as it was far away from the hustle bustle of the castle. Here, he could focus his thoughts and be alone with what he felt, unburdened by those around him, for only those who wanted to seek him out had reason to venture into this remote part of the ancient fortress.

Therefore, whenever someone drew near, whenever he sensed another's approach, Cormag knew that that someone was coming to see him.

That day, he had sensed Moira's remorse, her shame as well as her regret. He had known within moments that what she had done had not been done out of malice. She had been misled. She had been foolish and made the wrong decision, and he was certain she would not do so again. Was that why he had agreed to let her stay?

Because of a certainty that only he possessed.

Nevertheless, without revealing his gift to those around him, Cormag had not been able to provide a reason for his decision, and some of his clan members had been openly disapproving. They feared that she was a woman without scruples, that after betraying her own clan, nothing would keep her from doing the same to theirs.

Cormag could understand their concerns; still, he had been unable to send her away. A fact that still bothered him.

Returning his attention to the parchment on his desk, Cormag paused when he suddenly felt another's emotions approach.

A sense of unease, of nervousness drifted toward him, and he felt his chest tighten once more. Then, suddenly, warmth flooded his being, and he was surprised to also feel...a touch of longing. Or was he mistaken?

Rounding his desk, Cormag stepped closer to the door, curious who was coming to see him and why. His pulse sped up on its own accord as the one outside in the corridor stepped closer, then knocked. "Come in," he called, willing a mask of control back onto his face for despite his own intrusion into another's heart, Cormag feared nothing more than to have another look at him and know how he felt.

The door slid open, revealing-to his great surprise-the slender, young woman from Clan Brunwood.

Moira.

A frown drew down her brows, and her bright blue eyes were downcast as though she did not dare look at him. Then, rather absent-mindedly, her right hand rose, and he watched almost entranced as the tips of her fingers brushed down the side of her temple and then tucked a golden curl behind her ear. Her lips parted, and she inhaled a deep breath before finally lifting her gaze.

The moment her eyes met his, the air lodged in Cormag's throat, and he found himself altogether incapable of uttering a greeting.

Never had Moira come to see him. Whenever they had met, it had been coincidental. Out in the courtyard passing each other. In the great hall during a celebration. From afar when she had been down in the meadow and he had been up on the wall-walk.

Never had she sought him out. On the contrary, he always had the impression that she sought to avoid him for whenever they did happen upon one another, she always hurried onward as though afraid to linger.

Did she fear him?

Cormag swallowed the lump in his throat when he realised that he could not tell.

Instead of feeling overwhelmed by a flood of emotions crossing the barrier from her to him, all he felt in that moment was his own heart beating wildly in his chest. He felt nervous and unhinged, and yet, strangely intoxicated with her presence. He wanted her to leave, and he wanted her to stay. He wanted...

Why could he not feel her? Had he not felt her only a moment ago? Was it her gift? Did she somehow prevent his intrusion into her heart? To protect herself? Or had his own gift deserted him suddenly? Why else could he only feel what lived in his own heart?

"I apologise for the intrusion," Moira said, a slight tremble in her voice. She seemed hesitant and somewhat reluctant as though she thoroughly disliked being in his presence. Still, her blue eyes shone with determination, and it was clear that there was something specific she wished to address.

Trying his utmost to ignore the way his pulse quickened at the sound of her voice, Cormag stepped farther into the room, gesturing for her to follow. "What can I do for ye?" To his relief, his voice revealed none of his inner turmoil, and he silently thanked his father for his guidance.

Clearing her throat, Moira squared her shoulders and took a step forward. "I've come to ask for a favour."

A frown drew down Cormag's brows as he watched her, unfamiliar with the notion of not *knowing* what lived in another's heart. All he could do was guess based on the way her eyes held his, pride shining in them, refusing to let her back down. "A favour?" he repeated, stalling for time as he tried to make sense of her sudden appearance in his study. "What kind of favour?"

Her lips parted, and she seemed on the verge of replying when her mouth closed once again, and a hint of frustration came to her eyes. For a moment, she seemed lost in thought, clearly contemplating what to say, before she huffed out a breath in annoyance. "All I can say," she whispered as though afraid someone would overhear, "is that...that a situation will soon present itself and that the only one to solve it is Garrett MacDrummond."

For a long moment, Cormag stared at her, watching the way the muscles in her jaw tensed as she gritted her teeth. He saw her clasp her hands together tightly and steel come to her eyes as though she feared he would mock her. "A situation? What kind of a situation?"

Exhaling a long breath, Moira rolled her eyes. "I canna say more. I need to go." In a flash, she spun around and hastened toward the door.

Cormag's heart jumped into his throat, and without thought, he found himself rushing after her. "Wait!" Pushing the door closed before she could open it beyond a small gap, he placed a hand on her shoulder, urging her to turn around.

Her eyes were wide as Moira turned to face him. She instantly retreated until her back was against the door. Still, she did not drop her gaze nor lower her head.

"I'm sorry." Seeing the way her chest rose and fell with rapid breaths, Cormag took a few steps back. Although Moira was not a small woman, he still towered over her, and even without his gift, he could tell that he had...frightened her? "Why can ye not tell me more?"

Her sky-blue eyes roamed his face, weighing his words and searching for something that would tell her how to proceed. She was more than reluctant to share what she knew. She was clearly...afraid? Considering what little she had said, Cormag surmised that it had something to do with her gift. Had she seen something?

After a small eternity, Moira swallowed, then licked her lips. "Send him to the border," she said, an almost pleading note in her voice.

"Now?"

"Ye'll know when."

Cormag frowned, searching her face. "Why?" He could not deny that he was intrigued and desperately wanted to know more. Never had he spoken to another who shared such a gift. "Why is this so important to ye?"

Although Moira did not drop her gaze, she remained silent. Still, her lips seemed to move as though she too desperately wished to say more but did not dare.

"I canna do as ye ask without knowing why," Cormag said as he looked down at her. Her eyes still held his, and although he could not read her heart, he felt the warmth of her skin and smell the sunshine in her hair. The soft scent of wildflowers lingered near her, and he remembered how she had sat under the grove of trees earlier that day.

Her eyes were hard, but at the same time, they held something vulnerable. "I promise ye that this will lead to no harm. I swear it."

Cormag swallowed, reminding himself that he could not in good conscience grant her request without knowing more. Still, his heart told him that there was no deceit in her words.

Closing her eyes, Moira sighed, "My vow is not enough, is it? Not after what I've done." Shaking her head, she turned around, her feet carrying her back and forth between him and the door.

Watching her, Cormag saw her turmoil, saw how torn she was. Obviously, her request was important to her; still, she feared its consequences. Had a similar situation led to her banishment? Although Cormag knew the essence of what had happened back then, that she had betrayed her laird out of jealousy over his marrying an English lass, Cormag had always known that there were some things that eluded him.

Her feet stilled, and once more her blue eyes settled on his. "Garrett will find the woman he's meant to be with in Gretna Green in five days."

Cormag stared at her, seeing her jaw quiver as she waited for him to absorb her words.

"If he doesna go," she continued, "Fate will never lead them together again, and his son will never be born." Moira swallowed, and he could see a tear forming in the corner of her eyes. "It has to be now."

Cormag exhaled a slow breath. Then he stepped toward her, his eyes searching her face. "How do ye know this?"

Moira licked her lips. "I've seen it." Again, her jaw quivered, and she gritted her teeth. "I know ye're not one to believe in such things, but 'tis the truth."

Cormag almost laughed, wondering about the irony that he who possessed a similar gift was considered one to deem such things no more than fairy tales. "Do the things ye see always come to pass?"

The expression on Moira's face froze as she stared up at him, clearly shocked by this indication that he might believe her. "Nay, not always," she whispered, and a sadness darkened her blue eyes that spoke of pain and regret.

After a moment, her shoulders pulled back and she lifted her chin.

"Please, do this. I swear ye will not regret it." Then she turned and walked away, closing the door behind her.

As she hastened down the corridor, her footsteps echoing to his ears, Cormag still felt his heart beating wildly in his chest. A part of him wanted to go after her, but he knew even catching up to her would not bring him more answers. She had shared with him all she was willing to and would say no more. The question was, did he dare trust her?

Did he dare trust that she spoke the truth and send his oldest friend to the border? If something were to happen to Garrett, Cormag would never forgive himself.

The woman he's meant to be with.

Hearing Moira's words echo in his mind, Cormag turned to the window, his eyes once more gazing out at the green hills. What if he did not send his friend, and Garrett lost his one chance at happiness? Would he forgive himself for that?

Bracing his hands against the windowsill, Cormag wondered what he would do when the time came. Five days, Moira had said. So, the situation she had spoken of-whatever it was-would present itself soon.

And soon he would have to decide.

Cormag could only hope that he would not choose wrong.

Chapter Three

A RARE DAY

Standing in the courtyard around midday, Moira stared at the three clansmen mounting their horses, provisions and a bedroll strapped to their saddles. The look in their eyes was one of determination mixed with a hint of annoyance. Still, Finn and Garrett were chatting cheerfully with one another. Only Ian seemed glum, his eyes downcast, his thoughts clearly directed inward.

Moira clutched the basket with bread she held to her side, her fingers tightening on the handle, as she felt tears stinging the backs of her eyes. Were they deceiving her? She wondered, then blinked, only to see that the three riders where still there, now waving to their friends and families as they spurred on their horses.

Swallowing, Moira gritted her teeth against the overwhelming emotions that seized her in that moment. Never would she have thought that the MacDrummond laird would believe her, heed her words and act upon them. She had only gone to him to fulfil her duty, to avoid regrets, to know that she had done all she could to assist Fate.

Without thought, Moira followed the three riders until she reached the front gate, where she stopped and leant against the rough stone. There she stood for a long time watching them ride off into the distance, bound southward, toward the border and Gretna Green.

Moira hoped with all her heart that her gift would not betray her again, that no harm would come to Garrett as she had promised.

As she had promised Laird Cormag.

Moira remembered the shrouded grey of his eyes as though he too was concealing something from the world. He struck her as a man familiar with keeping secrets. Nevertheless, she doubted that his secrets went beyond the nature of everyday clan affairs. Still, from the first, she had thought him trustworthy, and so Moira had gathered her courage and gone to him with what she knew.

And he had listened to her. More than that. He had believed her, had he not? Or had she been mistaken? After all, she had hardly spoken more than a few words to the man in all her time with Clan MacDrummond.

Not since that first day when they had met in his study had Moira ever sought him out, and neither had he. She had sensed a certain apprehension in him whenever their paths had crossed by accident, and it had saddened her to think that he disliked her.

Still, she could not blame him, could she?

Again, Moira recalled the way he had stopped her from leaving his study. He had stood so close, his warm hand on her shoulder, urging her to look at him.

After the distance that had always been between them, Moira's senses had been overwhelmed by the way his presence affected her. Certainly, her heart had always skipped a beat whenever they had happened upon one another. However, to have him stand so close, to have his grey eyes looking into hers had been unexpected and... completely exhilarating.

And in that moment, Moira had once again wished she could erase her past and have a chance to find happiness. Aye, most days she was content, knowing herself to be fortunate to have been given the chance to live with Clan MacDummond. However, occasionally, a quiet little voice deep inside spoke up, whispering of a longing Moira had buried the day she had realised that she had indeed betrayed her own kin.

All her hopes had died that day.

Never to rise again.

Or so she had thought.

From the moment her gaze had met Cormag MacDrummond's that day two years ago, her heart had reawakened, and no matter how often she reasoned with it, it would not listen. It still wanted and wished and desired, and occasionally, Moira let it have its way, basking in the soft emotions she never thought she would ever know.

And now, Cormag had heeded her words, placed his trust in her, and she felt her heart warm with gratitude. To be considered trustworthy again after all she had done brought fresh tears to her eyes, and Moira realised how much she missed the warmth of her family, of her own clan, the companionship and respect that had always been a part of her life.

But that life was no more.

What Cormag had given her was a small mercy, and she could not hope for more.

She needed to find a way to be content with what she had and not long for anything beyond that or disappointment would find her yet again.

Turning away from the receding figures of the three riders, Moira once again prayed that all would be well. That Garrett would find happiness. That her dreams were not taunting her yet again. If so, her fate with Clan MacDrummond would surely be sealed.

Walking down the path into the village just outside the walls of *Seann Dachaigh* Tower where she shared a small cottage with her aunt, Moira heard voices as she approached the small structure. Quietly, she drew closer, and peeking around the side of the cottage, she spotted Fiona standing in the vegetable patch, her hand lifted to shield her face from the sun.

That was nothing unusual; however, her aunt was not alone.

Duncan MacDrummond, fair and tall like his nephew Ian, stood in front of her, a deep smile on his bearded face as the two of them conversed. Moira could not quite make out the words that were spoken; however, she saw the slight blush on her aunt's face and doubted that it had been caused by the sun.

The way the two of them gazed at one another, a hint of nervousness in their laughter, in the way their eyes flitted up and down, meeting and then not daring to, brought a welcome warmth to Moira's chest. After all her days of loneliness, Fiona deserved to be happy again and perhaps Duncan MacDrummond was just the man for her.

Moira could only hope so.

Sneaking into the cottage, Moira set down her basket in the small kitchen before rummaging through her herbs, selecting a few to be taken to Mrs. Brown for cooking. The old cook had been a bit apprehensive at first, but was now grateful for Moira's diligence in collecting, drying and delivering the herbs that would enrich her meals. Once again, this task gave Moira a sense of usefulness, and she could not deny that she revelled in Mrs. Brown's appreciation.

Glancing around the corner of the cottage, Moira smiled when she saw her aunt and Duncan still glancing at one another rather shyly, a youthful blush warming both their cheeks. Then she headed back up the path she had come, reminding herself that life looked better than she had ever expected it to.

Moira picked her way up the small slope and headed toward the tower. Crossing the courtyard, she suddenly heard her name called and froze as though someone had slapped her.

No one ever called her name.

No one.

Eyes wide, Moira turned, and fear crept into her blood before her gaze fell on little Blair, her blond hair in two plaits hanging over her shoulders. At the sight of the smiling little girl, Moira exhaled the breath she had been holding, her limbs trembling with the sudden relief that claimed her.

"Hello, Moira, I picked these for ye," Blair exclaimed as she drew to a halt in front of her. Her blue eyes shone with pride as she held up the bouquet of wildflowers, her little fingers clutched around their stems possessively. "They're beautiful, are they not?"

"They are indeed," Moira agreed, making a show of examining and praising each little blossom. "And they're for me? Would ye not rather give them to yer mother? I'm sure she had love them."

Blair shook her head. "I already gave her some. These are for ye."

Knowing she could not bring herself to refuse the eager, little girl, Moira thanked her for her kindness and took the flowers. Still, her fingers trembled, and she could not ignore the unease that gripped her as she lifted her gaze and found Niall standing at the other end of the courtyard, eyeing them with a scowl on his little face.

Never had Moira been so grateful to know that his father was not around as he was currently riding toward Gretna Green with Garrett and Finn.

After beaming up at her once more, Blair darted away; however, not toward her brother. Instead, she raced over to the baker's market stall where her mother stood with Emma Stewart. The two young women had been friends for a long time, and Moira envied the deep bond that existed between them. Oh, what she would not give for a friend to talk to!

Smiling, Maggie bent down to her daughter and brushed a gentle hand over the girl's bobbing head as her little mouth prattled on without pause, her finger pointing toward Moira.

An ice-cold grip settled on Moira's heart for despite Maggie's kindness toward her in the past, she still feared to see displeasure in the dainty woman's blue eyes. Fortunately, when Maggie lifted her head and turned in the direction her daughter indicated, a warm smile came to her lips and she nodded her head toward Moira.

Although somewhat rusty from disuse, Moira returned the woman's kind greeting, and she felt her heart warm at this small gesture of cordiality. Today was truly a rare day!

After crossing the courtyard, Moira finally entered the great hall, its vaulted ceiling echoing with the voices of those within. Keeping her head down, Moira moved with precision, avoiding those standing in small clusters, and stayed close to the wall that led to the rear corridor. She breathed a sigh of relief once she left the great hall, finding it easier to breathe away from the watchful and mostly disapproving eyes of others.

Weaving her way through the corridors, Moira was still replaying the moment outside in the courtyard in her mind when she rounded a corner and almost ran into their laird and his mother Maeve. Both pulled up short; however, the look on Cormag's face did not speak of surprise.

"Oh! I'm so sorry, my dear," his mother exclaimed, pressing a hand to her chest. "My goodness, you have a lightness of foot. I didna even hear ye approach." The smile on her face fell, replaced by a hint of mortification. "Please do not mistake my comment as criticism. 'Twas merely an observation."

Lost for words, Moira merely nodded her head, her eyes darting back and forth between mother and son.

While Cormag strongly resembled his father-as she had been told-tall and dark and brooding, his mother was a vivacious woman with lively green eyes and deep auburn curls. The few streaks of grey running through them seemed like silver threads, accentuating the paleness of her skin and rich colour of her cheeks. Her hands seemed always in motion, gesturing wildly, and her lips rarely ceased to speak whatever was on her mind.

Moira liked her instantly and was surprised to see no dislike in the woman's green eyes.

In fact, they were looking rather curiously at her son, who stood like a stone column beside her, silent and unmoving. "Have ye lost your tongue, my dear?" she asked him, humour in her voice. "Would ye not consider it right to offer a greeting as well?"

Considering that Moira had not uttered a single word either, she quickly waved Maeve's concern away. "There's no need. In fact, I must be on my way. I-"

"Where are ye headed?" Maeve asked, peering into Moira's basket.

Glancing at Cormag's stoic face, Moira quickly focused her attention back on his mother. "To see Mrs. Brown. She asked for these herbs."

"Oh, aye, she's a wonderful cook," Maeve beamed. "We're so fortunate to have her. What she creates out of a few simple ingredients..." She shook her head in awe, then peered into Moira's basket yet again. Then she stepped closer. "These dunna look like herbs," she observed, a slight curl coming to her lips as she lifted the small bouquet Blair had given Moira from the basket. "Were they perhaps a gift?"

Returning the woman's smile, Moira noted the strange way Cormag shifted his weight from one foot onto the other, the look on his face becoming even more stoic than before. "Aye, they were."

Maeve nodded, glancing up at her son, before she leant toward Moira. "Pray tell, who gave them to ye? Or is it a secret?"

Moira laughed, realising that she would have felt at ease in the woman's company had it not been for Cormag's rather disapproving scowl. What on earth had she done wrong? The day before he had seemed almost caring, but now... "'Tis not a secret," Moira told his mother, determined to ignore his disapproval of their polite conversation. "Little Blair picked them for me. She is such a delight."

"Aye," Maeve exclaimed, clapping her hands together. "I've seldom seen a more cheerful chil-"

Cormag exhaled a sharp breath before he clamped his jaw together tightly once more.

"Are ye all right, dear?" his mother asked, her narrowed eyes sweeping over him. "Ye look a bit out of sorts."

"I'm fine," he all but forced out through gritted teeth, hands linked behind his back. For a second, Moira felt his gaze flicker over her face before he turned to his mother. "Did ye not also wish to speak to Mrs. Brown, Mother?"

His mother frowned.

"To enquire after her sister?"

Understanding dawned, and his mother nodded her head vigorously. "Indeed. Thank ye for reminding me." A slight curl came to her lips, one that reminded Moira of someone aware of a secret, but reluctant to admit to it. "If ye dunna mind," she said turning to Moira, "I could deliver yer herbs for ye. 'Twould be no bother."

Although certain that something had passed between mother and son that she did not understand, Moira knew that she could not refuse the woman's kind offer, and so she handed her the basket, only holding on to Blair's small bouquet. "Thank ye. Ye're too kind."

"Think nothing of it," Maeve said, smiling at her as she gently squeezed her hand. Then, after glancing at her son once more, she headed down the corridor the way she had come and soon vanished around the corner.

Odd, Moira thought, wondering if Maeve truly had wanted to seek out Mrs. Brown or if her son had urged her to pretend. But why would he do so? And why would his mother comply? It was indeed a rare day.

Rare and strange.

Still, Maeve's exit provided Moira with an opportunity to speak to Cormag alone. Was that why he had seemed so tense? Because he feared she would address their conversation from the day before in front of his mother? Was he afraid that others found out that he had granted her request and sent Garrett after the two love-struck runaways?

Bracing herself for his displeasure, Moira turned back around to face the stoic man behind her. His grey eyes were still as hard as steel but watching her with an attention she had rarely known. "I wanted to thank ye," she said quietly, praying no one would overhear, "for sending Garrett to Gretna Green."

His shoulders tensed. "There was no reason not to," he replied calmly, but his hands remained linked behind his back. "Had ye not spoken to me, I might still have done the same."

Moira nodded, understanding that he needed a reason that was easier to grasp than the fleeting vision that had sent her to him. "I promise I shall not repeat to others what I told ye." Holding his gaze for a moment longer, Moira then turned to leave.

"Wait," Cormag said once again as he had the day before, his voice low and, yet, slightly hoarse.

Moira froze, feeling her heart pounding in her chest. She could not deny that she was pleased to remain in his company a little longer. Still, his request confused her. Only a moment ago, he had seemed rather displeased to have come upon her.

"Will ye not look at me?" he asked from behind her, his voice surprisingly gentle, before she felt his hand once more descend upon her shoulder. His touch was as light as a feather; still, it sent a jolt through her that made her flinch.

Instantly, Cormag retracted his hand.

"Is there something else?" Moira asked, doing her utmost to keep her voice even as she turned around to face him.

His hands moved to link behind his back once more, re-establishing the familiar distance that had existed between them from the first. Tension settled in his shoulders and steel returned to his grey eyes, and Moira wondered what he was thinking in that very moment as his gaze watched her with the same attention as before.

"Garrett is an old friend," he finally said, his voice even; still, Moira understood without a doubt what he was trying to tell her.

"I know," she replied, nodding her head in affirmation. "I swear I would never knowingly endanger him." She sighed, once more feeling the weight of her betrayal. "I know ye have no reason to believe me, but I give ye my word."

Cormag's eyes lingered on hers. "Knowingly?" he repeated slowly, testing the word and examining its meaning. Then he took a sudden step toward her.

Moira drew in a sharp breath but forced her feet to remain where they were and merely lifted her chin to keep him in sight.

"Ye said ye saw something." His words were almost a whisper. "What did ye see?"

Moira swallowed. Never had she spoken to anyone about her dreams, especially not a stranger.

At her hesitation, Cormag drew closer, slowly, carefully until the tips of his shoes almost touched hers. "I trusted ye, Lass," he whispered as his gaze locked on hers. "Now, 'tis time ye trusted me."

Swallowing, Moira nodded. He was right. She knew he was. He deserved answers, but her dreams had always been such a deeply personal part of her that she felt it was something too intimate to share with someone she hardly knew.

"I swear I will not repeat what ye tell me," Cormag assured her, his voice filled with kindness, but also with insistence, and Moira knew that he would not walk away from this.

Licking her lips, Moira allowed her mind to wander back to the dream that had found her only two nights before. "I saw him in a taproom," she whispered, and she could tell from the look in his eyes that he was hanging on her every word, "a dark-haired woman by his side. They were holding hands, and the way they were looking at one another..." Her breath hitched, and she suddenly felt uncomfortable with the way Cormag was looking at her.

Perhaps he sensed her unease for he took a step back. "I see," he mumbled. "What else?"

"I saw them married," Moira went on, a part of her regretting the renewed distance between them.

Cormag's face remained immobile. "Ye mentioned a son."

"The image changed, and I saw them together, arm in arm, gazing down at their child," Moira whispered as she closed her eyes, recalling the vision that had filled her with such joy and peace. They had seemed so happy, and the warmth that had engulfed her in that moment had been completely overwhelming. They belonged together. She had been certain of that, and the thought of them never finding one another was what had brought her to Cormag's study the day before.

"How do ye know when they will meet?"

Opening her eyes, Moira smiled. "That I canna say. I simply do." She exhaled a deep breath, feeling as though a small weight had been lifted off her shoulders. Perhaps it had been good for her to share her thoughts with him. Perhaps it was not wise to keep everything locked inside.

The look in Cormag's eyes became contemplative. "Ye canna say with certainty if what ye see will happen even without yer interference?"

Moira could not help but flinch at the last word, and the muscles in her jaw tightened. "I never know if my dreams merely tell me about what will happen or if they want me to act. I canna tell the difference." She sighed. "They come when they choose, and there is nothing I can do."

Cormag drew in a slow breath, and all the while his eyes remained on hers. "Ye feel helpless," he whispered. "At their mercy."

Moira frowned, wondering how he knew. "I never asked for them," she told him, feeling a sudden urge to share this with him, "but neither can I ignore them. What if I do, and then...?" She shook her head, feeling tears sting the backs of her eyes as a new wave of helplessness washed over her. "There is always the risk that someone will suffer because of what I do...or don't do. I never know beforehand."

Cormag nodded, and she could see that there was something on the tip of his tongue. Still, he hesitated, his grey eyes watchful, observing, assessing. Finally, she saw his jaw tense as he reached a decision. "Was it such a dream that led to yer banishment?"

Moira flinched as though he had slapped her across the face, and she stared up at him, her mind empty and her heart throbbing painfully.

Regret came to his eyes when he saw her reaction.

Moira swallowed as a tear spilled over and snaked its way down her cheek. Still, she clenched her teeth against the turmoil that reached for her once more. "I made the wrong decision," she finally said, her voice trembling with the memory of what she had done. "I thought I... I didn't know that...I..."

When he reached out a hand to her, Moira shrank back, her limbs trembling. "I need to go." Then she spun around and strode down the corridor, refusing to run, but frantically brushing the tears from her face. What had she done? Had he only asked to better assess the risk she posed to his clan? Would he send her away now?

Not since the day she had been forced to leave Greystone Castle had Moira felt this alone and unwanted.

Exiled.

Banished.

It would seem today was a bad day after all.

Chapter Four

A RARE WOMAN

Standing in his usual spot up on the wall-walk, Cormag looked out across the green hills surrounding *Seann Dachaigh* Tower. When he saw movement near the tree line to the south, he squinted his eyes.

Riders were approaching. Were his men returning? Had they found the runaways? Had Garrett gotten married?

Cormag allowed his gaze to wander from the distant riders to the young woman once more sitting beneath the grove of trees not too far from the outer walls. She sat with her back resting against a thick trunk, a basket of herbs beside her, and her hands resting leisurely in her lap.

She looked at peace, and yet, after their encounter a few days ago, Cormag doubted that she ever truly was at peace. It seemed-not unlike himself-she too often wore a mask, not allowing others to see what lived in her heart.

From the thicket near the small loch, little Blair came running across the meadow, once again heading toward Moira. For a reason no one could fathom, the little girl was utterly taken with her, seeking her out whenever she could.

Niall, on the other hand, was as always displeased with his sister's

42

obsession and tried his best to change her mind. He grasped her arm, his lips moving quickly as he no doubt tried to reason with the stubborn little girl. Blair, however, remained adamant and was skipping toward Moira only a moment later.

Cormag could not help but wonder why Ian disliked Moira with such vehemence for his reaction appeared fuelled by more than simple mistrust or a cautious nature. Indeed, it seemed personal as though something had happened between them, some grievance or confrontation that had spiralled out of control. Perhaps Cormag ought to speak to him; however, he doubted that Ian would be very forthcoming.

As the riders drew closer, Cormag saw that it was indeed Garrett, Finn and Ian, accompanied by the two young runaways, their faces drawn and filled with apprehension. In fact, the tension that had gripped them upon being discovered and forced to return home was almost palpable for Cormag, and with each step their horses took, bringing them closer, he felt his own heart ache with the pressure.

Inhaling a calming breath, he tried to regain his composure, knowing the coming days would be trying. Still, a solution needed to be found, and he needed a clear head to do so.

Allowing his gaze to sweep over the small group yet again, Cormag was surprised to see no additional rider. If Garrett had indeed gotten married, then his wife had not accompanied them.

Deep down, Cormag realised that he had expected Moira's prediction to come true. Had she truly been wrong? Or had something else interfered? Something she had not seen coming?

As the riders entered the courtyard, Cormag saw the worried parents rush toward their children, pulling them apart, angry words flying back and forth. A part of Cormag could understand what had prompted the youths to run off, trying to evade their parents' bickering. Still, judging by the hatred swirling around in the courtyard below, their decision had only made matters worse.

Drawing back his shoulders, Cormag stepped away, knowing that it would do no good to reveal himself in this situation. No, it would be better to speak to Garrett first and then begin mediation between the two families. Restoring peace would not be easy, and it would take time.

If only Moira had been able to keep the youths from running off in the first place! But her dream had told her something else, had it not? It had been about Garrett and not the two youngsters.

Returning to his study, Cormag concentrated on a few administrative matters before he finally sensed Garrett's approach. His friend's steps were fast and with purpose, and Cormag could tell that something had changed in him since they had last seen each other.

After giving a short knock, Garrett stepped into his laird's study, his dark hair unkempt and his clothes dishevelled from the long ride. "We're back," he announced, a wide grin on his face, "but ye already knew that, do ye not?"

Cormag nodded to his friend. "I saw ye," he confirmed, watching as Garrett strode to the window, the energy humming in his muscles not allowing him to sit down. "I hope all went well."

Turning around, Garrett sighed. "We found them," he said with a sigh. "Unfortunately, not before they had gotten married."

Cormag gritted his teeth. This would certainly complicate matters considering the young lass was already betrothed to another. Or had been. What made matters worse was that the two families had been fighting with one another for years. As far as Cormag knew, it had all started over ten years ago with a sack of grain. After that, more grievances and disputes had come up year after year as the families continued to argue, seemingly out of spite.

Still, in that moment, Cormag knew that what he wanted to know was whether Garrett had found the woman from Moira's dream in Gretna Green. Still, he did not dare ask, did not dare reveal what was on his mind. "I'd appreciate it if ye'd lend a hand in the negotiations. Ye know the families rather well, and I think 'twould be of some help."

Garrett heaved in a deep sigh, "I had hoped to leave immediately."

Cormag frowned as he sat forward, leaning his elbows on the table-top. "Why is that?" he asked, sensing the urgency to be off in the way his friend ran his hands through his hair. He felt his own heart mimic the excitement that course through Garrett's body and almost agreed right there on the spot.

Garrett gritted his teeth; still, there was a smile lurking nearby, tugging on the corners of his mouth. "Canna someone else talk to them? It will take weeks, perhaps even months to get them to see reason, ye know that as well as I do."

Cormag nodded. "That is most certainly true, which is why ye're the man to do it."

Beginning to pace the length of the room, Garrett rubbed his hands over his face, his gaze distant as he no doubt sought to choose his words. Then abruptly his feet stilled, and he turned toward the desk, his green eyes meeting Cormag's. "Something's happened," he said, and finally the smile that had been lurking nearby claimed his face, making his dark green eyes shine with joy.

"Ye look happy," Cormag observed, a question in his tone.

"I am," Garrett beamed, his booming laughter echoing through the room. "Ye might not believe it, but...I got married. To an English lass. Only a few days ago."

The air rushed from Cormag's lungs, and he shook his head. "So, she was right after all," he mumbled as no small measure of awe found its way into his heart. "She was right."

Frowning, Garrett stepped closer. "What are ye talking about? Who was right? And about what?" He laughed, "I admit yers is not quite the reaction I'd expected."

Sighing, Cormag leant back, wondering if he should say something. Moira had not sworn him to secrecy. Still, he knew that she had placed her trust in him. Still, Garrett was his oldest friend, and a part of Cormag simply wanted to share what he had learnt because...because he was proud of her. Of what she had done. Of what she had risked seeing it happen. She had been selfless, and she deserved recognition. "Moira knew ye would get married."

For a moment, Garrett simply stared at him. "The Brunwood lass?"

Cormag nodded.

Shaking his head, Garrett once more rubbed his hands over his face as though to clear his thoughts. "I've heard rumours," he whispered, his green eyes searching Cormag's face, looking for confirmation. "I've heard that she has the Sight. 'Tis true then?"

Cormag nodded. "So, it would see." He sighed, and his gaze held Garrett's for a long while. Only when the other gave a barely perceptible nod did Cormag dare continue, now certain that his friend would keep this confidential. "She came to me and said a situation would arise that only ye could solve."

Still staring at his friend, Garrett slowly sank into the chair opposite the desk. "She did? Did she see it? Truly?"

Cormag nodded. "She said she saw ye married and-" Breaking off, Cormag realised that he ought not speak of the son Moira had seen. The boy's promise had not yet been realised, and if something were to interfere, perhaps it would be better if Garrett did not know. What would it do to a man to hear the promise of a child that would never be fulfilled?

"And what?" Garrett pressed, sitting on the edge of his seat.

"She saw ye happy."

A large smile claimed Garrett's face, and Cormag realised that his friend was no longer adrift in a world full of possibilities, deciding on a whim which path to follow. No, now he was anchored to another, a woman who had claimed his heart in a single night...but she had not followed him home.

"I must say I'm surprised ye believed her," Garrett said, his eyes watchful as he looked at Cormag. "I wouldna have thought ye would."

Cormag swallowed, knowing he must not seem indecisive. As laird, he needed to remain in control and must not allow himself to be easily swayed. "I didna believe her," he replied, aware that his words were dangerously close to being a lie. "I simply saw no reason not to send ye. Considering yer connection to the families, ye were clearly the best choice, and if she hadna come to me, I would have sent ye all the same." Cormag felt his muscles relax with each word he spoke, finding relief in the fact that he spoke truthfully. "And that is the verra reason I would ask ye to assist in the mediations. Use what influence ye have and see that this matter is resolved peacefully. There's been animosity between the two families for too long. 'Tis time it came to an end." He lifted his brows for emphasis. "A peaceful end."

Even before Garrett opened his mouth to speak, Cormag felt his friend's reluctance to comply. Garrett knew his duty. Still, his heart urged him down a different path. Cormag wondered what had happened in Gretna Green. He sighed. "What of yer wife?"

Garrett's shoulders tensed. "I canna say for certain."

"What happened?" Cormag asked frowning.

Garrett gritted his teeth. "She disappeared." His jaw clenched, and Cormag felt fear grip his friend's heart. "I rose early to speak to Finn and Ian-I admit they were the ones who found the two youngsters as I had been otherwise occupied," a contrite look came to his face, "and when I returned, she was no longer in our room. From the innkeeper, I learnt that apparently her brother had come to take her back home."

"Ye said she's English?" Cormag mused as he considered the situation.

"Aye, a lady it would seem," Garrett replied with a large grin. "A feisty one who says what's on her mind." Booming laughter left his lips, and Cormag could hear deep affection ring within it.

Still, he felt the need to suggest caution. "Do ye think her family might disapprove of yer union? What was she doing in Gretna Green in the first place?"

"She ran off to be married to some English cad, who abandoned her there when *his* brother came and forbid the union," Garrett told him, no small measure of relief and anger in his voice. "She was furious when I met her."

"She came to marry another," Cormag rephrased, fearing that deep disappointment would be found in his friend's future, "and yet, ye saw it right to marry her yerself." He drew in a slow breath. "Perhaps she changed her mind?"

Gritting his teeth, Garrett shook his head with vehemence. "Nay," he growled out, certainty ringing in his voice. Still, his green eyes shone with fear, and Cormag felt the air squeezed from his chest as his friend's pain washed over him.

"Ye married her after only a few hours," Cormag said carefully, feeling the anger that was building in his friend's chest. "How well can ye truly know her after only so short a time? Perhaps 'twould be wise to give each other some time to analyse the depth of yer feelings for one another."

Garrett surged to his feet. "I need to go look for her. I dunna even know where she is."

"That is precisely my point," Cormag pointed out. "Ye dunna know her. Ye dunna know how she feels about what happened. Perhaps she has come to regret-"

"No!" Garrett snarled as he braced his hands on the tabletop, his green eyes piercing as he looked at Cormag. "She is like no other I've ever met. There's not a single doubt in my mind that we were meant to meet there that night." He drew in a deep breath and straightened. "And now after what ye've told me, I know that 'tis true. She's the one. I knew it the moment I saw her." Shaking his head, he swallowed, and a small smile came to his lips as he remembered the moment he spoke of. "It hit me like an arrow to the heart or a punch in the stomach. It almost knocked me off my feet. I feel...unhinged when I'm near her; yet, the world has never seemed more right." His gaze cleared and once more found Cormag's. "Ye might not know what that's like, old friend, but I know that she is the one, and I need to find her."

Cormag fought the wave of recognition that swept through him, bringing with it an image of Moira's face. He saw the kindness and vulnerability in her gentle features, her eyes shining a deep blue, full of secrets and fear, as the sun danced on her golden curls, bright and promising, whispering of a future that might still come to pass.

Immediately, Cormag's heart sped up and his breath lodged in his throat.

Until this very moment when his oldest friend spoke of the love he had for his wife, Cormag had not dared interpret the effect Moira had on him. He had not dared put into words what he had suspected somewhere deep down.

All reason seemed to vanish whenever she was near, and all he could think of was her. He felt drawn to her, and even now, he wished he could seek her out. It was a rather unsettling emotion as though he was no longer in control of his own heart and mind, no longer free to choose, but urged down a path he had not chosen of his own free will.

Looking up, Cormag found Garrett's eyes on him, his gaze slightly narrowed as he watched him with interest as though seeing his old friend for the very first time. Cormag swallowed, praying that Garrett could not read his thoughts or see into his heart. His jaw clenched as he forced his mask back into place. "Be that as it may," he said, willing his tone to remain unaffected, "yer clan needs ye at present."

Garrett closed his eyes, resignation coming to his face.

"Make enquiries," Cormag continued. "Write to Maggie's brother, Lord Tynham. Perhaps he can help ye locate yer wife's family." The look on Garrett's face pained him, but Cormag feared what would happen if Garrett rushed into this without thought. Hopes that soared to the heavens would plummet deep. He did not want that for his friend. Perhaps with time, the hold his wife had on him would loosen, and Garrett would not be devastated if he learnt that she had come to regret their hasty union.

Cormag could only hope so. Perhaps with time, Garrett would regain control of his life.

Perhaps with time, so would Cormag.

"Ye said she saw us happy," Garrett whispered, a plea in his voice that cut deep into Cormag's heart. "Do ye believe that she spoke the truth? Will what she sees come to pass?"

Cormag hesitated, afraid to give his friend false hope but equally wanting to ease his mind. "Not always," he replied, trying his best to remember what Moira had told him. "Her dreams have led her down the wrong path before."

Garrett stilled. "Her banishment?"

"I believe so."

Garrett sighed, and Cormag knew that his friend wanted to believe that Moira was right, that her dreams foretold the future. "I've heard whispers of her...*interfering*," he finally said, and Cormag knew exactly what he meant for he had heard them as well. "Once she sent for the midwife when no one could have known that the babe would be born early. Or that time she found Old Grannie Brown out in the woods." He sighed. "D'ye think she knew these things would happen? D'ye think she saw them in her dreams?"

Cormag nodded, remembering the times when Moira had veered off her solitary path as though she had known something would happen and stepped in to prevent it. People had noticed as well, and their whispers had begun to veer into two directions; some in awe and some in fear. Some were grateful for Moira's help while others feared the power her gift granted her.

"Despite what happened," Garrett began, his green eyes once more trained on Cormag's face, "d'ye believe her to be an honourable woman? Or d'ye think there's an ulterior motive behind her *assistance?*"

Cormag swallowed. "I've not seen evidence of a malicious mind."

Garrett snorted, humour curling up the corners of his mouth. "But what d'ye think of her?"

For a short moment, Cormag needed to close his eyes before once more meeting his friend's inquisitive gaze. "She's a rare woman," he finally said, knowing that he could not lie to his oldest friend.

Gift or no, Garrett would know.

"Indeed," Garrett mumbled as he gave a short nod in affirmation. "That she is."

Chapter Five

GIFT OF THE OLD ONES

Sitting in her usual spot under the grove of trees, Moira watched a group of children playing in the meadow, Blair and Niall among them. Their faces were flushed and their eyes glowing as they chased one another. A little boy of no more than two years stumbled after them, his little legs not yet secure enough to keep up with his playmates. Still, his scrunched up little face spoke of his determination not to be left behind, and so no matter how often he stumbled and fell, he always pushed himself back up, pursuing the others.

Just as he reached the small slope leading up to the front gate of *Seann Dachaigh* Tower, the others turned back around and raced downward once more.

A smile came to Moira's lips when she saw him double his efforts, his little legs almost tripping over one another as he surged down the slope after them. She felt certain he would stumble and fall at any moment, but to her surprise, he managed to stay on his feet.

The other children were splashing in the small stream that snaked through the meadow farther downhill, and Moira had to rise to her feet to keep them in sight.

Autumn was well on its way, and the air had a definite chill to it. The children shrieked as they splashed each other with the cold water, memories of hot summer days lingering in their minds. Soon, they would not be so foolish as to soak each other through, but with the sun shining overhead and no more than a soft breeze in the air, they lived in the moment, unconcerned by what lay ahead.

Moira envied them.

To not think about the future was an unfathomable concept. Always had her mind shown her images of what was to come. Always had she lived with her eyes firmly fixed on the future. What would it feel like to simply live in the moment? To not worry about consequences? To simply do what she wanted because her heart ached for it?

Never had Moira asked herself what it was she desired, not apart from the promises of the future she saw in her dreams. Always had her wants and desires been shaped by what she had seen. What would it be like to be free of th-?

Walking down the slope toward the stream, Moira saw the group of children racing back uphill, once again leaving the little boy behind. He stumbled out of the cold water and then tripped on the bank, pitching forward and breaking his fall with his hands.

For a moment, she thought he would push himself back up as he had before, but then he sighed as though in resignation and sat down in the grass. His little fingers dug into the ground, and he began pulling out blades of grass, throwing them around in frustration.

Then he paused, and his gaze drifted downward.

Moira quickened her step, her heart tightening in her chest as she relived the dream that had found her the night before.

The boy's hands held something in their grasp, and she saw him lift it higher as he inspected it in the bright autumn light. Then his hands moved toward his mouth, and Moira lunged forward.

The boy shrieked as she all but tackled him to the ground. Oh, why had she not moved sooner? Moira cursed as the boy's wails pierced her ears. She had been so intent on keeping her distance that she had been almost too late, or had she?

Scrambling to her knees, Moira gripped the child's chin but, to her relief, saw nothing in his mouth. Her gaze drifted lower and she spotted the root he had found lying by his feet. "'Tis all right," she said, trying her best to sound soothing. "I mean ye no harm." She picked up the root and held it up for him to see. "Dunna ever eat this. 'Tis poisonous."

Smiling, she nodded to him, and he slowly calmed down, gazing at her with big eyes.

"Only ever eat what yer family gives ye," she urged him, "but never something ye find. 'Tis not safe. D'ye promise?"

Still staring at her, the little boy nodded.

Then footsteps echoed closer, and Moira looked up to see the group of children rushing back down toward them. Their gazes flitted over her and the boy, and she could see the speculation in their eyes. No doubt, their parents would hear grand tales tonight, embellished versions of what had happened just now. Moira could only hope that it would not lead to any harm.

An older boy pulled the little one to his feet, and the kids rushed back the way they had come, all but dragging the little boy behind them. Only Blair remained with Niall standing a little higher up the slope. "Come! We need to go," he urged his sister.

But Blair stayed where she was, her round blue eyes trained on Moira.

Sighing, Moira held up the root for her to see. "If ye find these, dunna eat them. They're poisonous. D'ye promise?"

A smile came to Blair's face, and she nodded. "I promise."

"Blair, come! Father will be furious."

Shrugging her little shoulders, Blair winked at Moira, then spun around and rushed past her brother up the slope. Niall cast another wary glance over his shoulder before he hurried after his little sister.

As the children raced back up into the village, heading toward the inner courtyard of *Seann Dachaigh* Tower, Moira sank back down into the grass. Although her heart felt pleased that she had been able to save the child, she knew without the shadow of a doubt that this *interference* would lead to more whispers, more distrust, more animosity. Would this go on forever? If she continued to heed the warnings she saw in her dreams, she would spend the remainder of her days as an outsider. Moira was certain of it, and it was a thought that weighed heavily on her heart...as did the image of Niall trying his utmost to protect his little sister.

For he reminded her of her own big brother.

Alastair.

Always had he looked out for her, and now that she needed him the most, he was not here. And she could not even be angry with him for it because it had been her doing. He had been right to abandon her, but the wound still ached as though it had been inflicted only the day before.

For a long while, Moira sat in the tall grass staring out across the land, wishing she could go back and change what had happened, what she had done. Her thoughts grew dark, and her heart sank with each breath she took. She felt despair settle on her shoulders like a heavy blanket, weighing her down, and knew that if she allowed it, it would squeeze the last bit of life from her.

So, Moira gritted her teeth, drew in a deep breath and pushed to her feet. There was no point in mourning what had happened. There was no point in mourning the life she had lost. In pitying the turn her life had taken. She knew that, but occasionally, she needed to remind herself of it in order to keep going.

"I need to move on," Moira whispered to herself as she turned back toward the keep. "I need to let this go."

If only she knew how!

As Moira stepped through the large gate, she spotted Blair and Niall speaking to their father on the other side of the courtyard, and her heart tightened in her chest.

While Blair stood almost stock-still, her little arms crossed over her chest in annoyance and her lips pressed into a pout, Niall was gesturing wildly, pointing toward the gate and the meadows that lay behind it. His lips moved, and Moira knew without doubt what tale he was relaying, a tale that darkened his father's gaze.

Unadulterated hatred came to Ian's eyes, and Moira saw tension grip his shoulders and curl his hands into fists at his sides. Instantly, panic washed over her, and when he looked up and their eyes met, Moira was ready to bolt.

Ye did nothing wrong, a voice deep inside whispered. *Ye did nothing wrong. Not today.*

Moira pushed back her shoulders and lifted her chin, fighting down the panic that urged her to run. Still, would that not be an admission of guilt? To run when she had done nothing wrong?

Unfortunately, judging from the look in Ian's eyes, he needed no admission. He needed nothing from her to fuel the anger that burnt inside him. Moira wondered what had first started the fire that raged within him. Of course, many were distrustful of her, suspicious even, but Ian's hatred had always felt different. Although she had never met him before setting foot in *Seann Dachaigh* Tower, Moira could not shake the feeling that his dislike of her had been born out of a more personal reason than her betrayal of her own clan.

If only she knew what it was. How had she crossed him?

With her head still held high, Moira turned back the way she had come. She was determined not to cower, but neither did she wish to provoke a confrontation, a confrontation she would surely lose.

Feeling the need to be alone, Moira went for a walk across the green hills, trying her best to clear her thoughts and banish the loneliness from her heart. The soft breeze tugging on her curls almost felt like a caress, and Moira welcomed it. Over the past two years, she had learnt to make do with the comforts of nature, the gentle breeze in her hair, the warm sunshine on her skin, the soft ground under her hands.

Still, sometimes her heart ached for the simple contact of another's touch. It had been two years since last someone had drawn her into their arms. Two years since another's hand had brushed over her cheek. Two years since she had been able to lean onto another.

Tears streamed down her face, and her body shook with longing as her mind recalled the many moments of her past when Alastair had pulled her into his embrace, his strong arms coming around her. She remembered hugging Deidre as well as her aunt Rhona. Even Connor had embraced her now and then...in friendship as her cousin.

It had been a part of life, and back then, Moira had not thought twice about it. She had taken her family's comfort for granted. Now, she knew better. Now, she knew how priceless their love and devotion had been, how a simple embrace could heal the heart and ease the mind and how its absence brought a coldness not even the hottest summer day could chase away.

Always was Moira surrounded by people, and yet, she was alone.

Utterly alone.

Exiled.

Banished.

The sun was setting before Moira managed to gather enough strength to return home. The air had grown chilled, and she could smell the promise of winter lingering on the breeze still tugging on her hair. Rubbing her arms against the cold, Moira quickened her step, her eyes seeking the familiar little cottage that had been her home for the past two years.

As she walked up to it, the door suddenly swung open and she saw Duncan step outside. Immediately, he swung back around, his eyes finding Fiona standing in the door frame, an enchanted smile on her lips as she gazed back at him.

Duncan inclined his head to her, a deep smile coming to his lips. "Good night," he whispered gently before he stepped away and then turned around.

As his gaze fell on Moira, his features hardened, and in that moment, he reminded her of his nephew. Like Ian, his eyes were narrowed and full of suspicion. Hatred showed in the tension gripping his shoulders, and for a terrifying moment, Moira thought he would strike her.

But he simply walked by her, not uttering a single word.

Swallowing, Moira stared after him before her aunt called to her. "Come inside," Fiona hissed, grabbing a hold of Moira's arm and pulling her into the small cottage. She flung the door shut behind them, her hands on her hips as she stared at Moira in disapproval. "What were ye thinking? Are ye out of yer mind? D'ye not know the whispers that have started anew today?"

Although Moira understood her aunt's agitation, she could not in good conscience bow her head in shame. After all, she had done nothing wrong. Not today. "I saved his life. In my dreams, I saw him lying on the side of the bank, his cheeks pale and his eyes lifeless." Blinking back tears, Moira swallowed, and her jaw hardened. "What should I have done? Tell me, please. What should I have done?"

Shock rested on her aunt's features as she stared at her, her eyes wide and her lips trembling as Moira's words sank in. "Ye saw the boy come to harm?"

Moira nodded. "I dunna know what people are whispering, but I didna attack the lad." She sighed. "I tried to keep my distance-I always do because I know how people see me-but then I was too far away. I ran and..." Closing her eyes, she shook her head. "I dunna regret it." Meeting her aunt's gaze, Moira drew back her shoulders. "He's alive because of me. I was right to act. No matter what they may say, I did nothing wrong. Not today."

Pressing her lips together, Fiona nodded, her cheeks pale and her eyes filled with tears. "Aye, ye did right, Lass. Ye did right." Then she swallowed and gestured toward the kitchen. "Come. Ye look like ye could use some food between yer teeth."

Nodding, Moira watched as her aunt brushed the tears from her cheeks. "Thank ye," she said, gratitude warming her chest. Fiona's words were not an embrace, but they did ease the ache in Moira's heart, and for that, Moira was grateful.

That night, she slept without interruption. Her eyes remained closed and sightless. Her dreams chose to grant her a reprieve, not invading her heart and mind and forcing her to act. Every now and then, days or even weeks passed without an image of the future rising before her eyes, and for that too Moira was grateful.

In these moments, she felt less alone, less odd and almost, *almost* like one of many. A member of the clan. Someone who did not stand out. Someone who belonged. Or at least someone who could belong.

One day.

Still, she knew that her dreams would return as they always had.

Autumn turned to winter, and with the cold came a new warmth as people huddled together indoors, often gathered around the large fireplace in the great hall as the elders told stories about times past. They whispered of brave Highland warriors fighting for their cause, of daring lasses who stood to protect their homes, of the Old Ones who bestowed their gifts on those they deemed worthy.

A murmur went through the crowd at these words, and Moira could feel more than one set of eyes turn to her. Her skin crawled as she kept her head down, her back pressing into the wall behind her.

Panic swept through her, and she realised she had been foolish to join them, to think she could partake in their gathering. Was this the moment? Had it finally come? Would they turn on her now?

As her heart beat frantically in her chest, Moira gritted her teeth, bracing herself for hands that seized her.

But they never came.

Swallowing, she lifted her head and found the attention of those in the great hall not focused on her, but instead on the old white-haired woman seated in front of the fireplace. Her soft voice rang loud and clear as she spoke of the many wonders the world held, wonders that included gifts like Moira's.

Again, murmurs echoed to Moira's ears, but now she realised that there was no hostility in them. Instead, they rang with awe and enchantment. She saw smiling faces and glowing eyes as the young and old listened to the stories that had been told in the MacDrummond clan for generations.

Entranced, Moira watched those around her, wondering in that moment if it had solely been her betrayal that had turned the tide on how people perceived the gifts of old. Would they have been this distrustful if she had not betrayed her own clan? Had this indeed been her doing?

Moira sighed, and her heart grew heavy when she realised she had no right to be here, to disrupt this peaceful moment.

Sinking her teeth into her bottom lip to keep at bay the tears that threatened, Moira quietly stepped back in order to retreat from the gathering. However, the moment she turned to go, her gaze fell on silver-grey eyes that looked back into hers as though they knew the turmoil in her heart.

Moira froze as she found Cormag looking at her from across the large hall. His gaze was slightly narrowed, yet, fixed on hers in a way she had never noticed before. It was as though they were the only two people in the hall, and she felt his presence all the way to her toes.

Her heart pounded in her ears, and she blinked her eyes frantically to chase away the tears that rose. How long had it been since another had looked at her? Truly looked at her? And seen her?

Too long.

Moira swallowed, unable to avert her eyes, and yet, she knew she ought to for Cormag MacDrummond was no more than a stranger. A man she hardly knew. A man she rarely spoke to. A man who nonetheless seemed to see to the very core of her.

There was something in those hooded grey eyes that spoke of a knowledge he could not possess as though he could see into her heart and know how she felt. Always had she wondered why he had believed her when she had asked him to send Garrett to Gretna Green. Aye, he had given a reasonable explanation, and still, Moira was certain that he had in fact believed her.

But why?

He knew nothing about her, nothing beyond the whispers that circulated around her betrayal. Then why did she feel as though he was on her side? Was she mistaken? Was it simply wishful thinking? A deep desire to not feel all alone?

Or was there a spark of truth in it?

As he looked at her, Moira felt the chill leave her body, slowly replaced by a warmth she had not felt in a long time. She felt her being strive toward him, her feet almost twitching with the need to move, to carry her across the hall and to his side.

Cormag's gaze held something almost tortured as though he too felt overwhelmed by something he had no control over. Something that urged him in a direction he did not wish to explore. Something that worked against his will.

Moira swallowed as disappointment swept into her heart. Whether he truly felt something or not, it was clear that he did not *wish* to feel it.

Not for her.

For anyone else, but not for her.

Hardening her heart, Moira forced her gaze from his and then fled the hall with as much dignity as she could. She knew she had no right to ask for his heart, but neither would she allow herself to break into a thousand pieces because he rejected her.

No, she would stand tall. After all, she was a Brunwood.

Or had been.

Once.

Chapter Six

A LAIRD'S DUTY

With a deep sigh, Cormag sank into his chair, his head throbbing from the voices that still echoed in his mind. Harsh and loud and filled with disdain and pride, the runaways' families had argued for weeks on end before reaching an agreement. Never would Cormag forget the hatred that had stood in their eyes, their children standing in the middle, desperately begging their parents to be allowed to love one another.

It had been a torment on Cormag's heart as well, and he felt deeply grateful that Garrett had been there to mediate, to shoulder most of the burden. Cormag knew that alone he would have lost his mind, unable to shut out all the emotions that had come at him from all sides, his mind unable to remain detached and reasonable.

Without Garrett, he would have indeed been lost.

Still, Cormag knew that he had done wrong by his friend. Every day, he saw Garrett's longing to go after his wife. Time had done nothing to loosen her hold on him, and Cormag knew that the guilt he felt over detaining him was justified. If he had let his friend go, allowing him to search for his wife, would Garrett have found her by now? Would they already be happy again?

Cormag had considered consulting Moira on the matter. Still, he had not dared approach her for whenever she was near, he still felt utterly unhinged. His heart beat as though it wished to jump from his chest, and his skin crawled with the need to feel her touch. The day they had met in the corridor months ago, he had barely been able to keep himself from reaching for her. From drawing her into his arms.

He had linked his hands behind his back. Still, when she had turned to go, he had been unable to stop himself. He had touched her. He had placed a hand on her shoulder and felt her warmth through the fabric of her dress.

Cormag had known that if he wished to remain in control of himself, he would need to keep his distance.

So, he had.

And it had been agonisingly painful.

A few days ago, their eyes had met across the great hall when old Grannie Brown had told stories by a roaring fire, her whispered words drawing young and old to her side. Often, the old woman was confused, forgot the names of those around her as well as her own. However, occasionally, her mind was clear, and she remembered the great stories told by their clan, enchanting everyone who came to listen.

Cormag had sensed Moira nearby. That he could still do, even if he could not tell what lived in her heart. Although he had cautioned himself, his gaze had sought hers, and when her deep blue eyes had looked back into his, he had been unable to look away.

Like a fly caught in a spider's web, he had been unable to move. He had stood and stared, and his heart had warmed at the longing he had seen in her eyes. Did she feel something for him? He could not be certain, and it riled him that he did not know.

With everyone else, he could tell. He knew what lived in their hearts better than they did. He knew. He knew beyond the shadow of a doubt. But when it came to Moira, he could only guess. He saw the warmth in her eyes, the slight hitch in her throat as she drew in a quivering breath, the way her hands trembled, the way the colour of her cheeks deepened.

He saw all that, and yet, he did not *know*.

Shaking his head, Cormag sat back in his chair. Had he lost the ability to interpret the facial expression of others? The way they moved and spoke? Had he been relying too much on his gift and thus forgotten how to read another's heart without it?

Anger and frustration flared, and Cormag brought his fists down hard on his desk, sending parchments tumbling to the ground. He knew he was losing control, and that only stoked his anger. He surged to his feet and began pacing the length of the room, running his hands through his hair, trying his best to regain his balance. When that did no good, he rushed to the window, bracing his hands on the sill and looked out at the snow-covered hills surrounding his ancient home. He did his best to focus his breathing, and slowly, ever so slowly, Cormag felt his heartbeat calm.

Strangely, the emotions that had surged in his chest felt familiar, and Cormag knew that he had encountered them before.

Not in himself, but in another.

Once he had sufficiently calmed himself, his thoughts travelled backwards, trying to find the moment when he had felt that same longing followed by anger and frustration. Many similar emotions met him on his search, but it was not until he turned his attention to his childhood friend Finn that he knew he had found what he had sought.

More than once, Cormag had sensed these emotions in his old friend, seen his eyes grow hard and his lips press into a thin line as he had stared across the room...at Emma Stewart.

The young woman had a beautiful and kind face, and if Cormag was not thoroughly mistaken, her dark brown eyes often lingered on his old friend. She too seemed to draw in a steadying breath whenever their paths crossed, and yet, it seemed they both did their utmost to pretend that it was not so.

Cormag chuckled and hung his head when he realised how blind he had been.

While he had used his gift in matters pertaining to the clan, he had never considered using it for matters of the heart. Of course, he had felt the emotions of those around him, but he had never thought to dwell on them. Always had he sought to rid himself of them as quickly as possible. Partly because they overwhelmed him, but also because he did not think he had the right to know their hearts as he did.

Now, for the first time, he wondered if he had received this gift because he was meant to...interfere. Was that not what Moira did? She did not simply see what the future held, but she also acted upon the dreams that found her. Ought he do the same?

That thought stayed with Cormag in the coming days as he carefully watched Finn and Emma, for the first time willing to feel what they felt in order to understand the bond that connected them.

Christmas drew near, and the once green hills were covered in deep snow as an icy wind blew across the land. Garrett grew more and more restless now that the situation with the runaways was finally resolved, their joy a small reward for his efforts. Still, Cormag counselled him not to rush off as the deep snow made travel almost impossible, and with Garrett's head not where it ought to be, he feared that his friend might come to harm.

Two days before the Yuletide feast, Cormag and his friends followed an old tradition of handing out logs to the people of their clan. It was a promise, a reminder that no one was ever alone, that they would stand together, one able to depend on the other especially in times of need.

While Ian sulked as he often did these days, Garrett was driven by an eagerness Cormag understood only too well. Finn, too, seemed miserable, and Cormag sensed the same war within him that had waged in his own heart more than once since Moira had first come to *Seann Dachaigh* Tower.

Finn was in love with Emma, but he did not dare hope that she returned his emotions. Oddly enough, Cormag realised that Emma felt the very same way. Only Finn did not know.

Sighing, Cormag wondered what he ought to do.

For years, he had seen the two avoid each other like the plague. It was clear that something had happened, something that stood between them, and he suspected that whatever it was it had caused Finn to run off to Clan MacKinnear for a time, hoping that distance might heal his heart.

Clearly, it had been a futile wish.

Cormag remembered the day Moira had tackled little Robbie to the ground. He himself had stood up on the wall-walk, watching her as he did more often than he liked to admit. He had seen the tension in the way she had moved. He had seen the way she had watched the children, not with ease, but as though she knew something was about to happen.

And she had, had she not?

At first, Cormag had been confused regarding her motivation. But later, as the whole clan had been abuzz with what had happened that day, he had heard Blair speak of a root little Robbie had found. She had cautioned all the children, telling them how Moira had warned her.

Ian had been furious, but Cormag had been able to calm him down, making him see that Moira had indeed saved the child. Still, doubt had remained in Ian's eyes.

Moira had interfered.

Likely, she had seen the child come to harm, and she had stepped in to prevent it. Watching Garrett and Finn converse as they trudged through the snow from house to house, Cormag wondered if he ought to speak to his old friend. After all, Moira had spoken to him on Garrett's behalf, urging him to send him down a path that would lead him to the woman meant to be by his side. Ought he not do the same for Finn?

Slowly, he drew closer to where Garrett and Finn were speaking to one another, hoping the opportunity would present itself for him to say something.

Garrett laughed at Finn, shaking his head. "Ye can say what ye wish, Finn, but no one glares at another like that without deep emotions. The lass must've truly gotten to ye. Why else would ye care what she does or who she marries?"

Cormag paused, surprised to hear that Garrett had interpreted the situation the same way. Perhaps there truly was another way to know another's heart, but unfortunately, Cormag had all but forgotten how to use it.

"Aye, I can see verra well that she means nothing to ye," Garrett continued to mock Finn, who began to feel increasingly uncomfortable, his unease drifting into Cormag's heart as well. "A bit of advice, dunna wait too long. One of these days, ye willna succeed in turning away a suitor and then she'll be lost to ye. Why do ye think I married

Claudia right then and there on the spot? She's a fierce woman, beautiful and strong and so...so verra alive. I knew another man might snatch her up in an instant, and so I claimed her as my own as fast as I could. No matter where she is, I will find her and remind her that she's mine...as I am hers." He clasped a hand on Finn's shoulder. "Ye'd be wise to do the same...if indeed ye care for her." Then Garrett hurried away, grabbing another log from the cart to placate Ian, who looked increasingly annoyed with their delay.

Despite Garrett's words, Cormag felt the need to do his part, to help his friend reach for the woman he loved. "Ye'd do well to heed his advice," he said, and Finn spun around, clearly unaware that Cormag had drawn near.

"How long have ye been there?" he asked panting, a bit of red coming to his cheeks.

"Not long," Cormag replied, sensing Finn's unease. For a moment, he merely watched him, wondering why his friend had allowed years to pass without speaking his mind, without addressing the woman he so obviously cared for. And yet, Cormag understood. "What does she mean to ye?"

The muscles in Finn's jaw tensed, and his lips pressed into a thin line, refusing to answer. Still, Cormag felt the deep longing that lived in Finn's chest as though it was his own. "I see," he mumbled, frustrated with the way the heart often made one stumble even though one's path was so clearly laid in front of one's feet.

"What is it?" Finn demanded, displeased with his friend's short comments.

Cormag shrugged, keeping his tone even and firmly detached from the rolling emotions in his chest. "I canna help but wonder why people are so vehement in pretending that they dunna care, for it only seems to complicate matters." In truth, Cormag knew very well why, but it still riled him.

For a moment, Finn remained silent before his brows drew down into a frown. "People? Ye said, people? Who did ye mean?"

Cormag merely lifted his brows, knowing his friend would understand.

Finn stared at him with wide eyes. "Emma?" he whispered, hope seeping into his voice as well as the desperate need to keep it in check. "Did she...did she say anything to ye?"

"She didna have to," Cormag replied, "for the lass is as inept at pretending that she doesna care as ye are, Finn." He held his friend's gaze a moment longer, hoping that Finn would heed his words. Then he stepped away and went after Garrett and Ian, lending a hand where he was most needed. Was that not what a laird did? He glanced over his shoulder at Finn who stood stock-still, his eyes wide as though shock had frozen him to the spot. Had he done right? Cormag wondered, once again thinking of Moira. Had he been given this gift to interfere? To help? Or had it not been his place?

Cormag hoped with all his heart that Finn and Emma would find happiness. If only they dared reach for it!

Chapter Seven

A YULETIDE SEASON

Bracing himself for what lay ahead, Cormag strode toward the hall.

Although too many people at once were often over-whelming for him, a laird needed to see to his clan. He needed to know their hearts and minds, and he needed to give them the opportunity to speak to him. And so, he headed onward, exchanging a few words here and there, relieved to hear that no serious matter needed his attention. Most were in a festive mood, and he found Ian's wife Maggie flitting around the great hall like a fairy, decorating the ancient stone walls with evergreen boughs adorned with red ribbons and straw figurines.

Emma was by her side, indulging her friend despite the look of exhaustion that hung on her features. Finn, too, lingered nearby, and although Cormag could not read his heart with such a distance between them as well as the emotions of others nearby, the look in his green eyes spoke of a new determination. It seemed Finn had finally made up his mind to speak to Emma...once an opportunity presented itself.

Cormag hoped that it would.

The atmosphere in the hall was pleasant even for Cormag. Though most days many people meant an overwhelming variety of emotions. However, that night, most of his clan members were in a cheerful mood. Their hearts and minds were at ease, a hint of excited expectation lingering in the air as they laughed and chatted, enjoying a moment of peace and tranquillity.

Breathing a sigh of relief, Cormag leant back against the stone wall, his eyes sweeping over his people, as he enjoyed a rare moment of serenity among them.

The jolt that shot through his heart in the next moment was more startling as it was unexpected.

Feeling his muscles tense, Cormag fought the urge to spin around toward the entrance. Instead, he willed himself to remain immobile, his mask fixed in place as he slowly lifted his head and glanced at the large archway through which people moved in and out.

There she was.

Moira.

His heart paused as his gaze lingered on her gentle features, touching upon her golden curls before his eyes sought hers, drawn to the sparkling blue that shone like pools of water reflecting the hall's candlelight. She moved slowly, her head not bowed, but her eyes slightly averted, not lingering on another's face. She kept to the side of the hall, the look in her eyes one of pride and the determination not to yield. For although Moira often kept to herself, she did not shy away from people, refusing to lock herself away. No, she did mingle, but with care...and a certain reluctance. Still, a smile seemed to tease her lips as her gaze swept over Maggie's decorations, and Cormag knew that she was touched by the warmth and harmony that currently lingered in the hall.

The warm glow from the fire seemed to dance with the deep colours of green and red of the branches and ribbons hung around the large hall. In a corner, children were clapping their hands in rhythm to a soft melody travelling from their lips to the ears of those around them, and the scent of freshly baked bread and pastries hung in the air as Mrs. Brown slaved in the kitchen, ensuring that all would be readied for tomorrow's feast.

After a moment's hesitation, Moira proceeded further into the hall, her eyes touching upon Maggie as she continued to dance around like a fairy. He saw a moment of indecision on her face before her lips moved, and Maggie turned toward her, a smile on her glowing face.

Cormag had long since observed that while Ian seemed to detest Moira, Maggie in turn held no grudge whatsoever. Her smiling blue eyes shone with sincerity as she spoke to Moira, and she invited her to join her at the table where they continued to work on tying more red ribbons to more evergreen branches. It appeared there was no end to Maggie's enthusiasm for the Yuletide season.

Moira seemed to relax, and Cormag felt an answering sigh sweep through his own being.

Careful not to be too obvious, he watched her, enjoying the tender smiles that now and then tickled her lips. Her eyes often rose to meet Maggie's, and the two women were soon speaking to one another with ease.

Still, a growing tension lingered nearby, reaching out its talons toward Cormag's heart, and he turned his head, a frown on his face, as he tried to determine where it had come from.

Further down the hall, he spotted Ian, his eyes narrowed and a snarl contorting his face that spoke of hatred. Cormag knew that he ought to speak to his friend; clearly, there was a reason for Ian's disdain of Moira. Still, Ian was not one to share his thoughts and feelings with another-in that regard they were the same-and Cormag could only read his heart, not his mind. Even knowing how Ian felt, Cormag could not determine what had caused these emotions. That was something his gift could not reveal to him.

Running a hand over his face, Cormag tried his best to disentangle himself from the situation, knowing there was no upside in allowing these emotions to overtake him. He needed to remain in control, keep a clear head, and ensure that he remained watchful. It would not serve him if his people noticed his partiality toward Moira, and so he forced his eyes away.

Ever since she had walked into his home two years ago, Cormag had been wondering if the effect she had on him would ever wane. He had hoped it would be so with all his being, keeping his distance, convincing himself that she was only one of his people, one of many. That reasoning had worked until the day she had sought him out, asking for a favour.

Ever since then, Cormag had been unable to banish her from his thoughts. He spent more time than before up on the wall-walk, knowing she would be down in the meadow, looking for fresh herbs. Even now that winter had come, she still walked through the snow, her gaze fixed on the distant horizon, and he wondered if she ever thought about leaving.

Not long ago, Cormag would have welcomed her departure, knowing it would pull him away from the abyss he was knowingly walking toward. Now, however, his heart twisted painfully at the thought of losing her for good.

Out of the corner of his eye, he noticed Moira rise from her seat at the table, and although Cormag wanted nothing more but to watch her, he did not. He forced himself to remain where he was and not turn toward her. Nevertheless, he glimpsed her walking over to where Emma sat by the fire, watching over Niall and Blair as they slept deeply the way only children could. A few whispered words were exchanged, and then Emma rose to her feet.

Cormag swallowed, wondering what was happening when he saw Moira stride away toward the back end of the hall while Emma headed down a corridor that would lead her outside. Stopping in the small archway, Moira looked over her shoulder, the ghost of a smile coming to her face when Finn suddenly rose from the spot he had occupied all night and left the hall as well, following Emma.

Cormag froze, finally realising what was happening. Moira was interfering again, was she not? Had she seen Finn and Emma together and was now helping them along as she had helped Garrett?

Pride swelled in his chest as he watched her disappear through a back door, amazed by the quiet way she nudged people onto the right path. Never would they know what she had done for them, thinking their happiness had been their own doing. If only they knew! But Moira would never say a word. Cormag was certain of that.

For a long while, he stood lost in thought, contemplating all that he had observed when a familiar voice spoke out from behind him. "D'ye have a moment?"

Blinking, Cormag turned around and found Garrett standing in front of him. How had he not noticed his approach? Clearing his throat, Cormag forced his attention back to the here and now. "Aye. What is it?"

Garrett's eyes narrowed slightly as they took in the discomposure that no doubt clung to Cormag's features. "Are ye all right?"

Cormag nodded, willing his eyes to remain on Garrett's. "Aye. What did ye wish to say?"

Garrett swallowed. "I just wished to inform ye that I've made preparations to leave for England as soon as the snow lets up." He drew in an impatient breath. "I canna wait any longer."

Cormag nodded again, feeling Garrett's restlessness and longing grab a hold of his own heart. To his great shock, it felt achingly familiar, reminding him that not only Garrett had crossed paths with the woman he loved.

The shock of that realisation reverberated through Cormag's body, and he could barely keep up pretences, feeling his friend's lingering gaze. What did Garrett see when he looked at him? Could he read him? Did he know that...?

Cormag swallowed. "I understand," he finally said, nodding to his friend. "Ye've waited long enough. 'Tis true. I wish ye all the best and hope ye'll find her."

"Thank ye," Garrett replied, a deep smile coming to his face as his eyes lit up with relief. Soon he would be on his way. It was about time!

"Thank ye as well," Cormag replied, feeling the need to voice his regret to have detained Garrett for so long. "Thank ye for staying as long as ye have. I know 'twas not easy, but I doubt they would've reached a peaceful agreement if ye hadna-"

Another jolt-the same as before-surged through Cormag's chest, momentarily upending his balance, and he knew even without turning toward the entrance that Moira had returned to the hall.

"Are ye all right?" Garrett asked for the second time that night, his green eyes narrowed in concern. "Ye look...unhinged somehow?"

Cormag swallowed. "'Tis nothing. I...'Tis nothing."

"Is there anything I can do?" Garrett asked, clearly not fooled by Cormag's unconvincing denial.

"'Tis nothing," Cormag said yet again as words failed him. His heart thudded in his chest, and then he caught sight of her as she walked back to the table she had been sitting at before, Maggie across from her. Once again, the two women bent to work, exchanging a few words here and there. The glow on Moira's face spoke volumes about how deeply she was enjoying the simple pleasure of another's company.

"Ye've written to Lord Tynham?" Cormag asked when the silence that hung between him and his friend stretched on.

Garrett nodded. "Aye, he's agreed to aid me in my search. Though I dunna know her brother's title, I informed him of Claudia's maiden name. He didna know it, but he wrote that it sounded familiar. He promised to make enquiries."

"Good. I suppose as the season in London is to begin soon, 'twill be easier to find her, d'ye not think?" Cormag was concentrating hard to continue his conversation with his friend while his heart only had eyes for Moira.

Still seated across from Maggie, she tied ribbon after ribbon onto a large branch, her fingers moving swiftly while her lips moved in quiet conversation. Her blue eyes were bright, and the occasional smile tugged on her lips.

And then Maggie reached for another branch, knocking over a candle in the process.

The second the small flame touched Moira's sleeve, Cormag's heart stopped and every muscle in his body tensed. Images of a fiery inferno filled his mind, and he was about to lunge forward when Moira jerked her arm back.

Instantly, his body stopped itself as he saw that her sleeve only showed a small black mark.

No more.

Maggie was on her feet in a second, putting the candle back in its upright position before her hands reached for Moira's sleeve, inspecting the damage.

Smiling, Moira waved her concern away, and before long, the two women were back at work.

Still, Cormag could not so easily shake off the moment. The strength of her effect on him overwhelmed him, and he had to fight for control. Never had he felt so unbalanced as though he were no longer the one who determined his own fate, as though like the earth moved around the sun, his own world had shifted, drawn to her.

To her alone.

His muscles tensed, and he knew he needed to leave. He needed distance and a way to release the tension gripping him. Still, he could not bring himself to go. Like a magnet drawn to another, he felt her pull, aware that he was not strong enough to break free. So, he stayed, exchanging a word here and there without thought, without awareness, his whole being focused on her alone. He watched from the shadows, out of the corner of his eyes. He pretended to be disinterested. He acted as was expected of him as laird.

He prayed no one would realise how hard his heart beat in his chest.

Every now and then, Cormag thought to feel her gaze travel to him in the same way his lingered on her. However, he could not be certain, and frustration soon built within his chest. Was he only imagining her attention?

Cormag could not deny that on occasion he felt as though he were losing his mind. He cursed under his breath. With all the emotions of those around him he could feel-he had no *choice* but to feel-he could not tell what was in her heart.

That remained shrouded.

A mystery.

No more than a guess.

As the night wore on, Cormag continued to linger. He knew he ought to leave, but he cherished the rare opportunity to be near her. In the past two years, he had only ever watched her from afar, unable to make out the light reflecting in her eyes or the slight curl that would come to her lips occasionally.

Even though the doubt and distance between them was torture, he found a small measure of enjoyment in simply being close by. After all, that was all he could hope for, was it not?

Again, Cormag's thoughts drifted back to Finn and Emma as well as the advice he had given his friend. And in that moment, Cormag realised-belatedly! -that his own situation was not as different as that of his friend. He too...felt strongly for a woman, wondering if she returned his affections. Ought he take his own advice and speak to her?

The thought sent a cold shiver through his body, and a hint of panic sparked in his heart. For the first time in his life, Cormag felt uncertain about another's affections, and he felt overwhelmingly vulnerable not knowing. At this realisation, it was only too understand-able that Finn had held back from speaking to Emma for so long.

Doubt was indeed paralysing.

Ye should marry her, his mother's voice broke into his thoughts, and Cormag groaned.

While Cormag had always been someone to inspect all aspects of a situation with the utmost care before deciding his future and that of his clan, his mother had always had the *tendency* to look at the world at its simplest. She spoke her mind freely and had never been able to understand why certain things posed a difficulty for other people.

For her, if two people loved each other, they ought to marry. It was as simple as that. The circumstances did not matter and thus deserved no consideration.

In the past, whenever Cormag had been faced with a decision that he was of two minds about, his mother's voice had often whispered in his ear as though she stood right beside him. It spoke with the same carefree lilt her true self-possessed, and he had often wondered why his mind would conjure her in these moments as her daring suggestions stood in stark contrast to the careful advice his father had always given him.

His parents had been like day and night, different in every way, but a deep love had connected them all their lives.

Now, his father was gone, and he knew that his mother's heart was no longer as it once had been. Still, she had remained herself, always looking on the brighter side of life and urging others to see it as well. Nothing was ever lost or doomed in his mother's eyes, and Cormag could not deny that her outlook on life was...comforting.

Still, he often reminded himself that life was not as one wanted it to be simply because it was one's desire. So, even if he...wished to marry Moira, even if she wished it as well, would it be the right choice?

Cormag sighed. So much stood between them. He was laird of his clan, and Moira had been banished from hers. What would his people say if he were to make his intentions clear?

Pausing, Cormag swallowed, wondering at what point he had realised what it was he wanted. How could he know? After all, he had never spoken more than a few words with Moira. What if he made the wrong choice? What if a union between them would bring them both misery?

His gaze drifted to Ian and Maggie as they stood head to head, a quiet argument between them as they spoke to one another. While Ian's face held nothing but pain and regret, Maggie's spoke of guilt, and Cormag knew that theirs was a union that perhaps had better not come to be.

For Maggie loved another.

Or once had.

Cormag knew nothing of the circumstances; however, he had felt Ian's love for his wife as well as the absence of Maggie's. He had felt longing in her heart, the same kind of longing he had felt in Finn's and Garrett's chest, the same kind of longing he felt in his own. The longing for another who was out of reach, who was unattainable. The kind of longing that brought with it regret as well as fear of the future.

A future alone.

A future without that other person by one's side.

With each day that passed, Cormag began to understand these emotions more and more for they had sneaked into his own heart when he had not been looking and taken root. Now, it seemed as though they had been a part of him forever, and he knew not how to deal with them.

Suddenly, the wave of emotions of those within the hall was too much for him to bear and he found himself rushing from the peaceful gathering before he had even decided to do so. His feet carried him down the corridor to his study where he hoped to find the necessary peace and quiet to know his own heart, unaffected by the feelings of others.

Sometimes it was difficult to tell, and Cormag feared to make a wrong decision based on an emotion that was not even his own.

Gulping down a lungful of air, Cormag shut the door behind him and strode to the window without another thought. The snow-covered hills greeted him, and he felt his mind ease as the strain of the evening slowly fell away. It was the familiar routine that calmed him, and he sometimes wondered what he would do if his small sanctuary was ever lost to him.

The moon shone in the dark night sky; its silver rays reflected in the blanket of snow draped over a sleeping world. It was a peaceful image, and Cormag found himself breathing easier. Still, his thoughts remained in an uproar as he remembered the few moments he had shared with Moira. He remembered the hint of longing he had felt swell in her chest the first time she had sought him out in his study to ask for a favour. Had he been mistaken? For whenever their paths had crossed since, he had always detected a hint of nervousness or unease in her. Sometimes, she had seemed skittish, and a part of him wondered if she might be afraid of him. Could she tell that he…longed for her? Did that thought upset her because she did, in fact, not return his affections? Was that why she always sought to avoid him?

Frustration rose once more, and Cormag marvelled at how others managed their lives with this constant level of uncertainty. While he could at least most of the time be certain how some felt, others were always in doubt. How did this not drive them insane?

A sudden knock on the door made him spin around.

His brows drew down, and he shook his head. "How can it be that I didna sense yer approach?" he whispered to himself as he strode toward the door. Perhaps his preoccupation with Moira affected him more than he knew.

Opening the door, Cormag found none other than Finn and Emma standing before him, the glow in their eyes speaking volumes. Not that Cormag needed to read their expressions, for the love and joy that suddenly filled his heart nearly brought him to his knees.

Clearing his throat, he gritted his teeth, fighting for composure. "What can I do for ye?" he asked as he stepped back around his desk, motioning for the couple to enter.

Finn closed the door behind them before they stepped up to his desk, their hands linked as though they could not bear to be separated from one another...even if only by the air between them.

Cormag envied them. "I suppose congratulations are in order," he said without thought, still fighting to keep his expression even as their emotions in his chest urged a deep smile onto his face.

Finn and Emma exchanged a look, a slight frown on their faces. "Is it that obvious?" Finn asked laughing as he pulled Emma's hand through the crook of his arm.

Cormag nodded, allowing a small smile to show. "I'm afraid so." Still, he wondered how they had finally overcome the obstacles in their path, obstacles that had kept them apart for years. Had they simply spoken truthfully with one another? Had it truly been as simple as that?

"We came to ask for a favour," Finn said, glancing at Emma, who returned his smile with a dazzling one of her own. "We wish to be married...tomorrow."

Cormag stilled. "Tomorrow?" he asked, looking from one to the other. He was about to ask for a reason when he stopped himself, knowing that it was unnecessary. They could not wait. Not after all this time.

"Tomorrow then," Cormag finally said giving his agreement. He saw relief wash over Finn's face before he turned to look at Emma. "'Twould seem ye decorated the hall for yer own wedding day, Lass."

Smiling, Emma cupped her hands over her face in sheer disbelief of her happiness before she flung herself into Finn's arms. He caught her, his arms rubbing over her back, before he turned his head to look at Cormag. A silent thank-you flew from his lips, and Cormag was relieved to see that sometimes circumstances truly did not matter.

Whatever had stood in their path, it seemed it had never been of importance. But was that true for everyone? Or were they simply two of only a handful of fortunate ones?

A small smile came to Cormag's face as he watched them leave his study arm in arm, happiness emanating off them in waves, and he wondered what would have happened if he had not spoken to Finn, if Moira had not interfered, giving them an opportunity to speak to one another. Would they still be getting married tomorrow? Had they truly helped bring two people together?

Cormag wished he could speak to Moira about this. If only he dared!

Chapter Eight

OVER THE EDGE

When spring chased away the last of the snow, Moira felt relieved for the outdoors had always been her sanctuary offering her peace and quiet. Wrapped in a warm cloak, she ventured across the meadows, delighting in the children racing each other up and down the small slope, their little faces speaking of an equal delight to be no longer confined indoors.

The air smelled fresh, heavy with lingering rain but full of promise as a deep green reclaimed the land. Animals awoke from their slumber, and their voices echoed through the air, speaking of joy and a new year on the horizon.

Soon, Moira would spend most of her time in the hills and forests surrounding *Seann Dachaigh* Tower, searching the banks of lochs and glens for the herbs she needed to replenish. Her mind would be set to a useful task, a task that would keep her occupied and chase away the thoughts that had lingered all winter.

Thoughts she should not have entertained.

Thoughts that would only lead to heartbreak.

Thoughts of Cormag MacDrummond.

Although they had spent the past two years avoiding each other, something had changed since the day she had sought him out to ask for a favour. Ever since then, she had felt his gaze on her whenever they happened to pass one another in the courtyard or the great hall even if only from a distance. Still, he never spoke to her, his shoulders tense whenever she dared glance in his direction.

Mostly, however, Moira kept her eyes averted, afraid that the flutter of her heart would somehow be visible on her face. What was it about Cormag MacDrummond that made her feel...unhinged?

Walking through the tall grass, Moira felt the droplets clinging to the stalks soak through her hem, bringing with it a slight chill. Still, Moira could not return, not until she had sorted out the turmoil in her heart. She needed time alone. Time to think. Time away from suspicion and mistrust.

Again, she recalled the look in Cormag's eyes when they had happened upon one another only a few days ago.

Moira had walked around a corner and drawn up short, her heart hammering in her chest when she had found herself almost colliding with his broad chest. Her eyes had darted upward to meet his but had not dared to linger. She had stammered an apology and tried to slink away, but...

Closing her eyes, Moira remembered the feeling of his warm hand on her shoulder.

He had stopped her, his sharp grey eyes studying her face as though trying to see below, to understand something that eluded him.

Moira frowned, realising that unlike her he had not seemed startled in the least to come upon her so unexpectedly. Or had it not been so?

During the first two years of her stay at *Seann Dachaigh* Tower, Moira had rarely stumbled into his path. However, over the last few months, it seemed that wherever she went, he was nearby. Why? Was he watching her?

The thought that he might distrust her sent a jabbing pain through her heart. Moira could not say why, but for some reason, she had always felt as though...he knew that she had not acted out of malice. That she had made a mistake, aye, but that she had never meant to harm anyone.

Had something happened to make him doubt her? Or had she been mistaken about him?

Perhaps she ought to confront him.

In her old life, she would not have hesitated to do so. However, now, everything was different.

Still, Moira could not help but wonder why his suspicion should rattle her so. No, not rattle. It brought a flutter to her heart and often had her breath lodge in her throat.

Leaning against the thick trunk of an elm tree, Moira closed her eyes, recalling the moment their eyes had met. Indeed, he had been... watchful, but there had been something else in his gaze as well. Something that had made her skin crawl, not with dread, but with...something else. Something pleasant. Something enticing. Something...

And then he had touched her, and the world had stopped spinning.

Moira recalled with shocking detail just how his hand had rested on her shoulder, the pads of his fingers pressing against the fabric of her dress, warm and teasing, as though urging her closer.

Closer to him.

If Mrs. Brown had not happened upon them in that moment, who knows what would have happened? Moira could not deny that she longed to know. Was it possible that he cared for her? Or did he merely desire her?

"Moira!"

Flinching, Moira felt her eyes snap open as the shock of hearing her name called reverberated through her body. Would she ever get used to it? Once, it had been nothing unusual. Something pleasant. Comforting.

But now, it held a dark foreboding, making Moira's skin crawl.

"Are ye all right?" little Blair asked as she pulled to a stop in front of her. Her blue eyes swept Moira's face, and her brows drew down in concern. "I shall pick ye some flowers. They'll make ye feel better." A deep smile came to her little face.

Moira could not help but return it. "If ye can find any. It might be too early, mind ye." Despite her best efforts, Moira had been unable to keep the little girl from her side. No matter her brother's and father's disapproval, Blair had a mind of her own and she intended to use it the way she chose.

Grinning, the little girl dashed off, certain victory glowing in her eyes as she raced past her brother, who bore the familiar frown upon his face.

Moira smiled at him, but his brows only drew down more before he turned his back on her and followed his sister.

Her shoulders slumped in defeat, however, before the familiar wave of hopelessness and despair could engulf her, Moira consciously straightened her spine and lifted her chin, pulling her shoulders back. She steered her thoughts toward Maggie's enchanting smile, a woman who had only ever met her with kindness. She thought of Garrett, who had left shortly after Christmas to search for his wife. However, before he had left, their eyes had met across the hall, and he had inclined his head to her in gratitude. In that moment, Moira had realised that he knew, that Cormag had to have told him of her request, a request that had not led to disaster.

Not this time.

Although months had passed and they had not heard from Garrett, Moira was certain that he was still searching, that one day he would find his wife and be happy again. After all, she had seen it.

Then she directed her thoughts toward Emma and Finn, remembering their happiness as they had finally spoken their vows on Christmas Day. Then, too, Moira's *interference* had not led to anything harmful, judging from the unadulterated joy always sparkling in their eyes these days.

All had gone well, and Moira knew that there were a few people-even if only a handful-who did not look upon her with disapproval, with suspicion, with disgust. No, there were a few people in *Seann Dachaigh* Tower, who respected her, who liked her, who did not see her as a threat.

Moira reminded herself never to forget that as she strode up toward the village situated around the ancient structure that had provided a home to Clan MacDrummond for countless generations. She might still be a stranger, not one of them; still, she had a place among them.

Stepping into the small cottage she shared with her aunt, Moira called Fiona's name, but all remained quiet. Perhaps her aunt was still out with Duncan. Earlier that morning, Moira had seen the two of them strolling across the courtyard, eyes only for one another and completely oblivious to everything else happening around them.

The warm glow of Fiona's eyes had brought a smile to Moira's face, and she hoped that her aunt would find happiness a second time around. Moira would certainly miss her if she became Duncan's wife; however, she knew that it would please her to see Fiona happy again especially after the hardship Moira had brought into her life simply by being here, by being *her* niece.

For the remainder of the morning, Moira kept busy in the small kitchen, straightening up and noting down the herbs she would need to look for first. Then she began preparing the midday meal, hoping Fiona would be back in time.

As Moira was about to set the table, a sharp knock on the door drew her attention. Frowning, she turned toward it. *Fiona wouldn't knock, would she?*

Crossing the room, Moira flinched when the knock came again, this time with even more vehemence. Someone was angry, and for a moment, she wondered if she ought to even open the door. But what if something had happened to her aunt? What if she was needed? Or her herbs?

Fear gripped Moira's heart, and she all but lunged forward, grabbed the handle and pulled the door open. "What's hap-?"

The rest of the question died on her lips when she found herself face to face with Ian MacDrummond.

His face was a dark red, and his eyes had narrowed into slits, daggers flying from them as he glared at her.

Before Moira could gather her wits, Ian pushed inside, his right hand wrapping painfully around her throat. He shoved her backwards until the back of her head collided hard with the wall, and she saw bright lights dance before her eyes. "How dare ye go near her?" he snarled into her face as his hand tightened, his fingers digging into her flesh. "Stay away from her! Do ye hear? Stay away!"

Blinking her eyes against the blinding flashes, Moira tried to draw air into her lungs as her hands fought to loosen Ian's grip around her throat. "I d-dunno what y-ye mean," she gasped, beginning to feel the lack of air darken her sight.

"Blair almost drowned!" Ian spat into her face, his gaze only inches from hers as he glared at her in disgust, in hatred, in abhorrence. "Do ye hear me? She almost drowned because of ye!"

Moira's ears rang with his words, and panic swept into her heart. "What?" she gasped, her voice strangled and barely audible. She tried to swallow, but Ian's grip prevented it. "H-how?"

Ian's jaw clenched, and fear came to his pale eyes before he shook it off and anger returned, darkening his features. "She meant to pick flowers for ye," he snarled. "Water lilies, she said. She fell in and..." Pain contorted his face, and Moira saw clear as day how deeply he loved his little girl.

"I didna know," Moira rasped, remembering how Blair had spoken to her earlier that day. The little girl had wanted to cheer her up, and so she had looked for flowers that were not even in bloom yet.

"Isna it enough that ye turned my wife against me?" Ian hissed, and his hands dug deeper into Moira's flesh. "Ye also seek to harm my daughter? What kind of woman are ye? Harming children?" His jaw clenched, and he shook his head. "Ye're evil! A witch!"

Dark spots began to blur into her field of vision, and Ian's voice sounded as though it was coming from far away. Moira felt her hands cease their efforts as her body surrendered, her muscles unable to keep fighting without life-sustaining air.

Was this it? Moira wondered somewhere deep down. Was this how she would die?

Feeling her knees buckle, Moira sank down when Ian's grip suddenly vanished from around her neck. Instantly, air surged into her lungs, and her eyes jerked open in shock. She hit the floor hard, and her hands flew up to wrap around her neck protectively as she drew air back into her starving body.

Then Moira's gaze cleared, and she looked up.

With his back to her, Cormag stood between her and Ian, his feet firmly planted on the ground and his hands lifted in warning as he faced his friend. "What madness is this?" he demanded, his voice harsh and, yet, in control. Still, there was something in the way he glanced back at her that told Moira how deeply this confrontation affected him.

"Blair almost drowned!" Ian snarled, his eyes blazing with hatred as he shot forward again, his hands once more reaching toward her.

Moira drew in a panicked breath, and her feet pushed her harder against the wall, futilely trying to put more distance between her and the man seeking to avenge his child.

"Dunna dare lay a hand on her!" Cormag commanded as he shoved Ian back. "What happened was an accident. 'Twas no one's fault, do ye hear?"

Ian's glare moved from Moira to his laird. "Why would ye defend her? She's evil. She's betrayed her own clan." His jaw clenched. "Ye should never have allowed her to stay. She's a danger to us all."

Shivering, Moira watched as Cormag took a careful step toward Ian. "She made a mistake, aye, but she didna harm yer daughter. What happened to Blair was an accident, nothing more." He clasped a hand on Ian's shoulder. "I willna have members of my clan attacking one another, do ye hear?"

As though slapped, Ian jerked back. "She's not of our clan, or have ye forgotten that? Her own people banished her. She doesna deserve yer defence. How dare ye choose her over yer own people? Over my daughter?"

"I am not," Cormag replied, a dark tone in his voice as his shoulders tensed. "Always have I put our clan first, but that doesna mean I'll stand by and allow ye to harm her."

Disgust filled Ian's gaze as he took a step back, looking at his laird as though he had never laid eyes on him before. "How dare ye defend her after what she's done? Has she bewitched ye?"

Wrapping her arms around her bent knees, Moira watched the two men, her heart teetering between fear and awe. While Ian's hatred had not come as a surprise-long since had Moira feared that one day, he would find reason enough to attack her-Cormag's defence had stolen the air from her lungs in a most pleasant way. How had he known that Ian was attacking her? How had he known that she needed help?

"Dunna be a fool," Cormag replied, a forced chuckle rising from his throat deeming Ian's accusations ludicrous. Still, the tension in his shoulders never subsided, and Moira wondered if he truly believed his own words. Did he think her a witch as well? Then why would he defend her? Why had he interfered?

Ian's eyes narrowed, and he crossed his arms over his chest. "Ye've changed," he hissed, momentarily glaring at Moira. "Ye're different around her. Is that not proof that she's a witch?" He shook his head. "Never have I doubted yer ability to lead our clan, but now...What did she do to ye? What is it ye hope to gain by defending her? Do ye simply wish to bed her? Is that it?"

In the next instant, Cormag's fist collided hard with Ian's jaw, sending the fair-haired man flying backwards. He landed with a dull thud, and a cry of pain escaped his lips. Still, he was back on his feet the moment Cormag lunged forward and grabbed him by the collar. "Pull yerself together," Cormag snarled as he glared down at Ian. "Ye're allowing yer anger to cloud yer judgement."

Wide-eyed, Moira stared at the MacDrummond Laird, certain that he had never reacted quite so...passionately, without thought, almost without control, on instinct alone. Judging from the look on Ian's face, he too was surprised by his friend's reaction.

"Ye've been angry for a long time," Cormag spoke, his voice deadly calm and, yet, the pulse in his neck beat wildly, "and ye need to find a way to deal with whatever it is that boils yer blood. Ye canna walk around making accusations because of something ye canna handle. Do ye hear?" Releasing Ian, he took a step back. "If ye need my help, ye only need ask, but I willna tolerate this vicious hatred. Would ye have attacked yer wife if she had been the one whom Blair had sought flowers for?"

Gritting his teeth, Ian swallowed, calmer now; his eyes, however, still shone with unadulterated hatred, and Moira wondered what it would take to make him look at her differently. What had he said earlier? She had turned his wife against him. What on earth could he mean by that?

Turning on his heel, Ian stormed out of the small cottage, banging the door shut as a last act of defiance.

Moira flinched at the sound, her eyes filling with tears as she stared at the wooden door.

"Are ye all right, Lass?" Cormag asked as he knelt in front of her, his sharp grey eyes taking in the tears spilling from her eyes. There was warmth and concern in the way he looked at her, and Moira felt her heart respond to it with desperate need.

Her jaw quivered, and she cursed herself for allowing him to see her in such a desolate state. "I'm all right," she croaked, her throat sore, as she tried to push herself to her feet. Still, her knees felt as weak as her resolve to remain strong.

"Let me help ye." Holding out his hand to her, Cormag moved closer, his gaze drifting to her throat, her hands still wrapped protectively around it.

Again, Moira swallowed, and again, it hurt. Then she noticed his hand hovering in the air before her, and time seemed to still.

Although she had felt his hand on her shoulder a time or two, the thought of feeling his skin against hers, warm and alive, once more stole her breath. For a long moment, she looked at him, wondering why he was here, wondering if she simply ought to send him away, wondering if she was imagining the tender concern she saw in his eyes.

Eyes that had always seemed sharp and hard and unyielding.

But not now.

Slowly, Moira removed her right hand from around her neck and carefully slipped it into Cormag's. The moment their fingers touched, she drew in a shuddering breath, feeling the sensation in every fibre of her being.

A small smile teased his lips before his hand closed more strongly around hers and he rose to pull her to her feet.

Moira's legs still trembled with shock, and she swayed on her feet. Instantly, her hand tightened on his, seeking to steady her, and he stepped forward, his other hand coming to rest on her left arm.

"Did he hurt ye?" he asked, his jaw tensing as his eyes dropped down to where her left hand still lay wrapped around her throat. "Let me see."

Reluctantly, Moira unclenched her fingers, slowly removing her hand. She swallowed and immediately cringed at the pain. Pulling back, she dropped her chin, overwhelmed by the tenderness in his gaze. How long had it been since anyone-?

Gently, his hand grasped her chin, tilting it upward as he leant in, his gaze travelling over her exposed neck. Immediately, the expression on his face tightened, and she could see anger spark in his eyes. His fingers on her jaw tensed, and Moira felt her breath quicken.

Did this mean he cared? Would he still look at her the way he did if he did not feel the least bit of affection for her? Or was it simply compassion? Pity even?

Closing her eyes, Moira fought the need to sink into his arms and feel them wrap around her, holding her. It had been too long since she had felt close to another, since anyone had dared touch her in a gesture of comfort or affection. His right hand still held hers, and she could feel her skin tingle at the contact.

So warm.

So soothing.

So unfamili-

Moira held her breath when she felt his other hand move from her chin, his fingers skimming along the line of her jaw and down to her neck until they gently brushed over the bruises Ian's hand had left behind.

Drawing in a sharp breath, Moira's eyes flew open.

Instantly, Cormag retreated and his hand fell from her neck. Guilt etched into his eyes, and he gritted his teeth as her other hand slowly slipped from his grasp. "It'll heal," he murmured, his grey eyes not veering from hers. "Ye'll be fine."

Swallowing, Moira nodded as her throat burnt yet again. Still, her skin tingled with the way he was looking at her, and she wished...

Moira did not know what it was she wished for. It had been a long time since she had allowed her heart to dream, to hope, to long for something.

For someone.

Still, in that very moment, she could have sworn that her heart yearned for the taciturn man standing in front of her. Not because she was lonely, but because she knew she would never tire of having those dark grey eyes looking into hers.

If only she had met him in a different lifetime!

Chapter Nine

BURDENS

With a last glance over his shoulder, Cormag hurried from the small cottage, leaving Moira behind.

Every fibre of his being urged him to stay with her, to not leave her alone. Still, he remembered well the way she had cringed when he had touched her, when his fingers had travelled along the line of her jaw seemingly of their own accord.

Always had he been in control, but where Moira was concerned, Cormag could not trust himself. He had hardly noticed the way he had drawn closer before she had shied away. Did she fear him? He wondered, cringing away from the thought as it burnt through his heart.

With perfect clarity, he remembered Ian's words, *Do ye simply wish to bed her?* Was that why she had flinched at his touch? Or was it because he had so harshly attacked his friend? Not that he had not had good reason, but had she seen something in him that had frightened her?

Cormag wished he knew. He wished he knew if she had truly been afraid, afraid of him, or simply overwhelmed by the situation.

As he strode across the courtyard, trying to be unobtrusive, Cormag recalled the very moment he had come upon her and Ian. He had been nearby and sensed Ian's hatred, blazing like an inferno, as well as the fear that mingled with it. The closer he had come to Fiona's cottage, the stronger the emotions had seized him, and Cormag had known what would await him inside.

And then he had seen her.

Standing pressed against the wall. Ian's hand wrapped around her delicate throat. Her eyes wide with fear. The look on her face one of resignation.

Rubbing a hand over his face to chase away the image, Cormag hurried along the corridor toward his chamber. He needed to be alone, afraid of what he might do or say should he encounter someone as all his thoughts circled around what had just happened. His heart thudded wildly in his chest, and he knew how close he was to losing control.

"Are ye all right?"

At the sound of his mother's voice, Cormag cringed as though someone had struck him. Of all the people he needed to avoid, she was the one who was the most dangerous to him.

For she knew him well.

Too well.

"'Tis nothing," he replied over his shoulder, barely slowing down, worried to be drawn into a conversation. "I'll speak to ye later."

Before he turned away from her, his feet carrying him onward, Cormag noted the slight frown coming to her face. A sense of suspicion drifted into his being, and he knew he had not been convincing.

"Ye can run but ye canna hide," she exclaimed, a slight chuckle in her tone as she followed him, her footsteps echoing closer. "Ye might as well tell me the truth."

Pulling to a stop, Cormag gritted his teeth before he turned to face her. "What is it ye wish to know?"

Her green eyes swept over his face in that oddly unsettling way that made him wonder if she could read his thoughts. "Tell me."

Cormag sighed, "Have ye heard what happened to little Blair?"

The look in his mother's eyes grew sad, and she nodded. "Aye, 'tis awful." She exhaled a relieved breath. "I'm so grateful her brother managed to pull her out. He's always looking out for her."

Cormag nodded. Indeed, this once, Niall's watchfulness had been lifesaving.

"But that is not what made ye angry," his mother commented, her green eyes sharp once more as she looked at him enquiringly.

"Ian blamed Moira because Blair got hurt trying to pick flowers for her."

His mother nodded knowingly. "Aye, there's bad blood there," she whispered, and for a moment, her eyes became distant. Then she blinked, and her gaze returned to his. "Did he harm her?"

"I found him with his hand around her throat," Cormag whispered, feeling anger boil hot once more, curling his hands into fists by his side.

His mother's eyes narrowed as she glanced down. "But she is well?"

Unable not to, Cormag began to pace. "As well as can be," he growled, knowing his behaviour would only fuel his mother's suspicions. "His hand left marks on her neck."

"Did ye speak to her?"

Cormag halted in his step, then turned and looked at his mother.

"She might need someone to talk to," she suggested, stepping toward him. "A friend who can give her comfort." Placing a hand on his arm, she looked up at him, a soft smile curling up the corners of her mouth. "She shouldna be alone after what happened."

Cormag gritted his teeth. "She barely knows me and...would certainly not consider me a friend." He swallowed, taking a step back. "Her aunt will be home soon. She'll look after her."

His mother sighed, "Fiona is rather preoccupied right now. She willna know what-"

"I canna be her friend!"

The harshness of his words shocked Cormag more than his mother as she simply continued to look at him, that knowing half-smile on her face, and asked, "Why not?"

Feeling the muscle in his jaw twitch, Cormag drew in a slow breath, trying his best to calm the pulse that thudded in his neck. He knew he was acting rash and without thought. He ought to know better. He ought to know how to maintain his balance, how to avoid this emotional turmoil that now threatened to undo him.

But he did not.

In that moment, all he knew was that he needed to be alone. "I'll speak to ye later," he said, stepping away. "At present, I'm..."

"Go," she whispered, that knowing smile back on her face. "But ye might want to consider something other than the solitude of yer room. If ye dunna want to speak to me, perhaps a friend will serve ye better." Her green eyes twinkled with humour as she smiled up at him. "Finn is downstairs in the hall. Perhaps he'll know what to tell ye." She brushed a hand down his arm in that comforting gesture she had always used ever since he had been a lad before turning around and walking down the hallway.

Staring after her, Cormag paused, wondering if she could be right. Annoyingly, he had to admit that his mother had a way of being right about these things. He knew that if he were to spend the afternoon pacing the length of his chamber, it would only bring him closer to the edge of the abyss. Perhaps he ought to ask Finn for a quick training session.

Cormag would have preferred to speak to Garrett; however, his oldest friend was still in England searching for his wife. Still, Finn knew Ian better than anyone and could perhaps shed some light on the man's hatred for Moira. The thought of him attacking her again made Cormag feel sick to the stomach and he knew not what to do.

An hour later, the two men strode onto the meadow they had used for their training ever since they had been lads. It was a familiar surrounding, one that inspired calm and concentration, and Cormag felt his heartbeat slow.

The sun shone brightly, gleaming in the blades of their swords as they faced one another. Their feet stood secure on the ground, and their hands were wrapped around the hilts of their swords. A soft breeze brushed over Cormag's heated skin as he spun around to block Finn's attack.

His friend laughed; his gaze watchful. "Ye look distracted," he remarked after a while, lowering his sword. "Is something wrong?"

"Nay!" Charging forward, Cormag attacked.

Dropping down, Finn avoided the reach of Cormag's sword. He rolled sideways and jumped back up onto his feet, the look in his eyes more contemplative than before. "I canna say I believe ye," he commented as his frown deepened. "Quite frankly, ye're scaring me. I've never seen ye so...unfocused. What happened?"

Panting, Cormag thrust his sword into the ground, watching it reverberate with the impact. Then he ran his hands through his hair, not knowing what else to do with them. "Did ye hear what happened with little Blair today?"

Finn's gaze darkened. "Aye."

Seeing the question in his friend's eyes, Cormag swallowed. "Ian blamed Moira for it." His teeth ground together. "He attacked her."

Finn's eyes widened. "He did what? Are ye certain?"

Cormag nodded, feeling his control slip away once more.

"Tell me what happened."

Looking at his friend, Cormag nodded and described the scene he had all but stumbled upon. "Ye shoulda seen him. He was not himself."

Concern rested in Finn's eyes as he stepped closer. "He's never liked her, but..." He shrugged. "I always thought that was only because of his usual mistrust."

"So, did I," Cormag replied. "But now 'tis clear that 'tis more than that. Something happened." Again, his jaw clenched as his thoughts ran in all kinds of directions. What could possibly have happened to cause that kind of hatred?

"Did ye ask Moira?"

Cormag froze at the sound of her name. "I didna. She was too shaken, and I dunna think she knows."

Finn sighed, shaking his head. "Ian's been..." He threw up his hands. "Ye're right. He's not been himself lately. He's angry and...and now that..." Closing his eyes, Finn drew in a slow breath, and Cormag felt a wave of regret, of guilt wash over his friend.

"Now that what?"

"Now that I have Emma," Finn whispered, "I can see that 'tis not the same between him and Maggie." He shook his head. "I didna see it before. I was too...focused on my own misery. I havena been a good friend."

Stepping forward, Cormag placed a hand on his friend's shoulder. "Dunna blame yerself. Ye've always been a good friend to him. The trouble is that he doesna seek help. Whatever plagues him, he willna speak about it."

"I'll try," Finn promised. "I'll speak to him. Perhaps it'll help."

Cormag nodded, hoping that Finn was right. Still, he could not help but feel that Ian would not share his reasons with his friend. He could only hope that Ian's anger would wane before causing irreparable harm. If he attacked Moira yet again...

Yanking his sword from the ground, Cormag cursed his gift for it failed him here and now. If only he knew what fuelled Ian's hatred, he could protect Moira. However, the cause remained hidden, and so he was forced to wait and see how things unfolded.

Never had Cormag felt so powerless.

Chapter Ten

OPEN WORDS

S itting under her favourite cluster of trees, Moira found peace in the soft singsong of birds overhead as it mingled with the gentle caress of the breeze tugging on her hair. Nearby, she heard children laughing, and although Moira had always loved the echo of their joy, she felt herself tense.

Fear gripped her, and she glanced over her shoulder, afraid to find Ian standing there, his hands reaching for her throat.

When Moira saw nothing but the distant glen, she breathed a sigh of relief, and yet, her hand brushed absentmindedly over the bruised skin on her neck. Only an echo remained of Ian's attack, and each day as the bruises faded more and more, Moira wished her memories would do so as well.

Still, she could not deny that she cherished the memory of how Cormag had come to her aid. More than once she had relived the moment they had shared in the cottage in her dreams, seeing those dark grey eyes looking into hers, full of concern and compassion. She remembered the soft touch of his skin against hers, the tenderness with which he had reached out to her, brushed his fingertips over her bruised skin.

Moira remembered how she had flinched at his touch and how he had immediately retreated, guilt darkening his eyes.

The contact had been so unexpected and overwhelming that a jolt had gone through her. She could only hope that Cormag had not misinterpreted her reaction. She loathed the idea that he might think she had been repulsed by his touch.

More than once, she wished she could have spoken to him, but lately their paths did not seem to cross. It was as though he was staying away from her.

Moira's heart sank at the thought.

"Ye look sad."

Moira's head snapped up, and for a moment, she feared her worst nightmare had come true.

That Ian had found her and come to exact revenge.

Then she blinked and found Maggie standing off to the side, her auburn hair gleaming in the sun. Relief rushed through Moira, and she closed her eyes, willing her pulse to calm.

"Ye thought 'twas my husband," Maggie remarked as she walked over and then sat down beside Moira. Her blue eyes held regret as she reached out a hand to brush over Moira's arm. "I came to speak to ye about what happened. I came to apologise."

Moira smiled at the young woman. "There's no need. I-"

"Aye, there is," Maggie insisted, her fingers toying with the hem of her dress. "What he did was wrong, and I'm sorry ye got hurt. I tried to talk to him, to make him see that 'twas only an accident, but sometimes there's no talking to him." She scoffed. "He can be as stubborn as a mule."

"I'm sorry Blair got hurt. If I'd known she would-"

"Children get hurt," Maggie interrupted, a sad smile on her lovely face. "'Tis a fact of life. As much as we want to keep them safe, we canna always protect them. 'Twas not yer fault, and I dunna blame ye." Scooting to the side, she turned to face Moira. "And neither does Ian. Not deep down. He did what he did because he was terrified of how close we'd come to losing her. He felt powerless, and it was more than he could handle."

Moira nodded. "I understand." Despite her own terror in that moment when Ian's hands had closed around her throat, Moira had seen the fear and pain in his gaze. She had known that while it had been hatred that had made her a target, it had been fear that had forced him to act that day.

"When he..." Moira looked at the woman beside her, wondering about the words Ian had spoken that day. Words that still echoed in her mind. "He said, *Isna it enough that ye turned my wife against me?*" Her gaze swept over Maggie, seeing her eyes darken and her chin drop. "What did he mean?"

Tears pooled in Maggie's eyes as her fingers tore more roughly at her hem, seeking to release some of the frustration that now stood in her eyes. "I dunna love my husband," she whispered. "I never have. I thought I could at one point, but I..." Tears streamed down her face, and for the first time since Moira had come to *Seann Dachaigh* Tower, Maggie was not the flitting, dancing fairy with light in her eyes and a heart full of strength and laughter.

No, in that moment, she looked broken, her heart weighed down by regret and guilt. She too felt powerless, caught in a life, in a marriage, that was not built on love, but on a wrong choice. "He knows," she whispered, wiping the tears from her cheeks. "'Twas days after ye came here that I told him how I felt. I didna know it then, but I think 'tis the reason why he dislikes ye so. He believes ye did something to steal my love for him."

Moira reached for the other woman's hand, gently pulling it into her own.

"I tried to talk to him," Maggie continued, "but he doesna hear me. I think deep down he knows that I speak the truth, but I guess 'tis easier for him to think otherwise. It allows him to feel anger instead of regret, and..." She exhaled a shuddering breath. "Regret is so crippling; I know why he retreats from it."

"I'm sorry," Moira whispered gently, squeezing Maggie's hand. It was a comfort for them both, a connection to another who cared, who listened, who was simply there. "What happened?"

Maggie sighed, and the ghost of a smile flitted across her face as she turned toward her memories. "When I came to Scotland to visit my mother's clan, I was...I was in love." A chuckle escaped her, and her eyes took on a faraway look. At least for a moment. "I thought he loved me as well, but I suppose I musta been mistaken. Before we'd even returned home, my father wrote to me that he had gotten married." Fresh tears pooled in her eyes. "He didn't even write to me to tell me himself. I never heard from him again. Not a word."

"And so ye stayed in Scotland?"

Maggie nodded. "I was terrified of seeing him again...with...with his wife." She swallowed hard. "And so, I extended my stay again and again. Ian was there. He tried to cheer me up. He was so sweet, so full of life and laughter."

Moira felt her jaw drop.

"I know," Maggie replied. "'Tis hard to imagine, but he's not always been the man he's now. *I* did that to him. I knew that he loved me, and I thought perhaps one day I could love him as well. And so, I stayed and accepted his proposal." Her hand squeezed Moira's. "It took me a long time to realise the severity of my mistake. I should never have accepted him. I ruined his life, and there's no going back." A deep sigh left her lips. "I'm sorry for what happened. 'Twas my fault. I'm so relieved Cormag came when he did." Her gaze drifted lower to the faint bruises on Moira's skin. "I dunna want to imagine what might've happened if he hadna been there."

Moira nodded, feeling an echo of the relief that had swept through her upon seeing Cormag come to her aid. "Aye, he saved me. I wish I knew how he came to be there," she marvelled, still wondering about the many times their paths had crossed seemingly by coincidence. "It felt as though he had known that..."

"That ye needed him?" Maggie whispered, something teasing sparking in her eyes. "Aye, he's a quiet one, but he...he sees things others dunna. He knew of Ian's hatred for ye, and when he heard of what had happened to Blair, I suppose he knew Ian might blame ye."

Moira blinked, wondering if this could be true. Had he truly come for her? Or had he merely been nearby and happened upon them by chance? "But why would he...?" Again, she blinked and turned to look at Maggie. "I'm nothing to him while Ian is his fr-"

"Ye're not nothing to him," Maggie objected, her hand closing tightly around Moira's. "He cares for ye. Do ye not see that?"

All thoughts vanished, and Moira could do little else but stare at the young woman beside her.

Maggie laughed. "Aye, 'tis always hardest to see for those involved. 'Twas the same with Emma and Finn." A deep sigh left Maggie's lips, and although the smile still clung to her features, there was a deep longing in her eyes. "He's different around ye."

Moira felt a shiver run down her spine as she remembered how Ian had thrown those same words into Cormag's face. Could it be true? Did he truly...?

"I can see that ye care for him as well," Maggie whispered as she tried to meet Moira's gaze, a teasing smile tickling the corners of her mouth. "Perhaps ye should speak to him."

A shudder gripped Moira. "I canna," she stated forcefully, knowing how devastating it would be to hope and then have those hopes crushed. "He's the laird, and I'm...I'm an outcast, barely tolerated to live amongst ye. Nay, there's no future for us...even if ye were right."

Sighing, Maggie shook her head. "If ye believe that, I canna sway ye, but I urge ye to look a little closer next time ye see him." Then she rose to her feet and with a quick wave walked back up the slope toward the keep.

Moira stared after her for a long time, but in her mind's eye all she could see were those dark grey eyes locked onto hers, full of tenderness and concern.

If only there were a chance.

Chapter Eleven

A CALL FOR AID

T he great hall was abuzz with joyful voices as Cormag stood off to the side watching the happy couple receive congratulations and well-wishes, their eyes aglow whenever they looked at one another. Despite his advanced age and serious disposition, Duncan, a touch of red colouring his cheeks and the pulse in his neck hammering like a stampede, looked like a lad who had lost his heart for the first time. His hand held on to Fiona's, never once slipping from hers, as he guided her to their place of honour at the large table.

Taking her seat, Fiona smiled up at him, and Cormag saw her draw in a shuddering breath when her new husband's hand trailed down her arm until it once more reached for hers resting on the tabletop.

Both had loved and lost, and Cormag was happy to see that they received a second chance at love. They both deserved it, and he could only hope that their union would bring their families closer together.

Swallowing, Cormag glanced at the far corner of the large room where Moira stood in the shadows.

While Ian and his family joined in the festivities, Moira had kept away, only lingering on the fringes, casting glances at the festive celebration, but never once participating.

Cormag's heart sank when he saw the longing in her eyes as she looked at her aunt. There was joy there, joy to see someone she cared for find such happiness. Still, her hands clenched, and tension rested on her lovely features, and even though Cormag could not sense her heart's desire, he suddenly felt certain that she knew the meaning of regret. Had she once dreamed of a wedding of her own? Of a husband?

Swallowing, Cormag reminded himself of the few details he knew about her banishment. Connor Brunwood himself had informed him that while he believed that she had never meant to harm him, she had conspired to rid him of his wife. What had been her motivation? Had she thought as Old Angus had? That the English were the downfall of the Scottish clans even today? Or had there been another reason? A more personal reason?

Cormag gritted his teeth at the thought that Moira had given her heart to the Brunwood laird and wondered if the man possessed it still.

As the festivities continued, Cormag remained where he was, watching his people.

Watching Moira.

Lost in thought, she seemed oblivious to her surroundings, her teeth worrying her lower lip as though her mind was working to solve some problem. Her hands remained clenched, and every now and then, they would rise and cross over her chest, gripping her arms as though she needed comfort and knew not where else to find it.

Cormag frowned, wishing he could move to her side, wishing he knew how she felt in that moment, wishing...he could help.

And then her gaze rose and met his.

His heart paused as though hanging suspended in mid-air when he saw something in those blue depths. A flicker of...something. A message...as though...

Moira took a few steps sideways toward the arched doorway leading to the rear of the castle, and all the while her eyes lingered on his as though inviting him to follow. Then she turned and vanished down the corridor.

Cormag's heart slammed to a halt, and before he knew it, his feet carried him across the hall, following in her wake.

"Where are ye going?" Ian snarled from behind him.

Cringing, Cormag turned to face his friend. "It doesna concern ye," he snapped, instantly regretting his tone. "I'm sorry, but I needa go." However, when he turned to walk away, Ian held him back.

Glancing over Cormag's shoulder at the doorway through which Moira had left, he shook his head. "That woman is trouble, and ye know it. Why are ye being such a fool? After all she's done, how can ye-?"

Brushing Ian's hand away, Cormag stepped back. "I willna discuss this with ye again, old friend. I understand yer reservations, but the world is not black and white." Giving Ian a quick nod, Cormag headed out the doorway, disappointed to see that Finn had not been able to sway their friend from his path of hatred. What would it take for him to abandon it?

Hurrying down the corridor, Cormag glimpsed Moira's dark green skirts disappearing around a corner. His heart picked up the pace as his feet did as well, and he wondered if he had mistaken her intention. Had she truly wanted him to follow her? And if so, for what reason? In truth, they had very little to say to each other.

A fact, Cormag began to regret more with each day that passed.

Turning another corner, Cormag frowned when he saw her waiting down the corridor outside the door to his study. Her feet carried her a few paces up and then down again as she wrung her hands, agitation now clearly showing on her face.

The moment Moira noticed him, her feet stilled, and her blue eyes met his. She drew in a slow breath as she watched his approach, and despite the small tremble he saw grip her frame, she straightened her shoulders and lifted her chin, not shying away from what lay ahead.

"Is something wrong?" Cormag asked when he reached her side. His heart was beating frantically now, and he could not help but worry about what had urged her to seek him out this day.

She swallowed. "I need to speak with ye." Her eyes shifted to the door. "Alone."

Nodding, Cormag led her into the room, then closed the door. "Ye look worried," he observed, wishing he knew why her pulse beat so fast and her feet would not keep still. "What can I do?"

At his question, she paused, and her blue eyes sought his, a hint of astonishment in them. "Would ye help me if I asked?" she murmured, uncertainty in her voice, but her gaze held his, pride not to cower, not to plead.

Taking a step toward her, Cormag nodded, realising how alone she had to feel to be so surprised that another would dare offer his help. What was it like to be alone in the world? To have no one to turn to in a time of need?

Cormag could not imagine it for his clan had always stood as one. Certainly, there were disagreements-some harsher than others-but in the end, no one was left alone standing outside in the cold. Was that how Moira felt day in and out?

If only he knew!

At his affirmation, Moira's eyes closed as though to savour the moment, and the soft smile that teased the corners of her mouth made him want to reach for her. Still, he did not, and when her eyes opened once more, he stood there as before, his mask firmly in place.

"I need to ask ye for another favour," she whispered into the stillness of the room. Her eyes lingered on his face, and he knew that she was assessing his reaction.

"A favour?" Cormag mumbled as he had before, and a frown came to his face as he stepped closer. "Is it about Garrett?"

Swallowing, Moira nodded. "He needs help."

A deep chill seized his bones as he saw the concern on her face. "What happened? What did ye...see?" Weeks had passed since he had last heard from Garrett. Apparently, even with Lord Tynham's help, tracking down his wife was not an easy feat, and Cormag had long since begun to worry that this endeavour would not end well.

"He found her," Moira replied, her lips quirking with the hint of a smile. "He found her."

Joy tickled his lips. "But that is...good." His gaze narrowed. "Why does he need help?"

"When I saw him, he-"

In that moment, the door burst open, banging loudly against the stone wall, and Ian walked in, a dark scowl on his face.

Cormag saw Moira flinch and cursed himself for not having sensed another's approach. It would seem his gift completely deserted him whenever she was near. "What is this?" he demanded, turning toward his friend. Behind him, he sensed Moira take a step back, but then she paused and straightened, refusing to retreat...even in fear.

"Do ye truly believe a word she says?" Ian snarled, his pale eyes darting to the woman standing behind Cormag. "Why can ye not see that she's bewitched ye?" With his jaw clenched, Ian shook his head in frustration. "Ye were never a fool, Cormag. Ye've always done what was right for the good of the clan. But now? Why would ye believe her? She's a traitor! Every word out of her mouth is a lie!"

Hatred seeped into Ian's blood, and his face turned a dark red as he stood there, his feet in battle stance and his right hand absentmindedly moving toward his belt as though he was about to draw his sword.

Fortunately, he was unarmed.

Fighting against his friend's hatred as it tried to urge him into a reaction he would regret, Cormag drew in a slow breath, remembering his father's calming voice whispering to him to find his balance, the place where he existed and no one else.

Where he could be himself and act as he would without persuasion.

"Leave this room now!" Cormag demanded, his tone unyielding as he stared down the man who had invaded his study without so much as the courtesy of a knock. "Ye have no right being here, and I've told ye before I willna discuss this further. Leave." He took a step toward Ian. "Now."

Ian's jaw clenched, and Cormag could see the battle that waged within him. Hatred sparked in his eyes. Still, there was a sense of right and wrong in his friend that would not allow itself to be silenced without a fight. "What did she say about Garrett?" he demanded, his gaze sweeping over to Moira. "What did ye do to him?"

"I did nothing," Moira replied, a slight quiver in her voice. Nevertheless, she took a step forward and faced Ian with an unflinching look in her eyes. "He went to find his wife, and...although he's found her, there's...there's danger ahead. I came to ask that ye send help." Her eyes drifted to Cormag, and he nodded to her.

"And ye believe that?" Ian demanded, his hard gaze going back and forth between Cormag and Moira. "How can she possibly know if she isna a witch? And if she is, her word canna be trusted!"

"I'm not a witch," Moira stated calmly, a hint of annoyance in her blue eyes as she rested her hands on her sides, exasperation in the way she stood in front of them. "Sometimes I have...glimpses of what lies ahead, but nothing more. 'Tis the extent of what I can do. I dunna have the power to...bewitch anyone." For a split second, she turned to look at him, and Cormag felt his heart skip a beat. "I never did."

Ian snorted in derision, and Cormag could not help but think that there was some small truth in his friend's words. After all, did he not feel robbed of his senses whenever she was near? Did he not think of her even when he did not wish to? Still, that did not mean that she was a witch. It meant that-

Footsteps echoed closer, and a moment later, not only Maggie, but also Finn and Emma burst into the room. Maggie's gaze swept over them and she quickly took in the situation before turning to her husband. "Ian, please come back to the festivities. Yer uncle will miss ye." Then she reached for his hand.

Ian, however, stepped back and out of reach, his eyes hard as he looked at her as though she were a stranger. "I do what I must in order to protect ye, all of ye. Why can ye not see that? Why do ye believe her word over mine?"

Chapter Twelve

AN ABYSS AWAITS

Moira could see the loneliness in Ian's eyes and remembered what Maggie had told her not long ago as they had sat out in the meadow under the small grove. Though she still feared him, feared what he might do if provoked, Moira understood him now.

Ian had married a woman who did not love him, who *could* not love him, and because he had wanted her, had wanted the idea of a future with her, he had refused to see that marrying her would be a mistake. And now, he was trapped in a life he had foolishly chosen, and he needed someone to blame.

Moira knew that feeling. She knew what it felt like when anger surged in her blood, seeking to chase away the loneliness that lingered. She knew how easy it was to give in, to simply forget one's own fault and blame another.

It eased the pain.

But it was wrong.

"Her word?" Finn asked, and his gaze moved from Ian to Moira and back again. "What do ye mean? What's this about?"

Ian snorted, and his eyes settled on Moira, a challenge in them. "Tell them! Tell them yer lies!"

Feeling her heart thudding wildly against her ribcage, Moira glanced at Cormag. His face was calm and his eyes gentle as they rested on her. He gave an almost imperceptible nod, granting her permission to speak if she should wish to do so. And then, just as she was about to answer, Cormag moved and came to stand by her side.

Warmth flooded her at this simple gesture of comfort, and the loneliness receded if only a little. He did not even know what she had come to ask, not the details, and yet, here he stood in support of her.

Blinking back tears, Moira smiled up at him, grateful beyond words. Then she turned to face the rest of the room, fighting to stay in control as she prepared herself to reveal her gift in a way she had never done before. "Last night," she began, feeling all eyes on her, "I saw glimpses of Garrett."

While Ian snorted yet again, Finn's and Emma's eyes widened in confusion. Only Maggie seemed unsurprised.

"He's found his wife...and soon they'll be heading north-"

"He did?" Finn exclaimed as he turned to Emma, reaching for her hand.

"This is nonsense!" Ian snarled, crossing his arms over his chest as he began to pace, angry strides carrying him up and down the room.

Moira nodded, seeing contemplative faces looking back at her. "But there's danger ahead. If he doesna receive help, he will lose her again."

"How?" Cormag asked, his gaze searching hers as he looked down at her.

Moira shrugged. "I dunna know, but-"

"Ha!" Ian exclaimed. "Now, ye suddenly dunna know? How convenient!"

"Let her speak, Ian," Finn interfered before he turned to Moira. "If ye dunna know what that danger is, how do ye suppose we help him?"

"Ye canna truly say ye believe her?" Ian gaped at Finn, shock marking his features. "Has she bewitched ye as well?"

Emma's lips twitched. "Nay, that would be me."

Grinning, Finn squeezed her hand and she leant into him. "Aye, never was a truer word spoken." Then his features sobered, and he gave Ian a warning glance before turning to Moira once more. "What do ye know?"

"I know," Moira began, "that he'll be needing a ship."

"A ship?" Finn gawked. "What for?"

"To sail the seas, I suppose," Maggie said with a grin. "What else would ye be needing a ship for?"

Finn rolled his eyes at her good-naturedly. "When?" he asked Moira, surprising her yet again. Never would she have thought that he would accept her word so effortlessly.

"A fortnight at most."

"But we don't have a ship," Emma threw in, her gaze sweeping around the room as though hoping someone would object and pull a ship out of their pocket.

Finn nodded. "But Clan McKinnear does. They have several." He turned to look at Cormag. "We need to send word."

Moira felt her heart leap into her throat as she stared at Finn. Never would she have expected this. As she looked from one face to the next, she found no suspicion there, no doubt, merely surprise, and Moira wondered how this was possible.

"Ye canna seriously think to include Clan McKinnear in this?" Ian snapped. "They've been our allies for generations. They're our friends. Our kin. How dare ye endanger them?" His stare drilled into Moira as he approached, anger balling his hands into fists. "Have ye not done enough? Do ye seek to destroy one clan after another?"

Forcing herself not to retreat, Moira met his eyes. "I understand why ye would be suspicious of me, and I dunna blame ye. All I can say is that I speak the truth." She glanced at Cormag, who had moved closer upon Ian's approach. "The decision is yers."

Cormag nodded in acknowledgement. "'Tis not an easy decision for we know verra little," he said, and for a reason Moira could not name, she knew that he was merely trying to be diplomatic and not doubting her word.

"That is precisely why we should do nothing!" Ian insisted. "We have no facts. All we have are her claims." Again, he glared at her as though he wished the earth would simply swallow her whole so he could be done with her.

"We can't do that," Finn objected, and his hand tightened on Emma's. "If there is a chance that Garrett will lose the woman he loves again, then we must act!" He looked at his wife. "He would do the same for us."

Emma nodded.

As did Maggie.

Moira looked at Cormag. His jaw held tension, and she would not be surprised if the hands he held linked behind his back were clenched into fists. Indeed, this was not an easy decision to make. After all, they could not be certain, not the way she was.

"I canna believe ye all," Ian all but whispered, shock paling his features as he looked at his wife, his friends, the people he called family. Moira knew that he felt betrayed, and she knew that he would blame her for it.

As though he had read her thoughts, he turned his gaze to her, measured steps carrying him closer.

Moira cringed and fought the urge to avert her eyes. Although Cormag moved half in front of her, protecting her from any physical harm Ian might feel compelled to inflict, he could not shield her from the hatred that burnt in Ian's eyes.

"Ye dunna belong here," he snarled. "Ye're not one of us, and ye never will be. Ye dunna deserve to be."

"Ian!" Cormag warned.

"It might take time," Ian continued undeterred, "but one day people will see ye for the monster ye are. I will ensure that they do, believe me. I willna rest until ye're exposed for the liar and traitor ye are."

"Leave!" Cormag growled, stepping in front of his friend, his large body a towering wall between Moira and the man who hated her with every fibre of his being. "Now!"

With a last growl, Ian stalked from the room, his angry footsteps echoing down the corridor.

"I shall think on it," Cormag told the rest of them. "Thank ye for yer counsel."

One by one, Maggie, Emma and Finn left to return to the festivities, their whispered voices slowly receding as their feet carried them away. Moira could only hope her aunt's wedding would not be overshadowed by the emotions that had run high in this room.

"Are ye all right?"

Blinking, Moira looked up and found Cormag standing in front of her. His grey eyes swept over her face, and his brows crinkled in concern. "I'm fine," Moira whispered, feeling the corners of her lips rise in imitation of a smile. "I should...I should be going." A lump settled in her throat, cutting off anything else she might wish to say, and a familiar cold began to crawl up her spine.

Moira had felt it before.

Now and then.

As Cormag took a step toward her, his hand rising to reach for her, Moira shrank back, afraid to break down in front of him. She could feel her resolve weaken, feel the cold spread through her body, bringing with it the same hopelessness and fear that had overwhelmed her before.

Turning on her heel, she hastened from the room.

The moment she stepped across the threshold, tears began streaming down her face as Ian's words echoed in her head. *Ye dunna belong here. Ye're not one of us, and ye never will be. Ye dunna deserve to be.*

Ever since she had been banished from her own clan, Moira had felt alone, and she knew that she deserved to be. Ian's words, spoken out loud, had cut deep especially after the warmth of acceptance she had felt from the others if only for a moment.

A rare moment.

A moment she had hoped for but never dared believe in.

And then Ian had spoken up, destroying that little spark of hope, crushing it and pushing her over the edge into an abyss she had known before.

Most days, Moira managed to persevere. Despite her loneliness and her guilt, she knew not to dwell on what she had lost, on what would never be again, but to concentrate on the simple tasks of her daily life and be grateful for the small blessings she had received.

Most days, Moira was in control.

Most days, she knew how to keep the cold at bay.

Today was not one of those days.

Today, desperation pulled at her.

As Moira rushed down the corridor, her feet all but stumbling as she tried to see through the curtain of tears clouding her eyes, her heart beat wildly, painfully in her chest. It felt as though it might stop at any moment. A threat that lingered. A threat that all might be over soon. A threat, and yet, it was also a promise.

Of peace.

Of the end of her struggles.

Of the absence of loneliness.

A large staircase loomed before her, and Moira rushed toward it as she had before, her feet carrying her higher and higher as she hastened toward the spot that had seen her break down before.

Her limbs began to ache with the strain of carrying her upward, step by step, the hard-stone wall scraping against her skin as she tried to keep her balance with one hand out to the side. Her breath came fast and ragged, and her chest began to hurt-if from exertion or despair she could not say.

And then she burst through the door and out into the warm summer air, the bright sunlight momentarily blinding her. She stumbled onward until her body slammed into the outer wall and her ribs ached from the impact.

Still panting, Moira clung to the rough stone, her gaze reaching over the wall and downward until it came to rest on the courtyard far below.

Up on one of *Seann Dachaigh*'s tall towers, Moira knew that she had once more found a fork in the road. Thrice already she had found her way up here, a choice placed at her feet: to go on or to end it here and now.

A voice deep inside whispered that she was a coward, seeking the easy way out. Still, Moira wondered how much pain one could bear before losing any resemblance of the person one had once been. It was not the guilt or the shame that had brought her here, not now and not before. No, it was the loneliness, the distance to those around her, the cold that settled on her bones even in the height of summer.

If only there were one person-only one! -who still cared, who would take her hand and walk with her. One person to confide in. One person to whom she could turn. One person to embrace, to hold, to...love.

Moira thought of Alastair and knew that if he had not turned from her, she would have had the strength to stand against the despair that grew in her heart. Still, that thought alone-accusing in its nature-brought guilt to her heart as she knew she had no right to fault him.

No, it had been her doing.

Hers alone.

And loneliness was her punishment, fitting somehow, tormenting in a way nothing else ever had been.

So, why continue?

It was the one question Moira found harder to answer with each time her feet carried her up here, and one day, she was certain she would not find it anymore.

Was this day today?

Chapter Thirteen

A PRICE TO BE PAID

Pacing the length of his study, Cormag knew he ought to rejoin the festivities. Still, his thoughts lingered with Moira, contemplating all she had said, all she had asked him to do, knowing he needed to decide.

Deep down, he knew he believed her. He thought of Garrett and the joy his friend had felt upon returning from Gretna Green. He had been in love, and the way he had spoken of his new wife had resonated within Cormag.

That had been Moira's doing.

She had sent Garrett down a path that had led to his happiness.

Was that not reason enough to do as she asked once again?

For Cormag, it was. Still, he was not acting alone. He was the laird; he needed to do what was best for his clan. He knew he could not act without reason. He knew his clan would need an explanation or whispers would begin anew. Eventually, whispers would lead to doubt, and doubt was poison.

If his clanspeople doubted him, his competence, his dedication, then the stability and safety of their clan was threatened.

Cormag knew if he granted Moira's request, Ian would not remain quiet. He would make his displeasure known, and who knew what would come of that.

Still, if Cormag did not, what would happen to Garrett? Would he lose his wife for good?

Resting his head against the cool windowpane, Cormag blew out a long breath. Perhaps he ought to speak to Moira again. Perhaps there was more she could tell him. Perhaps there was another way.

A compromise: something to help Garrett and pacify Ian at the same time.

Cormag chuckled, knowing well enough that life did not usually work like that. No, he would have to decide, and he would have to pay its price.

Returning to his desk, Cormag sat down and leant back in his upholstered armchair, momentarily closing his eyes. He needed clarity, and so he concentrated on evening his breathing, on shutting out the dim sounds of the festivities drifting over from the great hall.

Slowly, his pulse calmed. The slight throbbing in his temple receded. He breathed in and out, feeling himself relax. His hands unclenched and rested calmly on the tabletop as a sense of peace came over him.

And then a jolt of something dark and threatening surged through his heart and his eyes flew open. "Moira!"

Cormag did not know how he knew, but he was certain beyond the shadow of a doubt that something was wrong. That she was in danger. That there was no time to lose.

All but lunging from his chair, Cormag rushed out into the corridor and hastened toward the sound of laughter and joy, his mind churning with what to do. Had Ian found her once again? Was he the threat Cormag had sensed?

A frown came to his face, and he wondered that he had felt anything at all. Usually, he could not feel her. Usually, he did not know what lived in her heart. What had changed? Why was it that he had felt her if only for a split second?

Stepping into the great hall, Cormag paused, willing himself to think. He needed to stay calm and act with thought, like his father had taught him. So, he allowed his gaze to sweep over the crowd, their faces laughing; their feet dancing to the cheerful tunes echoing through the vaulted room. He looked from face to face, along the walls and dipped into corners as he knew that Moira liked to keep to the sides.

Still, he could not find her among them.

Unlike Ian.

His childhood friend stood in the far back, Finn by his side, their faces taut as words flew back and forth from their mouths.

Cormag breathed a sigh of relief, and yet, the questions remained: where was Moira and what had brought such terror to her heart?

Not knowing what to do, Cormag stepped outside into the gentle evening air. The sun was slowly dipping lower, its warm golden rays casting a beautiful light over the green hills. Still, Cormag's heart was in an uproar, and his eyes swept over his surroundings with an almost desperate need.

And then, he felt it again, a mild echo of what had surged through his chest before, and his head jerked upward.

Why he did so, he did not know. All he knew was that the moment his eyes came to rest on the eastern tower of *Seann Dachaigh*, blind panic filled his heart.

Up there, on the parapet wall stood Moira, her arms stretched wide as the wind tore at her dark green skirts and pulled on her golden tresses as though it wished to tumble her into an early grave.

Moments later, Cormag found himself rushing up the spiral staircase, taking two steps at a time in his haste to reach her before...

He did not remember rushing to the side entrance, avoiding the large crowd that would have hindered his progress. He did not remember making a conscious decision. All he knew was that he needed to reach Moira before she would be lost to him for good.

His heart beat painfully against his ribcage as he pushed himself to go faster, his breath panting in his own ears. Upward, he surged, and a slight dizziness engulfed him at the spiralling movement. But he continued, doubling his efforts when he spied the wooden door at the top of the stairs.

In the last moment before he would have burst through it, Cormag cautioned himself, pulling short and stilling his feet, his breath, his heart lest he rush forward, startle her and...

Gritting his teeth, Cormag reached out a hand and forced himself to open the door slowly. He stepped out into the waning light and carefully turned toward the outer edge, knowing exactly the sight that awaited him. Still, the moment his eyes fell on her, balancing precariously on the parapet wall, his heart slammed to a painful halt.

For a second, he froze, unable to move, his eyes only seeing the way she swayed in the wind, her soft tresses dancing on the breeze like a leaf carried higher and higher into the sky. But then a gust caught hold of her skirts, and she tipped forward, her arms paddling frantically to force herself back.

Without thought, Cormag lunged forward.

Long strides carried him across the small distance, his arms stretched toward her as Moira righted herself, a sharp exhale of air rushing from her lungs. She was still swaying, but her footing was steady once more at least for the moment.

Nevertheless, the second Cormag all but slammed into the parapet wall, his arms closed around her midsection, pulling her against him and away from the early grave she had been toying with.

A scream tore from Moira's lips as she fell backwards into his arms, her heart beating like a drum of war against his own. Kicking and screaming, she tried to free herself from his hold, panic giving her more strength than he would have thought her capable of.

"'Tis me!" Cormag barked, spinning her around and grabbing a hold of her wrists. "'Tis me!"

The moment her wide, blue eyes fell on him, she stilled, her chest rising and falling with each rapid breath as she stared at him as though he was the last person she would have expected to see.

Cormag gritted his teeth, feeling a stab of pain at the realisation that he was not on her mind as she was on his. "What were ye doing?" he growled, yanking her closer as his hands tightened on her wrists. "What were ye doing up there?"

A gasp flew from her lips at his harsh treatment, and she began to struggle against his hold on her. "It doesna concern ye," she panted, the pulse in her neck still hammering erratically. "Release me!"

"I saved yer life," Cormag snarled, anger now mingling with the fear that had seeped into his blood. "I deserve an explanation."

Ceasing her struggle, Moira met his gaze, her own defiant. Still, there was a slight tremble in her lower lip that almost doused the flames of his anger. "I never asked ye to." Strength rang in her voice as she began to speak, but it quickly waned until the last word was nothing more than a whisper.

Her breath quickened as tears filled her eyes, and she dropped her chin, trying to hide her pain from him. "Please, release me," she whispered without strength, and this time, Cormag complied.

Drawing in a deep breath, he sought to calm the emotions that boiled in his own blood. "Tell me what brought ye up here, Moira," he demanded, but his voice rang gentle for his heart saw the despair that clung to her features.

Moving away from him, Moira kept her gaze on the stone floor. "Ye wouldna understand," she whispered before wiping her hands over her eyes to stem the flood of tears streaming down her face. "Leave me be."

Afraid of what would happen, of what she might do if he were to respect her wishes, Cormag went after her when she once more drifted closer to the stone wall. "I willna leave ye alone up here, Lass."

At the sound of his voice, Moira turned around, but her feet kept moving her backwards until the wall stopped her. Her arms spread to her sides, and she rested her hands on the rough stone as though it gave her comfort.

Cormag felt as though a dark abyss was opening between them. "Talk to me," he said gruffly as his eyes swept over her tear-streaked face, fighting to look deeper, to understand. Where was his gift when he truly needed it? "What brought ye up here?"

She swallowed hard, and her eyes became distant. "Ye dunna know what it is to be utterly alone and to know that ye deserve it." She blinked, and her eyes met his, fresh tears pooling in their blue depths. "I dunna deserve yer pity, but I canna live like this. Not anymore." She closed her eyes, and in that moment, she seemed frighteningly fragile, breakable that Cormag feared a gust of wind might carry her away.

Her words echoed in his mind, reminding him of how Ian had

spoken to her earlier that day, his voice full of hatred and accusation. "Dunna listen to what Ian says," he told her, carefully moving closer as he feared she might do something rash if her emotions should run high once again. "He's battling his own demons and canna see that his words are unjust."

"But they're not!" she exclaimed, her outburst a cry of pain. "I deserve what I got, and yet..." She swallowed, shaking her head. "How does one live without pride, without self-respect? I know I need to forgive myself, but I dunna dare for 'twould be wrong. What was willna be forgotten, and perhaps it shouldna." She inhaled a shuddering breath, pressing herself closer against the wall. "I canna live this life. I've tried, but...but this...this loneliness, it rips me apart." Sobs tore from her throat, and she clamped her lips shut to keep them contained.

Her despair echoed in his heart, but Cormag knew that it was not his gift that allowed him to feel her. He felt her pain because he cared. It was a simple truth, but it almost knocked him off his feet.

He cared for her, and the sorrow in her eyes was almost more than he could bear. More than anything, he wanted to take her in his arms and soothe her fears, promise her that all would be well, that she would never be lonely again.

That he would take care of her.

That he would be there.

Afraid to frighten her, Cormag approached with caution, noting the way she watched him, the way her shoulders tensed and the way she pressed closer to the wall. His stomach churned when a shiver gripped her, but he knew he could not walk away no matter how much she might wish he would. "Think of yer family before ye act, Lass. It might not feel like it now, but they love ye. Dunna do this to them."

A dark chuckle rumbled in her throat. "'Tis not true. They might have...once, but that is long gone. What I did destroyed the love they had for me." She swallowed hard. "I havena seen my brother in over two years. He wouldna know if I were gone. And my aunt only suffers because of me, because I am here, because..." Her shoulders pulled back as her features hardened. "Nay, I willna fool myself. No one," her voice caught, but she pressed on, "no one would miss me if I were no more. No one." Her gaze held his for a long moment before she suddenly spun around, ready to lift herself up onto the wall once more.

Cormag's heart lurched into his throat, and his hands shot forward, grabbing her by the arms and yanking her back, pulling her away from the wall. She struggled against him, tears misting her eyes. "Please, release me. I only want this to be over. Please."

His heart softened toward her, but he did not comply.

"No one would care," she promised, her wide blue eyes looking up into his. "I swear it."

Grabbing her chin, Cormag pulled her into his arms, his eyes locked on hers. "Damn it, Lass, *I* care!"

Staring up at him, she froze.

Chapter Fourteen

THE EASTERN TOWER

Dark grey eyes looked down into hers, and Moira knew not what to feel.

Only moments ago, she had been so close to the end, to giving up, and then Cormag had come, and her traitorous heart had soared at the sight of him. Never would she have thought that he would come for her, that he would fight to keep her in this world, that he would...care.

But did he speak the truth?

Oh, her heart wanted nothing more but to believe his words. The way he had pulled her away from the abyss that loomed before her, dark and all-consuming, had set her skin on fire. She felt his rough hands wrapped around her arms, holding onto her as though he truly feared to lose her. His grey eyes had darkened, and that calm, controlled expression that always clung to his features had shifted. Emotions lurked around their edges, and she could see from the way his jaw tensed that he was not pleased.

Perhaps she was only seeing what her heart wanted to see.

Cormag had not come because he cared for her, a deep-seated fear whispered, but because he was responsible for her. By accepting

Connor's request, she had become a clan matter, and he was the MacDrummond's laird.

Disappointment extinguished the flames that had warmed her skin only a moment ago, and Moira knew that she had been foolish to believe anyone could care for her out of more than duty and honour. Those days had long come and gone.

Her gaze slid from his and her head sank, suddenly feeling heavy like a boulder balancing on a twig. She felt her strength wane and was ready to sink to the ground and weep when a flicker of pride caught her off guard.

No matter what the circumstances, she was still a Brunwood, and she would not cower.

Not now.

Not ever.

Straightening, Moira lifted her head as she pushed that little flicker of pride to spark into something more.

Cormag's gaze narrowed, and she knew that he could see the change in her. The pressure of his arms around her lessened until he stepped back and finally released her. "Ye willna do anything foolish?"

Moira scoffed, trying her best to hide the shudder that claimed her at the loss of his warmth. "Have I not already done so? As have ye?"

A frown drew down his brows, and his eyes remained on her face, watching, assessing. "What d'ye mean?"

"Ye allowed me to stay," Moira replied, torn between putting more distance between them and abandoning all pride and rushing into his arms. "Ye shouldna have done so, for it only brought trouble on ye, has it not?"

His jaw clenched and unclenched before he nodded. "Aye, 'tis brought trouble upon me, but-"

"There!" Moira exclaimed. "I knew ye were lying." Still, hearing his admission, she felt fresh tears pricking the backs of her eyes. Deep down, a part of her had clung to the belief that he truly cared.

"Lying? About what?"

Shaking her head, Moira retreated, unable to bear being so close to him. Even five paces were not enough. Six. Seven.

For a moment, he watched her, indecision resting in his eyes, before he closed the distance between them once more, and his hand reached out to grab her wrist. "Will ye stop trying to throw yerself off the roof?"

Trying to jerk her hand free, Moira felt her earlier despair return. "Unhand me!" she demanded, shoving against him.

Instead of budging, he swiftly caught her other wrist, pulling her back against him.

Moira gasped. His face was so close, his grey eyes looking into hers in a way that... "Release me," she whispered, but it was more like a plea, and she felt disgusted with her own weakness.

It was not surprising, though, was it? After all, where would she have found the strength to hold her head high? There was nothing left. Nothing but tears and shame and loneliness.

"I willna walk away until ye've explained yerself," Cormag whispered, his voice deadly calm as his hawk-like eyes swept over her face. "How have I lied to ye?"

Willing her voice not to quiver, Moira looked up at him. "Ye...ye dunna care. I know ye dunna. Ye only said so to keep me from flinging myself off the ledge. From ruining my aunt's wedding. From causing more trouble for ye."

Anger flared in his eyes, and she gasped as his hands tightened painfully on her wrists. "Is that what ye believe?" He inhaled a slow breath. "Is that what ye think of me?"

A flicker of pain came to his eyes, and Moira knew that her words had wounded him. "I didna mean to say that...that ye have no compassion. Ye're a good man, and I thank ye for what ye did for me. But when I said that no one cared, I meant..."

His gaze softened as he watched her fumble for words, as heat stole into her cheeks and she dropped her eyes, unable to bear his nearness a moment longer.

Moira tried to step back, tried to spare herself the humiliation of having him look at her thus, but he would not release her.

"I do care for ye, Lass. Whether ye believe me or not, 'tis the truth."

Moira fought against the wave of warmth that flowed into her being, willing herself not to believe him, to not even hear him. Still, she could not keep herself from lifting her chin and meeting his eyes.

So grey.

And dark.

And warm.

And...

With his eyes locked on hers, he moved closer, slowly, carefully, almost like a hunter trying not to spook the deer. And then for a split second, his gaze dropped to her lips.

Moira drew in a sharp breath as his intention became clear, and for the first time that night, she was glad that he held her so tightly for if he was not, she would have sunk to the ground in a flutter of nerves.

"Tell me no," Cormag whispered as he leant in, his large body shifting closer to hers.

Even if Moira had wanted to refuse him, she would not have been able to force words past the tightness in her throat.

All she wanted in that moment was him. His warmth. His kindness. His comfort. Everything else faded from her mind as her heart revelled in the way he drew closer and closer, his warm breath fanning over her skin. His eyes held hers, still searching, a spark of concern in them that he might be overstepping, pressuring her into something she did not want.

His consideration and respect for her felt utterly intoxicating, and Moira found herself striving toward him, lifting her head to accept his kiss.

And then he did kiss her, his lips a gentle pressure against her own, and Moira knew that she would forever remember this night. Not because she had almost given up her life, but because for the first time in years, she felt a shred of happiness.

With a sigh, she sank into his arms, which finally released her wrists and moved to wrap around her. Slowly. Hesitantly. Almost awkwardly as though he did not dare, as though he should not, as though he knew better than to allow her close.

Moira knew exactly how he felt. Words of warning echoed in her head, reminding her that opening her heart to another made her vulnerable. Still, she was powerless against the tide that swept her into his arms. Her hands lowered to rest upon his chest right above his heart, and she felt it beating almost as erratically as her own.

And then the tentative manner of his touch changed as though he had finally made up his mind. His arms pulled her deeper into his embrace, and one hand rose to brush along her jawline before his fingers slipped into her hair. As he pulled her closer still, the pad of his thumb came to rest upon her cheek, brushing gently over her skin and sending shivers down her spine.

Moira returned his kiss, marvelling at the tenderness of his touch.

What simmered between them was not blind passion-as inexperienced as she was, Moira was certain of that. No, it was more than want and desire. It was subtle. Caring. Two people reaching out to one another, offering a bit of themselves, taking a risk in the hopes that perhaps, perhaps they would find something in the other that would speak to them, that they recognised, that they had been missing without ever being aware of it.

How long they stood there in each other's arms, gently exploring the fragile bond that had so unexpectedly formed between them, Moira did not know. However, when a crow called in the distance, its piercing shriek ripping through the haze that had shrouded them from the world around them, they almost jerked apart.

Panting, they stared at one another, a good bit of shock marking their features as the realisation of what they had done finally sank in. They had crossed a line and were no longer the people they had been before. At least not to each other.

Night had fallen, and Moira wondered how she could not have noticed.

Absentmindedly, she touched her fingers to her lips, feeling them tingle with the memory of their kiss, and found Cormag's gaze follow her movement. As inexpressive as his face had always been, in that moment, the look of longing in his eyes took her breath away, and she all but stumbled backwards.

Instantly, his features tensed, and his hand shot forward, once more reaching for her wrist.

"There's not need," Moira said quickly, pulling back her arm before his fingers could touch her. "I willna..." She glanced over her shoulder at the wall in her back, knowing the abyss that awaited beyond. "I willna try again, I promise."

For a long moment, his gaze rested on hers, once again searching, assessing, trying to determine if he could believe her, if he should. Then he exhaled slowly; nevertheless, his body remained tense as he took a step toward her. Then another until she once more felt his warm breath on her skin. "Ye are forbidden from ever venturing up here again, d'ye hear?"

Staring into his sharp, hawk-like eyes, Moira felt a spark of defiance spring to life. Her jaw tensed, and her eyes hardened as she fought the urge to lash out at him. Who was he to tell her what to do? If she wanted to end her life, then that was her Goddamn right! Why would he care?

And then she saw the touch of gentleness that still rested in his eyes, the way he slowly breathed in and out, strained somehow as though he was in pain, and Moira understood why he had spoken to her thus.

Because he cared.

He truly cared, did he not?

Joy surged through Moira, though it was accompanied by no small measure of disbelief and the fear to have her heart ripped from her chest should she dare to open it to another.

At her silence, his gaze hardened on hers, the hint of a threat in the way the muscles in his jaw contracted. "I swear I'll lock ye up if I ever see ye venture this way again, is that clear?"

Suppressing another surge of joy, Moira nodded. "I swear I willna do so again."

Cormag exhaled a long and slow breath, and she saw his shoulders relax and the tension leave his body. "If ye ever...feel overwhelmed again, Lass," he whispered, understanding resting in those dark eyes, "then come and find me. I swear I will help ye through it."

Staring up at him, Moira nodded, touched by his offer to be there for her. "Thank ye," she replied, knowing that those two words fell far short of the deep gratitude she felt.

Cormag nodded. "Let me take ye home," he said, gesturing to the door that led back downstairs. "Ye need rest."

Moira nodded and together they crossed the stone floor and passed through the door. Heading down the spiral staircase, she noted that Cormag was careful to keep his distance. He held his large body awkwardly angled as they passed through the narrow doorway, careful not to touch her. Moira wondered why after the way he had kissed her only moments ago.

The silence that lingered between them felt oppressive, and whenever their gazes collided by accident, they quickly averted them as though burnt.

Moira sighed.

Something had changed. As close as she had felt to Cormag up on top of the tower, now it seemed that what had happened had pushed them even further apart. Every now and then, she thought to see a desire to reclaim that closeness light up his eyes, but she could not be certain, and she did not dare ask.

All that mattered was that he had come for her. He had been the only one to notice...

Moira stopped on the last stair before reaching the ground floor as her thoughts ventured back to the events of that night.

"Are ye all right?" Cormag asked, turning back to look at her. His dark eyes swept over her face as he drew closer, his hand reaching to touch her face before he stopped himself and dropped it to his side once more.

Moira blinked. "How did ye know I was up there?" she whispered, noting the way his eyes dropped from hers for a split second. "How did ye know I was about to...?" Her gaze narrowed as she took a step toward him. "How did ye know?"

A muscle in his jaw twitched, and for a small eternity, he remained silent. "I...I saw ye," he finally said, his voice slightly hoarse. "From down in the courtyard." Then he took a step back, gesturing for her to follow him down the corridor to the side door that would lead them outside.

Slowly, Moira put one foot in front of the other, her mind churning with the subtle reactions she had observed in him, for although his words seemed honest, she could not shake the feeling that they were incomplete.

As they stepped out into the courtyard, Moira lifted her head and glanced up at the tall tower and the parapet wall where she had stood not long ago, ready to end her pitiful existence once and for all. It looked tall and threatening, but not as tall and threatening as it had from up there, and a shudder gripped her, making her hands grasp her arms in a sad imitation of a hug.

"Are ye cold?" Cormag asked, watching her as intently as he had before.

Moira shook her head, wishing she would not have to hug herself, wishing he would pull her into his arms once more. So warm and comforting and safe.

Cormag's eyes swept over her face, and he took a step closer, his hand rising as though to grasp her chin. Unfortunately, he once again thought better of it, his feet stopping mere inches from her. "Ye look shaken," he whispered, concern etched into his grey eyes. "Ye need rest."

Turning toward him, Moira allowed herself to simply look. Her eyes traced the line of his jaw, touched upon the curve of his lips and travelled upward to meet his gaze. He was like a book written in a language she could not understand; yet, there was something in the words before her that her heart recognised. "There's something ye're not saying," she told him, not surprised to see an almost imperceptible jerk in his shoulders. "What made ye look for me? Tell me the truth."

Chapter Fifteen

FOR THE GOOD OF THE CLAN

Cold fear gripped Cormag's heart as her words echoed in his head.

Never had he revealed his gift to anyone. Never. Only his father had ever truly known, and he had been the one to grasp the meaning of Cormag's odd behaviour as a lad. He had been the one to see, to look deeper and understand. There had been no need for Cormag to confide in him because he had simply known. The way fathers sometimes did.

Cormag had never been more grateful in his life.

"Why can ye not tell me?" Moira whispered, curiosity shining in her deep blue eyes as they travelled over his face, lingering here and there, almost a caress that he felt against his skin. Instantly, his body warmed, and the memory of their kiss resurfaced. His gaze dropped lower, and from the way she inhaled a quivering breath, he knew that she had guessed the direction of his thoughts.

Curse him! Why had he kissed her? Emotional entanglements only complicated matters, and now more than ever, he needed to keep a clear head. Especially with Moira, for he could not be certain how she felt. Even more so tonight, for the ordeal she had been through had clearly shaken her to her core.

If her mind had not been overshadowed, would she have refused him? Had she only accepted his kiss because he had been the one to find her? Because she had so desperately needed someone-anyone! -to care?

"Ye need not worry," he told her, hoping to put her mind at ease, "I willna...cross the line again."

At his words, she blinked a couple of times as though stunned or confused by what he had said. Then something in her changed. Her hands fell from her arms and came to rest on her sides, her chin rising a notch as her eyes reached for his, a demand in them that had not been there before. "Will ye not answer me then?"

"Answer ye?" he asked, trying to buy time, knowing exactly what she wanted to know.

A teasing smile flashed across her face as though nothing out of the ordinary had happened that night. "Ye know what I mean," she stated, and her gaze narrowed, trying to look deeper. "Ye're a very secretive man, Cormag MacDrummond."

Surprised by the lightness of her tone, Cormag nodded. "Aye."

"Ye never share much of yerself."

He simply held her gaze.

Inhaling a slow breath, Moira took a step forward, her blue eyes serious as she looked at him. "I thank ye for what ye did for me tonight. I never would've expected it, and...and it felt good." A shy smile teased the corners of her mouth. "If ye...ever change yer mind, ye'll know where to find me as well." A soft smile played on her lips, and she reached out and cupped a hand to his cheek. "Thank ye for finding me."

Then Moira stepped back and walked away, her feet carrying her across the courtyard and out the gate toward the small cottage that would be hers alone from this day on.

Cormag stared after her, his muscles painfully tense as he fought the urge to follow her, to break his promise only moments after he had given it. Not in a long time had his own emotions overwhelmed him thus. It had only ever been those of others that had overcome his heart, forcing him to fight to stay in control. Never had it been his own heart that had urged him down a different path than his mind considered reasonable.

She cares for ye as ye care for her.

Cormag frowned at the echo of his mother's voice, once again wondering why he would hear her in such a moment. Certainly, his mother tended to interfere, to meddle; however, he had never put much stock in her strong opinions. Why on earth would his subconscious force him to hear her now?

Feeling the tension of the evening catch up with him, Cormag rubbed a hand over his face, then turned and headed back inside. The wedding celebration was still in full swing, and he stole a glance at Fiona and Duncan their faces aglow with happiness.

Then he retired to his chamber, his own heart and mind still in turmoil over what had happened, over what he had felt that night, over what he had done. He had allowed himself to act upon his emotions, to feel them so deeply that he had not been able to keep them at bay.

Standing with his hands braced on the cold windowsill, Cormag stared out into the darkened night and finally admitted to himself that he had kissed Moira because he had wanted to. Not because he had wanted to prove to her that she was not alone, that someone cared. Not because he had responded to her need for comfort and warmth. But because he had wanted to. Because he truly cared for her.

Cormag hung his head, fearing what these emotions might do to his judgement. For the good of the clan, he needed to ensure he was in control. He always needed to keep his wits and ensure that he could make wise decisions.

And he feared he would not be able to do so when his heart longed for Moira. He needed to keep his distance, to regain his balance and ensure that his mind was unaffected by what had happened this night.

Even though his heart cringed at the very thought of it.

All through the next day, Cormag considered what to do about Moira's latest request, trying to determine if he desired to grant it merely because he desired *her*. He paced the floor of his study until he felt certain the rock would break away and a hole would open underneath him. He did his best to consider this case from all sides, recalled

Finn's as well as Ian's arguments, tried his best to weigh them and put them in perspective.

And then a knock sounded on the door.

"Aye," he called, feeling his heart pause in his chest as a desperate hope burnt through his body. It had been hours since he had last seen her, and a part of him could not bear to be away from her a moment longer.

Cormag cursed under his breath the moment Moira opened the door and stepped across the threshold. Seeing him, she frowned. "Are ye all right?" she asked, closing the door and plunging him into a world where no one existed but them.

Cormag swallowed. "I should be the one to ask that."

She inhaled a slow breath, a slight nod moving her chin up and down. "I suppose ye're right." Walking past him, she stopped in front of the window, her eyes sweeping over the green hills. "'Twas strange to sleep in that cottage all by myself," she whispered, a slight catch in her voice. "I never thought I'd miss her even during the night."

Cormag did not know what to say for anything he could say would once again weaken the barrier he fought to re-establish between them.

"Have ye made a decision yet?" Moira asked before she slowly turned around, her sky-blue eyes settling on his. The sun behind her glinted on her golden curls, making her shine in a way that tugged on Cormag's heart.

He cleared his throat. "I have not."

"Why?"

He shrugged, his hands gesturing without thought. "Because I fear it will split my clan in two."

Sighing, Moira nodded her understanding. "I dunna know the burden ye carry," she said, her voice soft and awfully enthralling as she ventured toward him, "and I know that one's own judgement can be... wrong," a shadow crossed over her face, "but if ye trust yerself, then ye know what to do." A half-smile touched her lips. "What is right is right, and that doesna change simply because others disagree."

Cormag nodded. "Aye, there's truth in yer words, but that doesna mean the consequences willna be dire."

"Do ye truly believe sending Garrett help will divide yer clan?"

"I dunna know what Ian will do," Cormag whispered, "but I worry."

"What if I," her voice broke off and a slight shiver gripped her before she continued on, "if I left?" Moira's eyes were round as they held his, unshed tears brimming in their corners. "With me gone, Ian would have no reason to speak ill of ye."

"No!" The vehemence of his response startled Cormag as much as her, and he felt his teeth pressing painfully together as he fought to calm the beating of his heart.

"But if it would help?" Moira watched him with wide eyes. "I don't belong here. Nothing would be lost if I-"

"No!" Striding forward, Cormag reached for her, gripping her arms the way he had the night before. "Ye willna leave. Promise me that ye willna leave!"

"Why?" she gasped, her chest rising and falling with each rapid breath as her eyes held his, demanding an answer. "Why do ye want me here?"

Cormag felt the barrier between them crumble to the ground, and he groaned at the mistake he knew he had made. Like his clan, he too felt divided, his heart and mind pulling him in different directions, and he knew not what to do.

What he needed was clarity, balance, distance, peace of mind; something he knew was impossible with Moira in his arms, her soft breath fanning over his skin and her warmth setting his blood on fire. Those deep blue eyes were his undoing, and he felt weakened to his core.

So, he lied.

For the good of the clan.

"'Tis as ye said," he whispered, taking a step back as his hands fell from her arms. "Ye're..." His gaze dropped from hers as he found himself unable to force the words past his lips while she was looking at him with such faith. "Ye're my responsibility, and 'tis my duty to look after ye, to ensure yer safety."

Cormag did not dare look at her face, and so he stepped past her and strode to the window. Still, he could hear the soft exhale of air as though his words had shocked her. Had they? He wondered. Did it truly matter to her what he thought?

"I swear I spoke the truth," she said after a while, her voice now taut and slightly hoarse. "If ye dunna wish for Garrett to lose the woman...the woman he loves, then ye need to send help as ye would have if Garrett had sent a messenger, asking for the support of his clan. Only he canna because he doesna yet know that he'll be needing it, and once he does, it'll be too late." She retreated a few steps toward the door. "There, that's all I came to say. The choice is yers."

Then Moira turned on her heel, and Cormag heard her cross the short distance to the door before pulling it open. "Oh!" she exclaimed, surprise quickening her breath.

Cormag spun around, relieved to see that it was only Finn who stood in the doorway, his green eyes travelling from Moira to him. "I hope I'm not interrupting," he said, a teasing gleam in his eyes that made Cormag worry that his partiality toward Moira was slowly becoming known.

"Not at all." Clearing his throat, Cormag greeted his friend. "What can I do for ye?"

"I came to ask if ye'd made a decision yet," Finn said, stepping across the threshold as his gaze continued to drift back and forth between him and Moira. "About Garrett."

As much as Cormag feared the consequences of his decision, he had known from the start that he could not refuse his help, not to Garrett of all people. And the truth of the matter was that he believed Moira. More than that. He knew that she spoke the truth, and he could not in good conscience rob his friend of the woman he loved. He had kept him from going after her for far too long-for his own selfish reasons-and now he owed Garrett his support.

"I have," Cormag said, straightening as he faced his friend, ignoring the wide-open gaze Moira bestowed upon him. "Send word to Clan McKinnear. Ask them to ready a ship." He paused, then turned to Moira, willing himself not to see the soft glow that shone in her eyes. "Where?"

"Port Glasgow," she replied, biting her lower lip as it began to quiver.

Cormag swallowed and quickly turned back to Finn. "Port Glasgow then. Ask them to make haste. Ye'll know best who to address."

Finn nodded. He had spent some time living with their allies in the past years, running away from his feelings for Emma, believing them to be one-sided. How wrong he had been!

Cormag sighed, "Ian willna be happy to hear this."

"I'll talk to him," Finn promised, the look on his face one of quiet assurance. "I believe 'twould be best if he and I headed down to Glasgow as well, to meet the McKinnears and to speak to Garrett." He sighed, "Perhaps 'twill help Ian see that she is not a witch." He grinned, looking at Moira. "At least, not an evil one." Then he turned and strode from the room to complete the task he had been given.

"I like him," Moira whispered before her eyes rose to look at Cormag. "He has a kind heart."

Cormag nodded. "He's a good friend. Has been all my life."

"So has Ian." A sigh escaped her lips. "I'm sorry that I came between ye." She paused, and her lower lip quivered once more. "Perhaps ye should reconsider. Perhaps 'twould be better if I left. Perhaps there's another clan or..."

Her voice trailed off as Cormag stalked closer, his eyes fixed on hers. "Ye willna leave, and that is final." He felt a muscle in his jaw twitch as he fought to stay in control-at least as much as that was possible at this point. "If ye try, I swear I will come after ye and drag ye back here. Is that clear?"

The ghost of a smile teased her lips. "I'd miss ye, too."

Chapter Sixteen

HOPE & FEAR

S eated in the shade of her small grove, Moira lifted her chin when voices trailed near. Looking up, she spotted Emma and Maggie walking arm in arm down the meadow toward the small stream, Blair and Niall racing ahead. Their heads were bent toward one another, and Moira could see their lips moving as they no doubt discussed a confidential matter.

Moira sighed. She missed her sister-in-law Deidre, who had been a loyal friend and confidante all her life. Always had Deidre known when something was weighing on Moira's heart, and she had poked and prodded in her own gentle way until Moira had felt compelled to confide in her friend.

And it had always eased the burden upon her heart.

Watching the two women, Moira flinched when Emma's gaze rose and suddenly met hers. Quickly, she averted her eyes, pretending to pick grass off her skirts lest the two women think her intrusive.

"Moira!"

At the sound of her name, Moira felt a cold chill grip her shoulders, and her muscles tensed as though preparing for an attack. It had become second nature to her, and although Ian had reluctantly accompanied Finn on his way to Glasgow, her instincts still responded as though he could come upon her at any moment.

Swallowing, Moira carefully lifted her chin and found Maggie and Emma looking at her, their faces smiling, before Maggie waved, gesturing for Moira to join them. A shiver went down Moira's back at the invitation, and she knew not whether to give in to joy or rather err on the side of caution. Still, the promise of companionship was none Moira could ignore, and so she pushed to her feet and walked over to the two friends.

"Would ye like to join us at the stream?" Maggie asked, nodding toward the spot where Niall and Blair were splashing one another. "Perhaps somewhere drier."

Emma laughed, "But I still want to dip in my feet. The afternoon sun's awful hot."

Moira looked from one to the other. "I dunna wish to intrude."

"Oh, but ye're not," Maggie exclaimed, and without another word, she slipped her other arm through Moira's and pulled her along as they proceeded down toward the refreshing riverbed.

"Careful, ye wee fishies," Maggie called to her children. "The rocks can be slippery."

Niall and Blair nodded their heads in affirmation and then continued to run and skid as before.

Moving a bit farther downstream, the three women sat down in the shade of a large oak and after slipping off their shoes and stockings dipped their heated feet into the cooling stream.

"Ah!" Maggie sighed as she leant back and closed her eyes. "Wake me when the sun goes down."

Emma chuckled, "And who will watch yer wee fishies in the meantime?"

"Ye," Maggie replied, propping herself up onto her elbows. "It'll be good practise for ye before yer wee one gets here."

Moira froze, and her gaze snapped to Emma before it fell from her eyes and dropped down to her flat belly. "Are ye...?" Then she caught herself. "I'm sorry. I didna mean to-"

"'Tis all right," Emma exclaimed, waving her concerns away. "I'm not certain yet, but..." A smile tugged on her lips as her hand fell to her midsection. "I hope and wish that 'tis true."

Moira smiled at her. "Ye'll make a wonderful mother, and Finn'll make a wonderful father. Ye'll have a verra happy baby."

Emma looked at her with glowing eyes. "I spoke to Maggie," she all but whispered, casting a sideways glance at her friend. "She told me that she never asked ye to send me out for more branches that night in the hall. The night Finn found me and asked me to marry him."

A question clung to her words, and Moira bowed her head, unable to ignore the sense of apprehension that came over her at the thought that someone might disapprove of her interference. Still, the joy and gratitude on Emma's face soon put her fears to rest. "Aye, I mightna have spoken completely truthfully. I hope ye can forgive me."

Emma laughed, "There's nothing to forgive. Without ye, who knows what would've happened? If Finn and I had ever found the courage to admit how we truly felt?" A deep sigh left her lips. "I'm verra grateful to ye, and I'm sorry I havena said so earlier." She reached out and squeezed Moira's hand. "I know that yer beginning here with us has not been easy-"

"I dunna blame anyone for mistrusting me," Moira objected, touched by Emma's kindness. "After all, I've earned the reputation I have."

"Still," Maggie agreed before she exchanged another meaningful glance with her friend, "ye've worked hard to redeem yerself, and we believe that ye've done so. Give it time, and ye'll see that more will come to trust ye, to see that we all make mistakes-some graver than others, I grant ye that, but mistakes nonetheless." Maggie smiled at her in that warm and utterly enchanting way. "Ye'll see all will be well."

Moira pressed her lips together as tears threatened to burst forth, and her heart ached with such longing that she knew not how to contain it. "Thank ye," she whispered, and her jaw trembled with the overwhelming relief to have found acceptance. Perhaps even friendship.

Emma squeezed her hand, and Maggie reached out to take her other. "Dunna mind my husband," Maggie counselled. "He's angry because of me, not ye. Ye'll see that we're not the only ones who have come to care for ye."

Emma nodded in agreement. "Finn spoke highly of ye before he left for Glasgow. He said there's honesty in yer eyes, and compassion." A teasing smile touched her lips. "He said that Cormag has noticed it as well."

While Moira felt herself still, shock freezing her limbs, Maggie laughed loudly. "I reckon he's noticed more than her honesty and compassion."

Emma nodded in agreement. "Aye, he seems verra...aware of ye. Always."

Moira swallowed, remembering how Cormag had spoken to her only a few days ago. "Nay, he's merely kind. I admit I'm surprised that he would heed my advice, but 'tis all there is."

"I dunna believe so," Maggie objected, shaking her head so her auburn curls danced from side to side.

"But he's told me so himself," Moira disagreed, terrified by the small spark of hope once more igniting deep in her chest. "I'm a duty to him, nothing more. After all, I'm...I'm an outcast. I canna expect-"

"Around the time ye came here," Maggie interrupted, "there were whispers that Cormag intended to wed the daughter of the McKinnear laird."

Every fibre in Moira's body stilled as she turned to stare at Maggie.

"And then from one day to the next, he seemed to have...changed his mind." Maggie shrugged, her blue eyes holding Moira's. "There was no more talk, and ever since, he's been...keeping his distance from Clan McKinnear as though worried that the old clan chief would hold it against him that he all but snubbed his daughter." A teasing smile curled up Maggie's lips. "I wonder why he did that. What changed his mind."

Moira felt her heart thudding wildly in her chest, and for a second, she thought she needed to lie down as the world began to blur before her eyes. Joy and fear and hope and terror surged to the surface, mingling in her heart, her mind, her soul until she no longer knew what to fear or hope for. All she remembered was the vehemence in Cormag's voice when he had told her not to go.

"Has he never said anything to ye?" Emma asked gently.

Maggie scoffed, "He's not the type to reveal what's in his heart. It'll have to be ye, Lass. If ye want him, ye'll have to be the one to take charge."

Overwhelmed, Moira leant back against the oak's thick trunk, almost grateful when Blair slipped and fell, howling loudly and clutching her knee. Instantly, Maggie and Emma scrambled to their feet and hurried over to her, inspecting the reddened skin and soothing the girl's tears.

In a daze, Moira sat in the grass, her heart and mind returning to the few moments she had spent with Cormag. Always had she felt an odd pull to inch closer, to sink into his arms and share with him her greatest fears and joys. She remembered the way he had kissed her, held her, full of tenderness and concern. That night, he had come upon her in a moment when she had needed him most, when no one else had even noticed her absence. How had *he* noticed? What had made him search for her?

Whatever it was, Moira was glad that he had for despite the darkness that had consumed her that night, deep down, Moira wanted to live...

...and love...

...and be loved.

If only there was a chance for them. If only Maggie and Emma were right.

If only!

Moira was so lost in her thoughts that she barely noticed how the time passed. Only when Maggie put a hand on her shoulder did she return to the here and now. Her chin jerked up, and she stared at the auburn-haired woman.

"'Tis almost supper time," Maggie said with a knowing smile. "Time to head home."

Nodding, Moira pushed to her feet and joined the other four on their way up the slope toward *Seann Dachaigh* Tower. As they approached the small village, the children ran ahead, and Maggie and Emma squeezed Moira's hand in a friendly goodbye as well as a promise that more days like this would come.

A warm smile clung to her lips as Moira walked up the narrow path to her aunt's cottage, a cottage that was now hers. The sun shone red in the sky, casting a warm glow over the land, and the scent of wildflowers lingered in the air.

Indeed, today had been a good day, and Moira hoped with all her heart that more like it would follow.

At the sound of a soft neigh, Moira frowned and looked up to see a chestnut mare tied to the pole outside her front door. Instantly, her feet stopped, and she felt every muscle in her body tense. Who had come to see her? And for what reason?

Swallowing the dread that had lodged in her throat, Moira carefully stepped forward and around the horse before her gaze fell on the small patch of white hair on the mare's left flank. It looked like a star and Moira had seen it many times before.

Her heart soared upward as she hastened on, her eyes searching for the gentle face she longed to see.

And then her wide eyes fell on the small bench by the front door and the young woman sitting there.

"'Tis about time," Deidre exclaimed as she surged to her feet. "It feels as though I've been waiting for hours." And then she flung herself into Moira's arms, hugging her with a fierceness that belied her slender form.

Shaking, Moira clung to her childhood friend as tears streamed down her face. Three years had passed since they had last seen each other, and yet, Deidre embraced her with a familiarity that took her breath away. A familiarity born out of shared memories. Memories that were alive today as much as they had been then.

"I've missed ye," Deidre whispered, her slender arms wrapped tightly around Moira.

Sinking her teeth into her bottom lip against the sob that threatened to escape, Moira buried her face in her friend's hair, her own arms tightening their hold as well. "I've missed ye, too," she whispered after a while, her jaw quivering with the emotions that assailed her. "I've missed ye every day for the past three years."

Chapter Seventeen

A FRIEND'S RETURN

Long into the night, Moira and Deidre sat in the little kitchen, unable to part ways no matter how much exhaustion tugged on their lids. Covering her mouth, Moira yawned and then lit another candle, dreading the moment they would have to cut their reunion short and head to bed. "And ye truly didna tell Alastair ye intended to come here?"

Deidre smiled, her warm eyes glowing in the dim light. "He wouldna have let me."

"He can be a bit boorish that brother of mine," Moira said with great affection, wondering if the abyss between her and Alastair could still be bridged.

Deidre chuckled, "Naw, not at all. 'Tis simply that...that I'm his greatest weakness," she whispered, a deep sigh leaving her lips. "He fears for me for he wouldna survive if something were to happen to me, and he's been on the brink of losing me more often than anyone ever should be. He's terrified."

Moira nodded, remembering how often Deidre had almost lost her life trying to fulfil her greatest wish: becoming a mother. She had miscarried countless times, and two or three times it had seemed as though she would not recover.

Alastair had been beside himself with worry. His face haggard and his eyes bloodshot, he had refused to leave her side, barely eating or sleeping, his hands clinging to the woman he loved as though he could keep her alive by sheer willpower alone.

"I'm with child again."

Moira's head snapped up at Deidre's softly spoken words, and cold fear gripped her heart. "No!" The word flew from her lips without thought, echoing the panic that swept through her being at the thought of losing her friend, her sister.

An indulgent smile played on Deidre's lips. "I know ye fear for me, but I..." Sighing, she shook her head, unable to explain the deep longing that lived in her heart. "I canna not be a mother," she whispered, tears misting her eyes. "I have to try."

Nodding, Moira reached for Deidre's hand. "I know," she murmured, looking into her eyes. She had always known. If there was a woman destined to be a mother, it was Deidre. Still, it seemed that Fate saw fit to play a cruel trick on her, granting her children and then ripping them away. It was a harsh life, and Moira knew that it had crippled her brother and his wife. Still, the love they had for one another lived on, untouched by the cruelty of Fate.

It had always been an inspiration to Moira. Ever since her brother had gone against their parents' wishes and married his delicate and seemingly fragile wife, Moira had dreamed of a love like theirs. For a long time, she had thought Connor was the man who would claim her heart.

Now, she knew better.

That night, Moira slept like a rock, exhausted from the emotional turmoil of the day before. However, upon waking, her memories reminded her of Deidre's presence, and she jump from her bed with a smile on her face.

"Ye look famished," Deidre commented when Moira finally stepped into the small kitchen, the aroma of hot tea welcoming her.

"Aye. Have ye been up long?"

Handing Moira a cup, Deidre sank into the chair opposite her, arms folded on the tabletop. "I always have a hard time sleeping without Alastair by my side." A look of utter longing came to her eyes. "It feels as though a part of me is missing."

Moira smiled. "I reckon he'll come for ye soon."

Laughing, Deidre nodded, the look on her face far from disapproving. "As soon as he returns to Greyston Castle and learns that I've left, he'll have a fit."

"Especially when he learns where ye went."

Reaching out, Deidre placed a hand on Moira's. "Make no mistake, yer brother loves ye fiercely, and he's suffered greatly these past three years. Yer loss pains him, believe me." A soft smile touched her lips. "I often find him down by the Falls."

Moira's heart tightened as hope assailed her anew. "Truly?"

Deidre nodded. "Truly."

Sighing, Moira closed her eyes, savouring the moment. Again, she saw the thin waterfall as it cascaded down a steep rock wall, pooling into a small stream that snaked its way through the meadows near Greystone Castle.

As children, Connor, Alastair, Deidre and Moira had dared each other to jump off the steep cliff. Not one of them ever had, though, knowing that such a fall would be almost impossible to survive. Still, it had been a game of childhood days long gone, and Moira remembered well how her older brother had taught her how to swim in the shallower areas of the stream. When she had grown more proficient, Alastair had attached a long rope to a thick branch reaching far into the stream on which they had swung across.

Now and then, they had not made it, but landed in the stream, sputtering and laughing.

Indeed, the Falls was a place that for Moira was irrevocably tied to her brother, and it seemed that he too felt that way.

"Thank ye," Moira whispered, squeezing Deidre's hand in gratitude for her words had bestowed a priceless gift.

Deidre nodded, then rose and reached for the plates of food she had prepared. "Let's break our fast and then go for a stroll. I long to see where ye've lived these past three years."

The grass was soft under their feet as the two women ventured along the bank of the small stream where Moira had sat with Maggie and Emma only the day before. She spied Niall and Blair and their friends splashing in the waters once more, now and then casting curious glances at Moira and her visitor.

"They remind me of us," Deidre whispered, her eyes watching the children longingly. "We were like them once, weren't we? Without a care in the world."

Moira nodded, feeling her heart yearn for those simple days long gone.

"I meant to ask ye something."

Turning to look at Deidre, Moira noted the way her friend's gaze had become downcast, her eyes tracing the way the tall grass swayed in the soft breeze. Her chest rose and fell with a deep breath, and her right hand settled protectively over her flat belly. Then Deidre lifted her gaze and looked at Moira.

"I know what ye wish to ask," Moira replied, feeling a stab of pain at the helplessness that seized her, "and I'm sorry, but I didna see anything that would lay yer fears to rest."

Swallowing, Deidre nodded, unable to keep the disappointment she felt from showing in her eyes. "I knew 'twas unlikely," she murmured, "but I had to ask."

Moira reached out and took her hand. "I would've written to ye, and I will if anything changes."

Deidre nodded. "I know. I never thought ye wouldna." A small smile came to her lips. "'Tis only I wanted to see ye."

"I'm glad ye came," Moira told her, gently pulling her friend into her arms. "I wanted to see ye as well."

For a long time, they stood on the stream's bank, savouring the feel of one another, the closeness, the comfort, the familiarity that needed no words before Deidre's head lifted off Moira's shoulder. "Someone is watching us."

"What?" Moira tensed, panic seizing her body. "Where?" Had Ian returned already?

Deidre stood back and then nodded her head toward the castle. "There, on the wall-walk."

Moira's heart paused, but this time not with fear but with hope.

"What is it?" Deidre asked, her eyes narrowing as she searched

Moira's face. "Ye look...There's something in yer eyes that..." Shock dropped her jaw. "Are ye in love?"

Heat shot into Moira's cheeks, and she immediately turned away, quick strides carrying her along the stream's bank. "That's nonsense! There's no one-"

"Then why are ye running away?" Deidre demanded, a teasing chuckle in her voice as she came rushing after her. "And yer face is burning like a flame." Grabbing Moira's arm, Deidre pulled her to a halt, then stepped around her, trying to look up into her face. "Why would ye run from it? Clearly, he cares for ye as well. Why else would he watch ye?"

Feeling Deidre's eyes on her, Moira closed hers, knowing that she could not lie to her oldest friend. Not because it would be wrong, but because Deidre knew her too well. "Ye're mistaken," Moira said none-theless and met her sister-in-law's gaze. "He doesna care for me. I'm a duty, nothing more. A clan matter."

Deidre frowned. "How would ye know?"

"He told me so himself."

Her friend laughed, "Then 'tis probably not true."

Goose bumps shot up and down Moira's arms. "Cormag wouldna care for me," she said, trying to convince her friend as much as herself. "He's much too-"

"Cormag?" Deidre frowned. "The laird?"

Moira nodded. "I...I told him about my dreams."

Deidre's eyes went wide.

"I had no choice. I needed his help."

"And did he grant it?" her friend asked, almost holding her breath.

Unable to fight it, Moira felt a small smile claim her lips. "He did," she murmured. "I think he truly believes me."

"That's good," Deidre exclaimed, a broad smile on her face as she grasped Moira's hands. "Why would ye think he couldna care for ye?"

Closing her eyes, Moira resigned herself to her fate and began to tell Deidre everything that had happened since the moment she had first set foot in *Seann Dachaigh* Tower three years ago.

Deidre's eyes alternately glowed with joy and widened in shock, particularly when Moira confided in her about the night Cormag had come upon her on top of the eastern tower. Tears filled her friend's eyes then, and yet, not a word of reproach left her lips. "I canna understand why ye believe that he doesna care for ye?" Deidre finally said, slipping her arm through the crook of Moira's as they headed back to the village.

Moira sighed, "Can we not speak about this? Believe me, 'twould not be wise to have hope."

"'Tis never wrong to have hope," Deidre whispered, gently squeezing Moira's arm with her own. "'Tis never wise to give up on it."

Deep down, Moira could not help but wonder how Deidre had reached that conviction after everything that had happened to her, after everything she had lost and might lose again. Oh, how Moira wished she could see what would become of Deidre's pregnancy!

However, her dreams always came when they chose...and stayed away when they chose as well.

Chapter Eighteen

A GIANT OF A MAN

From the way the two women clung to one another, Cormag could tell that they were close, probably had been since childhood. A deep bond seemed to connect them that went beyond words, and he rejoiced at the thought that someone from Moira's past had reached out to her, for the joy it brought Moira was clearly written on her face.

Together, they spent their days strolling the meadow near the stream, even venturing into the neighbouring woods, their heads always bent close in confidence, their arms always linked in comfort.

From Fiona, Cormag learnt that the young woman was Deidre Brunwood, her nephew's wife and Moira's sister-in-law. She spoke warmly of the slender young woman with the bright, warm eyes before whispering with sadness of the misfortunes she had had to endure.

Cormag wondered why Deidre had come and why her husband had not accompanied her.

Four days after the young woman's arrival, he received his answer.

The sun had long since passed its zenith when a rider appeared on the horizon.

Cormag was up on the wall-walk, urging himself to leave but unable to do so, his gaze lingering on the nearby woods into which the two women had disappeared.

The rider approached fast, and as he drew closer to the main gate, Cormag frowned at the way he sat in the saddle. This was a man driven by anger, but also by fear, and he hurried down the stairs and into the courtyard, approaching the man when he pulled his mount to a halt. "Greetings," he said, his voice tinged with warning. "What brings ye here?"

The man jumped off his snorting horse, his tall stature not in the least dwarfed by that of his mount. He moved with purpose, a strain in the way he pulled back his broad shoulders and lifted his chin. The moment their eyes met, Cormag suddenly understood the odd familiarity he had felt upon seeing the man's flaxen hair.

His eyes were the same deep blue as Moira's.

"I'm Alastair Brunwood." He stepped closer, before he nodded his head in greeting. "Ye're the MacDrummond laird."

"Aye, Cormag MacDrummond. Are ye here to see yer sister?"

The man tensed, displeasure contorting his features, but Cormag saw a hint of longing come to those deep blue eyes before the feel of it crossed over and settled in his heart. "I'm here to fetch my wife," he replied, his tone gruff. "D'ye know where she is?"

Cormag wondered about the unlikely couple: Alastair, a giant full of strength and hard edges, and Deidre, so delicate and fragile that the wind might carry her away. "Aye," Cormag replied, curious to see the dynamic amongst the three who were family. "Follow me."

Nodding his head, Alastair fell into step beside him as they walked out of the courtyard and headed down the slope to the small path leading through the village, past Moira's little cottage and down to the stream.

Alastair paused momentarily, a deep frown coming to his face when Cormag made to cross the stream in a narrow spot. "She went this far?" he demanded, doubt ringing in his voice. "By herself?" Suspicion gave his tone an edge.

Cormag stopped and turned to face him. "She came with Moira."

The man's jaw tensed, and a muscle in his temple twitched while he held himself immobile, refusing to react beyond that which he could not control. Cormag felt the tension that held him, tension that masked fear and insecurity, and he knew that at some point in his life, Alastair Brunwood had felt completely and utterly helpless, powerless, forced to watch as someone he loved endured unspeakable pain.

As they proceeded farther into the woods, the echo of soft voices soon reached their ears and they turned toward it. Alastair's head snapped up and his eyes narrowed as he pressed onward, striding past Cormag, his ears attuned to his wife's soft lilt. They came to a small clearing where the women stood arm in arm, their gaze directed upward at the shifting clouds.

"Deidre!" Alastair bellowed, and while Moira flinched, Deidre merely turned her head to look at her husband as though she had known he was there. A deep smile came to her face, and even from a distance, Cormag could sense the overwhelming joy that surged through her being at the sight of the man she loved so fiercely.

Staying back, Cormag watched as Alastair's long strides carried him to his wife and sister. Moira stood stock-still, her eyes fixed on her brother as he approached, her chest rising and falling with each rapid breath. Longing rested in her deep blue eyes, and Cormag saw the way the muscles in her arms twitched, wishing to reach out and embrace the brother she had not seen in too long.

Still, the dark looks on his face kept her where she was, watching as Alastair reached for his wife, pulling her away from the sister who had betrayed him. "I canna believe ye left without a word," he snarled down into Deidre's face, the muscle in his jaw tensing as he ground his teeth. "I canna believe ye-"

Reaching out, dainty Deidre pulled her giant of a husband into a deep kiss, her hands brushing gently over his cheeks and further down his neck. In an instant, he responded, crushing her into his arms, giving voice to the fear and longing that had driven him to follow her the moment he had learnt of her departure.

Quietly, Cormag moved closer to Moira, who was still frozen to the spot, tears pooling in her eyes as she watched the reunion of Deidre and her husband, no doubt wishing her brother would embrace her as well or at the very least acknowledge her existence.

"He loves ye," Cormag whispered, placing a gentle hand on her shoulder.

A shiver went through her, and the tears brimming in her eyes finally spilled over.

"But that was never the question, was it?" Moving closer, Cormag tried to look into her eyes. "'Tis whether or not he can forgive ye?"

Moira nodded, and then turned away from the scene that had cut deep into her heart. "He's a proud man," she murmured, wiping at her cheeks. "He's always been, and he follows his code of honour to the letter." Sniffling, she smiled through the tears streaking her face. "To him, the world has always been black and white. Simple. Straightforward. I've often wondered if he's ever felt doubt over what to do."

Cormag tensed as a low growl rose from Alastair's throat and his hands tightened on his wife's arms. Looking around Moira, he tried to determine if her brother might be losing control of his anger.

"He willna harm her," Moira whispered without looking. "She's... She's his weakness. He loves her beyond hope. He always has." Fresh tears shot to her eyes, and she turned to look at them.

Standing beside her, Cormag watched the way Deidre met her husband's angry gaze, her deep brown eyes unflinching. There was no fear or concern in them, no submission or distress. She stood tall, and Cormag realised that despite their differences, theirs was a relationship of equals. On the surface, Alastair might appear strong and domineering while Deidre seemed weak and submissive. However, deep down, they were both strong and weak at the same time for they were dependent on one another, each one half of a whole.

Smiling gently, Deidre reached out and cupped her hand to Alastair's cheek, whispered words leaving her lips. At his wife's touch, the tall man closed his eyes in surrender and tenderly rested his forehead against hers, their breaths mingling into one.

"They're an unlikely couple," Cormag whispered into the stillness of the late afternoon.

Moira nodded. "But they were meant to be."

"So, it would seem."

With her arm slung around her husband's, Deidre dragged the log of a man over to where Cormag waited beside Moira. Alastair's face held displeasure, and yet, he followed Deidre, his eyes rising and then reluctantly meeting his sister's.

In that moment, Cormag realised why Deidre had come, why she had left without speaking to her husband, why she had dared to frighten him with her departure.

As Moira had said, Alastair was a proud man who would never have agreed to visit his sister. Cormag did not doubt that Deidre had done her utmost these past three years to persuade him to open his heart to Moira once more.

Tried and failed.

And so, the delicate, little woman had chosen a different path, knowing that her husband would follow her, even if it forced him into enemy territory, even if it meant facing his demons, even if it would bring him face to face with his sister.

And she had been right.

"I'm sad to say goodbye," Deidre said to Moira, her warm eyes dark with sorrow. "I've missed ye terribly, and I shall again."

Moira nodded as her gaze carefully darted back to her brother. "I've missed ye as well." Her jaw began to quiver, and Cormag could see that she desperately wanted to reach out to him.

Alastair's posture remained tense. Still, the blue of his eyes seemed to soften as he looked at his little sister. Then he inhaled a deep, shuddering breath that said more than a thousand words before he finally turned away, pulling his wife along.

"Goodbye," Deidre whispered over her shoulder as they walked away, a look of encouragement in her dark eyes, before she glanced at Cormag. "Take good care of her."

Cormag nodded, aware of the magnitude of that promise.

Beside him, Moira stood frozen to the spot, her blue eyes watching as two people she had loved all her life walked away, perhaps never to return.

The moment they disappeared from sight, she broke down. However, she did not sink to the ground into a heap of misery. Instead, to his great surprise, she spun around and threw her arms around him, burying her face in the crook of his neck.

Feeling her warm body clinging to his own, Cormag could not

ignore the desire to comfort her. He knew it was foolish to allow her so close, but he knew that there was no force on this earth that could bring him to abandon her now. Not when she needed him, not when she clung to him as though for dear life, her tears soaking his shirt.

Gently, he enclosed her in his arms, his hands gently rubbing over her back, brushing damp hair from her face as she wept for a loss he wished he could have spared her.

How had this happened? That her pain hurt him more than his own? And what did it mean?

Chapter Nineteen

RETURN TO SEANN DACHAIGH TOWER

T he leaves were beginning to change from different shades of green to warmer colours of red and brown and gold, giving Scotland's rolling hills and dense woods a new face. The days started to grow shorter, and the heat of summer slowly retreated as colder winds began to sweep across the country.

Standing up on the wall-walk, Moira looked out at the vastness before her, remembering the day she had stood up here, watching her brother and his wife ride away, their eyes turned homeward.

"Home," she whispered to the wind as it tugged on her golden tresses and swept up the fabric of her cloak. Would she ever feel at home again?

Her hand rested on the rough stone of the parapet in front of her, and she remembered the many times she had seen Cormag stand up here. She could see the spot by the small grove of trees where she often sat, watching the children splash in the stream, and a deep smile came to her face.

"I care for him," she whispered softly to the wind, feeling a new warmth spread through her heart at the simple admission. She knew she did, and she had for a while. Still, it would forever only remain a dream, and she would have to learn to live with wanting something she could not have.

A movement on the horizon caught her eye, and Moira turned her head, squinting against the bright autumn light. Riders seemed to be approaching as well as a carriage.

Moira's heart banged against her ribcage as hope surged skyward. Still, she knew it could not be. Knew that Deidre's visit had been a rare gift and she could not expect more. Whoever was coming had not come from her old home, had not come to see her.

Waiting for her heart to calm, to accept the disappointment that always followed a moment of unrestrained hope, Moira watched as the small group drew closer.

And then she could make out their faces, and again, joy found its way into her heart, joy and relief.

Garrett had returned, riding at the head of the small procession, with the carriage following behind, flanked by Finn and Ian; although Ian had fallen a little behind, his face grim, while Finn chatted cheerfully with a dark-haired woman inside the carriage.

Squinting her eyes, Moira looked closer, her eyes gliding over the woman's smiling face, taking in the vibrant blue of her eyes and the undisguised love that shone on her face whenever she looked at Garrett.

Moira sighed in relief. She had seen this woman before; in her dreams, her smiling face turned toward Garrett, his own a reflection of hers.

For once, her dreams had not led her astray. For once, they guided her down the right path, allowing her to help, to assist, to lead two people who belonged together to find one another before Fate could rip them apart.

Garrett's smile spoke volumes, and Moira knew that all she had done had been worth it. He looked happy, in love, and the moment, his gaze rose to meet hers, Moira knew it to be true.

For a long while, they looked at one another, and his green eyes shone with gratitude as he inclined his head to her in deference.

A smile tugged on Moira's lips, and she remembered the way Finn had looked at her before he had left to call upon Clan McKinnear for help. A teasing grin had rested on his lips, and he had referred to her as a witch, but not an evil one. Moira had seen kindness in him that day, kindness and respect, the willingness to open his mind and accept that she was not so different from him.

Now, she saw the same glow in Garrett's eyes, and it gave her hope that she would not have to be an outsider for the rest of her days. Maggie and Emma had already welcomed her into their midst, and every day, Moira reminded herself that while false hope was devastating, the absence of hope was hell.

So, she dared to hope.

A little.

As the small group pulled into the courtyard, Moira stepped away from the wall-walk, not wishing to disturb the reunion as family and friends rushed forward to welcome them back home. She made to turn around, determined to head down the back staircase, when a large chest suddenly obstructed her view.

Taken aback, she stumbled backwards, her back colliding painfully with the hard edge of the parapet before her gaze snapped up to look into dark grey eyes.

"I'm sorry I startled ye," Cormag said, regret marking his features as he reached out to steady her. His hand was warm on her arm, and Moira felt that familiar flutter return to her belly.

"'Tis all right," she mumbled, watching him as he stood before her, a hint of indecision in his eyes. "Is something wrong?"

He shook his head. "I wish to speak with ye," he finally said before glancing around, taking note of those lingering nearby. "Alone." Then he offered her his arm, his gaze lingering on hers. "Will ye accompany me to my study?"

Determined to enjoy the moments she could spend in his presence-short-lived as they were-Moira smiled up at him, accepting his offer. "What do ye wish to speak about?"

His arm tensed as he guided her down the back staircase. "Ian."

Moira drew in a shuddering breath, remembering the dark look on the man's face upon his return home only a few minutes prior. Even though he now knew that she had not led them astray, he did not seem willing to grant her the benefit of the doubt. Distrust and suspicion still clung to him. Nothing had changed. What did that mean for the future?

Her future?

Closing the door behind them, Cormag released her arm, then took a step back, his dark eyes searching hers. "He's still angry," he began without preamble, "and I admit I'm concerned about what will come of it."

Moira nodded. "I know." She inhaled a slow breath. "Are ye saying ye changed yer mind?"

For a second, Cormag's brows crinkled in confusion before his lips grew tight. "I havena," he replied with determination. "Ye willna leave, d'ye hear? I will speak to Ian." He sighed. "I only mean to ask ye to...be careful."

Moira scoffed, "How? Do ye want me to lock myself in my home?" She shook her head. "He's found me there before as ye well know."

The memory of that day passed over Cormag's face, and once more, Moira saw his eyes darken with outrage. "Nay, I simply..."

Shaking her head, Moira stepped toward him. "There's nothing I can do to protect myself. If he loses his temper..."

The muscles in Cormag's jaw clenched. "I will speak to him," he growled out, frustration rasping in his voice.

"About what?"

"Maggie."

Moira frowned, noting the understanding in Cormag's eyes. "Did he tell ye that?" Never would she have thought Ian would confide in anyone, even a friend. She had thought him a man who would never dare reveal a weakness. A man who always believed he needed to be strong .

Cormag shook his head.

"Then how do ye know?" Moira whispered, noting the way Cormag's eyes did not quite meet hers as though he was trying to hide something from her, praying she would not notice.

"Ye knew where I was," she mumbled, oddly enough drawn back to the night of her breakdown. "Ye knew to look for me. Ye knew that..." She stepped forward, lifting her hands and settling them on his chest, urging him to look at her. "How?"

His jaw clenched, his lips pressing into a thin line. Still, there was something in his eyes that whispered of the desire to place his trust in her, to confide in her.

Moving closer still, Moira felt her heart beat fiercely, wondering if his did so as well. Therefore, she shifted her right hand, slid it sideways over his chest until it felt the powerful beats of a heart in turmoil.

He held his breath, his eyes watching her carefully.

Searching his face, Moira whispered, "Do ye see things as well?" Under her hand, his heart skipped a beat, and her eyes went wide as he paled. "Do ye?"

Gritting his teeth, Cormag closed his eyes, a battle waging over his features. "I dunna," he finally said, his grey gaze once more settling on hers. "But I feel things."

Chapter Twenty

WINDOW OF OPPORTUNITY

With wide eyes, Moira stared up at him, her hands still resting on his chest. He felt her soft weight leaning into him and fought the urge to close his arms around her and rest his forehead against hers. He remembered well the afternoon they had stood out in the small clearing in the woods when her brother had left, reducing her to tears. He remembered how he had held her, overwhelmed by the trust she had placed in him to allow him to see her so vulnerable. In her moment of need, she had turned to him, sharing her pain and allowing him to comfort her.

Did he dare do the same? Share what he had never shared with anyone?

"Tell me," Moira whispered as her eyes roamed his face as though she could see the answer if she looked hard enough.

Cormag swallowed, knowing that if anyone could understand, it was she. "My father called me an empath," he forced out through gritted teeth, his jaw clenching as panic over what he was doing began to spread through him. "I feel what others around me feel as though their emotions were my own."

Her wide eyes widened even more before a touch of red spread to her cheeks, darkening her fair skin, and for a moment, she dropped her gaze in embarrassment. "Ye can...Ye can feel what I feel?" When he remained quiet, her eyes rose to meet his.

Cormag exhaled a slow breath. "I canna."

She frowned. "But ye said that-"

"I can feel everyone's feelings...but yers."

A mixture of relief and disappointment swept over her face, and Cormag marvelled at how well he had learnt to read her, even without his gift. "Why not mine?"

Indeed, why not?

Afraid to answer that question, Cormag shrugged. "I dunno." Then he took a step back and her hands fell from his chest. Instantly, he wanted them back, wanted to feel her warmth again, but he did not dare. If she knew...

But he pushed that thought away, afraid to admit even to himself how deeply she affected him. "I need to go," he said instead, desperate to put distance between them, and yet, the thought of leaving her side brought regret to his heart and a longing that grew with each passing day.

Leaving her behind, Cormag strode from his study, his steps quickening as he passed through the great hall. Then he stepped outside into the sunlight, and his eyes fell on Garrett, carrying a small bundle in his arms as he peered up at the window to his chamber. Following his gaze, Cormag saw a dark-haired woman look back at him before she vanished from sight.

As Garrett turned toward the gate, Cormag went after him, calling his name. Instantly, his friend stopped, then looked back to watch his approach.

"Welcome back," Cormag greeted him, feeling as though the balance between them had changed now that Garrett was a husband and father.

"Thank ye. 'Tis good to be home." The usual smile rested on Garrett's face, and Cormag was relieved to see that Moira had indeed been right. His friend looked utterly besotted.

Happy beyond all measure.

Inhaling a slow breath, Cormag glanced down at the small bundle in Garrett's arm, a tiny face peeking out from under the blanket. "Ye have a son," was all he said, was all he could say as an image of his father rose before him, and his heart ached for the man's counsel.

Cormag had been a son once. As had Garrett, and now his friend was a father himself.

"Congratulations." Pushing away all thoughts of what he had lost, Cormag instead focused on that which he could change. "I'd expected ye to come and see me after ye'd returned."

Garrett nodded. "I meant to, but when I approached yer door, I heard voices." Cormag froze, his iron will forcing his face to remain expressionless. Had Garrett heard him speak to Moira? Had he heard how he had revealed to her that...? "I did not wish to intrude, so I decided to take my son for a walk first."

A moment of silence lingered before Cormag asked, "Would ye mind if I accompanied ye?"

Together, the two men walked out of the gate, and Cormag followed as Garrett's feet turned toward the small hill he had often sought ever since he had been a lad. Walking, Garrett slightly bounced in his step, carefully rocking his son as the boy closed his eyes, a wide yawn stretching across his face.

It was a peaceful sight, and surprisingly, it calmed the turmoil in Cormag's heart.

Standing on the soft grass as the wind tugged on their clothes, Cormag welcomed the silent companionship he had always shared with Garrett. Words were not needed. Still, the presence of someone he trusted felt soothing and helped Cormag regain his balance.

"I wanted to thank ye," Garrett said after a while as he glanced down at his sleeping child. "Without Clan MacKinnear, I wouldna have been able to retrieve my wife and son."

With his gaze fixed on *Seann Dachaigh* Tower, Cormag wondered what would have happened if Moira had not interfered. Would Garrett ever even have met his wife? Would Fate have found a different way to bring them together? Or was that why Moira had received her gift? To lend a hand? Was she part of the universal order that stretched across the world?

"Finn said 'twas Moira who insisted ye send for them," Garrett continued, his eyes watchful, and Cormag remembered well the hint of suspicion in his friend's gaze when Cormag had spoken to him of Moira's gift.

"Her reasoning was sound," he replied, willing himself to remain immobile, to not reveal his own emotional involvement in this matter. Indeed, he had ventured from the path of reason he had always pursued for far too long, and it was imperative that he found his way back.

Garrett chuckled, "Ian disagreed."

"Ian always disagrees," Cormag replied, surprised by the vehemence of his feelings. What would he do about his old friend? He could not allow him to harm Moira, and neither could he allow Ian to suffer the way he did for the rest of his life. *Something* had to be done.

"I keep thinking," Garrett began as his gaze returned to the ancient castle they called home, "that if I had gone to Gretna Green a day early or a day late, I would never even have met Claudia. The thought sends a chill down my spine. She almost slipped through my fingers, and I would never even have known what I would have lost." He looked down at his son. "Sometimes there is only a small window of opportunity, and sometimes the one person who completes us has been right there by our side for a long time. Still, no opportunity lasts forever. Eventually, it is lost."

Even though Garrett spoke without referring to anyone, Cormag well understood the advice meant for him. Garrett knew, or at least he suspected, and this was his way of offering his counsel, knowing well that a direct approach would only result in him banging his head against the wall Cormag had built around himself long ago.

So far, the only one to breach it had been Moira.

Was she the one person who completed him? Was this, here, now, his window of opportunity to ensure she would not slip through his fingers? What if one day she decided to leave after all, refusing to abide by his word? Would he force her to stay or allow her to choose her own path?

The more his thoughts circled around Moira, the more Cormag felt his balance slip away, and he all but bowed his head in defeat. "I have business to attend to," he heard himself say before taking a step back and leaving Garrett and his son to enjoy the cooling breeze of the late afternoon.

Garrett is in love, Cormag mused as his feet carried him homeward, *and yet, he seems calm, balanced, at peace. How is this possible?*

Chapter Twenty-One

WELCOME HOME

The whole castle was abuzz with Garrett's return, and Moira watched as men and women and children rushed around the courtyard, preparing a spontaneous feast to welcome the young family home. Tables were set up in the great hall, and once again, Maggie flitted about the vaulted room, decorating with what she had at hand, while Mrs. Brown slaved in the kitchen.

When Moira entered the hot, steaming room with additional herbs, the older woman's face was flushed, and her breath came in rapid gasps as she wiped sweat from her brows.

"Oh, thank ye, dear!" she exclaimed, all but jerking the small bags filled with dried herbs out of Moira's hands. "I'll forever be grateful to ye." And then she turned around and Moira knew she was dismissed as the stout cook began sniffing the small pouches, determining how to use their contents.

On her way back through the great hall, Moira smiled at Maggie, who stood with her hands on her hips, her eyes slightly narrowed as she surveyed her handiwork. "'Twas not enough time," she mumbled, her eyes sweeping over the flower bouquets and garlands she had fashioned from the armfuls of picked flowers and branches the children had gathered for her.

"Ye did a fine job," Moira told her, seeing the slight tension in Maggie's shoulders. "'Tis beautiful."

Looking up, Maggie smiled; still, her gaze held doubt. "D'ye truly think so?" She put a finger to her lips and glanced around once more. "I feel as though there's something I'm forgetting."

Moira laughed, "Nay, 'tis truly beautiful. They'll love it."

Maggie exhaled the breath she had been holding, and finally her shoulders relaxed as she smiled up at Moira. "Thank ye." She chuckled, "I know I can get a wee bit carried away." Then she stopped and looked at Moira, her eyes sweeping over her dress. "Now, go and change."

Moira paused. "I'm not sure I should-"

"Ye'll come!" Maggie exclaimed as her dainty, little hand snapped forward and grabbed a hold of Moira's arm. "Dunna think ye can get out of this!" she teased, an encouraging smile on her lips. "Claudia wishes to meet ye."

"She does?" Moira asked almost thunderstruck for although she always enjoyed the cheerful atmosphere of these festivities, she feared that her involvement in bringing Garrett and his family home might lead to unwanted attention. Especially Ian, he would be displeased to see her, and she did not wish to anger him.

Maggie nodded. "Aye, Garrett's told her that 'twas ye who had Cormag send him down to Gretna Green in the first place. She's curious to meet ye. She told me so herself."

Moira swallowed. "Do ye think...?" She glanced around the hall, relieved to find Ian absent. "Do ye truly think 'twould be all right for me to attend?"

"Aye," Maggie stressed with a grin. "Now, go and change." And she shoved Moira toward the door before calling for Blair and Niall to stop pulling the petals off a bouquet of flowers.

Returning to her cottage, Moira pulled on a dress of a gentle blue, modest and unassuming, determined not to draw attention to herself, but to remain in the background and merely observe the festivities. She had to admit she was curious to see the woman who had stolen Garrett's heart in a single night. The thought of such a love as theirs warmed her heart and made her yearn for something she did not dare name.

When the sun dipped lower on the horizon, Moira returned to the hall, finding it filled to the rim with people eating, laughing and dancing as a group of fiddlers played in the corner by the large fireplace, their jaunty tunes echoing through the air. Keeping to the sides, Moira saw smiling faces wherever she turned, and her heart ached as she felt reminded of happier times back home.

Greystone Castle had been a place of joy and celebration as well, and it probably still was. Only now, she was no longer one of them.

Across the hall near the main table, Moira spotted Garrett, his arm slung around a tall, young woman with mahogany curls and laughing, blue eyes. She leant into him as they watched the proceedings and whispered words between them. Garrett's hand reached out to touch her face before she stepped forward and all but fell into his arms. A deep bond tied them to one another, one that was there for everyone to see in the way they always lingered close, always aware of the other.

And then Garrett looked up, and Moira felt his gaze collide with hers.

Instantly, her heart slammed to a halt.

Although Moira knew that Garrett was among those who had come to accept her, perhaps even respect her as one of them, she feared that his attention would draw that of others. So, she drew in a sharp breath when she saw him whisper to Claudia, his chin nodding toward her.

The young woman turned, her eyes following his. Barely a moment later, she strode forward, picking her way down the long line of tables.

Moira swallowed and then lifted her chin, determined to stand her ground as people noticed the young woman crossing the hall, Garrett only a step behind her. Conversations stopped and heads turned. Moira felt countless eyes sweep from Claudia to her, brows drawing down in...confusion? Or disapproval?

"My husband tells me," Claudia began as she stopped in front of Moira, "that you're the reason we found each other." Smiling, she glanced at the man by her side, whose own face radiated the happiness she spoke of.

Moira swallowed, aware that countless ears were listening. "Perhaps," she said non-committally, "but the rest was all yer doing."

Claudia sighed, stepped forward and grasped Moira's hands, her blue eyes shining with unshed tears. The carefree joy that had clung to her features only a moment ago was replaced by a look of deep contemplation. "Thank you," she said, a quiver in her voice. "I know how close I came to losing it all: my husband, my son; it nearly killed me. If you..." She swallowed, pressing her lips into a thin line as a tear spilled over and rolled down her cheek. "If you hadn't sent Garrett, if you hadn't sent help, I..." She shook her head, unable to express the loss she had no doubt contemplated more than once.

Returning the woman's soft pressure on her hands, Moira smiled at her. "Ye're welcome. I'm glad to see ye happy."

A radiant smile came to Claudia's face, and she once more glanced over her shoulder at her husband before suddenly surging forward and embracing Moira in a way she had not experienced in years. "Thank you so much. I'll never forget it."

Returning the woman's embrace, Moira realised that her own eyes were suddenly brimming with tears. To be accepted like this, for her gift, for her *interference*, was something Moira never would have thought possible, and it warmed her deep inside, chasing away the chill that always seemed to linger.

After Garrett drew Claudia away to introduce her to more friends and family, Moira retreated into a corner of the hall, frantically dabbing at her eyes and trying to become invisible once again. She feared others would think she had bewitched Claudia as Ian thought her to have done to his wife. She feared Claudia's kind words would only prove to them that indeed Moira possessed an ability beyond those of others. She feared that now they would fear her even more than they already had before.

And fear often led to anger and hatred. She had seen it before, and she knew to fear it.

As her heart hammered in her chest, Moira found her gaze sweeping the crowd, looking, searching for dark grey eyes that possessed the unique and rather baffling ability to calm her, put her at ease and make her feel safe.

The breath caught in her throat when she found Cormag entering the hall, his eyes sweeping the crowd as though he too was looking for someone, and for a precious and shockingly intoxicating moment, Moira allowed herself to believe that he was looking for her.

Still, she did not dare reveal herself and stayed hidden in the small corner behind one of the large columns supporting the roof, her eyes following him as he made his way through the crowd, exchanging a word here and there.

Whenever they were alone together, Moira often felt an odd sense of recognition when she looked at him. There was something in his eyes that spoke of the same questions which plagued her, the same uncertainty which chilled her bones as well, the same desire to be understood which she longed for. Now, however, as he moved amongst his people, Cormag seemed like a man at ease with himself as well as the world, and Moira wondered if she had only ever imagined the connection she had felt to him.

Perhaps it had simply been a matter of wanting to believe it to be true.

Of needing it to be true.

To feel less alone.

"Will ye dance with me?"

Blinking at the sound of her soft voice, Moira looked down and found little Blair standing before her, a flower from one of her mother's bouquets in her outstretched hand. "Ye look sad again," Blair observed. "Perhaps ye should dance. 'Tis a lot of fun." Her round blue eyes shone with joy, but Moira saw something else there as well. Something she could not quite grasp, something that made her wonder about the little girl who refused to abandon her side.

"'Tis verra kind of ye to ask me," Moira told her, leaning forward to be understood over the roaring laughter echoing through the hall. "But...I admit I'm rather tired. Why don't ye go and dance with yer brother?"

Little Blair drew in a slow breath as her watchful eyes swept over Moira's face. The look in them was one of compassionate indulgence as though she knew very well that Moira's words did not reflect the truth but was willing to grant her a reprieve. "Verra well," she finally said, a gentle smile coming to her little face. "But if ye change yer mind, come and find me." Then she turned around and vanished into the crowd.

Straightening, Moira made to lean back against the wall, her heart overcome with regret, when a dark face suddenly appeared beside her.

Muffling a scream with a hand to her mouth, Moira shrank back, staring at Ian's contorted face as he forced her to retreat down the side corridor. His steps were measured, menacing, and the hatred that burnt in his eyes was almost painful to see.

Goosebumps shot up and down Moira's back as she pushed herself along the cold stone wall, her instincts urging her to retreat while her mind screamed at her that she was putting more and more distance between herself and someone who might come to her aid.

Cormag.

Like a lifeline, her heart clung to him, but it was too late, and she found herself in a darkened corridor, alone with Ian.

"I told ye to stay away from my daughter!" Ian snarled before his hand shot forward and clamped down hard around her wrist.

A gust of air rushed from Moira's lips as a dark memory resurfaced, overwhelming her in its vividness. Again, she felt Ian's hands squeeze her throat as though it were made of pudding. Again, she felt her lungs strain to provide her with life-sustaining air. Again, she began to see black spots dance before her eyes.

Moira knew she was not a woman to cower, to plead, to weep in the sight of danger. However, in that moment, she could not find the strength to stand tall and proud. In that moment, all she felt was worn and exhausted and weary.

When would this finally end?

"I swear," Ian growled into her face, "if I find ye near her one more time..." His voice trailed off as he gritted his teeth, fighting to stay in control as his other hand reached up, hovering near her face as though wishing to finish what he had started that day months ago.

Then he abruptly released her and strode away, his angry footsteps echoing in Moira's head, and her body flinched at each dull thud.

"I canna stay," Moira heard herself whisper repeatedly as she pushed off the wall and stumbled down the corridor. At its end, she pushed open the door and stepped out into the courtyard, her eyes moving over the closed stalls before coming to rest on the stables. "I canna stay."

Chapter Twenty-Two

INTO THE NIGHT

*S*omething was wrong!

Cormag could not say what, but there was a certainty in his chest that reminded him of a night a few weeks past. Unease settled in his bones as he lifted his head to see above the crowd, praying that he would find Moira's face amongst those laughing and talking, or at least hovering somewhere in the back. Still, as before, he could not find her, and his unease grew with each step he took around the large room.

"Is something wrong?" Garrett asked, his brows drawn down as he watched him.

"Have ye seen Moira?"

Garrett nodded. "Claudia and I spoke to her not long ago."

"And since?"

Garrett shook his head, then started to look around himself. "Why do ye ask?"

Cormag sighed, unable to explain even to himself why he needed to find her. "Did she seem upset?"

"Touched," Garrett replied, a deep sigh leaving his lips. "Claudia thanked her for aiding us in our search for one another. I think her words deeply affected Moira although she tried her best to hide it." His frown returned. "Is there anything I can do?"

Cormag shook his head and then quickly took his leave. After all, Moira was not here. But she had been in the hall before leaving sometime after speaking to Garrett's new bride. Why? Where had she gone? Home?

Halfway to the large oak door, Cormag froze as his mind conjured an image of the eastern tower, Moira standing on the parapet wall, swaying in the breeze tugging her forward.

"No!" Spinning on his heel, Cormag sprinted sideways into the darkened corridor and then raced up the stairs, his heart hammering as it had the night he had found Moira ready to fling herself off the wall. Had she not promised him to seek him out should she ever...?

Without thought, he burst through the door...only to find the roof empty, the parapet walls gleaming softly in the last rays of the setting sun. Slowly, his heart began to calm as he stalked around the stone floor, his thoughts running rampant, trying to determine what had happened and where she could have gone. Had Ian found her? Had he...?

Cormag's teeth gritted together painfully as he realised that he had not seen Ian either when he searched for Moira in the crowd. Had he merely overlooked him, his attention focused elsewhere? Or...?

Standing with his hands resting on the parapet wall, Cormag was about to push off and rush back downstairs to seek out his childhood friend and demand an explanation when movement caught his eye down in the courtyard.

Instantly, Cormag stilled, his gaze narrowing as he tried to see in the dim light of the approaching night.

"Moira." Her name flew from his lips as he stared at her golden tresses swaying in the wind. She moved swiftly and with determination, leading a horse from the stables and then swinging herself into the saddle. Before Cormag had even taken a single step, she urged her mount out through the open gate and they vanished behind the wall protecting *Seann Dachaigh* Tower from outside forces.

A moment later, Cormag all but flew down the stairs.

He finally had his answer.

Tears streamed down her face as Moira urged the mare onward, her hooves thundering through the small village and past the cottage that had been Moira's home these past three years. Still, it had also been the place where Ian had almost squeezed the life from her, and Moira once more felt his fingers tensing around her throat.

Willing the image away, Moira looked up at the horizon, which was slowly growing dimmer as the sun vanished behind Scotland's rolling hills. Darkness began to reach out its fingers toward the land, a threat which felt devastatingly familiar that Moira could not help but cringe at the thought. She knew she ought to head back. She knew it was madness to leave in the middle of the night. She knew she was not equipped to travel across country...especially since she had no idea where to go.

But she could not turn back. She simply could not. Yet, she could not stay.

Despite all the small wonderful moments she had shared with Maggie and Emma, Mrs. Brown's appreciation, Little Blair's tenacity in making her feel better, Garrett's and Claudia's gratitude, Finn's trust in her and...Cormag's way of looking deep into her soul like no one ever had before, Moira did not *dare* stay.

In this dark hour, she was once more reminded that even the smallest measure of happiness could be ripped away, leaving her alone and frightened and so weary. Aye, Moira was weary of fighting for acceptance every day. She could understand why people mistrusted her, and yet, in that moment, she did not have the strength to continue. She simply wanted it to be over, to rest her head and close her eyes.

In peace.

Thunder rolled in the distance, and Moira's head snapped up, her eyes gliding over the darkening sky, trying to see where dark clouds might have collected, threatening to soak her through should she proceed in that direction. Still, no matter how hard she strained to see, her eyes would not assist her.

Darkness was slowly falling over the land, hiding what had been visible only moments before.

The sound of thunder swept over her once more; only this time, it sounded less like thunder and more like-

Looking over her shoulder, Moira spotted a rider approaching from behind her, and panic swept through her like a wave. Was it Ian? Was he pursuing her? Seeing his chance far away from the castle?

With fear fuelling her blood, Moira leant farther over her mare's neck, urging the horse onward. Could she outrun him? Again, she glanced over her shoulder and saw a dim outline in the faint light of the crescent moon that hung crookedly in the midnight-blue sky.

The rider was gaining on her!

Pulling on the reins, Moira guided her mare to the left, closer to the woods where she might lose him in the thicket. Small groves stood here and there, and she tried her best to alter her course whenever they came in-between them, blocking his line of sight.

To Moira's relief, he soon vanished into the shadows, and she could no longer see him when she turned her head. Still, Moira did not dare slow her mare and continued as fast as she dared in the near-dark. Only when she came to the small stream where it snaked back around and travelled eastward once more did she slow her mount, allowing her mare to carefully pick her way across the slippery riverbed.

She had just made it to the other side when a dark shape suddenly appeared out of nowhere.

Shrieking in terror, her mare reared up, and Moira lost her balance, falling backward, her hands scrambling to find something to hold onto.

But there was nothing, and so she hit the ground with a hard thud, and she screamed out in pain. Panic urged her to her feet within seconds, and she immediately reached for her mare's reins as the horse pranced nervously in front of her, its ears flicking back and forth.

When rough hands grasped her, and a scream tore from her throat.

Terror gave her strength, and she struggled against her attacker with all her might. Still, he spun her around with little effort, his iron fists closing around her wrists in an oddly familiar way. Moira's head snapped up, and she found herself looking up into Cormag's dark eyes, a storm brewing in them as he yanked her closer, a snarl on his face. "How dare ye leave? Ye promised!"

Chapter Twenty-Three

HEART & MIND

As much as Moira had fought against him before, the moment their eyes met, her body ceased its struggle. Her breath came fast, and her hands were balled into fists, but she stood still, her wide blue eyes staring up into his.

Slowly, Cormag felt his blood calm. Aye, he had growled at her, given her a reason to be frightened of him...and he was coming to regret it. He ought not have lost control, no matter how angry he had been, how...frightened he had been. For if he were honest-at least with himself-he had been terrified at the thought of losing Moria, either to another place on this earth or to a tragedy that might have befallen her.

He could not lose her, and the thought tightened his grasp on her wrists.

Moira gasped, and her eyes narrowed, anger pushing away the hint of awe he had seen in her blue gaze the moment their eyes had met. "How dare ye follow me?" she snapped, yanking on her arms to free them. When she failed, a frustrated growl rose from her throat. "Release me."

Swallowing, Cormag complied, feeling the muscles in his jaw tighten at the loss of her touch. "What are ye doing out here?" he asked, willing himself to remain in control. "Where are ye headed at this time of night?"

Her lips pressed into a thin line as she rubbed her wrists. "That is none of yer concern. Leave me be." And with that, she spun around and stalked toward her mare, now grazing calmly nearby.

"Ye will answer me," Cormag demanded, his voice calm but tinged with a threatening growl.

Turning back to face him, Moira squared her shoulders. "I dunna owe ye an explanation, and ye have no right to demand one."

The tightness in his shoulders grew, and he felt his hands ball into fists by his sides. "Ye're my responsibility," he forced out through gritted teeth, his heart aching at the distance that now echoed between them. "I willna have ye come to harm. 'Tis foolish to leave the castle at night and on yer own." He tried his best to be reasonable with her, but he knew that his words were coming out differently.

Moira snorted, "Yer responsibility, aye?" She shook her head, and a grotesque imitation of a smile showed on her lips. "Then I release ye from that responsibility as it seems verra burdensome to ye."

Fear gripped him anew. "'Tis not that simple," he growled. "Ye-"

"I'm sorry ye had to pay the price for my wrongdoings," she interrupted, her dark blue eyes burning into his as though she was daring him to...react? "Ye did nothing wrong; still, ye had to put up with my presence all these years. I know it hasna been easy for ye, and so I think ye'll agree that 'tis in all of our best interests that I leave. Now. Tonight."

Cormag could not quite say what he was feeling in that moment. It reminded him of the day his father died; the sense of panic knowing that a tragedy awaited him around the next turn as well as the deep crater of loss that tragedy plunged him into. The helplessness. The need to do something. The fear that whatever he did would not be good enough. "Ye promised," was all he could get past his lips without losing control of the storm brewing inside him.

"I promised not to harm myself, nothing more." Inhaling a slow breath, Moira shook her head. "I never promised not to leave."

Anger sparked anew at this technicality, but he extinguished it quickly, reminding himself that nothing good had ever come from losing one's temper. "I dunna care. Ye're coming back with me."

Her lips thinned, and her nose crinkled ever so slightly, giving her the look of a feline baring its teeth. "Ye canna tell me what to do, Cormag MacDummond. Do ye hear?" Storming toward him, she tried to shove him out of her way, and her frustration grew when she failed. "Ye have no right meddling in my life. Why did ye come? 'Twould have been so easy for ye to rid yerself of this responsibility. It still is." She sighed, "Simply look the other way and let me leave." Her jaw clenched, and he thought to see a faint shimmer of tears in her eyes. "I promise I'll not return."

"That I canna do," he replied, wondering what had pushed her over the edge tonight. "Tell me what happened? What made ye leave?"

Her gaze dropped from his. "'Tis none of yer concern."

"'Tis my clan," he whispered, watching the way her lower lip began to quiver the same it had that night up on the eastern tower. "What did Ian do?"

Her head snapped up, and she stared at him with wide eyes. "How did ye-? Can ye feel what I feel...right now?"

Cormag shook his head. "I told ye I canna. But I know my people, and...I know ye." He took a step closer. "Tell me what happened."

"He hates me," Moira whispered, and the vulnerability that came to her eyes made him cringe. "He blames me for the loss of Maggie's love, and...and every time, Blair speaks to me...it riles him. Perhaps he fears that he'll lose her as well. I don't know." She inhaled a shuddering breath, and he saw the way her hands trembled before her arms rose and she wrapped them around herself. "All I know is that he blames me, and one day, no one will be there to interfere, to stop him from..." She swallowed, and a shadow crossed over her face. "I dunna want to die like that, and...and I canna live in fear." She shook her head as determination hardened her eyes. "I have to go." Again, she turned, her steps quick as she headed for her mare.

Panic gripped Cormag's heart, sending him after her. "I willna allow it," he snapped, his voice harsh as he reached for her arms, spinning her back around. He felt like an ogre, a barbarian, forcing his will on her when he could simply admit that...

But it was not simple, was it? It never had been.

She loves ye as well.

At the echo of his mother's voice, Cormag froze, cursing her influence on him. Never had they seen eye to eye on these matters, but instead gone head to head, her urging him on and him putting up barriers. Still, somehow, she always found her way into his mind.

Once more trapped in his iron grip, Moira stared up at him. Only this time, there was no fight in those deep blue eyes. Instead, he saw resignation and exhaustion, and he realised how close she was to giving up. Every day, she was forced to balance on the edge of a precipice, always fearing to fall, always fighting to stay upright. "Have ye never felt like getting away? Leaving it all behind? Do ye never feel overwhelmed? Exhausted?" Shaking her head, she straightened, a frown coming to her face. "How can ye always remain so calm? So controlled? Is there a beating heart in yer chest?"

There was. Cormag knew that there was, more so today than ever before, and that was the problem. "It doesna matter how I feel." He all but spat the words, afraid they would reveal him as a liar. "Ye will return to the castle with me."

For a moment, it seemed she would bow her head in defeat, but then her features hardened. "Why?" she demanded, and her voice grew in strength. "If ye want me to come, then tell me why. Why are ye here? Why did ye follow me? Why?"

Never in his life had Cormag been asked a more complicated question, or one more terrifying. "It doesna mat-"

"Aye, it does!" Moira yanked on her arms, but not as it seemed to free herself, but to pull him closer. Her eyes sought his, searching, demanding. "Tell me! Why do ye care? Why can ye not simply let me leave? 'Twould be better for everyone." She snorted, "Especially for ye, a man who adheres to reason at all times, this should be obvious." A moment of quiet fell over them, and the look on her face grew gentler. "Why?"

Cormag gritted his teeth until his jaw felt as though it would break apart. He wanted nothing more but to put distance between them, but he could not bring himself to look away, her blue eyes holding him trapped as though she had placed iron shackles on him.

"Why?"

"Are ye...," he swallowed hard, his breath coming faster and faster as his emotions fought to break his hold on them, "...never afraid that giving in to...to..." He broke off and forced himself to inhale a deep breath as his head began to spin. "That giving in will rob ye of yer control once and for all?"

Chapter Twenty-Four

A MOMENT OF SURRENDER

Moira stared up into his black eyes, taken aback by his question as it held countless implications and whispered of a caring heart, a heart he fought to hold in check, a heart straining to break free. If only he would let it.

Still, the tortured expression on his face spoke of a fight not yet ended. The battle still waged within him, and she could feel his struggle in the tight grip upon her wrists. "If ye don't allow yerself to feel," she whispered, noting the way his gaze held onto hers, "how do ye even know ye're alive?"

A dark chuckle left his lips, and she saw his resistance slip further through his fingers. Never had she seen him thus. Although she had glimpsed deeper emotions lurk beneath the surface of his controlled exterior every now and then, Moira had never felt certain that what she had seen had truly been there. For deep down, she knew what she wanted, what she wanted to see, and she feared that her eyes were fooling her, had been fooling her.

But perhaps not.

Perhaps there was something she could do to tip the scales, to win the battle, if not the war. Perhaps if she broke through his defences, she would receive her answer.

Moving closer until her body touched his, she watched as awareness came to his eyes and smiled as his breath momentarily lodged in his throat. "What are ye afraid ye'll say or do if ye allow control to slip from yer fingers?" she whispered, lifting her head to his.

His breath quickened as his gaze dropped to her lips, reminding her of the night he had found her on top of the eastern tower. "Ye dunna want to know," he rasped before he set his jaw in determination, and she saw his struggle to fight against the temptation she presented.

Joy and desire filled Moira's heart as it longed to relive the moment they had shared the night of her aunt's wedding. She recalled the warmth and comfort she had found in his arms. She remembered how the loneliness, her constant companion, had bowed its head in defeat. She knew that it had been a moment of peace and happiness.

A precious moment.

A moment that had stood against the darkness...and won.

"Ye're wrong," Moira whispered, and she pushed herself up onto her toes, bringing her mouth closer to his. "I do want to know." A smile curled up her lips as his warm breath teased her skin. "As do ye."

At what point the dam broke, Moira could not say. She did not even see a flicker in his eyes or a twitch in his jaw that told her he would answer her challenge.

From one second to the next, she found herself in his arms, his heart beating fast against her own, and his mouth claimed hers with a swiftness that stole her breath, demanding more than she had offered.

That night up on the eastern tower, Cormag had kissed her with such tenderness, his knuckles brushing softly along her jaw before his fingers had settled in her hair. She had been touched by his consideration, assessing at every turn whether she would grant him permission. He had been almost hesitant, careful as though she were made of glass.

Tonight, there was nothing hesitant about him. Nothing gentle.

His arms crushed her to him mercilessly as his mouth devoured hers. She felt his hands cup her cheeks, then roam lower, their pressure against her skin betraying his loss of control, his desire to feel her. Her feet barely touched the ground as he held her against him, his hands gripping her hips as his tongue invaded her mouth.

Moira gasped at the sudden sensations, unexpected and overwhelming, as she clung to him, swept away like a piece of driftwood and then brought back ashore by the power of waves crashing over her, threatening to pull her under. She had no control, and for a moment, a spark of fear lit in her heart at the familiar feeling of helplessness. She had felt powerless too many times in the past few years, and she could not bear it.

Her body tensed, but the fire in her belly burnt as strongly as before. She revelled in the feel of him, in the knowledge that at least a part of him longed for her as much as she longed for him. Her hands gripped his shoulders, needing something to hold onto, as she reminded herself that the waves throwing her about would never harm her. Would never take advantage.

Never.

Always had Cormag been there when she had needed him. Always had he listened even when he had not liked what she had to say. Always had she felt safe with him...because he cared, did he not?

He cared about her, could he deny that now?

As quickly as he had seized her, Cormag now almost pushed her from him, panting hard, his gaze wide as he stared into her eyes.

Moira felt weak, her legs threatening to drop her onto the ground, and yet, her heart raced with a strength she had not felt in years.

And then his gaze ventured lower, and she saw his jaw clench as his eyes travelled over her swollen lips to her bare shoulder, the fabric ripped and hanging down her arm, and farther over her crumpled dress.

He swallowed then, and his eyes closed for a long moment as he fought to regain control, guilt and remorse bringing a scowl to his face. "I'm sorry," he croaked, clearly shaken. "I'm sorry."

Moira shook her head, and her mouth opened to assure him that though a little unsteady on her feet, she was fine for the look of regret in his eyes sent a chill down her back. He was retreating once more.

"I'll take ye back," he stated gruffly as her mind was still contemplating how to reply. "Come." He turned to reach for her mare's reins and brought her over, careful not to step too close, not to touch her.

And then Cormag was gone, her view at him blocked by her mare, and she heard him trudge through the grass, soft murmurs leaving his lips as he approached his gelding. The animal snorted in greeting, and then silence lingered. For a long moment, Moira heard nothing but the soft chirping of crickets and the distant hooting of an owl. The breeze had grown colder in the absence of the sun, and Moira felt a chill raise goose bumps on her skin. Sighing, she rested her forehead against her mare's soft neck. "What should I do?" she whispered, still breathless from the depth of emotions she had experienced.

"Are ye ready?"

At the sound of his voice, Moira looked up and found him astride his gelding, waiting for her by the narrow spot where she had crossed the stream. Had that only been moments ago? For it seemed like a small eternity had passed since then.

Pulling herself into the saddle, Moira followed him back toward *Seann Dachaigh* Tower, wondering at what point she had abandoned the thought of leaving her life with Clan MacDrummond behind. Still, a lot had changed in the past few moments, and Moira could not bring herself to give up on the small hope he had granted her that night. For whether he liked to admit it or not, there was something between them. Something that Moira needed in order to step back from the abyss that threatened to topple her into its void.

It might be selfish of her to reach for him merely because she needed him. Perhaps he was right to fight for control, to not allow his emotions to overtake him. Was that not what had led Moira down a path of betrayal? Still, a life without...feeling something, anything that stirred her blood, was not a life she wanted.

A life she ever truly could live.

Had that not been the realisation she had faced up on the parapet wall? The realisation that not every life was worth living.

As they drew closer to *Seann Dachaigh* Tower and the threat that lived within, Moira glanced at the man riding ahead of her and wondered what was on his mind. She had seen regret in his dark eyes, but had that been brought on by his loss of control or the thought that he might have acted against her wishes?

Indeed, she had been overwhelmed by the fierceness of his desire, and perhaps he had interpreted her shock differently. Perhaps she ought to speak to him, to clear up misunderstandings. First, though, she needed to find out how she truly felt and what she wanted, how far she was willing to go and what she was willing to give up.

As they rode through the front gate, the dark stone walls looming like giants around her, Moira felt a familiar cold grip her and settle in her bones. No, she could not return to the life she had lived before. She could not bear it. Something needed to change.

Either she would leave or...

Chapter Twenty-Five

INTRUDER

After returning the horses to the stable, Cormag stalked toward the side entrance. The festivities were still ongoing as laughter and music echoed into the darkened sky, and he could not bear laying eyes on another soul now. He could barely look at Moira as she trudged after him, her head bowed, and her arms wrapped around her against the shiver that shook her body.

Cormag cursed under his breath, cursed himself for allowing her to break through his defences. She surely regretted her bravado now for the look on her face spoke of pain and fear. Cormag ran a hand over his face, unable to believe what he had done.

He had truly lost control and hurt the one person he cared about the most.

"Good night."

At the soft whisper of those words, Cormag turned to look at her.

Moira stood a few paces away from him, her face pale in the soft silver glow from the moon overhead, and he tensed at the hint of panic in her eyes. Did she fear him? He had to admit she had reason to.

At least now, she did.

Deep down, Cormag knew he ought to let her go, to grant her distance from him; however, the thought that she might try to sneak away again as soon as she was alone would not let him. "Ye canna return to yer home," he spoke into the dark as she made to turn back toward the village. "Not after the way ye ran off tonight." Afraid she might bolt, Cormag approached her slowly, his hands slightly raised as a promise that he would not get too close. Not again. "Ye'll sleep in the castle, and we'll sort out the rest tomorrow."

Her wide eyes remained on him, watching as he moved closer. "Where will I sleep?" she whispered as her gaze roamed his face, something lingering in their blue depths that Cormag could not grasp.

"There're unoccupied chambers reserved for visitors. I'm certain one of them will do."

Cormag thought to see a hint of displeasure in the way her lips thinned as though she disliked what he had said.

He swallowed. "I willna touch ye," he promised, and for a second, he thought she would cringe away. "But if ye give me no choice, I will throw ye over my shoulder and carry ye inside." His gaze held hers for he needed her to understand that he meant every word. "The decision is yers."

For a long while, they stood under a canvas of faintly glowing stars, the muted sound of music and laughter a barrier between them and the rest of the world. And then she suddenly nodded. "Verra well."

Not daring to question her sudden acceptance of his command, Cormag turned toward the side entrance that would allow them into the castle unseen by the celebrating crowd. Every few steps, he glanced over his shoulder to ensure that she was following him through the door to the back staircase and then upward. Neither one of them spoke a word, and to Cormag, the silence that lingered between them felt oddly oppressing.

Something had changed between them, and Cormag knew not how to get it back or if that was even possible. All he knew was that he had lost something that night, and his heart mourned.

Stopping outside a heavy door, Cormag glanced back at her, her head slightly bowed and her eyes distant as though she was lost in thought. Then he pushed open the door and invited her inside. "There are additional blankets in the cupboard," he told her, reaching for the key hanging on a little hook on the wall. He looked down at the small metal object in his hands before rising to meet hers. "I'm sorry, but I'll need to lock the door."

Her eyes narrowed. "Ye dunna trust me." Her words felt like a slap in the face, especially after the way he had betrayed her trust.

"Nay," Cormag said nonetheless, and then quickly stepped toward the door.

"Wait."

Looking back at her, Cormag followed her gaze as it shifted sideways and then touched upon her bare shoulder, the fabric hanging down in rags. "I'll need something to wear."

Cormag's lips thinned at the thought of how her dress had ended up in this condition. "I'll fetch something for ye," he said and then all but fled the room. Why was it that she made him feel so flawed?

Not wishing to leave her alone too long, Cormag hastened down the corridor to his own chamber and retrieved one of his shirts. Although she was a tall woman, it would still reach well past her knees. "Here, this should do for tonight," he mumbled, barely meeting her eyes before he once more made to leave.

"'Tis yers." Her voice was soft and did not rise in the way it would if she had asked a question. Her blue eyes looked down at the simple piece of clothing as her hands felt the fabric, her thumbs gently brushing over the material.

Cormag swallowed, remembering how those hands had touched him earlier that night, cupping the sides of his face and then skimming down along his neck. His skin began to tingle at the memory, and it took all his willpower not to reach for her. "I bid ye a good night," he croaked and then hurriedly stalked from the room, almost running as he retreated to his own chamber.

Once inside, he closed the door, leaning against it as he drew in a slow breath, seeking to calm his racing heart. Still, he spent the next hour pacing the length of his room, alternately raking his hands through his hair in frustration and cursing himself in anger. His mind kept replaying the moments by the stream, and he tried to understand how he had lost control, what it was about Moira that made him want to...feel, for lack of a better word.

What had she said? *If ye dunna feel how do ye even know ye're alive?*

As odd as it sounded whenever she drew near, Cormag did feel. He felt...more, more deeply, unable to maintain the distance he had always prided himself on. Her blue eyes had a way of looking inside of him, and as much as Cormag feared to have his innermost thoughts and desires revealed, he could not deny that he longed for her to know. For her to see him for who he was, and every now and then, when she had looked at him, her head slightly cocked to the side and her eyes narrowed in contemplation, he had felt weakened for he had known that in that moment she had seen him.

And now, he had ruined all that perhaps could have been.

All that he had hoped for without even knowing that he had.

Tossing his vest at the wall, Cormag sat down on the edge of his bed and yanked off his boots, then proceeded to hurl them across the room as well. He jerked on his collar, unable to bear the tightness around his throat a moment longer, and then heard the soft sounds of thread snapping and buttons tumbling to the floor.

A groan rose from his throat before he threw himself onto the bed, burying his face in the pillow to muffle the sounds that surged past his lips. He pulled the blanket over his head, not bothering to undress further, and forced his eyes closed, longing for the sweet oblivion of sleep.

It had been a truly agonising day, and he could only hope that tomorrow would be better. How that might be possible, he did not know, but a man could hope, could he not?

When sleep finally claimed him, Cormag did not know; however, it was still dark when he felt himself begin to stir once more, his consciousness slowly drifting back from the depth of slumber. The sound of faint breathing and the soft rustling of fabric nearby reached his ears, and his senses reared into alertness. His eyes flew open the moment he felt a small dip in the mattress as though someone had sat down on its edge.

Instantly, Cormag jerked upward, his hands reaching for the shadowy figure. He did not see the gleam of a blade in the dim light of his chamber; however, he did not hesitate.

Grabbing the intruder, he flung him around, and a startled cry escaped his...or rather her throat.

Cormag blinked, his eyes trying to focus in the dim light of his chamber as he stared down at the intruder and found himself looking into Moira's face. Her golden hair lay scattered about his pillow, and her eyes were wide as she stared up at him, her chest rising and falling with each rapid breath as he held her pinned down, his hands pressing her arms into the mattress.

For a moment, he remained still, unable to move as though still trapped in a dream. Then he felt her heartbeat against his own, felt the softness of her body beneath his and felt his own lips begin to tingle when he realised how close they were to hers.

As though burnt, Cormag rolled off her with lightning speed, his gaze jerking toward the windows, afraid to see fear returned to her eyes. "I'm sorry. I didna mean...I thought ye were-"

Her hand settled on his shoulder, warm and soft, urging him to turn back to her.

When he did, his head began to spin for he found her face only a breath away from his own. Her arms snaked around his neck as she pulled herself onto his lap.

"Moira? What...?" His breath quickened as he stared at her, felt her body move closer, covered in nothing but the thin fabric of the shirt he had given her. "How did ye get out of yer chamber?" Somewhere in the back of his mind, he wondered about the relevance of that question.

A small smile teased her lips. "Ye forgot to lock the door," she whispered as she inched closer still, her dark gaze locked on his.

Cormag felt his jaw clench. "Moira, ye shouldna-"

Before he could finish whatever it was he had meant to say, her head dipped lower and her lips captured his in a daring but heartbreaking, innocent kiss. Her fingers curled into his hair, and he felt her nails scrape against his skin, sending shivers down his spine.

Without thought, Cormag responded to her touch and pulled her into his arms, revelling in the gentle softness of her hands on him. Her caresses were soothing, chasing away the tension that had held him in its grip all night; they also made him yearn for more.

Tentatively, she deepened their kiss, testing, teasing, her hands moving down the side of his neck and below his collar. Then she suddenly shifted her weight, her hands locked around his neck, and rolled them back down onto the mattress.

When his weight landed on her, Moira gasped, but a moment later, her lips were back on his, her hands still locked behind his neck holding him to her as though she feared he might slip away otherwise.

Answering her demand, Cormag kissed her deeply, feeling the softness of her body through the thin barrier of his shirt. He felt her hands relinquish their hold on him and move down his neck once more, then grasp the back of his collar. With a swift movement, she tugged his shirt upward, and he moved so she could pull it over his head. Then he tossed it aside, his mouth once more finding hers.

Her hands began to explore his shoulders, drifting lower down his back and then up and over the planes of his chest. When his hand moved to cup her breast, she gasped and his mouth slid from hers, trailing kisses down her throat and onto her shoulder.

And then he heard it.

A faint sob that chilled him to his bones.

Lifting his head, Cormag tried to look down into her face, but she turned her head away, her hands once more reaching for him, urging him back into her embrace.

As much as he wanted to yield, Cormag resisted. "Look at me," he whispered, and his fingers gently grasped her chin when she did not. "Look at me."

After a long moment, Moira finally turned her head back to him, and he found that her eyes were brimming with tears. He saw her bottom lip quiver before she dug her teeth into it to keep the sobs at bay.

Cormag's heart broke seeing her thus, and he made to rise immediately, ashamed to have not noticed her emotional turmoil before. After everything that had happened, how could he have not seen this? How could he have thought-?

"Don't!" It was no more than a desperate plea, all her earlier bravado lost, as her hands settled on his shoulders, urging him to stay. "Dunna send me away. Please! I know...I know ye want me. Ye canna deny that. Please help me forget. Please!"

Shocked at her words and the despair that rang in them, Cormag looked down at her, his eyes searching her face, trying to understand. "Help ye forget what?" he asked, brushing his fingertips down her temple and tucking a golden curl behind her ear. "What do ye wish to forget?"

Tears ran out the corners of her eyes and vanished in her golden tresses. Her teeth dug deeper into her lower lip as she drew in a shuddering breath.

"Lass," Cormag whispered, gently skimming the pad of his thumb across her brow, then down over the bridge of her nose and along her cheek bone. "What do ye wish to forget?"

Slowly, her breathing calmed. She swallowed then, her lips straining into a brave little smile. "That I'm alone. That I dunna belong. That it'll always be thus." Her hand rose to cup his cheek. "I too want to feel...if only tonight." And with that, her head lifted off the pillow, her mouth reclaiming his.

Cormag groaned at the sensation, and his lips responded before he had even formed a clear thought. But then he felt the wetness on her cheek, and his heart clenched painfully at the thought of what he was doing. For the truth was that she did not want him. At least not in that moment. She was vulnerable and in desperate need of comfort, and he was taking advantage of that.

Of her.

Pulling away, Cormag sought her gaze. He saw her confusion, her regret, her need to feel anything but sorrow and loneliness, and he remembered the promise he had made her. If she ever were to feel pushed to her breaking point, she was to seek him out.

And Moira had.

A part of him still could not believe it that in her moment of need, she had come to him, and he knew he could not fail her.

He would not.

"Please!" she whispered once again, her hands tightening on his shoulders, urging him to continue what they had begun.

Slowly, Cormag shook his head, and she closed her eyes, pain marking her features as more tears streamed from her eyes.

Shifting off her, Cormag remained by her side, his free hand gently brushing a few stray curls from her forehead. Then he leant down and whispered in her ear, "I willna send ye away, Lass. But I canna do as ye ask for 'twouldna be right." He pulled back and looking down at her found her dark gaze searching his. "'Tis not what ye need."

A spark of curiosity lit up her eyes as she watched him settle down beside her, his head on the pillow. Then he held out his arm to her. "Come. Lie down with me," he whispered as he reached for her hand, his fingers trailing up her arm.

For a moment, Moira hesitated, but then she moved closer to him, tentatively resting her head on his shoulder. His arm rose and wrapped around her, pulling her closer still, tucking her into his embrace as her left hand came to rest on his chest where his heart beat at an erratic pace.

Never in his life had Cormag felt like this before: content and terrified at the same time.

"Sleep," he whispered, his lips brushing against the top of her head. "I'll hold ye all night if ye want me to."

With a sigh, she snuggled deeper into his arms, and he felt the hard tension leave her body as her breathing calmed. Her chilled skin began to warm where it rested against his, and Cormag reached out to pull the blanket over her, shielding her from the nip in the cooling night air.

His fingers trailed gently over her arm resting on his chest, and Cormag felt the tips of her fingers brush against his skin as though in answer. He knew she was not yet asleep, aware of the slight skip in her pulse every time his fingers settled back on her skin, skimming along the slim line of her arm from her elbow all the way down to her wrist, then onto her hand until his fingers slid in-between hers as though he wished to grasp her hand.

A shuddering sigh left her lips, fanning against his skin, and a part of Cormag wished he had re-donned his shirt before lying down. Still, he did not dare move now as the thought of leaving her embrace brought a deep sense of loss to his heart.

Instantly, his arm tightened around her, and his hand finally did grasp hers, holding on despite his determination to keep his distance. Cormag felt her smile, her head still snuggled onto his shoulder, and a part of him-quite another one-marvelled at the thought that Moira might be feeling the same.

A sense of peacefulness claimed him as they lay in each other's arms, and as he drifted off to sleep for the second time that night, he dimly heard his mother's voice whisper, *Hold on to her. Dunna let her go.*

Chapter Twenty-Six

A NEW MORNING

Warmth and contentedness engulfed Moira, and her limbs felt heavy in a most soothing and utterly relaxed way. She inhaled a languid breath as slumber slowly fell away, and her skin tingled with joy as she felt the sun's first rays on her skin. Her heart beat steady...below her ear?

Moira tensed.

For a second, she lay perfectly still, not even daring to open her eyes. Then she cracked one eye open, and in that very moment, the events of the previous night returned in a crashing wave.

Drawing in a sharp breath, Moira surged upward, staring down at the bare-chested man lying beside her. Unfortunately, her reaction drew Cormag from his own slumber with a sudden jolt. His eyes flew open, and he too jerked upward as though stung.

In the next instant, his forehead collided with hers.

Moira bit back a cry of pain as stars began to dance in front of her eyes. Her hand flew to her head as she sagged backwards and sank back down onto the pillow. Dimly, she heard Cormag suck in a sharp breath, mingled with a low growl deep in his throat.

Then silence followed, and Moira realised that her eyes had closed once more.

Drawing in a deep breath, she lay still, desperate to look at the man beside her, but not finding the courage to do so. Her head throbbed, but the pain slowly receded as every fibre of her body reached out to the man who held her in his arms all night.

The thought brought fresh tears to Moira's eyes, and she forced them back down. She had gone to him the night before as the coldness and loneliness she had found in the chamber he had taken her to had become too much for her to bear. Her heart had ached with an acuteness she had never known before, and her thoughts had time and time again returned to the man who would not allow her close but who equally could not keep away from her. She had remembered his tenderness and his fierceness. She had remembered how he had kissed her, his touch setting her skin on fire and chasing away the coldness that always lingered nearby. And she had known that his touch would help her find peace that night.

And so, Moira had sneaked from her bed and tiptoed to his chamber after finding her own unlocked. In the back of her mind, she had wondered if he had merely forgotten to lock her in or if a part of him had wanted her to come to him.

Whichever it had been, Moira had not cared.

All she had cared about had been the way his hands had seized her, bringing her closer. His skin had felt hot against hers, and she had reached for his warmth with every fibre of her being. She had been willing to give him anything he wanted if only he would not leave her alone in the cold.

That thought had terrified Moira to her core, and not until the moment Cormag had pulled back, urging her to look at him, had she realised that she had gone too far. That she had offered more than she had been willing to give.

But he had known. Somehow, Cormag had seen her longing, her need, and once again, he had been there for her.

All too vividly did Moira remember how gently he had pulled her into his arms, her head coming to rest on his shoulder. She had felt warm and safe and...loved even, and in that moment when his fingers had trailed across her skin, she had allowed herself to believe that he truly cared for her.

That there was still someone in the world, in her life, here and now, who wanted her close.

"Are ye all right?" Cormag's voice was a mere whisper, soft and soothing, and for a moment, Moira wanted nothing more than to hold onto the night they had shared. A part of her did not want to open her eyes, but stay like this, here with him, forever.

Gently, the tips of his fingers brushed over her forehead, and slowly, Moira surrendered. Her eyes opened, and she prayed that perhaps some of what she had felt the night before was still there.

Propped on one elbow, Cormag lay beside her, the fingers of his right hand trailing down her temple as he watched her, his grey eyes dark in the early morning light.

His warmth still lingered on her skin, and instinctively, she turned toward him. "I'm fine," she whispered before her own hand reached out toward him. "And ye?"

As his hand ceased its movement and came to rest upon her shoulder, Moira gently touched his face. Her heart raced, but in a way that felt utterly intoxicating.

Cormag drew in a shuddering breath. Then he swallowed; for a second his eyes drifted upward and away from hers as though he needed a moment to himself. "Ye slept like a rock," he remarked, a slight curl to his lips.

Moira smiled. "I havena slept this well in years," she confided, feeling the need to thank him for what he had done for her. "I...I hope 'twas not too uncomfortable for ye."

Slowly, he shook his head. "Nay, not at all. 'Twas verra...comfortable." A moment passed, and then another. "Are ye all right? Last night, ye were..." His grey eyes searched hers as though looking for injuries he had glimpsed the night before.

Moira dropped her gaze as heat shot to her face. "I'm sorry I burdened ye with-"

"Ye didna." His hand moved from her shoulder and settled under her chin, urging her to look at him. "I asked ye to come to me, and ye did." He swallowed. "I'm glad ye did, and I'm sorry I didna see right away what ye needed. I shouldna have-"

Moira smiled, wondering if they would ever be able to speak openly with one another, without hiding for fear of rejection, for fear of the consequences honesty might force upon them.

Cormag's brows crinkled into a frown. "What? I wish I knew what..."

Feeling suddenly daring, Moira pushed herself up onto her elbow, her eyes holding his as she moved closer. "I didna mind yer kiss or yer touch," she whispered, watching the way his gaze grew more intense at the memories her words conjured. "I admit I wasna ready for more last night, but I enjoyed being close to ye." She swallowed, and all humour fell from her. "I trust ye. I feel safe with ye, and I want..." Moira paused, seeing the way the muscle in his jaw twitched, and in the spur of the moment, she leant forward and gently pressed her lips to his.

Chapter Twenty-Seven

A MOTHER'S CALL

Her words brought joy to his heart, joy and longing, and Cormag knew in that moment that he had not been the only one affected by their shared night. Never had he allowed himself to be close to another in such a way. And to hear her say out loud what he himself had only realised moments earlier was a temptation he could not resist.

Her lips felt soft against his own, and he returned her kiss with the same tenderness she bestowed on him. Only when Moira leant closer, striving toward him, did he reach out and skim his knuckles along the line of her jaw, feeling her tender skin.

There was no passion in this encounter. Nothing desperate fuelled by fear or need or loneliness. Nothing that lingered in the blood and only knew the need for satisfaction.

Instead, it was something deep in his soul that answered her tentative touch, revealing and asking at the same time. Cormag felt vulnerable, exposed, and knew that he ought to pull back, shield himself and not let her see him. But he did not. He allowed her closer, allowed her to reach for him, allowed her to step past the barrier that now lay crumbled around him.

"I care for ye," he whispered against her lips, reclaiming her mouth the moment the last word had left his tongue, afraid to hear her response and learn that it did not match his own.

Perhaps fear lingered after all, but it was no longer all-consuming, and Cormag knew that he ought not allow it to control him any longer.

After all, had his father not also loved the woman he had married? Had he not also given his heart free rein to choose as it wished? And still, he had been a wise man, a good laird, guiding his clan with reason and compassion hand in hand.

Was there a reason Cormag could not do the same?

Lost in the moment, Cormag barely heard the soft knock on his door. Only when it flew open a moment later, hurried footsteps crossing the threshold, was he able to pull himself from the haze that lingered on his heart and mind.

His eyes went wide as he stared at Moira, the expression on her face a mirror of his own, before his head jerked around and he found his mother standing halfway between the open door and his bed, her green eyes as round as plates as she stared back at them. Before Cormag had a chance to react, to speak, to...do something, the corners of her mouth curled up into a teasing smile. "Now, this I wouldna have expected."

Sliding from the bed while Moira yanked the blanket up to her chin, Cormag found his shirt in a corner of his chamber and quickly pulled it over his head. "What are ye doing here, Mother?" he demanded, embarrassment giving his tone a hard edge. "How dare ye burst into my chamber?"

His mother cocked her head at him, her brows rising in challenge. "Now, dunna pretend to be angry with me," she chided, a lofty laugh spilling from her mouth before her expression sobered. Still, a spark of something Cormag could not quite make out lingered in her green eyes. "If ye must know," she continued, her right foot now tapping the floor as though in impatience, "I was worried about ye for 'tis not like ye at all to...sleep in." She glanced at Moira, and a teasing grin danced over her features. "All yer life, ye've been up and about the moment the sun rose, can ye truly fault me for being concerned about ye? I've been waiting in yer study for over half an hour."

Cringing, Cormag closed his eyes as he remembered that he had asked her to meet him in order to discuss Ian's return and how best to proceed. Unable to remain unbiased where Ian as well as Moira were concerned, he had thought to seek his mother's advice. Admittedly, it often went against every fibre of his being, but he had been desperate.

He still was.

"I apologise," Cormag gritted out. "I was-"

"No need to apologise." Chuckling, his mother turned to look at Moira. "Are ye all right, dear? Ye seem awfully pale."

Cormag saw Moira swallow, and her eyes darted to him for a split second before she sat up, her mouth opening to speak.

"I would ask ye to leave, Mother," Cormag interfered, stepping forward and taking his mother's arm, "and not a word of this to anyone. Do ye hear?" He held her eyes for a long moment, worried what his mother might do. Her reaction to finding Moira in his bed suggested that she was far from displeased. He also knew that his mother had long since urged him to tie the knot, and he feared that she would see this as confirmation that he had indeed chosen.

Had he? Cormag wondered. Perhaps so. However, he could not be certain how Moira felt, and he would not allow his mother to pressure her into a situation she did not wish to choose freely. He would not take advantage of her.

Never.

His mother chuckled, "And why not?" she whispered, glancing over his shoulder.

Cormag gritted his teeth. "Nothing happened, and I willna have ye spread rumours."

His mother's jaw dropped in mock outrage. "Are ye saying I'm a tattletale?" Her eyes narrowed, and she shook her head at him. "I resent that. I-"

"I should go."

Turning around, Cormag saw Moira step from the bed, her arms wrapped around herself as she tiptoed toward the door. Her gaze remained downcast, and he could see her teeth worrying her lower lip. "Wait! I-"

"Ye dunna intend to step out into the corridor like that, do ye?" his mother interfered, moving toward Moira as her eyes travelled over the simple white shirt she still wore. Then she looked at him. "That would certainly spread rumours."

Cormag rolled his eyes, hating the way his mother sometimes made him feel like a foolish lad again.

"I...eh...," Moira began, her gaze shifting back and forth between him and his mother. "My dress is..."

"'Tis all right, dear. Let me help ye." Unfastening the cloak from around her neck, his mother stepped forward and draped it around Moira's shoulders, pulling it tight in the front to hide her state of dishabille. "There. 'Twill do for now. Where is yer dress, dear, and yer shoes?" His mother cast him a questionable look before she guided Moira from the room after ensuring that the corridor lay deserted. "We shall speak of this later," she told him, sticking her head in through the door one last time.

Cormag groaned, raking his hands through his hair. Indeed, his mother would have a lot to say on the matter.

Chapter Twenty-Eight
A MATTER OF THE MIND

Finally, back in her cottage, Moira sank onto one of the chairs around the small kitchen table. Her knees felt weak and her breath came fast as she remembered all that had happened that morning. Her fingers curled into Maeve's cloak, hiding the torn dress beneath.

As much as Moira would have expected the laird's mother to lash out at her for seducing her son-After all, was she not the traitor? The witch? -she could not deny that the kindness in Maeve's manner had not come as a surprise.

Never had a bad word left Maeve's lips, and Moira wondered why that was. Instead of lashing out at Moira, would she later speak to her son, make him see reason?

Moira's heart and mind were a mess, and as she sat there staring out the window, she did not know how to feel.

I care for ye, Cormag had whispered, and yet, he had warned his mother not to breathe a word of their shared night. Was he truly afraid to ruin her reputation? Not that that was truly possible at this point. Or was he afraid that he would be honour-bound to marry her and thus ruin his own standing within his clan?

For even if Cormag did truly care for her, how long would they survive with something as dark and threatening as her past looming over them?

Not long was the sad and utterly devastating answer.

Ian would make certain of that.

Tears rolled down Moira's cheeks when she realised that although she might have found love after all, it was too late to claim it. She could not be selfish again and ruin the lives of those she cared for simply because she wanted Cormag.

She had done so with Connor, and it had led to disaster.

Then, too, she had been convinced to be doing the right thing, that all would turn out well, that the ends justified the means.

And she had been wrong.

So, so very wrong.

"I need to leave," Moira whispered into the silence of her kitchen, which once again echoed the loneliness she had fought to escape ever since coming to *Seann Dachaigh* Tower three years ago. She had known it before, and she had tried to leave only the night before, but Cormag had stopped her.

He truly cared for her, did he not?

Moira's heart smiled as more tears clouded her vision. "If only," she whispered, knowing that these thoughts served no purpose. In truth, it did not matter whether he cared for her or not. All that mattered was that he allow her to leave.

She needed a plan. She could not sneak away in the night. He would follow her, of that Moira was certain. He needed to allow her to leave. He needed to accept that it was for the best. But where could she go? Where would she be safe? To start over?

Moira blinked when she saw Maggie walk past her window, the woman's face taut and her eyes downcast, an echo of the deep ache in Moira's heart. *Was this a sign?* She wondered, pushing to her feet and hurrying toward the door.

"Maggie!" she called, flying out into the bright morning sun, her loud voice in stark contrast to the silence that lingered over the land. After the festivities of the night before, most of the MacDummond clan were still asleep, their limbs exhausted and their hearts and minds in need of rest.

Flinching at the sound of Moira's voice, Maggie turned, her quick hands brushing tears from her pale cheeks. "What are ye doing up so early?" she asked in a quiet voice when Moira reached her side. "Ye look...sad."

Moira swallowed. "As do ye."

Sighing, Maggie continued down the small path that led through the village. "Come, walk with me."

Moira fell into step beside her, and the two women walked on in silence until they reached the small stream. "Where are ye headed?"

Maggie shrugged. "Nowhere. Away." Gazing at the gently lapping water, she sank into the grass and wrapped her arms around her bent legs. Gone was the gleam that always rested in Maggie's eyes. Gone was that enchanting smile that always lingered on her lips. Gone was the flittering fairy that had always seemed so magical, almost out of this world.

"What happened?" Moira asked, seating herself beside the young woman.

"Nothing."

Long ago, Moira had sensed Maggie's sadness, a sadness she hid well, a sadness she kept locked away because it served no purpose. What good would it do her to break down? To mourn something that would forever remain lost to her? But to ignore the pain that lingered took strength, and sometimes there was simply none left.

Who had been the man who had broken Maggie's heart? Moira wondered, realising in that very moment that it was true; love did not always find a way. It did not overcome all obstacles. Sometimes love was not enough. Sometimes it failed.

It was a harsh truth, but a truth, nonetheless.

Maggie knew that, and Moira was coming to accept it as well. "Can I ask ye a favour?" she whispered into the soft silence that lingered over the gently rushing stream.

Sighing, Maggie looked at her. Then she nodded.

Moira gave her a small smile that spoke of deep gratitude for Maggie had been a true friend to her. It was more than Moira ever could have hoped for. "Ye were born in England, were ye not?"

A slight frown came to Maggie's face as she nodded her head yet again.

"D'ye still have family there?"

Maggie's frown deepened. "Why-? Ye wish to leave," she concluded, her blue eyes lingered as though trying to look deeper. "Why? Why now?"

For a moment, Moira buried her face in her hands. "I canna stay here. I understand that now. If I leave, all will be well here. There'll be no reason for..." She sighed as the thought sunk in.

"Ye dunna wish to go."

Moira shrugged. "I dunna know."

"He willna let ye leave."

Moira's gaze rose and met Maggie's, her blue eyes clear and seeing. "He will if he knows that I'll be well," Moira finally said, willing it to be so. After all, what other way was there? "Once he knows that I'll be safe. I'll explain it to him, and he'll see reason. He will understand it'll be the right thing to do. He'll see the wisdom in it. He always does."

Maggie snorted, "That doesna mean he'll let ye leave. He might understand, but he won't let ye go." She sighed, and a wistful smile came to her lips as she looked at Moira with distant eyes. "He canna. Not ye."

"Why not?" Moira asked, knowing full well what answer she wished to hear. It was foolish to ask, and it would be torture to know and continue down the path as she had reasoned would be the right course of action. But foolish or not, Moira wished to hear it, nonetheless.

"Because he loves ye," Maggie whispered, and her blue eyes sparkled, suggesting that she knew equally well why Moira had asked and what her answer meant to the other. "Do ye love him as well?"

Moira hung her head. "Do ye not know?"

Maggie laughed, "I do, but he doesna, and he might care to know."

Clasping her hands together until her knuckles stood out white, Moira fought the urge to give in, to hear Maggie's words and the promise that echoed within them. She knew she had to be strong. This was a matter of the mind after all. Was that not what Cormag had told her? That once out of control the heart would be almost impossible to rein in again. Was that not what he had feared? What he still feared?

"I wish to go to England," Moira whispered, her gaze focused on her clenched hands. "It'll be far enough away, and perhaps one day I'll be able to forget what I left behind." She turned to look at her friend. "Can ye help me?"

Maggie sighed, "If 'tis truly what ye wish."

Moira nodded, not trusting herself to speak.

For a long while, the two women sat side by side, gazing out at the soft ripples of the water, each lost in their own thoughts. It was peaceful, but lonely as well, and Moira could not deny that she wondered how Maggie made it from one day to the next and had for the past years.

A strong heart beat in the dainty woman's chest, but how much longer could it shoulder the loss she had suffered.

When the sound of children's voices echoed closer, Maggie rose to her feet, brushed the tears off her cheeks and met her son and daughter with a smiling face. "How can ye be hungry, ye wee rascals? If I'm not at all mistaken, ye ate half the food coming out of the kitchen last night. Is that not true?"

Both Niall and Blair laughed as the three of them headed back up the small path. Looking after them, Moira knew that she had made the right choice.

She needed to leave.

Rather today than tomorrow.

Chapter Twenty-Nine

A FUTILE CONFRONTATION

"Enter!"

The door opened, and Ian stepped across the threshold, his face grim and the look in his eyes one of utter betrayal. He walked with quick, measured steps, approaching Cormag's desk without hesitation. Still, from the suspicion Cormag sensed within his friend. he knew that Ian was aware why Cormag had asked him here.

"Tell me why," Cormag demanded, his gaze hard as he looked at his friend, knowing that Ian responded to strength alone.

"Why what?" Ian retorted; still, from the look of defiance in his eyes, Cormag could tell that his question had merely been asked to shift the balance of power. To point out that he had something Cormag wanted.

Needed.

As headstrong and impulsive as Ian could be, he was far from a fool.

"What is yer grievance with Moira?"

Ian scoffed. "Grievance?" he demanded as a dark red crept up his cheeks and his hands balled into fists, trembling with the rage that took him once more. "The woman is a witch. She-"

"I've heard all I want on this subject." Lifting his hand to stop his

206

friend before he could once again work himself up into a frenzy, Cormag stepped around the desk, his gaze seeking Ian's. "I know all yer reasons for hating her, for mistrusting her, for speaking out against her at every turn." His jaw clenched. "For frightening her. For attacking her." Cormag knew that his mask was slipping, that anger began to shine through. He saw it in the slight widening of Ian's eyes, in the spark of surprise that flashed across his face.

Still, Cormag remembered only too well the marks on Moira's neck. He remembered the way she had stood upon the parapet wall, ready to fling herself to her death. He remembered the night she had run from the castle, fear in her eyes, and how she had later sought him out, her heart desperate for comfort and safety. He remembered countless other things, but they had no bearing in this matter.

And Cormag knew that above all, he needed to keep a clear head.

"How can ye deny that she's bewitched ye?" Ian snarled. "How can ye-?"

"I willna hear this again!" Cormag thundered in a way that closed Ian's mouth instantly. "I've heard ye. Be assure of that. However, I've not heard all ye have to say for the true reason why ye hate her with such fervour remains to be seen."

Ian swallowed; however, the look of defiance remained. "The reasons I've given ought to be enough for ye to see that I'm right. There's no need-"

"Is it about Maggie?" Cormag asked, remembering what Moira had told him the night Garrett and his family had returned home.

The wave of shock that engulfed Cormag as Ian's face all but fell apart was answer enough. So, it was as Moira had said, as he himself had begun to suspect. Still, he did not know what on earth Moira could have done to sever whatever bond might have existed between Ian and his wife.

If ever there had been one, for Cormag could not remember ever having felt love in Maggie's chest. At least not toward her husband.

Unfortunately, Cormag could not reveal his own conclusions to his friend. Or could he? Would it do any good if he confided in Ian and told him the truth? Or would it turn his friend against him for good?

Ian's lips thinned into a hard line, and Cormag knew that he would not reveal whatever had turned his heart against Moira.

"Fine. Keep yer secrets," Cormag told him, his eyes full of warning. "However, I insist that ye treat her with respect." Ian's lips turned into a snarl. "If ye dunna wish to speak to her, then dunna. However-"

"How can ye demand this of me?" Ian asked, his face suddenly pale. "She went after my daughter. Blair almost-"

"She didna," Cormag thundered, exhaustion washing over him at the futile attempt to make his friend see reason. "'Twas an accident. And," he lifted a finger, "if I recall correctly, 'tis yer daughter who seeks out Moira. Not the other way around. So, if ye dunna want them speaking, talk to Blair."

Ian rolled his eyes, and Cormag almost laughed for as young as Blair was, the lass had a fierce spirit, and he was certain that she would only ever do what she deemed right.

Never mind her father's warnings.

"Ye've changed," Ian commented dryly, a hint of sadness in his voice. "I canna believe ye dunna see this." Then he turned and left.

Sighing, Cormag strode to the window, his eyes gliding over the familiar green hills, and he knew that Ian was right. He had changed. He could feel it every time he laid eyes on Moira. Every time he thought of her. Every time he heard her name spoken out loud.

I care for ye, he had told her, baring his heart and soul, and it had felt right.

Oddly enough, it had.

Still, since that morning when his mother had stumbled upon them, Cormag had barely seen Moira. More so than before she kept to herself as though she feared to meet his gaze, and he had to admit that it hurt. Not only did his heart ache for her, ache to hold her again, to look into those endless blue eyes, but it also shuddered at the thought that he might have misunderstood after all.

Moira had said that she trusted him, but she had never once said that she cared for him. Perhaps avoiding him was her way of letting him know that his feelings were one-sided.

Perhaps, he truly ought to let her go.

Hanging his head, Cormag rested his forehead against the cool windowpane and closed his eyes, fighting the pain that cut into him at the thought of never seeing Moira again. Still, was that not what one did for someone one cared about? To be selfless? To think about them more than about oneself?

Perhaps, it was.

But it would also cripple him in ways he had never thought possible.

Chapter Thirty

THE ESSENCE OF LIFE

A knock on her door roused Moira from her thoughts.

"Coming!" she called as she rose from the chair, her gaze sweeping over the list she had made, detailing all that needed to be done before her departure. Maggie had promised to write to her brother, asking him to find her a position within his household. Moira could only hope that she would not disappoint and that this would be a new beginning.

Opening the door, Moira stilled, eyes wide as she found Maeve standing on her doorstep. "G-Good morning," she stammered as her cheeks began to warm with the memory of the last time she had seen Maeve.

"Good morning, dear," Maeve greeted her, a knowing smile gracing the woman's lips. "Would ye mind terribly if I came in?"

Shaking off the daze that had claimed her, Moira stepped aside. "Of course not. Please do." Still, a frown tugged on her brows as she realised Maeve had a very specific reason for seeking her out. If only Moira knew what it was.

Seating herself in the chair across from the one Moira had vacated a few minutes before, Maeve glanced around the small kitchen before her eyes settled on the small sheet of paper on the table. "I see ye truly intend to leave."

Shocked, Moira snatched up the paper. "How do ye know?"

Maeve chuckled, "'Tis my clan, my home. Nothing happens here without me finding out about it." She sighed, and her dark green eyes swept over Moira's face in a way that made her skin crawl. "Why?"

Moira frowned, slowly sinking onto her chair. "Why what?"

"Why do ye wish to leave?"

Staring across the table, Moira watched the other woman with care. There was something deeply powerful and fearless in her gaze as though nothing ever surprised her, as though nothing ever dared to go against her plans. Maeve was a kind, generous and cheerful woman, but behind that smiling facade lived an iron will. Moira could see that now. "That is none of yer concern."

An amused smile came to Maeve's lips, and she leant back in her chair, her eyes intent on Moira. "There's no need to be defensive, dear. Believe me, I have no intention of conspiring against ye."

"Then why are ye here? Why do ye care whether or not I leave?" Crossing her arms, Moira wondered if Cormag's mother would answer her honestly. Always had she wondered about Maeve's kindness toward her when the rest of their clan had watched her with distrust.

"Because of my son, of course," Maeve replied without hesitation as though the answer should have been obvious. "He cares for ye, and it'll break his heart if ye leave."

For a long moment, Moira simply stared at the woman across from her, her heart torn between joy and regret.

"Come now, dear, dunna act as though ye dunna know," Maeve chided. "I believe he has said as much to ye. Has he not?"

Moira swallowed. "That is none of yer concern." She made to rise, but Maeve reached out and grasped her wrist, urging her back down.

"Ye've spoken to Maggie," Maeve said, her green eyes softening as she spoke of the dainty, young woman. "Ye've seen what a broken heart can do to one."

Moira swallowed, and her eyes closed as the image of Maggie's heartbreak drifted before her eyes. "Aye," she whispered, feeling a cold chill travel up and down her arms, sending a shiver through her body.

Maeve sighed, and her hand released Moira's wrist as she sat back in her chair. "Ye'll survive," Maeve whispered, and her gaze grew distant with memories, "but the wound will never close. It'll pain ye daily. Occasionally, ye will manage to ignore the pain, praying that the day will come that ye can forget." She shook her head, and her eyes once more focused on Moira. "But that day doesna come. The pain always returns and stronger after a longer absence."

Watching a myriad of emotions dance over Maeve's face, Moira wondered about Cormag's father. A man she had never met. A man who had been a kind and strong father. A man who had been a beloved husband. "It doesna always have to be like th-"

"But it is," Maeve objected, a rather indulgent smile on her kind face. "Ye dunna wish to see it because ye're afraid, but if ye do love my son, I promise ye that no matter how far ye run, ye will never be free of him." She sighed, "Believe me, ye'll waste yer life ignoring something that could've brought ye happiness."

Moira stared at her. "Do ye think I want to leave?" she demanded, anger mixing with the hopelessness that had begun to sneak into her heart once she had realised how much Cormag meant to her. "I am leaving because I dunna have a choice."

"But ye do."

"How?" Moira snapped as she pushed to her feet. "Ye know as well as I do that...that yer people will never accept me, not as one of their own, not as..." Swallowing, she bowed her head, her hands clasped together as longing tore at her.

"Oh, but they will," Maeve whispered as she too rose to her feet. "Ye might not have noticed for fear of disappointment, but people dunna see ye the same way as they did three years ago. Ye've made friends, have ye not?"

Looking up, Moira found the other woman standing in front of her, her hands reaching out to grasp Moira's. "Perhaps, but...then there's Ian. He-"

Maeve shook her head. "Ian is one man."

"He hates me!" Moira had to fight the urge to cringe at the memory of how his hands had dug into her throat. "There's no knowing what he'll do. It'll divide the clan. Yer son said so himself. He worries that-"

"Cormag always worries," Maeve interrupted with a slight roll of her eyes. "He doesna like to take risks. But sometimes," a soft smile lit up her face as her dark green eyes looked deep into Moira's, "sometimes ye have to or ye'll gain nothing but lose everything."

Staring at Maeve, Moira did not know what to say as her heart warred with her mind, oddly reminding her of Cormag's greatest fear: to lose control without ever getting it back.

"I think my son is slowly coming to see that," Maeve told her, "but if ye leave now, it might be too late. He'll need more time. He needs ye to trust him, to believe that ye belong together."

"How can ye say that?" Moira exclaimed. "Ye dunna know me. Ye dunna know-"

"I know my son," Maeve replied, "and 'tis true what Ian says; he has changed."

Maeve's words felt like a slap in the face. "All the more reason for me to leave," Moira sniffed as her courage began to wane.

"Ye misunderstood me," Maeve said, holding onto Moira's hands when she tried to pull them away. "Lately, I see his mask slip more and more, especially when ye're around because ye make him feel. I canna tell ye how worried I've been that he had insisted on spending his life alone. All he knows is his duty to the clan, his responsibility. He's so concerned to do right by everyone that he forgets to do right by himself." Maeve squeezed her hands. "He needs ye as much as ye need him. Even if I were blind, I could see that."

Balling her hands into fists, Moira fought to cling to her resolve. "I dunna believe ye."

"Then go to him," Maeve whispered, her dark green eyes daring Moira to accept her challenge. "He deserves to know that ye're planning to leave. He deserves to hear it from ye."

"I know that."

"Then go and speak to him," Maeve urged. "Ask him how he feels about ye, or better yet, ask him for a kiss." A devilish grin curled up her lips. "Men can be frightfully ignorant sometimes, unable to read their own hearts, but ye'll know."

Moira swallowed, unable to deny that the thought of kissing Cormag again, even if for the last time, was terribly tempting. "But even if ye're right, even if he truly cares for me, the clan-"

Maeve laughed, "Love is the essence of our clan, of any family. Aye, we fight and argue, but deep down, we love each other. We stand as one because we care. Without love, our clan would wither and die." Patting Moira's hand, Maeve stepped back. "Think about it."

Watching Maeve walk away, Moira stood in her small kitchen, listening for the front door to close and for Maeve's soft footsteps to disappear as she headed back up the small path to *Seann Dachaigh* Tower.

Feeling her knees buckle, Moira sank back down onto her chair, afraid that if she did as Maeve had asked, she might not have the strength to leave.

But it was the only way, was it not?

Chapter Thirty-One
JUST BECAUSE

Striding down the corridor toward his study, Cormag turned a corner and paused as he found Moira there. With her head bowed, she was pacing up and down the floor in front of his door, her hands clenched and her teeth worrying her lower lip. She seemed oblivious to his presence, her eyes downcast and overshadowed. There was something strangely vulnerable about the dark shadows that drifted over her face as though something pained her greatly.

And then she looked up and saw him, and for a split second, her face lit up like the morning sun, her deep blue eyes aglow with joy.

Cormag's heart skipped a beat, and he felt an answering smile claim his own face.

And then the shadows returned, and her face fell as she headed toward him, urgency in her step as though someone were after her.

Cormag tensed. *Ian?* "Are ye all right?" he demanded, reaching for her hands when she stopped in front of him.

A shuddering breath left Moira's lips when his fingers brushed over hers and her blue eyes fluttered upward to meet his. "I'm fine," she whispered, and her gaze held his, lingering as though she could not bring herself to look away.

"Ye seem nervous," Cormag observed, still not convinced that she was telling him the truth. Something was clearly upsetting her, and he needed to know what it was.

"I've spoken to Maggie," she said, and her eyes fell from his as though in shame. Cormag knew that whatever she was about to say would not find his approval.

"Why?"

For a long moment, she remained quiet, increasing his torment. "I asked her to help me find a position in England."

Her words seized his heart, trapping it in an iron vice, squeezing it painfully. He felt wounded, weakened, as though his knees could no longer support him, and his eyes fluttered closed as he wished with every fibre of his being that all this was merely a bad dream.

"Are ye all right?" Her soft whisper reached his ears a moment before he felt her hand brush over his cheek.

When Cormag opened his eyes, he found Moira standing barely an arm's length away, her blue eyes full of concern as she looked up at him. Her hand stayed where it was, the pad of her thumb gently skimming over his cheek. "Ye dunna need to leave," he croaked, willing himself to remain calm and not succumb to the panic that surged through him. "I swear ye'll be safe here."

Her gaze darkened, and her hand fell from his face, taking her warmth with it. "'Tis not that," she whispered, and he could see that she was searching for the right words to explain herself.

Cormag tensed, and he wondered if this time it was not Ian who sent her running from *Seann Dachaigh* Tower. Was she uncomfortable being near him after he had so foolishly revealed his affections for her? Still, the look in her eyes spoke of sadness and...

Cormag gritted his teeth, wishing for the thousandth time that he could read her heart. "Why are ye leaving, Lass?"

"There...there are many reasons," Moira began before her head rose and her eyes tentatively sought his. "I think 'twould be for the best. For all of us." A brave, little smile teased her lips; still, her gaze remained shrouded in sadness and regret. "Ye were right when ye cautioned me not to...feel too deeply. I think it best that I put some distance between myself and...and the clan. To begin again somewhere far away." Tears brimmed in her eyes, but she forced them back.

"Are ye certain?" Cormag asked, wanting nothing more but to lock her up and throw away the key. Still, she was right, and he knew that her words were meant as a request for *him* not to feel too deeply, to be reasonable and see that she needed to go.

Moira nodded. "I've been thinking about it for a long time, and while ye were right that I shouldna have left that night without thought, without a plan, I know that I must leave. 'Tis the right thing to do. Ye know that."

Cormag could not bring himself to answer. All his strength went into keeping him rooted to the spot lest he do something she did not want.

"Thank ye for everything." Her voice shook as she spoke. "If ye hadn't looked out for me the way ye did, I dunno..." She shook her head, blinking back tears. "Thank ye. Ye're a wonderful laird. Yer clan is fortunate to have ye." Then she turned around and walked away.

Staring after her, Cormag once again felt as though he had strayed into a nightmare. Did she truly think of him thus? As a laird looking out for his people? For her? Did she not know how much he had come to care for her? Had he not made it clear after all?

Still, somewhere in the back of his mind, Cormag remembered an afternoon in his study when she had asked him why he was looking after her, and he had told her that it was his duty as laird. How could he blame her for thinking that when he himself had told her so?

And then Cormag felt himself move, his feet carrying him down the corridor after her, knowing that he could not allow her to leave without her knowing the truth.

He had almost caught up with her when Moira suddenly paused, her feet still as she stood in the corridor. A moment of silence lingered before she suddenly turned, her eyes widening as she found him right in front of her. A smile flitted across her face, and swallowing, she took a step toward him. "There's...there's a favour I would ask ye." Her voice held little strength, and Cormag frowned at the rosy blush that touched her cheeks.

"Aye?" Was this about another vision? He wondered. Whenever she had asked him for a favour before it had always been in connection to something she had seen in her dreams.

"Would ye...?" she paused, closing her eyes as though to gather her courage, and Cormag felt something deep inside twitch in anticipation. "Would ye kiss me? Again? B-Before I leave?" Her eyes drifted from his as a nervous chuckle spilled from her lips. "I know 'tis a strange request, and ye dunna have to if ye-"

"Why?"

Her eyes snapped back to his at the harshness in his tone. "Just... just because," she whispered, uncertainty in her voice. Still, there was something in her blue eyes that drew him near.

Cormag hesitated, but no more than a second before the need to hold her became too overwhelming, and he found himself reaching for her without another thought.

Her body moulded perfectly to his own as she stepped into his embrace, his arms holding her to him. A smile rested on her lips as she lifted her head, her hands reaching for him, pulling him closer.

In that moment, everything seemed simple, and Cormag knew that he could not let her go.

Still, neither could he force her to stay.

When his mouth claimed hers, *just because*, Cormag could have sworn that the world shifted off its axis. His heart calmed and sped up at the same time, and he felt utterly unhinged, and yet, perfectly balanced.

Returning his kiss, Moira clung to him, and he felt her hands urge him closer, rising to brush over his shoulders and upward until they vanished in his hair. There was a desperate need in her as though any moment could be her last.

Their last.

Cormag knew how she felt as the threat of her departure hung over them, and he did not know how to make her stay. How to make her *want* to stay. She clearly did as much as she did not.

Confusion filled Cormag's heart and mind, and a tortured growl rose from his throat as frustration washed over him. His hands on her tightened, unwilling to ever release her, and he pushed her up against the wall, kissing her with a desperate need he had held in check for far too long.

Nothing and no one existed but them, and Cormag did not hear the voices that approached from around the corner until it was too late.

Chapter Thirty-Two

A MOTHER'S INTERFERENCE

Moira lost herself in his kiss, understanding with perfect clarity the longing that lived within her as Cormag held her close.

And then closer.

Words had not come, could not express how she felt when he looked at her and knew how she felt. He had told her that he could not sense what lived in her heart, and yet, she could not believe that to be true. There was something in the way he responded to her, not only her words, but the subtle emotions that sparked to life now and then, whispering of a longing, a deeper bond that existed only if it received an answer.

And he did know. Somehow, he always did.

Never in her life had Moira felt so overwhelmingly complete, and her heart broke at the thought of what she would lose once she left *Seann Dachaigh* Tower behind. Maeve's words echoed in her mind, and she saw Maggie's face drift in front of her eyes, sadness and regret clinging to her like cobwebs. Something she could not escape. Something that would stay with her every day for the rest of her life. Would this be Moira's life as well? A life filled with regret and longing that could never be fulfilled?

Panic surged through her, and her body urged her closer, deeper into his embrace, desperate to feel him, to know that he was there.

That he was still here.

At least for now.

And then Cormag froze, and dimly, Moira noticed the faint echo of voices nearby. Close. Too close. Their echo grew louder as her focus shifted from the man who held her in his arms to the world around them, and Moira knew that they were no longer alone.

"How marvellous to see ye two together!" Maeve exclaimed, clapping her hands, her voice almost shrill to Moira's ears. "Ye'll make a wonderful couple, don't ye agree?"

A cacophony of voices washed over Moira, and she realised in that moment that Maeve had not come upon them alone. Indeed, half the corridor was filled with people, friends, who gawked at them, some faces smiling while others looked rather taken aback.

Her aunt stared at her open-mouthed; still, after the initial shock passed, a slight curl came to Fiona's lips that spoke of something other than disapproval and disappointment. Something warm and affectionate rested in her eyes, and she clasped her hands together as though in joy.

Emma and Finn as well as Claudia and Garrett had found their way to this place and time as well. They each stood close to the one they loved, exchanging knowing glances before once more turning to smile at her and Cormag. It was as though they had come upon something they had always suspected but never dared hope to see.

Maggie, too, smiled at her; however, her smile held something wistful and heart-breaking, whispering of a longing unfulfilled, urging Moira to not be reckless with the happiness within her reach. After all, everything could be lost.

Cormag looked from face to face, his hands still lying gently on her waist as though they simply belonged there, as though they were a part of one another, and Moira wondered at the warmth she felt. If he had stepped back, if he had released her, she would have felt shaken to her core under the scrutiny of those who had come upon them so unexpectedly.

Everything was different with him by her side. Did he feel the same?

Cormag tensed, and his gaze met hers for a split second before he dropped his head as though in defeat. Still, his hands remained around her, holding on.

Moira bowed her head. "I'm sorry," she whispered when realisation found her, and the cold returned. "I shouldna have asked ye for a kiss here...out in the open. I..." Had Maeve known?

Glancing at his mother, Moira frowned. She could not imagine how Maeve could have known to find them here, now, in this moment, but she was certain that Cormag's mother *had* known, and Moira had played right into her hands.

As though echoing her thoughts, Maeve strode forward, hands raised in jubilation. "'Tis been about time that our laird chose his bride!" she exclaimed, turning to look at the small crowd she had somehow coaxed into accompanying her. "We're overjoyed that ye've found one another."

On cue, voices rose, their joyful echoes resonating within the corridor as they wished them well, offering their congratulations.

Moira had never felt so ill in her life.

Swallowing, she looked into Cormag's face, not surprised, but shocked, to see the frighteningly furious gleam that shone in his dark eyes. His jaw was clenched, and she only now realised that the hands that still held on to her had tightened to the point of pain.

A cold shiver gripped her as she sought his gaze. "I'm sorry. I didna know."

Cormag exhaled a slow breath, forcing his anger back under control. Then he stood back, and his hands fell from her waist. Tension held him rigid as he slowly turned to stare down at his mother. "I need a word with ye," he all but growled, the impact of his tone showing in the frowns springing up on multiple faces.

Maeve, however, looked unperturbed as her son grasped her arm and all but dragged her down the corridor and into his study, shutting the door with a loud bang that spoke clearly of his anger.

Left alone, Moira wished the earth would open and swallow her whole. Instead, she found herself swept into one embrace after another as more congratulations were uttered.

"I always knew he cared about ye," Garrett told her with a wink, drawing Claudia closer into his arms. "I'm glad he's finally admitted it to himself."

Had he? Moira wondered when Garrett and Claudia stepped back, making room for Emma and Finn. "After the way ye've helped us," Emma beamed, her eyes aglow as she looked at her husband, "I'm doubly happy to see that ye've finally found one another."

Next came Fiona, her eyes wide and her mouth opening and closing, before she threw up her hands with a smile and simply pulled Moira into her arms. "Ye've done well, dear. I'm proud of ye."

Tears began to mist Moira's eyes. She could not help but feel touched by the kind words and affectionate smiles granted her on this day. Never would she have expected to find people in this place that would come to care for her. And yet, they had. But how would they feel if they knew that-even unknowingly-she had helped Maeve trick her son into marriage?

For that was what Cormag's mother wanted. She had made that clear the day she had come to seek Moira out in her home, and now, her words had been final proof that she had pushed and prodded to see her son married.

Even against his will.

Only too well did Moira remember the furious glow in Cormag's eyes when he too had realised his mother's intentions in coming upon them with an audience following on her heel. But did he believe that she, Moira, had been complicit? How could he not? After all, she had been the one asking for a kiss!

Slowly, everyone took their leave, their happy voices echoing down the corridor until only Maggie remained. Her blue eyes were watchful, and Moira knew that she had an inkling of what had just transpired.

"For a blushing bride, ye dunna look happy," the other woman observed, a question in her words.

Moira's shoulders slumped as she pulled Maggie away from Cormag's study, afraid to hear his angry voice echo to her ears. "We never...I..."

She inhaled a deep breath. "He never asked me to marry him. 'Twas only a kiss. A kiss goodbye." Stopping in her tracks, Moira shook her head in disbelief. "What have I done? He'll never forgive me for this."

Maggie chuckled, "He mightna forgive his mother, but even that I doubt." Reaching out, she grasped Moira's hands. "He loves ye. D'ye not see that?"

"He cares for me," Moira whispered, remembering the moment he had whispered those words to her. They had touched her deeply, made her hope and yearn; still, they did not mean that he loved her, that he wished to marry her. He liked her. He cared about her. He desired her. That much Moira was certain of, but love?

If Cormag loved her, would he have been so furious when they had been discovered?

Moira doubted it.

Chapter Thirty-Three

A FOOL FOR LOVE

"How dare ye?" Cormag snarled under his breath, struggling to keep his voice low. Never had he felt so close to strangling his mother.

"Come now. Dunna be so verra dramatic," she chided with an amused chuckle, and Cormag felt like losing his mind. "What happened was hardly my doing."

Gritting his teeth, Cormag strode to the window, needing a bit of safe distance between himself and his mother. His hands had balled into fists, and he pushed them hard against the stone wall, feeling the rough rock scrape his skin, to keep himself from crashing them through the window.

Only too well did he remember the resigned look on Moira's face, full of regret and dismay, when she had realised his mother's intentions in bringing a small crowd to witness their kiss. How on earth had she known? Cormag wondered, knowing with perfect clarity that if he were to ask, she would only laugh, shake her head and speak of something else.

"I dunna see where the problem is," she spoke out from behind him, a gentler tone to her voice now. "Ye love her, and she loves ye. This should be simple."

Fighting not to allow his mother's observation to drag him down a path that would only lead to disappointment, Cormag turned to face her. "Ye had no right to interfere no matter what ye might believe."

Crossing her arms over her chest, his mother fixed him with an exasperated stare. "I've been watching the two of ye do yer best to ignore one another for almost three years." She threw up her hands, a look of sheer bewilderment on her face. "And for a reason I canna understand nor ever will for there is none, is there?"

"That is none of yer concern," Cormag hissed. "Ye dunna have the right to make decisions for me...or for her. 'Tis not yer place." With his gaze fixed on hers, he stepped closer. "How did ye know, Mother? For ye did, didn't ye? Ye had yer hands in this, I know it." There was a slight twitch of her lips, a sense of triumph unable to keep silent. "What did ye do? Did ye...did ye say anything to Moira? She acted strange today, not like herself."

His mother snorted, "And how would ye know that? Ye rarely speak to the lass, and when ye do, ye dunna say what's in yer heart. Neither one of ye does." Anger began to spark in her green eyes. "Ye're a fool, Cormag. Do ye hear me? A fool. If ye dunna act, she'll leave, and ye'll lose her for good."

Cormag swallowed as fear began to permeate his anger. "'Tis her decision," he gritted out, then spun on his heel and marched back over to the window, focusing his attention on the green hills in the distance.

"Why did ye kiss her?" his mother asked from behind him. "I know that she asked ye for a kiss, but why did ye do it? Why did ye not simply wish her well and tell her to take care on her journey?"

Tension gripped him, and Cormag felt his head sink forward as though it was suddenly made of lead. He felt the cool windowpane against his forehead, a stark contrast to the heat that coursed through his body.

"What did ye feel in that moment? For it tells ye everything ye need to know."

Cormag knew what he felt. He knew what he wanted as well. He knew what lived in his heart and mind. He had always known. But life was not as simple as his mother made it out to be. There were other factors to consider, not only his clan, but also Moira. He could not be certain what it was she wanted and...he did not dare ask.

"The moment she first set foot in this place, ye knew she was the one, did ye not?" Placing a hand on his arm, his mother urged him to look at her, her bright green eyes seeking his. "Look at me for I willna leave until ye've heard all ye need to hear."

Steeling himself, Cormag did as she requested, never having known his mother to leave something be. "Verra well. What is it ye think I dunna know?"

A chuckle flew from her lips. "I know ye've never placed much stock in the way I see the world, and I've always accepted that." She set her hands onto her hips, and he could see her resolve strengthening. "But I willna stand by and watch ye throw yer life away."

"Throw my l-?"

"Aye, ye are," his mother insisted, gripping his arm tighter. "I'm yer mother, and I wish to see ye happy. Ye canna deny that ye need her for that, can ye?"

Cormag's lips thinned, knowing he could not lie to his mother. She would know. She always did.

"Marry her," she told him then, her jaw set and her eyes determined. It was not a question, nor was it a request or a suggestion. It was a command, and she expected to be obeyed. "I'll have the wedding planned within a week. All ye need to do is attend and say the right words." Her brows rose in challenge, and in that moment, Cormag did not have the strength to fight her for deep down he wanted all that she *asked* of him.

If only he could be certain it was what Moira wanted as well.

Chapter Thirty-Four

FOR BETTER OR FOR WORSE

From the safety of her home, Moira watched as the whole clan prepared for her wedding.

Almost in a trance, she sat by the window as people hurried up and down the path that led by her cottage. She heard voices shouting and children singing. She watched freshly cut branches carted up the small slope, no doubt upon Maggie's request, who had taken over decorating the great hall yet again.

On the second day after their fateful kiss, Maeve had paid her a quick visit, informing her when and where she was expected to appear. Outraged over the woman's callousness in this matter, Moira had yelled at her, demanding an explanation, demanding at the very least an admission of guilt for luring her son into a trap. Maeve, however, had merely chuckled and gone on her merry way, completely unperturbed by her future daughter-in-law's outburst.

The next day, Moira's wedding gown had been delivered to her, including a reminder of the when and where of her wedding. As though Moira could ever forget!

The days passed in a blur as Moira continued to look out her window, her heart and mind strangely detached as though she truly had no part in this. And then slowly, as the sun made its way across the sky on the fourth day following their kiss, some things began to register.

People still looked as they made their way past her home the way they always had. Only now, Moira thought to see curiosity rather than suspicion. And the more she watched, the more she thought to detect a faint shimmer of hope in their eyes. A sense of a new beginning, and the shedding of an old fear. There were sparks of joy here and there, and on occasion even a friendly wave.

Shocked, Moira stood by her window, staring out at the people she had avoided these past three years. Aye, when she had first arrived, they had been displeased to see her, no doubt fearing she would disturb their peace. Moira had never blamed them for it, and so she had simply kept her eyes down and gone about her life, pretending that they were not even there, refusing to see their rejection day in and out.

However, now, she realised that somehow along the way, something had changed.

And hope began to blossom in her heart.

Moira knew that if Cormag had asked for her hand, she would not have refused him. However, he had not, and she feared that he did not truly want her. At least not as his wife.

Still, the very reason because of which Moira had been determined to leave seemed to be dissolving before her very eyes. Perhaps her marrying Cormag would not divide his clan. Perhaps his people had somehow reached a point where they were willing to give her a chance. Perhaps eventually she could be one of them after all.

A new home.

A new family.

A new clan.

And then her gaze drifted over Ian as he lingered a few paces down the path, his ice-cold eyes fixed on her, a snarl on his face as he stood with his feet apart and his arms crossed, like a man readying himself for battle.

Indeed, Ian was the problem. Moira knew that now. In her mind, his rejection, his distrust and suspicion had stood for all the others.

She had only ever seen him and assumed, feared that he was but one of many.

Could it be that he was the only one who wished her gone? And if that were so, was it truly a reason for her to leave?

He frightened her, aye! The moment his hands had closed around her throat was imprinted upon her mind, and every time he glared at her, her throat threatened to close yet again.

Still, she could not allow him to intimidate her, to run from the chance to be happy again. Perhaps, there was a way she could...speak to him, make him see that she had no power over Maggie's heart, that she was not to blame for his loss.

The thought sent a cold shiver down her back, and Moira immediately turned away from the window, sinking into the nearest chair as her knees threatened to buckle. "Not alone," she whispered, trying to reassure herself. "Not alone."

Perhaps, Cormag would help her. Of course, he would. He always had. Always had he come to her aid, stood by her side...even against Ian.

Was that not the answer she sought? Or had he merely done so because it had been the right thing to do? Still, Moira remembered well the bond she felt connected them every time he drew near. Did he feel it as well?

The night before her wedding, Moira drifted off into a fitful sleep as all her doubts and fears returned to torment her. She saw distorted faces, their eyes hard and unyielding, the accusation in them brutal and painful. Snarls flew from their lips as hands seized her, dragging her from her bed and out into the cold where she lay shivering, alone and forgotten.

And then she heard Cormag's voice. *I care for ye.*

Instantly, her nightmare vanished as though it had never been, and Moira felt herself pulled toward a bright light, a barrier, a threshold to another place and time.

Her muscles tensed as she braced herself for what she would see, for the burden once more placed upon her shoulders, the decision forced upon her.

And then her eyes cleared, and Moira found herself not looking down at another's life, another's future, but instead she found herself thrust into her own. She felt herself move, her skin tingling in anticipation as she stepped forward, her eyes gliding over a man who stood with his back to her.

Moira instantly knew it to be Cormag. She knew the breadth of his shoulders. His midnight black hair tied in the back. The tension that had him link his arms behind his back.

Sensing his need, Moira reached out to him, wrapping her arms around his shoulders, offering the same comfort he had always given her.

And then he turned, a smile on his face and swept her into his arms.

Stunned, Moira clung to him as his lips found hers, kissing her gently as he held her tight against his chest, his heart beating rapidly under the palm of her hand.

The tension she had sensed before vanished, and a joyful lightness engulfed Moira as Cormag carried her to the bed, gently setting her down upon the mattress. He kissed her deeply, and she lay back, feeling the cool sheets against her heated skin.

With a start, Moira shot upright as her dream slowly drifted away, the emotions it had brought lingering deep inside her heart. Panting, she brushed a hand over her face and tried to clear her thoughts, but her heart hammered with such vehemence that she could not calm herself, urging her to hear it.

And then Moira listened, listened to the emotions that lingered, whispering of a beautiful future if only she dared believe, if only she dared reach for it.

Was this a promise? Moira wondered, afraid to hope. Was Fate once more dangling something in front of her, urging her to reach for it only to snatch it away? Did she dare believe that her dream could one day come true?

Moira did not know, but she did know that she wanted Cormag.

And tomorrow, he would be hers.

For better or for worse.

Moira prayed that it would be for better.

Chapter Thirty-Five

AS ONE

Cormag knew he ought to have spoken to his mother. More than that. He ought to have spoken to Moira. Cancelled the wedding if she had wanted him to. However, he had not. Instead, he had gone about his business as usual, pretending that his wedding day was not approaching with fast steps. He had not even seen Moira since that fateful kiss, afraid that he would see regret in her eyes.

She had only asked for a kiss, a kiss goodbye, and now, she was trapped here, unable to leave. Thanks to his mother.

And him, he had to admit.

For he could have stopped this wedding. Of course, he could have. But he did not want to. He wanted to marry her. He wanted Moira to be his wife, and so selfishly, he had not said a word.

To her, or anyone else.

He had simply allowed things to run their course.

And now the day had come.

As Cormag stepped into the great hall, his gaze swept not only over the beautiful decorations that were no doubt Maggie's doing, but also over his people.

For the hall was filled to the rim; men, women and children chatting and laughing, their faces a mirror of joy and hopeful expectation. Garrett and Finn strode toward him, their eyes aglow as they each clasped a hand on his shoulder, offering their congratulations with wide grins.

"Dunna look so worried," Garrett chided. "Today's a happy day. If we think so, then ye certainly should."

"Perhaps 'tis disbelief," Finn commented, his green eyes narrowing as he watched him, "that a woman like Moira would accept him." He chuckled, "I know I felt the same way when I married Emma."

Garrett nodded in agreement as his eyes travelled across the hall to where Claudia stood, rocking their son in her arms. "We're lucky men, are we not?"

More nods followed as Cormag continued to stare at his people, his clan. "I never thought they..." His voice drifted off.

"We're all here to celebrate with ye," Garrett told him, a deeper meaning swinging in his voice. "With the both of ye. Let the past be the past and start a new chapter today."

Cormag blinked. "I always thought they'd disapprove. I always thought I couldn't...because..." Again, his gaze swept over the crowd assembled in the hall.

"Things have changed," Finn told him, exchanging a glance with Garrett. "We're not the only ones she's helped, the ones she's taken a risk for. We're happy because of her, and people have noticed. The whispers have changed, have grown hopeful, for no one wants to doubt and mistrust all the time. People want to feel safe and they want to be happy, and Moira hasna given them any reason to think that she'll stand in the way of that. On the contrary."

Cormag swallowed, overwhelmed by what he had thought impossible only the day before. Then he caught sight of Ian, standing in the back of the hall, his blue eyes hard as he glared at him.

Following his gaze, Garrett sighed, "Aye, he's not come around. Finn's spoken to him, but..."

"'Tis as though his anger is all he's got left," Finn remarked, compassion warming his voice as he looked at his friend with sad eyes. "I wish I could help him, but I dunno how."

"We'll figure out a way," Garrett promised, looking from Finn to

Cormag, his green eyes determined as he waited for them to agree. "Together."

Cormag and Finn nodded. "Aye, together."

Ian deserved happiness just like the rest of them, and Cormag knew that there would be no peace in his clan if his friend despised the very sight of his new bride. Indeed, even with the distance between them, Cormag felt a sense of betrayal rolling off Ian, and he wondered if there was anything in this world that could persuade Ian to look at Moira with fresh eyes.

If so, Cormag did not know what it was.

But he prayed that they would find out.

And then Moira stepped into the hall, and Cormag saw only her.

Her golden hair flowed freely over her shoulders, gleaming in the bright sunlight, its rays reaching inside the vaulted hall through its many windows and open door. Her dress was a deep azure, a perfect match for those utterly captivating eyes of hers that always sparkled like a lake at midday.

Soft murmurs went through the crowd at her entrance, and Cormag's heart calmed as the joy and hope his people felt echoed within his own heart. They glanced back and forth between the two of them, and Cormag knew that they wished them well.

Never would he have expected such devotion from his clan. It made him proud, and he smiled at them with gratitude in his heart before his gaze was once more drawn to his beautiful bride.

Their eyes locked as the crowd parted to allow her through, and the tentative smile that came to her lips sent a jolt through his heart. He heard Finn and Garrett chuckle beside him, and for the first time in his life, Cormag knew that his heart's desire showed on his face for all to see.

And he did not care.

All he cared about was Moira: in his life, by his side, in his arms. He wanted her. He loved her, and finally, Cormag was ready to admit that.

Even if only to himself.

The world went away, became distant, no more than a mild echo of what it had been only moments before as Moira came to stand beside him. Her hand trembled as he took it in his own, and the look in her eyes almost brought him to his knees.

More than that, it gave him hope.

Hope that she felt something other than regret to find herself bound to him after a few whispered words.

Cheers went up in the hall, and as they turned to face their guests, everyone seemed to rush forward at once, offering their congratulations and well wishes. Cormag felt overwhelmed at the onslaught of emotions until his eyes settled on his mother's, a sense of victory in their green depths. Still, the smile on her face spoke of happiness, and even from steps away, Cormag could see the soft mist clinging to her eyes.

Ye did well, he heard her voice in his head, and not for the first time in his life, Cormag wondered if there was more to his mother than met the eye.

As the music began to play, the cacophony of voices died down somewhat. Dancers collected on one side of the hall while others sat down to eat. Cormag saw Garrett take their son Aiden from Claudia's arms so that she could fetch herself a plate while Maggie and Emma helped hand out the food, ensuring that all would get their fill. Blair and Niall raced around the room with their friends, weaving through the guests like little mice, their faces heated from exertion as laughter spilled from their lips.

It was a happy scene, and yet...

Turning to his wife-*his wife!* -Cormag found her step toward him in that very moment, her blue eyes seeking his, a similar sense of urgency in them that he felt in his own heart. "Is there anything ye need?" he asked, leaning close to whisper in her ear.

Her hand came to rest over his rapidly beating heart as she turned her head, her lips brushing by his ear, and whispered back, "I need to speak with ye. Alone."

As she pulled back, their eyes met, locked, held, and Cormag felt the air around him grow thin. Then he nodded, and she slipped her hand through the crook of his arm as he led her toward the arched doorway that would guide them outside.

Apparently, their intention to retreat so soon after speaking their vows did not go completely unnoticed, for teasing remarks and laughter erupted around them, bringing a deep flush to Moira's cheeks. Cormag gritted his teeth and pulled her away as fast as he dared.

Guests even lingered in the hallway, glad to have a chance to offer their congratulations, and more people poured in and out of the side entrance, returning for food or leaving for a spell of fresh air. Turning toward the stairwell, Cormag guided his new bride upward, thinking that a walk on the battlements might grant them an opportunity to speak.

Moira, however, stopped him with a hand on his arm when they reached the corridor that led to his chamber. "I dunna wish to be overheard," she told him and then proceeded onward, heading toward his door with a certainty that surprised him.

Following in her wake, Cormag watched her as she opened his door and stepped inside. Then she paused, and he saw her gaze sweep over his room before settling on the bed where they would share a night in each other's arms not long ago.

"Are ye all right?" Cormag asked, worried that all these hasty developments had overwhelmed her. The last thing he wanted was for her to feel frightened, cornered, trapped, without options or choice.

Moira drew in a slow breath, momentarily lost in thought, before she turned to face him. "I'm fine." Then she looked past him. "Would ye mind closing that?"

Stepping back, Cormag did as she asked and closed the door, shutting out the world, before approaching her once more. Her gaze met his, and a nervous smile flitted across her face. Her feet moved then, carrying her around the room, indecision suddenly marking her face.

"We can leave if ye wish," Cormag offered, wondering if the memory of what had happened here in this room between them, of how he had almost taken advantage of her vulnerability was bothersome for her to remember.

At least for him, it was.

Turning from the window, Moira met his gaze. "Nay, I..."

"Ye seem nervous."

She nodded. "I am."

"Why?" Tension gripped him, and he feared that the hope he had held onto for the past week would finally be shattered. He had avoided her to not hear her say that she did not want to marry him, that she had only agreed to do so out of lack of options, to feel safe again, to belong, to have a home.

But not because she wanted him.

Moira swallowed. "I keep wondering why ye let this wedding take place, why ye didna stop it."

Cormag cringed, seeing his worst fears realised. His feet moved backward, putting distance between them, worried that his closeness might be threatening to her. "There's no need for us to share this chamber," he told her, trying to sound reassuring. "There are others ye can chose from. One that will be yers alone."

A slight frown came to her face as she watched him. "Why would ye make such an offer?"

Cormag squared his shoulders, linking his hands behind his back. "I know ye're vulnerable, ye're lonely, and I swear I willna take advantage of that again." His jaw clenched, but he forced himself to hold her gaze. "I'm sorry for what happened the other night. I shouldna hav-"

"The night *I* kissed *ye*?" she asked, her blue eyes lingering on his face. "After *I* came to *yer* chamber?"

Something odd reverberated in her voice, and Cormag was not certain what to make of it. "Ye needed comfort, Lass. Nothing more. I should've seen that right away."

A long sigh left her lips. "I felt many things that night, and I admit that what I needed most was comfort. Ye were right about that. I didna even know, not in that moment." A soft smile teased her lips before she drew in a long breath and then moved toward him. Her steps were slow, cautious, a bit hesitant, and yet, her eyes never fell from his until she came to stand not an arm's length in front of him. "Ye didna do anything I didna want, Cormag, not then, not ever," she whispered, lifting a hand and bringing it to his face, her fingers trailing over his skin. "Believe me."

His hands clenched more fiercely behind his back as he fought to remain in control. Why was it that she managed to strip him of every little bit of self-control within a matter of seconds? She could not possibly be doing this intentionally, could she? She could not know how her soft caresses drove him mad. How her nearness made him long for her more. "I disagree," he gritted out, wishing she would return to the other side of the room. "Ye were in tears, Lass, and I was selfish to-"

"I was selfish as well," she interrupted, and her hand slipped lower, down the side of his neck and over his shoulder until it came to rest over his stampeding heart. "I was selfish when I married ye today without..."

"Without what?" Cormag pressed, confused by the soft changes in her manner, back and forth between bold and nervous.

"Without speaking to ye, without asking if ye even...*wanted* to marry me," she whispered, pressing closer, her breath brushing over his skin as her blue eyes looked up into his in a way that stole the breath from his lungs. "I was selfish because I wanted ye. I wanted ye to be mine, and I was afraid that if I asked, ye might change yer mind, and so I didna." A shy smile curled up her lips. "Can ye not see that I want ye? That I have wanted ye since the moment I stepped into yer study three years ago?"

Unable to breathe, Cormag stared at her, doubting his ears, doubting his sanity, doubting...everything. "Ye needna...I..." Shaking his head to clear it, he reached for her, his hands bringing her closer, trying to see if there was truth in her words because if there was not, and he allowed himself to believe her, it would cripple him. "It canna be true," he mumbled. "I canna feel ye at all. There's nothing. All I feel is..."

"What?" she whispered as her hands snaked up his chest and came around his neck.

As though struck, Cormag stepped back, removed her arms from him and crossed to the other side of the room. His breath came fast, and his mind spun as he stared at her.

"What is it that ye feel when ye think of me?" Moira asked as her eyes lingered on his face, gliding over his taut features and down to the hammering pulse in his neck. "Do ye feel unhinged, and yet, strangely balanced? Do ye feel drawn closer like the pull of a magnet? Do ye feel the air stolen from yer lungs and yer blood set on fire? Do ye feel safe and warm and complete at the same time? Do ye feel all that? Because if ye do," tears misted in her eyes as she stepped forward, her gaze determined, but also deeply vulnerable as she faced him, "then ye do feel what I feel." She swallowed, and her lower lip trembled with the emotions streaming down her face. "Perhaps ye simply canna tell the difference for we feel the same."

Dumbfounded, Cormag stared at her as he listened to the faint echo in his heart. It felt as though there were two beats, and not one, hers and his beating together. Her words echoed within him, and he all but recognised them as his own. Could it be that she truly felt the way she had said?

"Why did ye marry me?" Moira demanded when he remained silent. "Out of duty? Because ye thought ye had to? To protect me because that is what a decent man does?" She paused and drew in a shuddering breath, hope and fear warring within her eyes. "Or was there another reason?"

Looking across the room, seeing her standing there, so vulnerable and brave, Cormag finally realised that his mother had been right after all. Deep down, love was simple, and in that moment, he could not remember a single reason why he had hesitated for so long.

But no more.

In a few large strides, Cormag closed the distance between them and all but yanked her into his arms. His mouth claimed hers in a daring kiss for he no longer feared that he was crossing a line. Her arms snaked around his neck once more, holding him close, and she kissed him back with equal measure, their hearts beating as one.

"I married ye, Lass," Cormag panted as he stared down into her blue eyes, "because I love ye, and ye were right, I have since the day ye arrived."

Tears flooded her eyes then, and a violent tremor shook her. Cormag pulled her into his arms, knowing that it was neither fear nor regret that had brought it on, but utter relief. For deep in his heart, he felt an echo of it, uncertain whether the emotion was hers or his own. In the end, though, it did not matter for they both felt the same.

Still, clinging to him, Moira lifted her head, warmth and longing shining in her eyes. "I love ye as well, and I have for a long time."

Closing his eyes, Cormag rested his forehead against hers as they all but breathed as one, their arms wrapped around the other, holding on. "Ye seem different today," Cormag whispered after a while, unable to shake the feeling that something had changed. "Brave, almost fearless. Why?"

A soft chuckle rumbled in her throat before she lifted her head. "I had a dream last night."

"A dream?" he asked with a frown before his eyes widened in understanding. "Ye mean...?"

Moira nodded, the smile on her lips one of deepest joy.

"What...what did ye see?" Cormag asked, not certain if he wanted to know.

She sighed, a deep, contented sigh. "I saw us, together and happy." One corner of her mouth curled up as her eyes became distant, returning to the moment in her dream. "But 'twas more than simply seeing us thus. It was the ease that existed between us. It felt simple, and when I woke, I could no longer remember why we were still apart." She blinked. "I knew that I wanted ye, and I could finally admit that to myself without fear. 'Twas... 'twas liberating."

Cormag swallowed. "Does that mean ye're here because-?"

"No!" came her answer like a shot, fired without hesitation or the slightest bit of unease. Grasping his hands, she met his eyes, holding on until he felt trapped in her deep blue gaze. "I'm not here because of what I saw. I know now that what I see is nothing more than a choice, and I would have left long ago if I did not care for ye. I'm here because I choose to be, and I married ye because 'tis what I want, not because of yer meddling mother, lack of choices or the whispers of fate." She inhaled a slow breath. "Can ye trust that? Can ye trust me?"

"Aye," Cormag whispered against her lips as he leant forward, drawing her back into his arms...where she belonged. "Aye, I trust ye. I always have." The smile that teased her lips warmed his heart, and he kissed her then without a moment of doubt, not in the least wondering if she wanted him as well.

Her eager hands raked through his hair and then began pulling on his shirt as he held her tightly in his arms, reluctant to allow even a breath of air between them. Only for a second did he lift his arms so she could pull his shirt over his head and toss it to the side before he reached for her again, his hands now eager to loosen her laces.

Soon, Cormag felt her bare skin against his own. He could not remember ever having felt more at peace with himself than when Moira's laughter echoed through his chamber as they lost their footing and tumbled onto the bed.

Love truly was simple...if one did not complicate it, of course.

Chapter Thirty-Six

A FATEFUL NIGHT

The first few weeks after their wedding were nothing short of a dream for Moira.

For so long, she had been alone; more than that, she had been lonely, the only comfort the reassuring words she had whispered to herself in the dead of night, longing for someone to hold her. Anyone, even if it was not Cormag.

Only to feel. To have that bit of contact that healed the soul and soothed the heart.

And now, she fell asleep every night, nestled in the warmth of his embrace. He was there when she closed her eyes and he was there when she woke, his soft silver gaze seeking hers with such tenderness that it robbed her of speech. Often, she simply flung herself into his arms, desperate to show him how fulfilled she suddenly felt.

Love.

Family.

Home.

All that Moira had thought lost to her was now slowly returning.

With Cormag by her side, she began to walk through the castle and its surrounding village with a raised head and open eyes. And on her way, she met friendly faces and exchanged kind words here and there.

At first, these exchanges were a bit strained and felt tense, but over time, Moira felt herself settle more into her role as the laird's wife. She took an interest in the people around her, freely offering her knowledge of herbs and their uses, helping where she could, be it with a sick child or when a cottage's roof needed to be re-thatched.

Maeve often brought her along when she made her round through the village, giving Moira the opportunity to speak to her people, to listen to their thoughts, their concerns, but also their joys. Soon, their names no longer slipped her mind, and she felt her heart swell with pride when one afternoon she was asked to look after the three children of a family whose mother was tied to her bed, struggling to bring another one into this world.

And every night, Moira fell into bed, grateful for the turn her life had taken. Still, every now and then, she shed a tear for those lost to her, for the family far away, who should have been there and shared in her happiness. Certainly, she had found new friends in Maggie and Emma and even Claudia as the young, English woman proved a wonderful companion; however, they could not fill the void left by Alastair, Deidre and even Connor.

Aye, Moira now knew that she had never truly loved him, at least not in any way different from how family simply loved one another. Sometimes she still wondered about the dream that had destroyed her life, trying to understand what purpose it had been meant to serve and how else she could have interpreted it. However, Moira had come to realise that without acting as she had, she would never have been banished, and would never have come to Clan MacDrummond and met Cormag.

In the end, although Moira regretted the pain her actions had brought upon her brother and her old clan, another part of her could not regret that it *had* happened.

For she could no longer imagine a life without Cormag.

"Are ye all right, Lass?" he asked one night when she awoke with a start, her heart hammering so fast that for a moment she feared she would faint.

His hand gently brushed a lock from her forehead as he pulled her close, wrapping his arms around her, holding her tightly until she began to calm down. "Was it a dream?" he whispered, his warm breath tickling her ear, the deeper meaning in that simple question loud and clear.

Moira nodded for her throat felt dry, and she rose to pour herself some water, immediately regretting the distance it put between them. Nevertheless, her pulse still beat fast, and her limbs urged her to move as though it would help clear her head.

"What did ye see?" Cormag asked as he leant against the head-board, his grey eyes almost black in the dim silvery light of the new moon. His gaze stayed with her as she paced, and Moira smiled at the thought that he knew her well enough to leave her be.

At least for the moment.

"I'm not certain," Moira whispered, fighting to hold on to the images as they began to slip away. "'Twas about Deidre and..." Her brows drew together almost painfully as her mind stretched to reach for the elusive images she had seen. "I saw a blue flower." She shook her head. "I didna recognise it. It looked strange somehow, blurred, as though 'twas not real."

"D'ye know what it means?" Cormag asked, a frown drawing down his brows to match her own as he tried his best to help her make sense of the warning she had received. For it was a warning, of that Moira was certain.

Stopping at the window, Moira looked out at the vast land stretching out toward the far sea. "It marked a day, I believe." She rested her hands on the rough stone and gazed out at the darkened world.

"What day? When?"

Moira shrugged. "I dunna know."

"D'ye know why 'tis important?" His voice sounded tentative as though he worried about pushing her too close to frustration. In truth, his simple questions helped direct her mind, focus it so she could hold on to the images that threatened to dance out of reach.

"'Tis the day, she'll find a great love." Cold shivers ran down her back as the words flew from her lips without thought. "Up by the ruins, near the cliff." Shock froze her limbs, and she turned slowly inch by inch until she met her husband's eyes. "What about Alastair?" she whispered into the dark, fear for her brother twisting her heart painfully.

Rising from the bed, Cormag crossed the room, his strong arms reaching for her, pulling her into the comfort of his embrace. "Was there anything in it that suggested that yer brother was in danger?"

Holding onto her husband, Moira shook her head. "Nay, nothing of the sort." She lifted her head and met his eyes. "D'ye think it could mean that Deidre will lose her heart to another?"

The deep frown on Cormag's face was a balm to her soul. "I canna imagine for it to be so," he whispered, brushing a finger over the soft ridge of her left brow, trying to chase away the frown line that lingered. "I've rarely felt a deeper love than I did between yer brother and his wife. They were utterly besotted with one another even after years of marriage."

Moira nodded, her heart beating a little easier. "Aye, I've always thought so as well. But then...," her heart jerked to a halt, "does it mean that he will come to harm?"

For a moment, Cormag seemed to consider her words before he shook his head. "I dunna believe so," he replied, "or do ye think that yer brother's death would cost him his wife's heart?"

"Nay," Moira replied without hesitation. "She's always loved him, and she always will." A gust of air rushed from her lungs. "Then how can she find a new love?"

"'Twas a different kind of dream than the ones ye had before," Cormag mumbled as his silvery gaze swept over her. "Have ye had such a dream before?"

Moira nodded. "Once or twice, I've had a dream that I felt rather than saw, not an image of a future event, but a sign pointing to something that remains unclear." Frustrated, Moira shook her head as her lips pressed into a hard line. "'Tis hard to interpret." She sighed, "Rhona, my aunt, Connor's mother, she has the gift as well, and she told me once that she thought our dreams were only meant to prepare us. Nothing more."

"She doesna believe ye're meant to change what ye see? Or help bring it about?"

"I'm not certain," Moira mumbled as she rested her head against his shoulder, her fingers curling into his shirt. "Perhaps not all dreams are the same. I've come to realise that the dreams that are the hardest to read are the ones that pertain to myself." She looked up at him. "I think 'tis because my own heart is involved and I canna be objective." A smile touched her lips, and she reached up to cup his cheek. "Perhaps 'tis the same with yer gift."

Understanding, Cormag nodded his head. "Ye mean I couldna feel ye because my own heart cared deeply about how ye felt, and I couldna distance myself from that."

"Aye." Moira heaved a deep sigh.

"What will ye do now?"

"I dunna know." Her eyes ventured to the window once more, gazing toward the horizon where far away her brother lay in his own bed, Deidre by his side, in his arms. "I will write to her," Moira whispered then before her gaze returned to Cormag. "I'll write to her, and if anyone can understand, it'll be Deidre. She's often helped me make sense of what I'd seen. She'll heed my words, and at the very least, she'll be prepared for whatever is to come." Closing her eyes, she exhaled a long breath. "There's nothing else I can do."

Without her vision, Moira only felt Cormag lean closer. She felt his hands settle on her waist and pull her toward him. Then his lips brushed over hers, a small comfort, a gentle reassurance that she was not alone, that he was here, beside her, holding her hand.

Moira smiled, returning his kiss, and her heart beat with more ease. "Go back to bed," she whispered, brushing the pad of her thumb over his lips. "I'll need some time."

Cormag held her gaze for a moment before he nodded and then kissed her once more. A part of her did not want to let go, and her heart ached the moment his arms released her. Still, Moira knew that she would never find peace if she did not do all she could to warn Deidre.

As Cormag returned to their bed, Moira seated herself at the small desk in the corner by the window. It had become her favourite spot for it promised peace and solitude while at the same time offering her a view of the world, proof that she was not alone after all.

Moira's eyes swept over the sleeping village, and a deep sigh left her lips before she turned her attention to the empty parchment before her.

Dearest Deidre,

This is not an easy letter to write for I fear I must warn you of something that lies ahead. I will do my best to share with you all that I know, but I'm afraid the images I saw were shrouded as though hidden in a heavy fog. You will have to trust your heart to guide you as do I, for I know that there is no better compass than the gentle soul that resides within you.

Once again, Moira willed her mind to travel back and reach for the images she had seen. The quill moved fluidly across the parchment as she attempted to describe the blue flower as best as she could as well as the meaning she believed it held.

Indeed, Moira had sensed a warning in her dream. There had been no fear though. Only sadness. Could that mean that no harm would come to any of them? Moira could only hope so as she paused for a long moment, torn about whether to urge Deidre to seek out the old ruins near the cliff on the day marked by the blue flower. What if seeking out that place would lead to disaster? What if not seeking it out would?

Burying her face in her hands, Moira knew not what to do. There was always a risk; however, it felt far greater when it was a risk to someone she loved. What if something happened to Deidre? Alastair would never forgive her for that. Nor would Moira herself.

And yet, she knew she had no choice for deep down she once again was beginning to believe that her gift would never intentionally lead her astray. It served to help and protect, to warn and prepare, and only human failure to see the truth in those dreams would lead to an unintended place.

When Moira finally rose from the chair, she found Cormag sleeping, one hand stretched out toward her side of the bed as though even in sleep he was reaching out for her.

Moira smiled, but knew that she could not join him. Her nerves were too rattled, and so she dressed quietly, knowing that the new day was not far away, and carried her letter downstairs to be sent out.

Then she slipped through the side entrance and stepped out into the night. The full moon cast a bright shimmer over the world, and Moira could see it glistening here and there as it touched the stream snaking its way through the land. Crickets chirped and an owl hooted now and then as she made her way out of the gate and down the small path. As she walked by her old home, Moira stopped, and her mind wandered back to a time that suddenly seemed long ago.

A smile touched Moira's lips, and she pulled her shawl tighter around her shoulders as the cool night air sent a shiver down her back. Then she paused, and a frown tugged on her brows.

Something was not as it ought to be, and she glanced over her shoulder as though expecting to see something out of place.

The castle and the village, however, continued to sleep peacefully, cast in the silvery light of the watchful moon.

Feeling the need to move, Moira continued to her destination, the small grove where she had often sought refuge. In the moonlight, the path was hard to see, and Moira walked slowly, careful to lift her feet over roots rising above the ground or dips left behind by moles as they expanded their underground residences.

The soft murmur of water drifted to her ears, and a moment later she found herself on the river's bank, her small grove only a few paces behind her right shoulder. Peacefulness washed over her, and Moira sank down into the tall grass and pulled her shawl forward to cover her knees as she hugged them to her chest.

Moira did not know how long she sat there, enjoying a rare moment, a moment of solitude that did not rest heavily on her heart, but rather served to ease the strain her dream had placed on it. Slowly, fatigue began to tug on her, and her eyelids grew heavy.

Longing for her bed as well as her husband's embrace, Moira pushed to her feet...and froze.

Her heart clenched in fear, and she realised in that moment that she was not alone.

Wheeling around, she gasped when her eyes fell on Ian, his face distorted into a grotesque mask of anger and resentment as he stormed toward her.

Terror gripped Moira, and she stumbled backwards toward the water's edge. However, before she felt its cool waters seep through her shoes, Ian's hands grasped her arms, yanking her toward him. "Ye betrayed us all," he hissed, the snarl on his face seeming otherworldly in the silvery light of the moon. "I'll make sure ye'll never do so again."

And then his hands once more closed around her throat, pressing inward, their grasp tightening.

In panic, Moira clawed at his arms, his chest, his face, but he could not be moved. He held on, and with each second that passed, her vision blurred and darkened more and more, her body screaming for air.

"Ye dunna deserve mercy," Ian hissed as he brought her face close to his, his ice-cold gaze drilling into her, "and ye willna get it." As he shook her, his right thumb moved, slid a little sideways, and suddenly, Moira felt her knees buckle as her vision darkened.

Blackness engulfed her, and then everything else went away.

Chapter Thirty-Seven

TO SENSE ANOTHER

As the sun streamed into their chamber, Cormag woke only to realise that his wife was not beside him. Nonetheless, his arm moved over the mattress on her side as though he could still find her if only, he looked hard enough. Disappointment darkened his mood, and he wondered at the deep longing he felt in his chest. Never had he needed another's presence as he now needed hers. A life without Moira had become unimaginable, and every fibre of his being urged him to go and find her.

To come home together.

To reunite them.

To be as one.

His gaze rose to look about the room only to find it empty as well before he pushed from the bed and quickly dressed. Then he headed downstairs, offering a few words here and there as the castle began to wake. However, no one had seen Moira, and so he stepped out into the early morning light, his eyes sweeping over the courtyard.

It was a bright and friendly day, but Cormag could not shake the feeling that something was utterly wrong. It reminded him of the night Moira had climbed the eastern tower as well as the night she had tried to leave *Seann Dachaigh* Tower, and a dark fear settled in his heart.

Was he simply seeing things that were not there? Or was this his gift, his connection to Moira? Was he feeling what she felt? Where on earth was she?

Striding across the courtyard, Cormag called out to everyone he saw, but no one had seen his wife. When he noticed Maggie, Emma and Claudia, he turned toward them, his pulse hammering frantically. "Have ye seen Moira?" he demanded, noticing the slight frowns that came to their faces at his harsh tone.

"Why? 'Tis something the matter?" Maggie asked, her blue eyes narrowing.

Cormag shrugged. "I canna say," he replied, knowing that there was no rational reason for him to think that something *had* happened. Still, he could not shake the feeling that something was wrong. That Moira was in danger. "She rose early, and no one's seen her since."

"It might have been her then."

At the sound of Claudia's mumbled words, Cormag turned toward her, his heart hammering painfully in his chest. "Ye saw her?"

Claudia's gaze cleared. "I'm not certain. Aiden woke in the middle of the night, and I was walking with him, trying to get him to settle down." She glanced up at the window to her and Garrett's chamber. "I came by the window, and I saw someone leave the castle. I couldn't see who it was in the dim light." She looked over to the gate before returning to look at him apologetically. "Whoever it was went down the path toward the village." She shrugged, glancing at the other two women. "It might have been her."

"Perhaps she went down to the stream," Emma suggested before she moved to look at Maggie, who nodded in agreement.

"Thank ye," Cormag mumbled before he hurried out the front gate, his feet moving as fast as he dared without drawing overmuch attention to himself. Perhaps she had ventured there to clear her thoughts. Perhaps she had even fallen asleep in the small grove where she liked to sit. Perhaps he would find her there, safe and sound.

Still, Cormag knew he did not believe he would. Something was wrong; he was certain of it.

Even from afar, he could see that the banks of the stream were deserted, and although he had expected as much, the stab through his heart was still crippling. He kept walking, not knowing where else to go, his eyes scanning the peaceful spot, wishing Moira would simply step out from behind a tree, a smile on her face as she flung herself into his arms.

But she did not.

Instead, Cormag's breath lodged in his throat when his eyes dropped to the ground, taking note of the boot prints that led to the water's edge. Here, the ground was soft, free of grass as the children loved to play in this spot, their little hands merciless when it came to the vegetation. From the way the prints were smudged, he suspected that there had been a struggle of some kind, resulting in feet being dragged rather than set down. There were two sets, one fainter than the other: Moira's.

Cormag moved forward, following what he saw until he took note of a large imprint as though someone had lain there. His heart clenched as panic gripped him, and for a long moment, he could do nothing but stare at the spot where Moira had lain.

Had she been hurt? At least, that would mean she was alive, but what if...?

"Cormag!"

Spinning on his heel, Cormag found Garrett and Finn hastening toward him, no doubt alerted to Moira's disappearance by their wives. "Has anyone seen her?" he asked knowing the answer would not satisfy him.

As expected, both men shook their heads, their faces taut as they stepped closer. Their eyes narrowed as they swept the ground the same way Cormag's had only a moment earlier.

"There's been a struggle," Finn stated before his gaze rose to meet Cormag's. "But ye already know that." Again, he turned his eyes to the ground.

"She was dragged," Garrett uttered, his voice distant as his mind worked, "but only up to here." He walked along the water's edge to where a thicket barred his way. "There're broke twigs here."

Cormag gritted his teeth as dark images found him, images that turned his blood to ice and twisted his heart in a way that threatened to rip it from his chest. "Who could've done this?" he whispered, fighting the image that drew near, unwilling to believe that it could be true.

"I dunno," Garrett replied as he turned and walked back to where Cormag still stood. "I canna-" He broke off and looked past Cormag's shoulder.

Turning around, Cormag spotted Maggie, her face pale and her eyes wide, hastening toward them, and in that moment, Cormag knew that what he did not want to believe could be nothing else but the truth.

"I canna find him!" Maggie panted, tears brimming in her eyes as she looked up at him. "Ian," she mumbled, barely glancing at Garrett and Finn, who had hastened over, the tension in them speaking to the shock they felt. "I canna find him. He's gone, and there are horses missing from the stables." She swallowed, and her jaw trembled. "He wouldna...He..." Staring up at him, she shook her head, unable to believe what she knew to be true.

Cormag knew only too well how that felt.

Gritting his teeth, he forced the panic that threatened to consume him back down. If there was any chance for him to find her, to get her back, then he needed to calm down and think. "Where would he take her?" he mumbled, trying to be reasonable, to remember what places Ian favoured, what route he might have taken.

"There's no way to know," Finn muttered, his jaw tight and his eyes pained as he looked at Cormag. "How can we figure out where he took her when I canna even believe he would do such a thing?" He shook his head, shock marking his features. "Ian's a good man. This," he pointed at the scene of the struggle, "is not like him. He would never...He..."

Maggie closed her eyes, burying her face in her hands, and Cormag felt her guilt grab his heart and squeeze until he thought he could no longer breathe.

Stumbling, he took a few steps backward, trying to put some distance between himself and the rest of them as he fought for control.

"The night I returned," Garrett spoke up as he came walking over to him, his green gaze fixed on Cormag's, a hint of speculation in them, "ye were looking for her as well."

Remembering the night Moira had almost slipped from his grasp, Cormag nodded. "Aye."

"Did ye find her?"

Cormag nodded, confused why his friend would ask him this now.

Garrett's gaze narrowed. "How?" he whispered as his hands settled on Cormag's shoulders and his eyes looked deep into his. "Did ye stumble upon her by accident? Or...?" The question hung in the air between them for a moment or two, and then as though lightning had struck him, Cormag understood with perfect clarity what his friend was asking.

Cormag's eyes widened, and his jaw all but dropped as his mind turned inward, remembering not only the night she had tried to leave *Seann Dachaigh* Tower, but also the night she had sought to end her life. He remembered how he had felt Moira's panic, her despair, and how he had rushed up the stairs to the tower's battlements. Somehow, he had known where to find her. Somehow, he had sensed where she was.

We feel the same, he heard Moira's voice.

Aye, he could feel her after all. His gift had not deserted him. Indeed, he felt her stronger than anyone else around him to the point that he had thought he could not feel her at all because the emotions in his chest had been so true that he had thought them his own alone.

But they had not been his. They had been theirs. And only when there was a change, when she felt something he did not, then he could tell them apart.

"Can ye find her now?" Garrett asked, squeezing Cormag's shoulders, no doubt to gain his attention. "Can ye?"

Cormag swallowed, terrified to feel nothing but his own fear for her. "Give me a moment," he whispered then and walked away, his feet guiding him to the spot under the tall oak where he had seen Moira sit countless times, watching the children splash in the stream.

Taking her seat, Cormag closed his eyes and rested his forehead on his bent knees. With his heart, his mind, with everything he was, he reached out to her, praying that the increased distance between them would not bar his gift.

For a long time, all Cormag sensed was a mild echo of his own fears. No matter how determinedly he tried to push them aside, they would not move, remaining where they were, calling forth disappoint-ment as well as an utter sense of failure.

And then a stab of panic surged through his heart, and Cormag knew-*knew!* -beyond the shadow of a doubt that it had been Moira's, not his own.

Gritting his teeth, Cormag pressed his eyelids closed, fighting to shut out the soft murmur of the water nearby, Maggie's heavy breathing as well as the sound of shuffling feet as Garrett and Finn moved about.

And then he felt her.

Her kindness.

Her strength.

Her unyielding will.

Her fear, her panic...and her longing for him.

Overwhelmed by her need for him, Cormag felt tears prick the backs of his eyes. Not since his parents had he ever felt such utter love and devotion, and he could not help the smile that tugged on his lips when her longing echoed within his own heart, matching what he felt.

A jolt went through him in that moment, like a tug on the bond that connected them, and Cormag urged himself to focus. He did not need to know how she felt. Not here and now. What he did need was to figure out where she was.

Allowing the soft tug to guide him, Cormag felt his head turn of its own accord, his thoughts striving unerringly toward her. "West," he mumbled as his eyes flew open and he pushed to his feet.

"What?" Garrett asked, a touch of incredulity in his green gaze as he hastened toward him, Finn not far behind.

"West," Cormag repeated as he met their eyes. "Ian took her west, toward the sea."

Finn frowned. "How can ye know that?"

"Never mind that," Garrett answered, his gaze never leaving Cormag's. "Then we should hurry."

Cormag nodded, feeling his limbs hum with the need to reach her. "Aye, we do."

As they headed back up the small slope, they spotted Maggie standing halfway up toward the village. She was leaning down to speak to Niall, her hands holding his as words flew from his lips, his little face white with concern.

Cormag's gut clenched as he felt a wave of fear reach out toward him. "Something's wrong," he whispered, cursing the timing.

Then Maggie straightened and took in her surroundings.

"Are ye all right?" Finn asked as they drew near; he placed a hand on her slender shoulder, offering comfort.

Turning toward them, Maggie swallowed, her face paler than before, and a sense of resignation clung to her being that Cormag had never seen before. "We canna find Blair," she whispered as tears filled her eyes.

"I've looked everywhere," Niall blurted out, eager to assure them that he had done all he could.

Cormag nodded as a sense of foreboding came over him. Perhaps it was nothing. Perhaps it was simply the fear that lingered in his heart. Perhaps Blair had simply found a way to finally escape her brother's watchful eyes.

But Cormag doubted it. After all, Niall clung like a shadow to his little sister, protective in a way that often threatened to smother the little girl in her thirst for adventure. Could she truly have slipped through his fingers?

"Do ye think...Ian took her?" Finn asked, his jaw tightening at the thought.

Garrett frowned. "Why would he? He's always tried to keep her away from Moira." He shook his head. "Naw, I dunna think her slipping away has anything to do with what Ian did. Perhaps 'tis simply a coincidence."

"We still need to find her," Finn stressed, and Cormag could feel the first stirrings of fatherly protectiveness sneak into his friend's heart. "We canna be certain that she will return on her own. Perhaps she wandered off too far and fell, hurt her ankle or something of the sort." He glanced from one to the next. "We should look for her."

"I agree," Cormag replied, noting the relief that found Maggie's heart at his words. "We'll find her." As well as Moira.

"Thank ye," Maggie mumbled, guilt clinging to her blue eyes. "What can I do?"

Cormag tried his utmost to focus his mind as fear threatened to urge him to act without thought. "Finn, ye'll gather some men and search the area." After his friend nodded in affirmation, he turned to look at Maggie and Niall. "Tell them where she likes to go, what places she favours, anywhere ye think she might have gone."

Maggie's and Niall's heads bobbed up and down, and then they hurried to fall into step with Finn as they returned to the castle, eager words flying from their lips. Cormag could only hope that no harm would come to the little girl.

Then he turned to Garrett. "I'll go after Moira. She-"

"Not without me," his friend stated, his voice brooking no argument.

A small smile teased Cormag's lips. "Thank ye. I might need the help." Garrett gave a short nod, and then they were rushing toward the castle as well, their feet carrying them toward the stables, and Cormag realised that Garrett had not asked him how he knew where to go.

He had not pressed for answers, and Cormag wondered how long his friend had been suspecting that there was something not quite *normal* about him.

Chapter Thirty-Eight

WRONG ALL THE SAME

T he first thing Moira noticed when the world slowly came
back into focus was that it was unsteady, swaying like a ship
tossed about by waves and...upside down.

Her stomach rolled, and nausea washed over her, making her groan
in agony.

"I see ye're awake."

At the grating sound of Ian's voice, Moira froze and within seconds
the events that had placed her in this precarious situation came
rushing back. Her dream. The letter to Deidre. The moonlit night.
Ian's hands around her throat.

Swallowing, Moira winced at the pain in her throat. Her mouth was
dry, and her head throbbed, which was not in the least bit surprising
considering that she was tied across a horse's back, her legs and upper
body dangling on either side of the large beast.

"Please, I need to sit up or I'll be sick." The blood rushed in her
ears, and for a moment, Moira feared she had pass out again. "Please, I
swear I willna run. Please!"

Her mount took another step or two before it stopped. She heard
Ian slide out of the saddle and to the ground, his footsteps soft as he
moved through the tall-stemmed grass. A moment later, his shadow fell

over her, and she flinched at the sensation of having him so close, looming over her.

"I'll cut yer throat if ye try," he snarled not far from her ear, sending a cold shiver down her back. And then his hands tugged on the rope, brushing against her skin as he undid the knot that kept her strapped to the saddle.

When the rope finally fell away, Moira slid off the saddle like a sack of grain, her legs unable to catch her as she crashed to the ground. Her limbs felt weak, and her skin burnt where the rope had cut deep into her flesh.

"Up!" Ian hollered as he stepped around the horse, his hands reaching for her. They closed around her wrists like iron shackles before he yanked her to her feet, his snarl now only a hair's breadth away from her face. "Ye will do as I say, or I swear I'll tie ye back down, do ye hear?"

Gritting her teeth, Moira nodded as she felt her body leaning away from him, from the hatred in his eyes and the burning anger in his touch.

Ian's eyes narrowed as he watched her. "Ye should never have come to *Seann Dachaigh* Tower," he hissed as he pulled her back toward her horse. "I canna fathom why yer laird left ye alive after what ye did." For a second, it seemed as though he would toss her up onto the horse, but then he spun around, shoving his face back into hers. "Did ye bewitch him as well?" he demanded, and his right hand gripped a fistful of her hair, yanking it back.

Moira sucked in a sharp breath as tears began to pool in her eyes. "No matter what ye choose to believe," she gasped, fighting to keep her wits about her at the sight of the threat that loomed over her, "I have no such power, and I never did."

Ian scoffed in disbelief. Then he released her hair and grabbed her around the waist, thrusting her back into the saddle, this time in an upright position.

Moira's legs tightened around the horse to keep herself from sliding off again as Ian once more reached for her hands, tying them to one another and then to the saddle. His movements were rough and intentionally harsh, his anger urging him to lash out at her, to hurt her as he believed she had hurt him.

Remaining still, Moira gritted her teeth against the pain and fear that rolled through her as she watched him pull tight the last knot. Then he grasped her reins and walked over to his own mount, pulling himself back into the saddle.

As they continued onward, Moira glanced around. However, her surroundings did not look familiar, and she could not even spot *Seann Dachaigh* Tower as a tiny dot on the horizon. How long had they been riding? She wondered, glancing up at the sky where the sun stood high above her. "Noon," she mumbled, but instantly lowered her head when Ian glared at her over his shoulder.

Hours had passed since she had left the safety of her bedchamber and walked down to the stream. Cormag would be up by now. He must know that she was missing.

Moira cringed at the thought of what he must be feeling. No doubt he was frantic with fear, with concern for her, and the thought that there was someone in the world who loved her with such ardour warmed Moira's heart.

At least for a short second.

Then guilt swept away the warmth, and for a desperate moment, Moira wished she had never come to *Seann Dachaigh* Tower. If she had not, Cormag would not have lost his heart to her, and he would not have had to suffer the agony of losing his other half. For that was how he felt. Moira knew it beyond the shadow of a doubt for it echoed within her own heart.

After finding the one man whom she truly loved, the one man who completed her in every way, she would now lose him after only so short a time. It had not been enough, not nearly enough time, and Moira knew if she were to die now, today, she would feel nothing short of deepest regret.

"Where are ye taking me?" Moira asked, knowing that the truth could not be worse than the fears that slowly built within her chest.

Glancing at her through narrowed eyes, Ian pushed onward. "Ye'll see soon enough."

"But I wish to know now."

At the sound of her voice, steady and demanding, Ian brought his mount to a halt. His gaze met hers, hard and threatening, as he pulled on her horse's reins, urging the animal closer to his own. "What ye wish is of no concern to me," he hissed, his nose barely an inch from hers, "and ye'd be wise not to test me."

Moira swallowed, fighting down the urge to drop her gaze. "No matter what I do, ye'll not let me go, will ye?"

Sitting back, Ian looked at her, his eyes narrowing in thought. "Have ye seen that?" he asked, a touch of honest curiosity in his voice. "Have ye seen what will happen to ye?" Then confusion drew down his brows. "But if ye did, why were ye fool enough to venture outside...alone?"

"I didna see anything," Moira told him, knowing that lies would only make her situation worse...if that was even possible. "Aye, I had a dream last night, but not about me or about ye. About a friend." She swallowed. "And it pained me to see something dark looming in her future. I needed some air, and so I went outside." She sighed, "I didna know ye'd..."

A moment passed as they continued to look at one another. Then Ian gave a short nod, and Moira knew that he believed her. It was but a small victory, but it was nonetheless a step in the right direction. Perhaps, there was a way to reason with him after all.

Their journey led them westward across Scotland's green hills as they wound their way through the countryside and closer to the sea. The touch of salt lingering in the air intensified, and Moira felt reminded of her old home, of Greystone Castle, and the family she had left behind.

"Why are ye doing this?" she asked after an hour of silence, an hour of considering her options, an hour of realising that none looked promising.

"To protect my clan, my people," Ian scoffed. "The exact opposite of what ye've done, of what ye're doing still."

Moira sighed, cursing herself for her failure of judgement that had led to her banishment. Could she truly fault Ian for believing the worst of her? "I regret what I've done," Moira whispered more to herself than him. "I never meant to harm anyone, least of all Connor, but at the time I...I was convinced I was serving my people, my clan." She looked up and found his blue eyes fixed on hers. "The same *ye* feel right now."

Ian's gaze hardened as her words sank in.

"I too believed I was doing the right thing," Moira pressed on. "I looked at Connor's English bride, and I knew, *I knew*, that she would bring harm to our people. I couldna believe it when everyone else remained blind to the threat she posed. I couldna believe that no one saw what I saw." Sighing, Moira closed her eyes, feeling the soft swaying of her mount as it picked its way across the land. "I felt compelled to act. I thought I was my people's last hope. I thought once I'd revealed her to be a thorn in our midst, they'd be grateful, they'd be relieved that I'd protected them when they had not been able to do so themselves." She met his eyes once more, surprised that he had remained silent all this time. "I believed that with every fibre of my being. I believed that I was right to do as I did. As ye do now."

Ian swallowed, and she could see the muscles in his jaw clench.

"Ye canna deny that I'm right," Moira said gently. "Ye feel the same as I did then, and ye're as wrong now as I was then."

Anger darkened Ian's face. "Dunna pretend that we're the same," he hissed, his tone rough and threatening; still, Moira detected a touch of defensiveness in his voice and knew that a small part of him now had doubt, fearing that her words might be true. "I would never act against my laird. I-"

"Ye're stealing his wife!" Moira exclaimed. "As I acted against Henrietta. I never meant for Connor to be in danger. I only ever meant to frighten his wife away. Everything else that happened, 'tis was Angus' doing. He betrayed me. He used me." Moira drew in a deep breath as all the emotions of her past came rushing back. "And I let him. I did not see his intentions because I did not want to see them." She shook her head as tears streamed down her face. "And it cost me dearly."

"Ye're wrong," Ian hissed. "Ye didna pay for what ye did. Ye came here and started over. A new life while the lives of others lay shattered at their feet."

"I know I didna deserve it," Moira admitted, "but I-"

"Ye came here and ye spread yer lies, yer evil tongue whispering in

the ears of my people, turning their hearts toward ye and away from..."
He swallowed, and for a split second, heart-breaking loss rested in his
blue eyes.

"'Tis Maggie, isn't it?" Moira asked, knowing that there was no way
around it for it clearly lay at the root of Ian's hatred of her. "Ye blame
me because she canna love ye."

"She did!" he snarled; his face now contorted with something that
sent cold, dark fear into Moira's heart. "She did love me until the day
ye came! Ye turned her against me! Ye bewitched her! 'Twas yer doing,
and ye're going to pay for it!"

Moira swallowed. "What will ye do to me?" she whispered, afraid to
hear the answer, but equally afraid to remain in the dark. "If ye wanted
to kill me, why didn't ye do so then? Ye had yer hands around my neck,
why didn't ye kill me then?"

A dark sneer came to Ian's face. "Because a witch canna be killed
like that," he all but whispered. "A witch must be drowned."

Panic gripped Moira at his words, and for long moments, she did
little else but stare at the back of his head as he urged their horses
onward.

Toward the sea.

Far away from *Seann Dachaigh* Tower.

Far away from anyone who might come to her aid.

Far away.

With his eyes to the ground, Cormag surged across the land, panic
urging him on, urging him to hurry. His mount's hoof beats thundered
in his ears as his gaze moved from the ground to the horizon and back
again. He felt a sudden tug on his heart, a flare of panic as though
something had changed, as though Moira had just...

Cormag gritted his teeth, afraid to trust his own heart, afraid that
it might lead him astray, that he would not be able to tell the difference
between her and himself.

That he would not find her.

Not in time.

And so, when he and Garrett came across two sets of hoof prints, Cormag decided to rely on his tracking skills rather than trust in the gift bestowed upon him by the Old Ones.

Still, time was of the essence, and so they pressed their horses, only pulling to a stop now and then to ensure they had not lost their tracks.

"Wait!" Garrett called, reining in his horse and jumping out of the saddle.

Staring at his friend, Cormag did the same, urging his mount back to where Garrett was now crouched in the soft grass. "What is it? What d'ye find?" He too jumped to the ground, his feet carrying him to his friend's side.

"Look," Garrett urged, his finger pointing at one hoof print overlapping another.

Cormag frowned. "Aye, 'tis proof of two horses."

Garrett shook his head as he rose and pointed down the way they had come. "For the most part, the prints have been side by side. Aye, overlapping here and there, but never for long." Again, he turned to the prints before them. "Now, look here. These seem to be overlapping continuously, sometimes on the left and sometimes more on the right as though-"

"Another rider?" Cormag exclaimed, confusion marking his face as he stared at the evidence before him.

Garrett nodded. "So 'twould seem. But who could it be? And why?"

"I dunna know," Cormag whispered, wishing he possessed Moira's gift, wishing he could see where she was and how to save her. "But it doesna matter. We canna linger here." Striding back to his horse, he pulled himself into the saddle. "Whoever it is, we need to continue on and see what we're dealing with when we get there." Hopefully, it would not be too late.

"I agree," Garrett said as he pulled up alongside Cormag. "I only sought to bring it to yer attention. We need to be watchful," he continued, voice imploring, "if we rush into this without thought, we willna be of any help to her."

Hearing his friend's words of caution, Cormag nodded, grateful that at least one of them was able to think clearly. "Aye, ye're right. Thank ye."

Without another word, they continued their journey, praying that somehow, they would catch up. However, Ian had half-a-day's head-start. What were their chances?

Chapter Thirty-Nine

DEEPER THAN BLOOD AND CLAN

"What are we doing here?" Moira asked as Ian pulled her out of the saddle and shoved her toward a thick pine tree. His hands were rough as he undid the knot that kept her hands together. Then he pushed her onto the ground, her back to the trunk and pulled her arms behind her, tying the rope around the tree.

Moira gritted her teeth at having her arms bent backwards in this fashion, her shoulders aching from the strain. Her breath came fast as fear settled deeper into her bones, and she knew that whatever Ian had planned for her was not far off.

Swallowing, she looked across the small level area around her to the spot where the land fell away in a steep drop. She could hear waves crash below and saw sea gulls circle overhead. The smell of the sea, clean and salty and invigorating, tickled her nose as her gaze swept over the rocky cliffs rising and falling to the right and left of this small plateau where Ian had pulled to a stop. Even settled under the pine, the wind tugged on her hair and brushed with chilling fingers across her cheeks, whispering of her impending end.

Would he simply push her over the edge? Moira wondered as fresh tears pooled in her eyes. But then why had he not simply done so? Why was he tying her to a tree?

Rising to his feet, Ian stood back and surveyed his handiwork. Satisfied that the bonds would hold, he turned back to their horses, hitching their reins to low-hanging branches. Then he turned toward the rocky cliffs, his gaze travelling over the large boulders as though searching for something.

"What are we doing here?" Moira demanded once again, fear now turning into anger that he would simply ignore her, that he would not even grant her the mercy of an answer. "Tell me!"

His ice-cold eyes settled on hers; his lips curled into a hateful snarl. "How does it feel not to know?" he asked in a quiet voice; still, it vibrated with the same hostility she had sensed in him from the beginning. "Stripped of yer power, ye're like the rest of us. 'Tis about time ye found out what it is to be vulnerable."

Closing her eyes, Moira laughed at the absurdity of his words. "As little as I know about ye, ye know even less about me." She swallowed. "I know well what it is to be vulnerable, to feel tossed about like a piece of driftwood on the high seas. Ye may not believe me, but my life hasna been easy either or free of heartbreak and sorrow. Aye, I suppose I deserved what came to me, but that doesna mean it was any less crippling."

Shaking his head, Ian stared at her, a dumbfounded expression on his face. "What came to ye? Nothing came to ye! Ye simply went on yer merry way and started over. Ye-"

"I lost my family!" Moira yelled, feeling her jaw begin to quiver. "I lost my home. I lost everyone I've ever loved. My brother won't look at me, and I...I can't even blame him." Tears now streamed down her face, and Moira wished she could brush them away. "I've thought about ending my life more than once, not out of guilt, but because I couldna bear it any longer."

"Ye lie!" Ian snarled, his blue eyes pale as he watched her. "'Tis a trick to twist my mind into believing something that isna true."

"The night of my aunt's wedding," Moira pressed on, her teeth chattering painfully against one another, "I...I almost jumped off the battlements of the eastern tower."

Ian's gaze widened for a split second before it once more narrowed in suspicion. "Ye lie," he said again, only this time there was less force behind his words.

Moira shook her head. "Ask Cormag. He was the one to find me. He pulled me away from the ledge and saved my life."

Ian's jaw clenched, and the deep, dark cold returned to his gaze. "He shouldna have done so."

"Perhaps," Moira whispered, wondering if Cormag had loved her even then. If she died today, she would never now. "But he did nonetheless." For a long moment, Moira looked at Ian and allowed him to see her, frightened and vulnerable, hoping that a part of him still knew the meaning of compassion.

A gust of air rushed from Ian's lungs when he turned away abruptly as though no longer able to bear her eyes on him. "I'll be back shortly," he hissed; nevertheless, the words did not sting as they had before. Perhaps a part of him had finally come to see her as human, a person with flaws and fears...just like him.

Resting her head against the rough bark of the pine, Moira watched him walk away, his steps measured and his gaze scanning the ground. Now and then, he stopped, his hands running over the rock here and there, pulling and pushing as though trying to see if a boulder would come loose.

The moment he vanished from her sight, picking his way higher up the jutting rocks, Moira finally realised what he was doing, and her heart froze in sheer terror.

Indeed, he did not simply plan to throw her over the edge. Moira did not know what the bottom of the cliff looked like. Perhaps the sea was deep there, not punctuated by deadly boulders. And if that was the case, what if he pushed her in and she were to survive the fall? What if she managed to swim to safety?

It would seem Ian did not dare risk that.

Closing her eyes, Moira could not help but picture herself dropping into the sea, the water closing above her as the heavy boulder tied to her feet pulled her down. Again, she felt the air forced from her lungs, her body straining to breathe, but unable to do so. What would it feel like to drown? To know that there was no way to return to the surface?

Moira's body began to shake uncontrollably at the thought, and she wished with every fibre of her being that she could hug her arms around her legs and sink into herself, drawing on what little comfort she could muster.

But it was impossible. With her hands tied behind the tree, she felt exposed and vulnerable, unable to protect herself, and the panic that lingered in her blood began to spread, seeping into every cell, chilling her bones and lodging the breath in her throat.

"Moira."

At the sound of her name, Moira jerked forward as far as her binds would allow her. Her eyes widened, and she stared straight ahead, unable to look away from the steep drop in front of her as her muscles tensed, and her heart threatened to jump from her chest.

The sound had been faint, soft like a whisper carried to her on the wings of the wind. Not truly there, but only something her mind had conjured, reaching for something to hold onto, something to give her comfort.

Moira's heart sank, and she slumped back down against the tree.

The sound of footsteps, soft and almost weightless, carried to her ear, and even though Moira could not turn her head far enough to see, she suddenly knew that she was no longer alone. Was it Ian? Had he rounded the site and was now returning from the east?

A whinny echoed over from the same direction, and Moira stared at the two horses tied to the branch not far from her. They were both grazing, but their ears flicked at the call of one of their own.

"Cormag," Moira whispered, wishing with all her heart that it would be him. Still, her mind insistently pointed out that something was not adding up. If it had been Cormag, he-

"'Tis me," came the soft-spoken voice again, and Moira's head snapped sideways in time to see little Blair step forward from behind the tree, leading a pony by its reins. Her deep blue eyes shone warm and caring as they met Moira's, and the smile that came to her little face could have melted ice. The wind tugged on her blond tresses and painted a rosy glow onto her cheeks as she dropped the reins and knelt in front of Moira.

"Blair." Feeling as though she had strayed into a dream, Moira stared at the little girl, unable to make sense of what she saw. "It canna be true."

A smile tickled Blair's lip. "Aye, 'tis true." Then her gaze drifted to the bonds that held Moira captive. She moved, her eyes shifting sideways, and Moira felt her little hands brush against her own as she inspected the knots. "I canna open these. We need a knife." Then she pushed to her feet and strolled over to her father's horse.

Still staring, Moira fought to find her voice. "What...?" she croaked as Blair stepped into the stirrup, pulled herself up and then standing on one leg, rummaged through the saddlebag. A moment later, she had obviously found what she had been looking for because she slid back down to the ground and headed back toward Moira. A small dagger rested in her hand, and she pulled off the sheath as she once again knelt next to the pine.

"What are ye doing here?" Moira finally managed as the sound of the knife sawing through her bonds drifted to her ears. Could this be truly happening? Had little Blair truly come to her aid? A girl of not even five years?

The thought was preposterous! This had to be a hallucination of some kind!

And then the bonds fell away, and Moira's hands dropped forward, her wrists aching with the sudden relief. Rubbing them, Moira scooted away from the trunk and turned to look at the little girl, who slid the blade back into the sheath with an ease that belied her years. "What are ye doing here? How did ye find me?"

Blair swallowed, and for a moment, she looked as young as she was. "I came to save my father."

"Yer father?" Moira repeated, unable to make sense of the girl's simple statement. "But...but why? Save him from what?" The thought was quite ludicrous considering that Ian was the one threatening *her* life and not the other way around.

"I saw him in danger," Blair whispered, her blue eyes wide with fear now. "I need to help him."

"Ye need to help him," Moira repeated yet again, her mind numb and sluggish, momentarily unable to process what she had heard. But then a single word stood out from all the others, and her mind pounced on it like a wildcat. "Ye saw?" she demanded, reaching for the girl and grabbing her by the shoulders. "Ye saw?"

Blair nodded. "Aye, in my dreams."

Moira's eyes closed when the last piece of the puzzle fell into place. Her heart skipped a beat before she found the strength to look at Blair once more.

And in that moment, Moira saw herself.

A spark of recognition flared, and the kinship she had always felt toward Blair suddenly made sense. Always had the girl sought her out, her wide blue eyes looking at her as though searching for something. Always had Blair seemed to understand the past Moira had never shared with her. Always had the girl been on her side.

Always.

Now, Moira understood why. They were the same, connected by something that went deeper than blood and clan. "What did ye see?" Moira whispered, remembering how overwhelming her dreams had been when she had been a child. They had loomed over her like a monster in the dark, and her child's mind had looked at them with different eyes, seeing things in a simpler light.

"I saw a shadow," Blair whispered as a shiver gripped her body, and she clung tighter to Moira. "It walks behind him, but when he turns, Father doesna see. He's blind." Her little hands dug into Moira's arms. "He doesna see 'tis coming for him."

Confused by the cryptic nature of Blair's dream, Moira pulled the girl tighter into her arms, trying to soothe the fear that lingered in her blue gaze. "Hush, hush, little one. All will be well." Her attention drifted back to the cliff where Ian had vanished among the rocks, reminding herself that he would not remain gone forever. Or had something happened to him already? Was that what Blair had seen? Had he...fallen? Or...?

"I'm sorry he took ye," Blair mumbled before she lifted her head to Moira's face. "I didna know he would. I would've told him not to."

A warm smile came to Moira's face, and she brushed a grateful hand over the girl's head. "Thank ye. Ye're a good friend. But how did ye know where to find us? Did ye see it in yer dreams as well?"

Blair shook her head. "Naw, I was up when Father left last night. I was afraid the shadow would come for him and so I followed." She sighed, her eyes becoming distant as she drew forth her memories. "I lost him near the stream and then saw him again when he headed back to the stables. When I saw what he was doing, I had to hurry. I almost didn't catch up, but then I found yer tracks...and followed them." She blinked, a proud smile tugging on her lips. "Niall taught me how."

Moira hugged Blair close as her mind spun. "I'm proud of ye," she whispered, grateful for Blair's interference, but concerned with what to do now.

Her own survival instincts urged her to get on the horse and put as much distance between her and the man who wished her dead. However, Blair would not leave her father, and Moira knew she could not leave the girl out here on her own.

After all, she did not know if something had happened to Ian or not. What could that shadow be that Blair had seen? Was someone else out here? Someone who wished to harm Ian? But for what reason?

Moira's head spun as she pondered what to do. Perhaps she could-

"Ye witch!"

The words cut through the stillness and resonated within Moira as though she had suffered a blow to the stomach. Spinning around, Blair still in her arms, her eyes found Ian standing high up on the cliff above them, a snarl on his face and a darkness in his eyes that knew no bounds.

"I'll kill ye for this!"

"The shadow," Blair whispered as her hands clenched, her fingers digging into her palms.

And in that moment, Moira understood.

A sea gull swooped over the land, and Cormag squinted his eyes, trying to see the horizon where land met sky. Wind whipped across the plain, and he thought to hear the faint echo of waves crashing against timeless rock, which jutted out higher as the hills rose and the country sloped upward. Trees grew denser, blocking their view, and the ground hardened as they approached the western end of Scotland.

"We're getting close," Garrett called over the thundering echo of their horses' hooves as they pushed them onward without mercy. Then his gaze swept back to the ground, narrowing as he tried to peer at the tracks they had been following for the better part of the day.

Seeing the frown on Garrett's face, Cormag signalled to his friend and then reined in his horse, knowing that speed meant nothing if they were heading in the wrong direction. Reluctantly, he slid from the saddle and surveyed the ground. "Anything?"

Garrett shook his head. "The ground is too dry here," he mumbled, continuing his search. Then he sighed and straightened, his gaze coming to rest on Cormag. "Where is she?"

Cormag inhaled a deep breath, knowing exactly what his friend was asking. It was this moment Cormag had feared ever since they had set out. The moment when everything tangible was ripped from his grasp, and he had to rely on his gift alone.

Instantly, doubt pushed to the front, whispering of the consequences of failure, whispering that if he made a wrong choice, Moira would suffer for it.

"Ye can do this," Garrett counselled, his voice calm as he stood in front of Cormag. "I know 'tis not easy with what's at stake, but ye've done it before. Ye can do it again."

Cormag nodded and then turned away, resting his forehead against his horse's neck. He breathed in slowly, trying to slow the erratic beating of his heart. He reminded himself that he had always sensed her...even before he had known her.

Days before Moira had first arrived at *Seann Dachaigh* Tower, Cormag had felt a shift in his heart. It had confused him then, that deep sense of expectation that had grown stronger with each step she had taken toward his home, toward him. Day by day, his awareness of her had increased. He had known that she was coming without ever knowing who she was and what she would come to mean to him.

And then she had stepped into his study, and all had become clear with a single look into her blue, bottomless eyes.

Moira had truly turned his world upside down.

Pride surged through his chest, and a smile danced over his lips before he froze, realising that the pride he had felt had not been his own.

But hers.

Cormag's head snapped up and he turned and stared in the direction he suddenly knew her to be.

Garrett chuckled behind him. "I always knew ye were hiding something, but I never would've thought it was something like this." He stepped forward and clasped a hand on Cormag's shoulder. "Ye know where she is, d'ye not?"

"Aye," Cormag confirmed before he pulled himself back into the saddle. "Something odd is happening though." He frowned, wondering about the sense of pride he had felt from her. It was something he would not have expected under the circumstances. "I dunna know what to make of it."

But he would know soon.

They were getting closer.

Chapter Forty

THE SHADOW

"**I** told ye to stay away from her!" Ian hissed, his hands balled into fists at his sides, his body trembling with barely controlled rage. He stood on the edge of a precipice that loomed high above them, his blue eyes staring down at where Moira huddled with Blair in her arms. "Get away from her! Why is she here? How did ye call for her?"

Moira swallowed, her throat dry as she searched for words to explain, to pacify Ian, to get out of this alive. But there were none. Ian was lost in his rage. He did not even fully acknowledge his daughter's presence. Although his gaze swept over her now and then, it never lingered as though he feared that his concern for Blair might lessen the strength of his anger.

And anger was all he had left.

Moira knew that now. It was not hatred that drove him, but desperation, hopelessness. That, she understood.

"Dunna be angry, Father," Blair called as she left the safety of Moira's embrace, her little feet carrying her closer to the steep rock. She craned her neck upward, and Moira prayed with every fibre of her being that Blair would find a way to reach her father's heart.

The snarl on Ian's face lessened when his gaze dropped and fell on his precious child. A warm glow came to his eyes as he looked at her, and yet, there was a deep fear lingering there as well. "Step away, Blair," he said gently, but with urgency in his voice. "Dunna get too close to her."

"She's not a witch," Blair told him before she cast a gentle look over her shoulder at Moira. "She made a mistake, but she's not bad. I promise. Ye dunna need to be afraid."

Ian's jaw clenched as he listened to his daughter defend the woman he saw as the root of all his troubles. "Ye bewitched her as well," he hissed, his gaze hardening as it left Blair's.

Moira's heart sank. It did not matter what anyone said for Ian had made up his mind, and it seemed there was no changing it.

With his body still tense, Ian's movements were jarred and seemed somewhat uncontrolled as he made his way down the cliff toward them. He stepped from rock to rock, choosing those that jutted out from the wall of granite, his hands holding tightly to smaller ledges.

"Careful, Father!" Blair called to him, wringing her little hands in agitation.

Glancing over his shoulder, Ian almost lost his footing.

Torn, Moira stepped forward and placed a gentle hand on Blair's shoulder. "Hush, little one. Dunna distract him or he'll fall."

"But he needs to know," Blair said, turning fearful eyes to Moira. "He needs to know about the shadow."

Before Moira could answer the girl, Ian's voice lashed out like a whip. "What shadow? What is she talking about? What did ye do to her?" His hands clung to the ledge, tightening with each word he spoke, the sinews standing out white as anger gripped him anew.

"I saw it," Blair rushed to explain, her little feet carrying her toward him again. "I saw it in my dreams. It walks behind ye. It wants to hurt ye, Father."

Ian froze, and Moira felt her heart speed up as the blood seemed to drain from his face, his skin turning a ghastly white. His fingers seemed to slacken, and all tension left his body.

For a second, Moira thought he might drop like a stone.

Then his gaze cleared and swung to meet hers, and what she saw there broke Moira's heart for it was utter and sheer betrayal. In his eyes, she had not only stolen his wife's love but now also corrupted his daughter, turning her into an image of herself and against him.

Pain and loss darkened his gaze, and for a short moment, his eyes closed as though he no longer had the strength to keep going.

The shadow Blair had seen.

It was not a person, but the hatred and disappointment that rested in Ian's chest, changing him a little bit every day, altering him, turning the cheerful and kind man he had once been into a snarling monster.

"Father, please, be careful," Blair implored, and her little hands rose as though to reach for him.

Moira knew not what to do. Her heart was torn between self-preservation and the compassion she felt at the sight of Ian's pain. Pain she understood and knew only too well. Perhaps she could try-

A soft rustling in the bushes opposite them drew her attention, and Moira's gaze narrowed as she took a step to the side, trying to see over them. Had it merely been the wind? She wondered, doubting it the moment she felt the little hairs in the back of her neck rise, sending a shiver down her spine.

An agitated snort came from one of their horses, still tied to one of the low-hanging branches, and both lifted their heads, their eyes slightly widened and their ears flicking nervously.

Moira felt herself tense as she watched, saw their hooves dance back and forth, agitation clearly visible in the way they moved, stretching the reins as though wishing to get away.

Away from what?

Glancing at Blair, she saw the little girl watch her father as he stood up on the ledge, carefully picking his way down. His eyes remained downcast, and Moira feared that Ian would never again look at Blair with the same love and devotion he always had until today. Would Blair's gift sever their bond forever?

A low snarl drifted to Moira's ears, and her head whipped around again, her eyes once more focused on the bushes not far from where Blair stood, her little hands clasped tightly around one another.

As though in answer, the horses began to prance nervously, their ears almost flattened to their heads. One tried to rear up but was hindered by the short rein.

Moira's skin tingled with awareness as she surveyed the area before her, blind to what hid not far from them. Was someone lurking in the bushes? No, not some*one*.

Some*thing*.

The breath caught in her throat as Moira once more turned to look at their horses and saw fear in their eyes. Clearly, their senses had picked up on something that people often overlooked, and they reacted to it on instinct alone.

Something was very wrong.

The thought had barely formed in her mind before a grey blur shot forward, tearing a shriek from Blair's lips as it landed not far from her, its fangs bared and a low growl emanating from its throat.

A wolf!

The shock almost flung Moira backwards. Her eyes went wide as she stared at the snarling animal, its fur dull and scraggly and its ribs visible through its pelt. It was thin, mal-nourished, starving, and it looked at Blair and saw easy prey.

For a moment, Moira thought she was dreaming, truly dreaming, for there had not been a wolf sighting in decades. Their kind had been slowly hunted to extinction and was now only whispered about in stories of old.

"Blair!" Ian yelled, fear changing his voice as he stared at his daughter and the growling animal slowly advancing on her. The horses neighed in panic, trying to break their bonds again and again until one of the branches snapped under the strain.

The freed horse instantly bolted, its thundering hoof beats echoing across the plain.

Shaken from her trance, Moira tried her utmost to remain as still as possible, her gaze sweeping over her surroundings. She needed a weapon. Anything to ward off the wolf.

Dimly, she remembered that Blair had taken a knife from her father's saddle bags, but where it had ended up was anyone's guess. It probably lay hidden in the dirt somewhere. A rock, perhaps? Or a branch?

Seeing the animal's sharp fangs, Moira thought a branch might be the better option and so when she saw Ian lunge himself from the ledge, aiming for the space in-between Blair and the wolf, Moira moved quickly. She reached for one of the lower-hanging branches, one that looked dry and brittle, and put all her weight on it.

Moira heard a groan slip from Ian's lips, and holding onto the branch, which slowly bent under her weight, she turned to see that he had hit the ground hard, the momentum propelling him sideways...and he hit his head on a large bolder sticking out of the ground.

For a moment, his limbs went slack, and Moira feared that he had lost consciousness.

Blair shrieked. "Father!" She surged toward him, but then stopped when the animal growled, snapping its jaws at her.

"Blair, stay back!" Moira yelled before the branch suddenly surrendered and she fell onto the ground. Her hands burnt from the effort and the scrape of the rough bark, but none of that mattered.

Out of the corner of her eye, she saw Ian stir. His eyes opened, and his head turned toward his daughter. "Blair." It was no more than a whisper, feeble and without strength.

Pushing herself up, Moira gripped the thick branch and crossed the small area in quick strides, holding the branch like a sword in front of her. Ian tried to push himself up, but he could not keep his legs under him. Blood stained the hard ground and the boulder that had broken his fall.

Moira knew that she was on her own.

As though the wolf sensed a threat approaching, it gave another menacing snarl and then lunged itself at Blair. The girl shrieked, and Moira surged forward, lifting the branch and swinging it over her shoulder. It struck the wolf in the face, pulling short its lunge, and dropped it onto the ground.

The animal yelped, but desperation and the instinct to survive had it back on its paws in no time.

"Stay behind me, Blair!" Moira shouted at the child, who cowered on the ground, her eyes wide with fear as she looked from Moira to the wolf and then to her father.

Again, Ian was trying to push himself to his feet, a hand pressed to his head, and again, he fell back down.

The wolf snarled, pawing the ground, and Moira knew it was only a matter of time before it would attack again. She gripped the branch with both hands and kept her eyes fixed on the animal.

Suddenly, it sprung.

It shot forward with surprising speed, and although she whacked it with her branch, yet again, it did not stay down long. Again, it came at her, and this time, Moira barely managed to bring the branch up, so the animal's teeth sunk into the brittle wood and not into her flesh.

The attack threw her backwards, and the animal's weight pushed her into the ground as its jaws tightened on the branch, the only barrier between them. A growl tore from its throat as it shook its head, trying to move the branch out of the way.

But Moira held on tight, knowing that without it, she would be utterly defenceless.

Still, how long would she be able to keep the wolf at bay?

Not long was the terrifying answer as she felt her arms begin to tremble with the effort. The animal's claws scratched her arms and dug into her legs, and she felt warm blood flow down her skin. With nowhere else to turn, she looked at Blair then, the girl's blue eyes wide as she looked up at Moira.

And then Ian staggered to his feet, unsteady and swaying, but he remained upright. He stumbled to his daughter's side and drew her into his arms.

For a moment, Moira thought they would both crash to the ground, but Ian managed to keep his feet under him.

Step by step, he moved forward, away from Moira and the wolf and toward the remaining horse. It was still prancing nervously, but Ian's presence seemed to calm it. He grasped the reins and drew it forward, lifting Blair into the saddle.

Averting her gaze, unable to watch them ride away and leave her behind, Moira fought the hopelessness that engulfed her as she found herself alone, abandoned. Without even lifting a finger, Ian had found a way to rid himself of her, and Moira knew she was done for.

Once more, she looked up at the snarling beast, its jaws slowly closing in on her throat. Soon, it would rip her to pieces, but at least Blair was safe. Ian would see to it. After all, there was no one in this world he loved more than his daughter.

If only Moira could have seen Cormag one last time.

Her eyes closed once more, and regret filled her heart.

Chapter Forty-One

LIGHT & DARK

Mmore and more sea gulls screeched nearby as Cormag and
Garrett drew nearer to the water's edge. A large outcrop
rose into the sky some distance ahead of them as they
made their way through a shallow dip in the land, the tall grass swaying
in the strong breeze.

As they crested the next hill, their eyes fell on a grazing pony. "'Tis
carrying a bridle," Garrett exclaimed, confusion clinging to his voice,
as they urged their mounts closer.

Lifting its head, the pony neighed as though in greeting and then
once more returned its attention to the lush grass at its feet.

"'Tis one of ours," Cormag said, allowing his gaze to sweep their
surroundings. "How did it get here? It couldna have carried Moira."

"The third rider!" Shaking his head, Garrett leant forward and
peered at the animal's hooves. "The third prints were smaller, but I
didna think of a pony."

"Still, that doesna explain what it's doing here."

A piercing shriek cut through the air, and Cormag's blood froze in
his veins.

"What was that?" Garrett exclaimed as he tried to calm his
prancing mount. "*Who* was that? Did that not sound like-?"

"Blair," Cormag finished for him before they pulled their mounts around and urged them in the direction from which the scream had come. "What on earth is she doing here?" Cormag mumbled as he flattened himself to his gelding's back, urging it to go faster still.

With thundering hooves, they flew across the land as the strong breeze tore at their clothes and whipped their hair into their faces. To shield his eyes from the sting of the harsh gust, Cormag squinted into the wind, his body tense with the need to know.

To reach his destination.

To act, to help, to be there.

Something moved on the horizon, and Cormag squinted his eyes further. "Another rider?" he yelled, pointing ahead of him.

The horse stormed toward them, and as it drew closer, Cormag realised that it was riderless as well. Its eyes were wide, and the way it moved spoke of flight.

"Something spooked it," Garrett echoed Cormag's thoughts. "What d'ye think-?"

"There's no time!" Not pausing, Cormag pushed onward, his thoughts scrambling to make sense of everything he had seen but coming up empty. How on earth had Blair ended up here? Why was she screaming? What was Ian doing to Moira?

Fear once more gripped his heart, more acute this time, and as though on cue, another scream cut through the peaceful stillness around him. Cormag flinched, and his mount slowed, but he quickly urged it back into a gallop.

There was no time to lose. Whatever was happening, Cormag needed to be there.

Now!

His blood pounded in his ears, and his heart tightened in his chest as though a heavy boulder rested atop it. His muscles fought to move, yearning for confrontation, but he forced them to remain still, to wait as his gelding thundered across the land, which levelled out toward the cliff's edge.

A line of trees blocked his view, and Cormag pulled up his mount, approaching it carefully as a deep snarl reached his ears.

"What was that?" Garrett panted the very moment another horse broke through the underbrush. Only this one had Blair clinging to its back, her eyes wide with fear and her face tear-streaked. The moment she saw them, her little hands reached forward. "Ye have to help! Please! There's a wolf!"

"A wolf?" Cormag could not believe his ears; however, the look of terror on the girl's face instantly wiped away his doubts. He spurred on his gelding, sending it flying across a thick cluster of brambles, and then urged it onward past the trees and into the small clearing.

What he saw then nearly flattened him - Moira pinned to the ground by a snarling wolf snapping its jaws at her throat.

For a moment, time seemed to stand still as Cormag stared across the clearing at his wife fighting for her life.

No more than a second passed, and yet, Cormag took note of the slight trembling in her arms, the fear etched into her eyes as well as the hard line of her jaw speaking of the determination not to surrender.

The wolf was a scraggly beast, thin and with little flesh on its bones, but desperation and the need to survive gave it strength. Its claws tore into Moira's clothes, laying bare her flesh, and he saw blood seeping into the ground beneath her.

And then there was Ian.

Blood stained his blond hair in the back of his head, and his movements were sluggish as he staggered toward Moira and the wolf. Then he stumbled and went down, bracing one hand on the ground to break his fall. Fatigue and no small measure of pain marked his face. Still, he reached for the knife in his boot, his eyes determined as they rose and fixed on Moira.

Fear grabbed Cormag's heart, and he all but dropped from his horse. The second his feet were under him, he pushed off and lunged forward, long strides carrying him toward his wife. His gaze darted back and forth between the two threats to her life: the wolf, which was still struggling to get past the branch she used to defend herself, and Ian, who was again pushing to his feet, the blade in his hand gleaming in the late afternoon sun.

Cormag felt sickened at the sight, and anger surged through his veins, giving him strength and pushing him onward. Moira could barely keep the wolf at bay. Soon, it would overpower her. And yet, even now,

Ian could not let go of his hatred. Would he truly end her life if the wolf did not beat him to it?

Cormag did not wait to find out.

And then the branch broke in two.

Moira screamed as the wolf's fangs grazed the skin on her throat, and Cormag felt his heart stop at the thought that he would not reach her in time.

A second or two was all he needed.

More than he had.

And then Cormag stared in shock as Ian lunged himself onto the wolf's back and sank his blade deep into its flank. The animal howled in pain and slumped forward, landing hard on Moira. Her eyes rolled backwards, and all colour drained from her face.

Ian's arms and legs came around the snarling beast, and he rolled them sideways, off Moira and toward the cliff face. His eyes were closed as he held on tight, waiting for the animal's strength to wane.

But so, did his own.

Still, Ian held on, never releasing his hold even for a second as the animal struggled to regain the upper hand. They rolled through the dirt and over small rocks jutting out of the hard ground. A groan left Ian's lips, and Cormag saw him grit his teeth.

Without thought, Cormag changed direction and then hastened toward his friend, knowing that Ian would not last much longer.

And then the wolf conjured his last bit of strength, twisting to free itself, and flipped sideways...over the edge.

The moment man and wolf went over the side of the cliff, Ian opened his eyes and for a long second they met Cormag's.

Guilt and shame and remorse lay in their blue depths, but below those, Cormag recognised the man who had been his loyal friend all his life.

And then Ian was gone.

Chapter Forty-Two

A FUTURE FORETOLD

A scream tore from Moira's lips as she saw Ian and the wolf disappear.

Her body ached, and every fibre of her being felt bruised and battered. The deep scratches left by the wolf's claws stung and burnt, and she began to feel lightheaded, her vision blurring every so often.

Still, something primal gave her strength, and she managed to push to her hands and knees and scrambled toward the edge.

Never would Moira have expected that Ian would come to her aid. She had thought herself alone, abandoned. She had thought he had left with Blair, taking his daughter to safety. It seemed that last part was true, but then he had returned for her.

Moira could not believe it.

And then she looked up, and her gaze fell on Cormag.

Still as a statue, he stood at the edge, his upper body leaning forward as he peered down at the sea where the waves crashed mercilessly against the steep rock. The sound of their movement was deafening, and Moira shivered at the thought of what had brought them here this day. Ian had intended for her to end in a watery grave, and now, he had taken her place.

Still, Moira felt no relief.

In that moment, she felt nothing, her heart and mind numb from the ordeal she had been through.

And then Cormag turned to look at her.

Moira blinked. The spell broke, and the world came rushing back.

For a moment, nothing made sense. When had Cormag come? Shaking her head, Moira could not recall seeing him. All she had been focused on had been the wolf...until Ian had interfered.

"Cormag," she whispered, and the strength that had swelled in her chest only a moment ago vanished as though it had never been. Relief and sadness broke over her, and she slumped down, tears flooding her eyes.

In an instant, Cormag was there, pulling her gently into his arms, his strength soothing the shivers that gripped her. She clung to him, burying her face in the crook of his neck, and felt the beat of his heart against the palm of her hand.

His presence was reassuring, comforting, and Moira felt the panic retreat until only sadness and regret remained. Then she lifted her head and looked up into his dark grey eyes. "I'm so sorry," she whispered as more tears streamed down her face.

Cormag nodded, his jaw clenched as he reached out and gently brushed the tears from her cheeks. "As am I." Then he pulled her back into his arms, and for a long moment, they simply sat there on the rough ground, their emotions torn between relief and regret, between joy and sadness.

Aye, Moira was still alive. Although her body ached, she knew she would recover and have a chance at a future with Cormag.

Still, the price had been steep. Although Ian had been the threat that had loomed over her ever since she had arrived at *Seann Dachaigh* Tower, Moira had come to understand him. He had not been a bad man, but a misguided one. Not unlike she herself had once been, and she could not help but feel sadness at the loss of his life.

"Are ye all right?" Cormag asked, his voice thick with emotions barely held in check. He lifted her chin and peered into her eyes before his own wandered lower, taking in the cuts and scrapes covering her body.

"I will be fine," Moira assured him as she placed a hand on his cheek, her thumb gently brushing away the lone tear that had escaped his iron will. Her blue eyes held his, and for the first time, he allowed her to see him, to see to the core of his heartbreak and loss, to see the vulnerable heart that beat in his chest and the pain that he suffered. His walls came down, and the trust he placed in her, revealing himself to her unguarded, warmed Moira's heart.

"Are ye all right?" Garrett's rough voice cut through the silent moment, and Moira felt them both flinch. Then she looked up and found her husband's friend standing not far from them, Blair in his arms, her limbs listless and her red-rimmed eyes staring into nothing as she rested her head on his shoulder. His face was taut, and his green eyes held the same sadness that rested in her own chest.

Moira nodded, not knowing where they were to go from here. A part of her felt like spending the rest of her life sitting on this cliff, wrapped in her husband's embrace. Everything else felt...wrong, inappropriate, as though leaving this place without Ian was simply not possible.

And so, they remained where they were.

While Cormag tended to Moira's wounds, following her instructions on how to clean them, Garrett took Blair into the thicket to the northeast to look for firewood. The girl moved without sound, her face haggard and her eyes directed at something only she could see.

Darkness fell slowly as they huddled together around the fire, shielded from the harsh wind by the outcrop that rose into the sky. Only Blair fell asleep, exhaustion forcing her lids shut, while the rest of them remained awake, unable to abandon the day's events. Garrett held Blair tightly in his arms, keeping her warm, a father's watchfulness in his gaze as he looked after her.

Moira and Cormag clung to one another, holding each other during those first few hours when Ian's loss slowly sank in, when their hearts and minds warred with the acceptance of it.

Come morning, they made their way down the slope of land that led to the beach below, unable to leave without seeing the very place where Ian had vanished. Nothing remained of him but their memories. A part of Moira had feared that they would find his body, washed up on the shore, and the thought had pained her throughout the night. She wanted to remember him the way he had been, the way he had looked at Blair, his eyes warm and full of love, the way he had come to her aid, selflessness and determination marking his features.

Moira wanted to remember the good man he had been, not the weak moments, not the ugliness of death. One glance at Cormag told her that he felt the same, and they all breathed a sigh of relief when they found nothing but an empty beach.

No sign of Ian or the wolf.

Hunger finally sent them to their horses, and with heavy hearts, they headed back east, toward home.

Blair rode with Garrett, and he did his best to distract her, pointing out hares as they dashed through the tall grass or finding shapes in the clouds that drifted past overhead. Now and then, a small smile crossed her little face, and Moira knew that she was trying to move on.

There was something overwhelmingly strong in that little girl, and in rare moments, Moira could almost glimpse the woman she would one day become.

Strong and fierce and utterly fearless in her devotion and loyalty to those she loved. Blair would be a force to be reckoned with, and the MacDrummonds would be stronger having her as one of their own.

"Ye feel warm," Cormag whispered in Moira's ear, his arms draped around her as they rode homeward. Although they had retrieved the runaway horse as well as the leisurely grazing pony, there was a need for closeness in all of them.

Moira sighed, aware of the slight fever that lingered. "I'll be fine," she said, resting her head against his shoulder. "'Twas to be expected. It'll pass in a day or two."

Cormag drew in a slow breath, and Moira knew that there was doubt in him.

"I promise," she whispered, turning her head into the crook of his neck and placing a gentle kiss on the echo of his heartbeat there. "How did ye find me?" she asked after a while, wishing to direct his thoughts elsewhere. "How did ye know where Ian had taken me?"

A slow breath left his body, and for a moment, he did not reply. Then he shifted the reins into one hand before the other moved to grasp hers, his fingers threading through her own. "I felt ye," he finally whispered, his words brushing across her skin.

Moira felt herself shiver despite the warmth his words evoked. "Ye felt me? From so far away?"

"I always feel ye." His lips brushed against her skin as he spoke, his warm breath increasing the delicious shivers that tingled up and down her body.

"How could ye be certain 'twas me?"

She felt him smile before the tip of his nose skimmed over the soft skin of her neck. "There's no one like ye," he whispered in her ear. "I've felt ye even before I first laid eyes on ye. Only I didna know it then." His teeth tugged on her earlobe, and Moira drew in a sharp breath. "But I do now, and I'll never let ye go again. No matter what, ye belong with me as I belong with ye." His hands tightened possessively on her, and Moira closed her eyes in bliss. "'Tis the one thing I'm certain of, the one thing that'll never change."

"Aye," Moira breathed, and her head began to spin, not from the fever, but from the overwhelming certainty that his words were true.

The Old Ones had foretold a different future, one that had led Moira down a path she could not help but regret. And yet, it had led her here, to this man, to this clan, to this home, and she knew that there was nowhere else she had rather be.

Epilogue

Summer 1810

Almost One Year Later

The sun shone brightly on the large gathering tucked into a lush valley halfway between *Seann Dachaigh* Tower and Greyston Castle. Tents had been set up in a wide circle, leaving a large space free where competitions would be held. The soft notes of a fiddle drifted through the early morning air as the people of clan MacDrummond and Brunwood began to rise.

Moira smiled as she stepped from their tent, her eyes sweeping over the people gathered here, and her heart swelled with love, for her husband had been the one to work tirelessly to bring this about.

"We were allies once," Cormag had said countless times to her, to his clan, to clan Brunwood, "and we can be again."

Although thoughts of Moira's betrayal still lingered, the two clans had begun to take steps toward one another in the hopes that the future might look brighter than the past.

Smiling faces met Moira as she walked through the camp. Children dashed in and out of tents, weaving through the temporary village as they laughed and shouted. Dogs joined in, their barking rousing even the late sleepers.

Fires were stoked and breakfast prepared, and before long, delicious aromas drifted around the camp, drawing old and young near to fill their bellies.

Garrett and Claudia sat with Finn and Emma around a small fire, a pot dangling over it. While little Aiden stared almost hypnotically into the flames, his little feet carrying him closer before he would spin around and retreat squealing into the safety of his mother's embrace, Finn and Emma's little daughter lay sleeping soundly in a make-shift cradle.

Niall and Blair chewed with vigour on their food, their eyes darting to a group of children heading toward the competition area. Impatience rested in both their eyes, and the moment the last morsel went down their throats, they darted away to join in the fun.

While the adults of both clans kept a certain distance, eyeing each other with care and testing the waters, their children felt no such inhibitions. Even after only a single day, one could no longer tell them apart

MacDrummond? Brunwood?

Why would it matter?

"Ye no longer look green around the nose," Maggie remarked as she came walking over to where Moira stood on a small hill, a sparkle in her blue eyes.

Moira chuckled, placing a hand on her belly. "Aye, the morning sickness has passed. In fact, I feel wonderful." Standing a bit off to the side and out of the way of the busy comings and goings of their clan, Moira surveyed the bustling people-*her people!* -before turning to look at her friend. "Isn't it wonderful to see them all together?"

Sighing, Maggie nodded. "Aye, 'tis enthralling. 'Tis the way it ought to have been all along."

"Sometimes, mistakes lead ye the long way around," Moira said, reaching for Maggie's hand and squeezing it gently, "but I've come to believe that we'll always get where we're meant to be."

Again, Maggie sighed, and Moira wondered what had been occupying her friend's thoughts of late. Cheerful by nature, Maggie had seemed a bit distant these past few weeks, her eyes unseeing as she had gone about her day.

Ever since Ian's death, the small family had drawn even closer together. Friends and family had offered their help, their compassion, their support, but in the end, it had been Maggie's iron will that had painted a smile on her children's faces yet again.

Moira knew that her friend still mourned Ian's death, not because she had loved him, but because she felt guilty for not being able to. Still, lately, her guilt seemed to have lessened, and as they stood together on the small slope overlooking the gathering, Moira noticed the way Maggie turned her gaze southward, a shuddering sigh leaving her lips.

"Are ye thinking about him?"

Maggie blinked, a slight confusion marking her features.

Moira smiled at her. "The man ye once loved."

Maggie fought hard not to drop her gaze, but she could not keep a slight blush from stealing onto her cheeks. In the end, she said, "Aye, now and then." Again, her eyes became distant as she once more lifted them to the far horizon as though drawn to a place of her past. Whatever had happened all these years ago, Maggie had not yet been able to put it to rest.

"Will ye come and eat something?" Maggie finally asked as she turned toward the small fire where Emma and Claudia sat together, laughing and chatting while keeping a watchful eye on their children.

"Soon," Moira told her, strangely reluctant to leave this spot. Certainly, it was a wonderful vantage point from where she could see far across the land and survey the beautiful reunion of two clans which should never have drifted apart.

Still, that was not all it was. For Moira knew beyond the shadow of a doubt that there was something else. Another reason. A strange sense of belonging. Of needing to be in this spot here and now.

As Maggie returned to the camp, Moira moved to look over the tents farther to the east. It was the Brunwood side of the camp, and when she looked closely, she could make out Connor's tent at the centre of it. He had come with his family: his wife Henrietta and their two daughters, spirited Bridget and shy Aileen.

The past was not forgotten and never would be. However, the day before, Moira had stumbled upon Henrietta by the stream. While neither one of them had said much, Moira remembered well the watchful eyes of Connor's wife. Henrietta was a cautious woman, but one who had learnt to look deeper and not be satisfied with first impressions.

For long moments, the two women had merely looked at one another and spoken not a single word. Still, a part of Moira was certain that Henrietta had understood, that she now knew that Moira was no longer the woman she had been four years ago.

It was a start.

"Are ye all right?"

At the concerned edge in Cormag's tone, Moira turned and cast him a deep smile, one meant to reassure for he tended to worry about her. Even more now that she was with child. "I'm perfectly fine, Husband," she whispered, sneaking her arm through the crook of his while leaning her head against his shoulder. "I was merely..."

"Thinking?"

"Aye," she chuckled, as always warmed by the thought that he knew her so well.

Cormag exhaled a deep breath, and Moira felt his arm tense. "I'm sorry that Alastair didna come," he whispered against the top of her head, "but I need ye to know that it had nothing to do with ye. After what they'd suffered, 'tis only natural to shy away from these kinds of festivities."

Moira nodded, feeling the rough fabric of his shirt brush against her skin. "Aye, I know," she said as sadness returned to squeeze her heart.

Earlier that year, Deidre had given birth to a beautiful little girl. She and Alastair had been mad with joy to finally hold her in their arms...and devastated to lose her only three months later.

The thought still sent cold chills into every cell of Moira's body, and her heart ached as she thought of losing the little one she carried. How much more would Deidre and Alastair have to bear? Would Fate never be on their side?

Occasionally, Moira still thought of the dream she had had almost a year ago of the blue flower and the ruins by the cliff top. When would this dream come to pass? Or had the future somehow been changed?

No doubt sensing the change in her mood, Cormag shifted and pulled Moira against his broad chest, wrapping an arm around her shoulders to hold her tight, assuring her that she was not alone, that he was here and always would be.

A smile played on her lips as Moira once more rested her head against his shoulder. Her gaze drifted over the two clans as they finished their breakfast and began to prepare for the Highland Games. From where they stood, she could see the Brunwood colours flapping in the wind...

...and the smile died on her lips.

Shock froze Moira's limbs as her mind drew forth a dream of long ago. A dream that had led her to believe she was meant to guide her clan by Connor's side. A dream that had sent her down a path of betrayal. A dream in which she had seen herself as Connor's wife.

Moira swallowed when the truth finally sank in. Oh, how wrong she had been! The air rushed from her lungs, and she felt Cormag's arm tighten around her.

Not Connor.

Cormag.

It would seem she had been more wrong than she had ever thought possible. Her dreams had not led her astray, had not meant to taunt her, but it had been *she* who had misinterpreted *them*, only seeing what she had wanted to see.

Closing her eyes, Moira snuggled deeper into her husband's embrace. *Sometimes Fate leads ye the long way around, but in the end, ye'll always find yerself where ye were meant to be.*

"Aye," Moira whispered with a smile, "how verra true."

THE END

Thank you for reading *Banished & Welcomed*!

· · ·

In the next installment, *Haunted & Revered - The Scotsman's Destined Love*, Deidre Brunwood embarks on a fateful journey that is prophesied to cost her her husband's love. However, Alastair has never been a man to give up...easy or otherwise, and he will most certainly not lose the woman he's loved all his life!

Read a Sneak-Peak

Haunted & Revered
The Scotsman's Destined Love
(#4 Highland Tales)

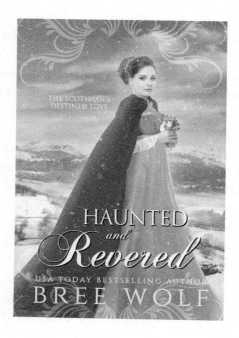

Prologue

GREYSTONE CASTLE, SCOTLAND

AUTUMN 1809

"Will nothing keep you from your little sanctuary? Not even the child in your belly?"

Standing on a small ladder, Deidre Brunwood felt her hand pause as she heard Henrietta's voice call out to her, a teasing chuckle following her words as the tall woman stepped out of the thick hedge growing around the small, lost garden Deidre had made her own.

Situated between the outer wall and the castle wall itself, it could only be reached through a small gap in the tall-growing hedge. A gap one could not see if one did not know where to look. Untended for years, it had grown wild, and Deidre remembered well the day she'd first stumbled upon it; an oasis of greens of all shades mingling with bright yellows, dark reds and stunning violets. Her soul had soared to the heavens upon seeing it, and Deidre had known in that moment that she'd found a piece of her heart.

"Why don't you ask someone to help you with the apple harvest?" Henrietta suggested as she came walking over, her short flaxen hair dancing upon her shoulders. She bore a tall, striking figure despite her slender build, an Englishwoman by birth, but a Scot at heart. Married to Deidre's cousin Connor, Laird of Clan Brunwood, Henrietta had been a close friend for many years.

"Mama, fwower!" Henrietta's two-year-old daughter Bridget exclaimed, pulling on her mother's skirts and pointing at a pale rose, still at bloom this late in the year. Her blond hair shone as brightly as her mother's, and her deep blue eyes whispered of a daring spirit, eagerly reaching for the wonders the world promised her.

Smiling, Henrietta brushed a hand over Bridget's head as she shifted her balance to accommodate baby Aileen, who lay sleeping peacefully in the crook of her other arm. At three-month-old, Aileen knew nothing of what her big sister spoke so ardently. Her little head sprouted dark brown curls, and her eyes glowed in a striking green whenever she dared to open them, her little heart far more content to look inward than to face the world. The girls were like fire and water, different in temperament and appearance, but the glow on their little faces never failed to make Deidre's heart ache.

Plucking the apple she'd been reaching for, Deidre climbed down the ladder and laid it down in the basket that was already half-full. "I find it soothing," she told her friend as her hand came to rest upon the small bulge under her dress.

Henrietta stepped closer, the look in her blue eyes tense. "Are you not worried that it might...?" her voice trailed off as her gaze dipped lower to where Deidre's hand rested protectively over her unborn child.

Deidre swallowed as she remembered the many pregnancies that had ended in loss. "I dunna believe it makes a difference. I've stayed abed before and it didna help." Her insides clenched. "I still lost my babe." Her hand brushed softly over her belly. "I believe the best I can do is to not be afraid, to live and smile and laugh as much as I can. I dunna know whether I'm meant to hold this babe in my arms or not, but I will love every moment I have with him or her." Tears filled her eyes, but Deidre quickly blinked them away. She'd already shed a lifetime's worth of tears over the loss of her children, not one of whom had ever drawn breath. She would not cry today when there was no reason to do so.

Drawing in a deep breath, Deidre lifted her head, willing the sadness back down. "What brings ye here? Have ye come to lend a hand?"

Henrietta chuckled, glancing at Bridget chasing after a butterfly, her little legs carrying her through the tall grass. "I'm afraid all my hands are currently occupied," she said, rocking little Aileen as the girl began to stir. A soft melody drifted from her lips as she hummed, brushing the pad of her thumb over her daughter's crinkled forehead, soothing the sorrows that had found her in her dreams until the little girl slept peacefully once more.

A lump settled in Deidre's throat as longing tugged on her heart yet again. She loved Henrietta's children dearly, but they only strengthened the yearning for a child of her own.

"I brought you this," Henrietta whispered, reaching into her apron and withdrawing a letter. "It was delivered this morning, and I've been looking for you ever since." Her blue eyes met Deidre's. "It came from *Seann Dachaigh* Tower."

"Moira?" Deidre asked, her hand reaching out for the envelope.

Henrietta nodded. "It seems to be her handwriting if I'm not mistaken." Her jaw tensed at the mention of the woman who'd tried to steal her husband. "Connor confirmed it."

Deidre nodded, her gaze gliding over Moira's flourished handwriting. They'd been friends since childhood, and they'd grown closer still when Deidre had married Moira's elder brother Alastair. Nothing had ever come between them until the day Moira had gone too far.

For her betrayal, she'd been banished from her home, sent to live with her mother's old clan at *Seann Dachaigh* Tower. Life had not been easy for her, but Moira had come to see the error of her ways and fought hard to make amends and regain people's trust. Ultimately, her devotion and loyalty to Clan MacDrummond had won her the laird's heart and they'd been married only a few weeks past. Still, Alastair had never forgiven his sister for her betrayal, and ever since, Deidre had stood in the middle, trying her best to mend fences.

Breaking the seal, Deidre opened the envelope and pulled out a single sheet of parchment. She unfolded it, her eyes drawn to the words written there as an odd sense of foreboding fell over her.

Dearest Deirdre,

This is not an easy letter to write for I fear I must warn you of something that lies ahead. I will do my best to share with you all that I know, but I'm afraid the images I saw were shrouded as though hidden in a heavy fog. You will have to trust your heart to guide you as do I for I know that there is no better compass than the gentle soul that resides within you.

Deidre's blood ran cold at Moira's words.

Three months ago when she'd first learned that she was with child, Deidre had travelled to *Seann Dachaigh* Tower to speak to Moira, to ask her if she knew what fate her unborn child was destined for. Would it live? Or would she lose it as she'd lost all the others?

Ever since she'd been a lass, Moira'd had the Sight. Dreams that whispered of future events, some clear and some shrouded in mist, impossible to understand until they came to pass. One such dream had led her to conspire against Connor's and Henrietta's marriage. A dream she had misunderstood.

As hopeful as Deidre tried to be, she could not deny that she feared for her child's life. How could she not? And so she had gone to Moira, asking for help. Only Moira had not been able to tell her anything as no dream whispering of her child's future had yet found her. Still, Moira had promised to write should anything change. Should she see anything in her dreams.

Deidre felt her hands begin to tremble.

"Are you all right?" Henrietta asked, her voice full of concern as she came to stand by Deidre, her unburdened arm coming around her friend's shoulders. "You've gone awfully pale. What does she write? Is everything all right?"

Unable to speak, Deidre held up the letter, gesturing for Henrietta to read along.

The images that found me were blurred and shifted quickly, and I'm afraid I'm far from certain as to their meaning. I pray you will be able to make more sense of them.

At first, I found myself looking upon a blue flower, its petals strangely tined and not smooth but as though wrinkled. The colour moved and shifted into different shades in stark contrast to the bright light surrounding it. I felt blinded, my eyes seeing nothing but white.

As far as I can tell the flower is nothing more but a marker. It marks the day when something will come to pass. As to what that is, I cannot say for certain. All I know is that I saw you up on the cliffs by the old ruins, brightness around you. A sense of utter sadness washed over me, making my heart ache. Still, it only lingered for a short while before all of a sudden my heart felt ready to burst with a new love.

"A new love?" Henrietta whispered beside her. "What does she mean?"

Deidre shook her head, her heart torn. "I dunna know." She'd expected news about her child, and yet, Moira's words spoke of something else. Could this be about her husband? About Alastair?

As you well know, my interpretation of these dreams is not free of error. I do not know what will happen. I can merely speculate.

Of course, I worry about what they could mean for I cannot deny that the images I saw echoed with warning. However, I've recently come to understand that my ability to interpret these dreams is less accurate whenever I myself am emotionally involved. If that is the case, I can no longer be objective and my interpretation becomes flawed.

I love you as I would my own sister, dearest Deidre, and so I fear that I'm not of much help. All I can tell you is that on the day marked by the blue flower, you're to seek out the old ruins and there you will stumble upon a great love.

I will not say more and leave all else in your trusted hands.

Be safe.

Moira

By the time, Deidre reached the end of the letter, her limbs were shaking so hard, she sank down into the leave-covered grass, Henrietta beside her. Her eyes closed, and one hand reached out to her unborn child as her mind pictured her beloved husband.

Was that what Moira had been reluctant to say? That harm would befall Alastair? That at some point in the future Deidre would stumble upon a new love?

"Impossible," she whispered into the stillness of her sanctuary, feeling Henrietta's arm tighten upon her shoulders. "Even if..." Her eyes opened, and she felt tears run down her cheeks as she turned to look upon her friend. "Even if he were..." Deidre swallowed. "I could never give my heart to another. Never."

Blinking back tears, Henrietta nodded, her hand seeking Deidre's, squeezing it gently. "I know," she whispered, then cleared her throat, casting a watchful look at Aileen. "Perhaps Moira is wrong." Her jaw tensed. "After all, she's been wrong before. Perhaps whatever she saw will not happen to you, but to another."

Deidre nodded, wishing she could grasp the lifeline Henrietta was offering her. Still, she knew that if Moira had not been certain she would not have written this letter. Like no other, Moira knew the bond that connected Deidre and Alastair, the love that had bound them to one another ever since they'd been children.

It was unbreakable.

Forever.

Destined.

"Will you tell Alastair about this?" Henrietta asked, aware of the tension between brother and sister. Even though Deidre had all but forced her husband to follow her when she'd slipped away to *Seann Dachaigh* Tower three months ago, brother and sister had barely spoken a word to each other when he had arrived to fetch his wife home. Alastair still had not forgiven Moira. Could not.

He was a proud man.

Stubborn.

Unyielding.

"'Twill only anger him," Deidre said, knowing from the look in Henrietta's eyes that her friend agreed. "He'll be furious with her, and it'll push them even farther apart." She sighed, feeling exhausted. "I still have hope that one day they'll find their way back to each other."

Henrietta swallowed, the look in her eyes wary. "What about...your new love? The man you will meet by the ruins?"

Deidre shook her head. "I dunna care. My heart belongs to Alastair. It always has, and it always will."

A smile came to Henrietta's face and she squeezed Deidre's hand. "There's not a single doubt-"

"None!" Her heart beat strong, and yet, her jaw quivered. "But what if...?" Both her hands reached for Henrietta's. "What if harm comes to him? What if that's the warning Moira felt? What do I do?"

Henrietta heaved a deep sigh before her gaze moved from the letter in Deidre's lap to the small bump under her dress. "It is as you said, you do not know what will happen. None of us do. All any of us can do is be happy and enjoy the time we have. What else is there?"

Deidre nodded, knowing Henrietta was right. Still, a new fear settled in her heart, and she knew it would haunt her for all the days to come. The fear to not only lose her child, but her husband as well. For although nothing could ever make her love another, her heart would break into a thousand pieces, never to be mended again, if Fate dared to separate her from the man she loved.

Series Overview

LOVE'S SECOND CHANCE: TALES OF LORDS & LADIES

LOVE'S SECOND CHANCE: TALES OF DAMSELS & KNIGHTS

LOVE'S SECOND CHANCE: HIGHLAND TALES

FORBIDDEN LOVE SERIES

HAPPY EVER REGENCY SERIES

THE WHICKERTONS IN LOVE

For more information visit www.breewolf.com

About Bree

USA Today bestselling and award-winning author, Bree Wolf has always been a language enthusiast (though not a grammarian!) and is rarely found without a book in her hand or her fingers glued to a keyboard. Trying to find her way, she has taught English as a second language, traveled abroad and worked at a translation agency as well as a law firm in Ireland. She also spent loooong years obtaining a BA in English and Education and an MA in Specialized Translation while wishing she could simply be a writer. Although there is nothing simple about being a writer, her dreams have finally come true.

"A big thanks to my fairy godmother!"

Currently, Bree has found her new home in the historical romance genre, writing Regency novels and novellas. Enjoying the mix of fact and fiction, she occasionally feels like a puppet master (or mistress? Although that sounds weird!), forcing her characters into ever-new situations that will put their strength, their beliefs, their love to the test, hoping that in the end they will triumph and get the happily-ever-after we are all looking for.

If you're an avid reader, sign up for Bree's newsletter on www.breewolf.com as she has the tendency to simply give books away. Find out about freebies, giveaways as well as occasional advance reader copies and read before the book is even on the shelves!

Connect with Bree and stay up-to-date on new releases:

facebook.com/breewolf.novels

twitter.com/breewolf_author

instagram.com/breewolf_author

amazon.com/Bree-Wolf/e/B00FJX27Z4

bookbub.com/authors/bree-wolf

Printed in Great Britain
by Amazon

45550650R00179